Robert Muchamore was born in 1972. His books have sold millions of copies around the world, and he regularly tops the bestseller charts.

He has won numerous awards for his writing, including the Red House Children's Book Award. For more information on Robert and his work, visit **www.muchamore.com**

Praise for CHERUB and *Henderson's Boys*:
'These are the best books ever!' Jack, 12

'So good I forced my friends to read it, and they're glad I did!' Helen, 14

'The CHERUB books are so cool, they have everything I ever wanted!' Josh, 13

'Never get tired of recommending CHERUB/ *Henderson's Boys* to reluctant readers, because it never fails!' Cat, children's librarian

'My son could never see the point of reading a book until he read *The Recruit*. I want to thank you from the bottom of my heart for igniting the fire.' Donna

BY ROBERT MUCHAMORE

The CHERUB series:

1.   The Recruit
2.   Class A
3.   Maximum Security
4.   The Killing
5.   Divine Madness
6.   Man vs Beast
7.   The Fall
8.   Mad Dogs
Dark Sun
9.   The Sleepwalker
10.   The General
11.   Brigands M.C.
12.   Shadow Wave
13.   People's Republic
14.   Guardian Angel
15.   Black Friday
16.   Lone Wolf
17.   New Guard

The Rock War series:

1.   Rock War
2.   Boot Camp
3.   Gone Wild
4.   Crash Landing

The Henderson's Boys series:

Start reading with *The Escape*

PEOPLE'S REPUBLIC

Robert Muchamore

*Hodder
Children's
Books*

HODDER CHILDREN'S BOOKS

First published in Great Britain in 2011 by Hodder Children's Books
This edition published in 2016 by Hodder and Stoughton

14

Text copyright © Robert Muchamore, 2006

The moral rights of the author have been asserted.

A CIP catalogue record for this book is available
from the British Library

ISBN 978 0 340 99920 2

Typeset in Goudy by Avon DataSet Ltd,
Bidford-on-Avon, Warwickshire

Printed and bound in Great Britain by Clays Ltd, Elcograf S.p.A.

The paper and board used in this book are made from wood
from responsible sources.

MIX
Paper from
responsible sources
FSC® C104740

Hodder Children's Books
An imprint of Hachette Children's Group
Part of Hodder and Stoughton
Carmelite House
50 Victoria Embankment
London EC4Y 0DZ

An Hachette UK Company
www.hachette.co.uk

www.hachettechildrens.co.uk

WHAT IS CHERUB?

CHERUB is a branch of British Intelligence. Its agents are aged between ten and seventeen years. Cherubs are mainly orphans who have been taken out of care homes and trained to work undercover. They live on CHERUB campus, a secret facility hidden in the English countryside.

WHAT USE ARE KIDS?

Quite a lot. Nobody realises kids do undercover missions, which means they can get away with all kinds of stuff that adults can't.

WHO ARE THEY?

About three hundred kids live on CHERUB campus. They are usually recruited between the ages of six and twelve, sometimes younger if they join with an older sibling. They are allowed to work as agents from age ten upwards, provided they make it through a hundred days of basic training.

Key qualities for CHERUB recruits include high

levels of intelligence and physical endurance, along with the ability to work under stress and think for oneself.

CHERUB STAFF

With large grounds, specialist training facilities and a combined role as a boarding school and intelligence operation, CHERUB actually has more staff than pupils. They range from cooks and gardeners, to teachers, training instructors, technical staff and mission specialists. CHERUB is run by its chairwoman, ZARA ASKER.

CHERUB T-SHIRTS

Cherubs are ranked according to the colour of the T-shirts they wear on campus. ORANGE is for visitors. RED is for kids who live on CHERUB campus but are too young to qualify as agents. BLUE is for kids undergoing CHERUB's tough one-hundred-day basic training regime. A GREY T-shirt means you're qualified for missions. NAVY is a reward for outstanding performance on a single mission. The BLACK T-shirt is the ultimate recognition for outstanding achievement over a number of missions, while the WHITE T-shirt is worn by retired CHERUB agents and some staff.

PART ONE

1. LAPS

July 2011

Three women sat in the chairwoman's office on CHERUB campus. Blinds shut out low evening sun as the air conditioner battled high summer.

'Tell me about him,' Dr D said, speaking in a brash New York accent as she studied a photo of a twelve-year-old. 'He's a good-looking boy. Do I see a touch of Arab in him?'

Dr D was tiny and the wrong side of sixty. Despite the heat she wore a tartan cape, thick grey stockings and knee-high boots. She looked like someone's cranky old secretary, but was actually a senior officer with the American intelligence service – the CIA.

Zara Asker was another spy who didn't look the part. CHERUB's forty-year-old chairwoman sat opposite Dr D, wearing a three-quid plastic watch and her youngest son's dinner down the front of her dress.

'Ryan joined CHERUB fourteen months ago,' Zara explained. 'His grandparents were a Syrian, a German, an Irishwoman and a Pakistani.'

Dr D raised one eyebrow. 'Sounds like the first line of a bad joke.'

'Ryan was mainly brought up in Saudi Arabia and Russia. His dad was a geologist in the oil industry, but drink and gambling problems led to debts and he turned up dead under some rubbish bags. Nobody knows if it was murder or suicide. Ryan reached Britain in 2009 with his mother and three younger brothers. She'd bluffed her way into a private treatment program for a rare form of cancer, but got kicked out when she hit the limit on her credit cards. Immigration tried sending the family back to Syria, but she was too sick. She died penniless in an NHS ward, with four boys under eleven and no known family.'

'Are they all here at CHERUB?' Dr D asked.

Zara nodded. 'We never split families. Ryan's the eldest, he's got twin brothers who are about to turn ten and Theo who's seven.'

'You said Ryan's not had much mission experience,' Dr D noted.

'Just a couple of one-day things,' Zara said. 'But he's chomping at the bit, and the operation you're proposing should be well within his capabilities.'

Dr D nodded as she reached forward and dropped Ryan's photo on to a glass coffee table. 'So when do I get to meet him?'

Ryan didn't know he was being talked about as he strolled off the campus athletics track. It was baking hot and he had a six pack showing as he stretched up the bottom of his grey T-shirt and used it to mop sweat off his face.

The twelve-year-old was muscular but not bulky. He had brown eyes, straight dark hair in need of a trim and a silver stud in a recently pierced ear. After two mouthfuls from an underpowered drinking fountain, Ryan went up three paved steps towards a tatty shed used by the athletics staff.

It was gloomy inside because the frosted window was boarded following an encounter with a football. There was nobody home, but the coaches' smell lingered in tracksuits and musty all-weather gear on wall hooks.

A clipboard on the window ledge bulged with crumpled forms. You could flip back and read through four months of minor crimes paid off with punishment laps.

A bead of sweat pelted the A4 page as Ryan grabbed the Biro-on-a-string and started filling boxes on the first blank page: *Time, date, name, agent number, laps run, reason for punishment.*

This last box irritated Ryan and he was tempted to write *No good reason.*

He had no problem accepting the tough discipline faced by agents who broke CHERUB rules, but having to run five kilometres because he'd got a fit of the giggles was ridiculous. Especially when other kids doing the same had got off.

'You holding on to that all night?' someone asked irritably.

Ryan's heavy breathing meant he hadn't heard the girl in the red CHERUB shirt and pink Nikes step up behind. He reluctantly scrawled *Laughing in class*, signed his name and passed the board over.

'All yours,' he said sourly.

Ryan jogged along a gravel path towards campus' eight-storey main building. Campus was dead because loads of kids were holidaying at the CHERUB summer hostel. A lift took him up to the seventh floor, but he broke off before reaching his bedroom to get a drink from a small kitchen.

'Ryan, you reek!' Grace complained, wafting in front of her nose as he squeezed by.

Grace was Ryan's age, but a full head shorter. Her best friend Chloe sat bare-legged on the worktop between a microwave and three dessert glasses, which were halfway to becoming trifles.

The vibe was awkward because Grace was the closest Ryan had ever come to having a girlfriend and their weekend of holding hands and awkward silences had ended with Grace lobbing macaroni cheese at his head.

'Can't help stinking,' Ryan explained, as he grabbed a pint glass from a cupboard and quarter filled it with ice chips from the dispenser in the fridge door. 'Punishment laps. In this *bloody* heat.'

The girls seemed curious as Ryan took a bottle of Diet

Pepsi from inside the fridge door and poured it over the ice. As he gulped fizz, Grace bashed up pink wafer biscuits before sprinkling the crumbs over custard in the dessert glasses.

'It's not like you, Ryan,' Chloe said, with a slight tease in her voice. 'You're usually a good boy.'

'Blame Max Black,' Ryan said, before ripping off a vast Pepsi-fuelled belch.

'Dirty pig!' Chloe protested, before Ryan began his story.

'We were in Mr Bartlett's maths class. Bartlett goes out of the room to fetch something. Max and Kaitlyn had been rowing all through morning break. Kaitlyn calls Max a *mongoloid*. And you know how oranges shrivel up when they're really old?'

The girls looked mystified by this turn in the story, but nodded anyway.

'Max has got untold crap in his backpack,' Ryan said. 'I mean, he's had the same school bag for years and I don't think he's cleaned out once: snotty tissues, socks, leaky pens. It's basically a biohazard. So he reaches down his bag and comes up with this shrunken old orange, about the size of a ping-pong ball. He throws it really hard at Kaitlyn.

'She dives out of the way, tilts off her chair and bops her head on the desk behind her. The orange whizzes on. It hits the handle of the cup on Mr Bartlett's desk. Max's throw was so hard the dried-out orange explodes and the mug does this little pirouette before toppling over.

'Earl Grey tea, almost a full cup. It goes *everywhere*. All over Bartlett's paperwork, and the desk drawer's open, so it's running in there: hole punch, staple gun, calculators, whole pack of squared paper and exercise books. Bartlett comes back inside. Kaitlyn's bawling and waving her arms around and totally milking it. Bartlett starts screaming at Max.'

Chloe and Grace were both into the story, and Ryan felt more relaxed. It was the first time he'd spoken to either of them since the macaroni incident six weeks earlier.

'So Bartlett was venting steam, going ape,' Ryan said. 'He gives Max a hundred punishment laps and sends Kaitlyn off to first aid. Then he gets everyone to calm down, but I can't stop. Like, I'm swallowing and trying to keep a straight face, but me and Alfie are wetting ourselves laughing. So Bartlett kicks us both into the corridor and gives us five kilometres of laps.'

'Harsh,' Grace said, as she topped each trifle off with aerosol cream and Maltesers. 'Bartlett's usually mellow. I can't even remember him raising his voice.'

Ryan tipped more Pepsi on to the ice. Chloe put on a serious voice. 'Well *I* don't think it's funny. Kaitlyn needed three stitches in her head.'

Ryan looked shocked. 'Seriously? Max's an idiot. He never knows when to stop.'

Chloe raised one eyebrow and burst out laughing. 'Had you going there, Rybo.'

Ryan shook his head, then smiled with relief. 'I was gonna *say*. Her head barely glanced the table. Gimme some Maltesers. Who's the third trifle for?'

'Not you, that's for sure,' Grace said, tipping brown balls into Ryan's outstretched palm.

Ryan dropped six Maltesers in his gob and crunched as he grabbed his half-drunk Pepsi glass off the worktop and headed out.

'Oi,' Chloe shouted. 'Where do you think you're going?'

Ryan backed up to the kitchen doorway and saw Grace pointing at the Pepsi bottle.

'What did your last servant die of?' she asked. 'Put it back in the fridge.'

Ryan stepped back grumpily. He was knackered and the girls had loads of stuff out on the worktop already.

'Putting one bottle back's hardly gonna kill you,' Ryan said.

'We might kill *you* if you don't,' Chloe said, as she jumped down off the cabinet. She was barefoot and Ryan's eyes fixed on her painted toenails as he opened the fridge door and bent forwards to slot the Pepsi back inside the door.

If he'd looked the other way he might have seen Grace before she yanked the elastic of his shorts and fired a long blast of cream towards his butt crack.

'Yuk, it's all sweaty down there,' Grace yelled, shielding her eyes as the aerosol whooshed.

Ryan tried backing out, but Chloe was pushing on the fridge door, wedging him in place until the can gave its last gasp.

'Cameraphone, cameraphone!' Grace said.

Chloe let go of the fridge as the empty can clanked against the floor tiles. As Ryan straightened up Grace smacked his bum, making the whipped cream explode out of his shorts. Then an iPhone camera flashed.

'Psychos,' Ryan shouted. 'What was *that* for?'

'The hell of it,' Grace said.

The second photo was the best shot, showing Ryan's face halfway between laughter and fury, with cream streaking out the bottom of his running shorts and dribbling down his thighs. The third showed Ryan lunging towards the iPhone, while Grace leaned into the frame with a mad grin and a double thumbs-up.

'You wait,' Ryan yelled, as he waddled towards his room like he'd crapped himself. 'You'd both better watch your backs.'

'We're really scared, Rybo,' Grace shouted, between howls of laughter.

They both knew he hated being called Rybo.

'Rybo, Rybo, Ryboooooo!' Chloe said, making it sound like a football chant.

Ryan slammed the door of his room and turned the key so the girls couldn't get in.

If tough training and punishments were the downside of being a CHERUB agent, the bedrooms were the biggest perk. Ryan had a comfortable space, with a leather sofa and TV one side of the door and a mini fridge and microwave on the other. His bed was a double and a large desk with a laptop and schoolbooks on it stood by the window.

Not wanting the cream streaking down his legs to end

up on his carpet, Ryan took three long strides and cut into his bathroom. Rather than mess up the floor, he stepped into his bath fully clothed: any gunk left in the tub would wash away when he turned the taps on.

Once his trainers were off, Ryan turned on the shower head. As the water got warm he stripped off, letting sweaty, cream-soaked clothes rinse in the swirling pool around the plughole.

His T-shirt was clingy and stuck halfway over his head when a phone started ringing.

'Tits!'

There was a handset mounted on the wall beside his toilet. Ryan was in two minds about answering. It was probably Grace and Chloe on a wind-up, but could also be something important. He almost slipped as he reached over and stretched the curly-corded handset across the room.

'Ryan, it's Zara.'

Ryan jolted. The chairwoman only called individual agents for serious business, like an important mission, or the kind of trouble that earned punishments far graver than laps. It was hard to hear so he used a soggy-socked foot to turn off the shower.

'What do you want?' Ryan asked nervously, as his brain flipped through possibilities.

'Just yourself,' Zara said. 'I've got two people down here who'd like to meet you.'

2. CLAN

Ryan wasn't particularly messy, but there always seemed like better ways of spending free time than on cleaning up his room. He left his running gear festering in the bathtub as he squirted deodorant, combed hair and swished mouthwash. Then he hunted through the mounds around his bed until he'd found clean underwear, a clean grey CHERUB T-shirt and cargo pants.

Before heading out Ryan toyed with the idea of taking the stud out of his ear. He'd had it pierced the previous weekend, hoping it would make him look cooler and more rebellious. But every time he went out he got all self-conscious and imagined that everyone was staring at it thinking he looked like a dick.

In the end Ryan left it in, because Zara was waiting and the ear got really sore when you fiddled with it.

When he reached the double doors of the chairwoman's office Ryan took a deep breath and realised that his arms were shaking. It might be trouble, or it might be the proper mission he'd been craving since he'd finished basic training eight months earlier.

'A-ha, the man of the hour!' Zara said, getting off her sofa.

The office had a high ceiling, with a large angular desk and filing cabinets at one end, and leather sofas in front of a fireplace at the other. Ryan appreciated the chill of the air-con as he stepped in.

Zara stood up and introduced Ryan to a stunning-looking woman in her early twenties. 'I don't think you've ever met Amy Collins?'

Ryan was awed as Amy shook his hand. She had blonde shoulder-length hair, a perfect face, perky tits and a heavenly, tanned bod with a thong showing above the waistband of cut-off denim shorts.

'Hi,' Ryan said.

'Cute earring,' Amy said. 'I've read your file and it's good to finally meet you.'

'Hi,' Ryan repeated, as his brain turned to mush. He jolted when Zara put a hand on his shoulder.

'Ryan, you look so nervous,' Zara said. 'We don't bite, I promise.'

Ryan was mortified that his state of mind was so obvious.

'Amy is a former CHERUB agent,' Zara explained. 'She retired back in 2005 and she's recently taken a job in Dallas working for TFU – a new international taskforce, which is being led by Dr Denise Huggan.'

The caped woman stood up, but even in high-heeled boots she only reached Ryan's eyebrows.

'Nice to meet you, Dr Huggan,' Ryan said politely as he shook a gnarly hand, covered with antique silver rings.

'You gotta call me Dr D,' she replied, with her shrill New York accent. 'That's the only handle I answer to.'

'Take a seat, Ryan,' Zara said, as Dr D let out a loud false laugh. 'Amy and Dr D have full security clearance, so you can talk freely about your training or experience as a CHERUB agent.'

As Ryan sat on a leather sofa next to Amy, he glanced at the files and documents spread across the coffee table. In particular he noticed one of the distinctive red folders in which CHERUB agents receive mission briefing documents.

'So am I finally getting a proper mission?' he blurted.

Zara laughed. 'Yes, *finally*. You've been a little bit anxious about that, haven't you?'

Ryan felt embarrassed as Amy and Dr D joined the laughter.

'I know exactly how Ryan feels,' Amy said sympathetically. 'You finish basic training and you think you're hot shit, but then you've got to go out in the world and do it for real.'

'Exactly,' Ryan said. 'And some of the guys I did basic training with have already done big missions, while I've been twiddling my thumbs on campus for *eight* months wondering if the mission control staff have forgotten I exist.'

'I waited eight months for my first big mission,' Amy said, smiling at the coincidence.

'Trouble is you never have the right agents,' Zara explained. 'For instance, I've had a very talented agent who speaks Urdu and Pashto sitting on campus for over a year. He's just gone on a mission, and within a week I've had to turn down another operation for which he'd have been ideal.'

'I do understand,' Ryan said. 'I'm not having a moan or anything.'

'I know you're not,' Zara said warmly. She paused for a mouthful of coffee, then changed the subject. 'Dr D is the head of a new international taskforce known as TFU, which stands for *Transnational Facilitator Unit*. The unit is relatively small, but it's being funded by the United States government, and supported by additional agents and resources from friendly countries, including the UK.'

Amy noticed Ryan's pained expression. 'Any idea what a transnational facilitator is?' she asked.

'Not really.'

Dr D made a screechy laugh. 'Nobody does!' she said. 'Including half my bosses in Washington. Basically, you have terrorists who want to blow stuff up. You have organised criminals like the Italian Mafia or the Japanese Yakuza, but at the top of the tree you have transnational facilitators. They're wealthy, well-organised and they run illicit transportation and smuggling networks that enable global crime to function.'

'Sort of like FedEx for bad guys?' Ryan said.

'That's a good way of putting it,' Amy said. 'A transnational facilitator might be one or two well-connected individuals, or a larger body with its own transport networks and powerful political connections. The thing all facilitators have in common is the ability to put together criminal operations in different parts of the world.

'They might link a drug producer in South America together with a street gang in the Philippines, or sell fake pharmaceuticals produced in India to a corrupt health official managing a disease outbreak in Africa.'

Dr D took over from Amy. 'The problem for law enforcement and intelligence agencies is that transnational facilitators almost always operate from poor and corrupt countries that don't have the resources or legal system to deal with them.

'They generate billions but are virtually untouchable. TFU is the first taskforce to target this top tier of organised crime.'

'Interesting,' Ryan said, as he looked at Amy. 'So you work for TFU as well?'

Amy nodded. 'I lived in Australia until six months ago, but now I'm based at TFU headquarters in Dallas. We're a small team with limited resources, but Dr D has recruited excellent people from all over the world and we've already had some success.'

'And now we have a lead on the biggest facilitator of them all,' Dr D said dramatically.

'Who's that?' Ryan asked.

'The group is most commonly known as the Aramov Clan,' Dr D explained. 'They're based in Kyrgyzstan, in Central Asia. The core of their operation is a fleet of seventy transport planes. They carry some legitimate cargo, but the real money is in trafficking: drugs, weapons, high-value counterfeits and illegal immigrants.'

'With so many planes, why can't you stop them?' Ryan asked. 'Send a few drones to Ker . . . Kergee . . . I mean Kyrg-ist-whatever-it's-called and blow up their aircraft.'

Dr D laughed. 'If only. The Aramov Clan has powerful political connections. Everyone knows what they get up to, but Kyrgyzstan lies in the politically sensitive buffer zone between China and Russia.

'Irena Aramov has been paying off Russian and Chinese politicians, military and bureaucrats for two decades. If America or Europe took action against the Aramov Clan in Kyrgyzstan it would cause a huge political stink with the Russians and Chinese.'

Ryan didn't even know where to find Kyrgyzstan on a map, but he'd understood enough of what Dr D and Amy had explained to make another observation.

'So the only way to bring down the Aramov network is to infiltrate and destroy from within?'

'That's right,' Dr D said brightly. 'You know, Ryan, I feel so *positive* about your aura. I sense we're going to work really well together.'

Ryan noticed Amy and Zara exchanging an awkward glance. Dr D was clearly an oddball.

'So what's my role?' Ryan asked.

Amy leaned forward and turned towards Ryan before explaining. 'Three weeks back, CIA monitoring stations in Afghanistan picked up an encrypted telephone conversation between the Aramov Clan's main office in Kyrgyzstan and a woman named Gillian Kitsell, who lives in Santa Cruz, California. It's unusual for criminals to communicate internationally by encrypted telephone.'

Ryan knew why and jumped in to show that he did. 'Because the coded signal is suspicious in itself. The conversation must either have been really urgent, or a mistake.'

'Exactly,' Amy said.

'What was said?' Ryan asked.

'Oh, you wish, Ryan!' Amy laughed. 'The Aramov Clan uses a sophisticated encryption algorithm. It's unbreakable, unless you happen to have eight months' exclusive access to a hundred-million dollar supercomputer. However, the FBI have begun surveillance on Gillian Kitsell's home and workplace. We now believe she's actually Galenka Aramov. She's the estranged daughter of clan head Irena.'

Ryan mulled this over. 'An estranged daughter may know nothing about the family business.'

'Possible,' Amy agreed. 'But Gillian Kitsell owns and runs a Silicon Valley-based company that specialises in advanced data protection and encryption systems. So even if Kitsell knows nothing about day-to-day clan operations, she almost certainly has technical knowledge that would enable us to start decoding

Aramov Clan e-mails and voice communications.'

'This has to be done in baby steps,' Dr D explained. 'If the clan gets the *slightest* hint that Gillian Kitsell is under investigation, they'll change codes and methods of operation within hours. Gillian has a twelve-year-old son named Ethan and your job is to become his new best friend.'

'Does Ethan know who his mother is?' Ryan asked.

'We're not sure,' Dr D said. 'But they live in an eight-million-dollar beach-front house and they don't employ any domestic staff.'

Ryan nodded. 'Rich people don't clean their own bathrooms unless there's *something* to hide.'

'Amy and a TFU agent called Ted Brasker will work alongside you,' Dr D said. 'Ted will be your father, Amy your half-sister.'

'That's if you're up for the mission,' Amy said.

'Of course I am,' Ryan said happily. 'When do we fly out?'

3. NING

Six weeks later, Dandong, China
Fu Ning hated a lot of things about her life, but she liked pulling her pillow up over her head and snuggling up to the wall when her alarm went off. She imagined having a feeding tube in her arm and another tube up her bum. Then she'd stay in bed forever: never have to study, never get moaned at for slacking, never have to put up with her step-parents rowing with each other.

But if Ning couldn't stay cosy forever, she'd settle for a ten-minute snooze instead of the compulsory six a.m. shower.

'Wakey wakey, sun is shining,' her room-mate Daiyu screeched cheerfully as she entered.

Daiyu was stick thin and at eleven the same age as Ning. She wore a pink Hello Kitty robe and had dripping-wet hair. Her other room-mate Xifeng was right behind, and gently threw her vinyl toiletries bag at Ning.

'Do you want the old battleaxe in here, yelling and criticising our mess?'

'Bog off,' Ning said, as she pulled her covers tighter.

'Can we get through one day without you causing trouble?' Xifeng asked, before grabbing a hairbrush from the metal locker beside her narrow bed. 'Miss Xu will make you sorry.'

'Sod Miss Xu,' Ning shouted. 'I need sleep.'

Xifeng and Daiyu sat on the edge of their beds, virtual mirror images as they combed damp hair and pulled on school uniform.

'I memorised European capitals and population last night,' Daiyu said, as she pulled a thick white sock up to her knee. 'Can you test me?'

Xifeng was a brainbox and enjoyed catching her best friend out. 'France,' she said.

'Paris,' Daiyu replied. 'Population two point two million.'

'Oslo?'

'Oslo, Oslo,' Daiyu said, drumming a finger against a dimple in her cheek. 'Don't say! I know this . . . Oslo: Norway, population six hundred and seventy thousand.'

'No, stupid!' Xifeng said happily. 'Four hundred and eighty thousand. Moldova?'

Eleven-year-olds in China have to remember thousands of facts for their middle school exams: European capitals, Chinese provinces, birthdates of revolutionary leaders, chemical compositions. A high grade gets you into an elite middle school, opening the path to a top high school and leading universities.

Daiyu knew Moldova and smiled. 'Capital is Chisinau, population six hundred and seventy thousand. One for you, Bosnia and Herzegovina?'

Xifeng answered instantly. 'So easy! Sarajevo, five hundred thousand.' Then she leaned across and jabbed Ning in the back. 'Ning, Miss Xu will rip into you.'

'Damn that lice-ridden frump,' Ning said, her voice muffled by duvet and pillows. 'Why be so scared of a little old lady?'

Xifeng was getting cross. 'If Miss Xu comes in here she'll be on at all of us. Get out of bed, *now*.'

Ning rolled away from the wall and shielded her eyes from the first light. 'Two more minutes,' she groaned.

'I'm not taking the blame any more,' Daiyu said, as she stood decisively. She strode towards the doorway, leaned into a long corridor and yelled above the sound of girls running back and forth between the shower and their bedrooms. 'Miss Xu. Fu Ning won't get out of bed again.'

A shocked Ning sprang from beneath her covers. A line had been crossed: they'd never gotten along, but snitching was a new low.

'What did I ever do to you?' Ning shouted.

Ning was big for her age. She wasn't fat, but probably weighed as much as her two waiflike room-mates combined. Daiyu was intimidated and ran to the corridor, but Xifeng stood her ground, placing her hands on her hips.

'We're tired of you,' Xifeng shouted. 'You play headphones too loud when we try to study. You get us into trouble when you eat in the room and make mess.'

Ning rose up from her bed, a full head taller than Xifeng. Ning's face was pretty, but broad shoulders and muscular arms gave her a masculine quality, of which she was self-conscious.

Xifeng feared a punch in the mouth, but was determined to speak. 'Mr Fang says we have collective responsibility. A class can be no stronger than its weakest member.'

Ning groaned with frustration. 'Don't repeat stupid school slogans,' she yelled. 'You think you're smart because you can memorise lists, but have you ever tried thinking for yourself? Who cares about clogging your head with facts, just so you can get into another school where you'll have to work even harder? Class pride, school pride, national pride. It's all a big bucket of crap.'

Xifeng couldn't have looked more shocked if you'd chopped her nose off. 'Society works when people conform to rules. Without rules there is anarchy.'

Ning laughed as she got right in Xifeng's face, punched a revolutionary fist in the air and screamed, 'Go anarchy, baby!'

Xifeng was trembling. 'I think you're mentally defective. You bring shame on our class and our school.'

'I fart on our school,' Ning said.

'Fu Ning,' a crackly voice shrieked. 'Causing trouble

again, no surprise!'

Miss Xu was old, but robust enough to keep up with the girls who lodged in her cramming school. She grabbed the back of Ning's nightshirt and pulled so hard that a button popped from around the neck. Towel-wrapped girls hopped out of the way as she yanked Ning down a puddled corridor to her office.

The tiny space was also Miss Xu's home. It had an old lady smell. There was an elevated metal bed frame, with space beneath for a desk. She shoved Ning back against the window and slapped her sharply across the cheek.

'Disgrace, disgrace!' Miss Xu roared. 'Why not shower like every other girl?'

Ning didn't answer, she just stared at her bare feet.

'You have gifts and opportunities. You were adopted by an excellent family, but act like the lowest ragamuffin. You got accepted into national school because of your strength, but you're kicked out for the worst behaviour. Fu Ning, look at me when I speak to you.'

Miss Xu put her hand under Ning's chin and forced her head upwards.

'Tell me why your father pays for you to live in these rooms?'

'Study,' Ning said reluctantly.

'If you don't get into a good middle school, you're throwing your life away at eleven years old. Do you crave failure, Fu Ning?'

'You don't need school for anything I want to do,' Ning said defiantly.

Miss Xu drew a sharp breath. 'Really? And what is

this job requiring no status or qualification?'

'If rock star doesn't work out, I'll become a terrorist,' Ning said.

Miss Xu raised her hand, threatening another slap. 'Maybe I should call your father and see what he says to his little rock star?'

Most Chinese girls would weep and beg rather than face the wrath of their father. Ning's stepdad was stricter than most, but she wouldn't give Miss Xu any satisfaction by showing fear.

'If I'm really bad, I expect my dad will send me away to live in a rotten little room, where I'm not allowed to go out, play sport, or watch TV and all I can do is cram for my exams before and after school every day and all weekend. But wait, he already did that, *didn't* he?'

Miss Xu could take no more of Ning's lip and swung her hand. But Ning had spent four years studying boxing at Dandong's National Academy of Sport.

Ning ducked swiftly beneath the hand. Miss Xu was so surprised that she overbalanced, while Ning thrust upwards, jamming two fingers hard under Miss Xu's ribs and sending her into spasm.

'Ker-pow!' Ning shouted, as Miss Xu stumbled backwards, clutching her sides.

The elderly woman was too stunned to react as Ning reached under the bunk and swept an arm across Miss Xu's desk. A pen pot, papers, telephone and spider plant all crashed to the floor. Ning opened the office door, making the girls who'd been nosing outside spring backwards.

'Mean old cow,' Ning shouted. 'No wonder nobody ever married you.'

Back in her room, Ning found Daiyu cowering on her bed with her knees tucked into her chest. 'Are you mad?' she asked nervously.

'None of this would have happened if you'd left me alone in bed,' Ning said. 'But don't worry, I doubt you'll have to put up with me any more.'

Ning pulled her nightshirt over her head and dressed quickly in a T-shirt with the logo of her favourite Korean rock band, ripped black jeans, scuffed black snow boots and a leather jacket. Xifeng stood watching in the doorway.

'Where are you going?'

Ning shrugged. 'Anywhere but here.'

'Don't do anything stupid,' Xifeng said nervously. 'There are people who can help with your problems.'

'My only problem is not wanting to spend fourteen hours every day studying for a stupid exam,' Ning screamed.

As Xifeng sheltered in the next room, Ning considered packing a backpack, but she had nowhere to run away to, so she just grabbed her phone, wallet and a pair of sunglasses. Heads disappeared inside rooms as Ning stepped into the corridor.

Miss Xu was back on her feet at the far end of the hallway. Rather than face her again, Ning jogged back towards the showers. She cut through steam and kicked open a blue fire door. The concrete stairs led down to a courtyard filled with children's bicycles.

News had spread to the boys on the floor below and a few of them yelled stuff like *Get 'em, psycho* and *Go Ning* through the barred windows of their rooms. For an instant she felt like the hero in some movie and when she reached the courtyard, she spun around and gave Miss Xu's cramming school a two-fingered salute.

'Screw the world,' she shouted.

Ning crashed through a metal gate and walked fifty metres up an alleyway towards a main road. It was twenty past six, but the four lanes were already busy with trucks and bicycles. She thought about going into a café for breakfast, but Miss Xu might send someone after her so she kept moving.

Without thinking, Ning had walked the short route to her school and found herself at the front gates of Dandong Lower School Number Eighteen. A carctaker and a young teacher were on stepladders raising a sign painted by little kids: *LS18 Welcomes All for Joyous Parents' Day.*

The thought of parents sent a shudder down Ning's back. Her stepfather would go bananas when he found out what she'd done.

4. STANDARD

As China woke up, the sun was going down on the opposite side of the world. Ryan studied his toes as he walked away from the ocean, his soles coated with soft white sand. He'd been living in Santa Cruz, California, three and a half weeks but his new home still made him feel like he'd moved into a TV commercial.

The eight sculpted concrete homes stood back from the sea on sandy dunes. Each had panoramic windows, giving views of the ocean, and a rooftop terrace fronted by a glass-bottomed swimming pool which allowed you to sit in your vast living room and watch swimmers overhead.

The home owners shared several acres of private beach and a harbour. An electric fence kept the rabble out and the guard on the front gate had a shotgun, just in case.

Squeals came up from the ocean, as the retired basketball star who lived in house six splashed his toddler son in the waves. Ryan was heading in the other direction, towards a couple of twelve-year-olds squatting over a timber deck.

Ryan's target, Ethan Aramov, was a stick boy. Even on a warm autumn night, he kept covered in jeans and a baggy hoodie. He had messy shoulder-length hair and he always squinted, even though he wore contacts.

Yannis was Ethan's best friend and constant companion. Morbidly obese, with an oily Mediterranean complexion. He got teased at school, but Ryan felt no pity because he was utterly obnoxious.

'Hey, guys,' Ryan said, as he strolled up, acting like bumping into them was a big surprise. 'How's the 'bot coming along?'

Ethan and Yannis were uber geeks. Their only school activity was chess club. They spent entire weekends playing online games, and when that wasn't nerdy enough, they built robots. Or more accurately, Ethan, who was smart, built robots, while Yannis sat about scratching himself and eating cheese puffs.

'Our robot is top secret,' Yannis said.

The tone was *we're better than you*, but the fact that Yannis was twelve and using a line you'd expect from a pouting six-year-old made it pathetic.

The robot was based on a radio-controlled car. Ethan had adapted it with optical sensors and a small handheld computer so that it could drive itself at high speed across the beach, tracking a course mapped out by cones, while swerving around puddles and unexpected obstacles like a kid running into its path. You could buy a four-hundred-dollar robot vacuum cleaner that did the same stuff, but it was impressive for a twelve-year-old.

Ryan sidestepped Yannis and approached Ethan, who was on one knee, cleaning the robot car's steering with a toothbrush.

'Must get pretty clogged up with all the sand,' Ryan said.

'D-uh, it's sand, retard,' Yannis said.

Ethan was shy. He'd usually let Yannis talk for him, but seemed keen to tell someone other than Yannis about his robot.

'I based it on a cheap fifty-dollar RC car,' Ethan said ruefully. 'Should have got a proper Taimya kit, with a waterproofed shell.'

Ryan had now spent three weeks trying to become Ethan's friend and this was the longest conversation they'd had.

'Would it be a lot of work to switch to a different car now?' Ryan asked.

Yannis hauled his fat arse up and wedged himself in front of Ryan before Ethan could answer.

'Let's carry the stuff inside,' Yannis said, with his flabby back in Ryan's face. 'It's getting dark. You can see better inside.'

Ryan sidestepped Yannis. 'This robotics stuff looks cool. Is there a club or something you go to?'

Ethan was about to reply, but Yannis blared over him. 'We learned ourselves from books and online. It's taken *years* to learn all that we know. We're not interested in working with a rookie.'

Ryan was easy-going, but he'd done a lot of combat training since he'd joined CHERUB and at that moment he'd have happily used his Karate black belt and kickboxing skills to beat Yannis to a pulp.

'Nighty-night, Ryan,' Yannis said, waving his porky hand as he followed Ethan up the beach towards house number five.

Ryan turned to face the sea and swore under his breath. On the way back to his house he encountered the little boy sitting proudly on the shoulders of his enormously tall father.

'How's it hanging, bro?' the retired basketball star asked.

'Been worse,' Ryan said, but his smile was fake and he was scowling by the time he reached house eight. He was living there with pretend half-sister Amy and FBI agent Ted Brasker, who was their pretend father.

Ryan pushed a sliding door and stepped inside on to the metal-grilled floor of a beach shower. After hosing the sand off his feet he padded into a huge basement room, kitted out like a proper health-club gym.

CHERUB agents are expected to maintain high levels of fitness when they're undercover. Ryan thought about the treadmill or the weight bench, but the heavy bag hanging from the ceiling seemed the best outlet for frustration.

After some warm-up stretches and toe touches, Ryan exploded upwards, pirouetting on the ball of his foot and smashing the bag with a powerful roundhouse kick. As the bag swung back towards him, he dodged it, then launched a stream of heavy left and right hooks, accompanied by grunts.

After five minutes Ryan's knuckles hurt, the tops of his feet were bright red, his torso glistened and the bag had a huge dent from the pounding.

'Give the poor bag a break,' Amy shouted, as she came down the stairs.

Ryan backed up and tried to catch his breath. Amy was the kind of girl who'd look hot if you put a tent over her head, but fresh from the pool in a lime green swimsuit she was off the Richter scale.

'Sorry, I was pushing the envelope, you know?' Ryan said.

He was trying to sound macho, but Amy sensed his frustration.

'I was floating,' Amy replied. 'I could hear your grunting two floors up.'

She inspected the dent in the heavy bag, before launching a heavy kick, spraying Ryan with chlorinated drips.

'You're not bad,' Ryan said, as he matched Amy's move.

Amy didn't appreciate having her combat skills referred to as *not bad*. She threw a kick so hard that it pushed the bag violently upwards. As it crashed down, the chain holding it up made a clank followed by a hollow boom as the entire ceiling flexed.

Ryan gawped upwards, half expecting to see cracks in

the plaster. He'd seen a heavy bag lifted up before, but only by a training instructor with thighs broader than Amy's waist.

'God help any guy who messes with you,' Ryan laughed.

'So why the naked aggression?' Amy asked.

'Nothing in particular,' Ryan said.

Amy didn't buy that. 'I saw you with Ethan and Yannis while I was swimming. Can I assume it wasn't the breakthrough you've been waiting for?'

Ryan looked depressed as he sat down on a weight bench.

'I've got to pull this off, but I'm screwing up,' he admitted. 'A good agent should make friends with their target within a day or two – a week at most. I've done hours of role play, I know all the psychological tricks for making someone like me. But we've been out here almost four weeks. I'm getting nowhere with Ethan, at home or school.'

'Is Yannis still the problem?' Amy asked.

Ryan nodded. 'I hate that fat dick, but they suit each other. Like, Ethan's really clever, but he's weedy and shy. It suits Ethan to have Yannis around. Yannis mostly does what Ethan tells him to, and the way Yannis brushes people off means Ethan doesn't have to deal with his shyness. It's like an impenetrable geek force field.'

Amy straddled at an overhead press machine and paused to think.

'What about physically?' Amy asked.

'Physically what?'

'Yannis gives Ethan what he wants, by fending off questions. But would Yannis be able to protect Ethan in a physical confrontation?'

'A bit. I mean, Yannis is such a lard arse that most average kids wouldn't start because he'd just end up sitting on them.'

'But the tough guys, the jocks, football players or whatever you have at your school?'

Ryan laughed. 'No way Yannis could fight them. You should see him in Phys Ed. He runs like a jelly having a seizure and sweats like a fountain.'

'Well that's it then,' Amy said brightly. 'Problem solved.'

'What, you're saying that I should beat Yannis up and then somehow take his place as Ethan's protector?'

'No,' Amy said, showing off sparkling teeth as she laughed. 'If you beat up Ethan's only mate, he'll hate you for it. You need a situation where Ethan is threatened but Yannis can't help him. It won't guarantee that you'll become best buds, but it will make Ethan feel that he owes you something.'

'So Ethan-the-wimp is about to get his arse kicked and Ryan-the-good-looking-hero steps in to save him,' Ryan said, half smiling.

'We tried something similar on a CHERUB mission when I was about your age,' Amy explained. 'An agent was trying to befriend the son of some mad Saudi terrorist but they didn't hit it off.'

'Couldn't you have mentioned this a week ago?' Ryan asked.

'I said we *tried* something similar,' Amy said. 'But it didn't exactly work.'

'What do you mean, *didn't exactly work?*'

'Well, the whole mission went down the pan and my fellow agent spent three weeks in hospital recovering from a head wound. But on the up side I have a pretty good idea where we went wrong.'

5. NOODLE

It was a quarter to eight, but the day felt old already. Ning sat in the remotest corner of a food court, less than a kilometre from her school. The place ached with pastel shades and newness, but had never caught on. Seven of the ten food stands had gone bust and the only regular customers were high school kids, who liked the deserted space because they could hang out for hours without getting moved on.

The high-schoolers put huge effort into looking cool. They had dyed hair, carried fake designer bags and wore leather jackets over their school sweatshirts. Ning watched one lad showing off a new mobile, before it got snatched and thrown about.

But the conversations Ning caught were hardly different to her eleven-year-old classmates': exams, teachers, TV. They made Ning feel that the future held nothing but more of the same. Depressed, she sat with her head on a plastic tray, while her deep-fried shrimp bun congealed.

She tried keeping her mind blank, but that's tough when you're troubled and getting in deeper. Miss Xu's rooms were privately owned and had no connection to Ning's state-run school. But while she faced no consequences at school, she'd suffer a huge loss of face arriving in class less than an hour after storming off so dramatically. Also, Ning didn't have her books or uniform and to make matters worse it was parents' day, which she'd been dreading for weeks.

Parents' day was a huge deal. Mums, dads and grandparents toured the school in the morning, looking at displays of work and listening to class presentations. In the afternoon, parents gathered in the assembly hall to hear lengthy speeches by the headmistress and school's communist party representative, followed by a stage show with a small role for every child in the school.

For Ning, the best thing about parents' day was that hers never turned up. Her stepfather Chaoxiang ran a large business and was always too busy to attend, while her stepmother Ingrid was an Englishwoman who preferred to stay home with vodka and badly dubbed American cop shows.

But the fact Ning's step-parents weren't attending didn't excuse her from having to dress up in tights and ballet pumps and clomp her way through a twelve-minute routine, lined up with girls who were mostly half her size.

Her dad would yell at her for what she'd already done, so how much worse would it get if she skipped a day's school as well?

Ning's eyes glazed as the high school kids started moving off for the beginning of school. She began to daydream, imagining some high school punk starting to flirt with her and taking her on his moped. Or hanging out in his room, listening to really loud music. Maybe they'd smoke some weed.

She liked the thought of causing a huge scandal, with everyone in her class hearing that she'd been busted by cops, with a cute, stoned, sixteen-year-old riding a stolen moped.

By God, that would freak everyone out!

But it wouldn't happen. Cute guys always went for skinny rakes like Xifeng, for starters. Ning sat up, feeling ugly and wondering how to pass the hours. She'd have to stay off the main streets because the cops would pick her up. But she needed to buy a book or sneak into a cinema, otherwise she'd die of boredom. Or maybe the best thing would be to call her dad and get it over with. He might not be so mad if she got her side of the story in first.

Ning slid a little Samsung out of her coat pocket. She'd switched it to silent in case her school rang. She half expected to find missed calls, but there was just a single text message from a boy in her class called Qiang: *Ms Xu has packed all your things and put them in the lobby. At least if your dad beats your face you can't get any uglier!*

Qiang was a troublemaker. He could be hilarious but

he was cruel to the weaker boys. Ning didn't exactly like him, but at least he wasn't a zombie like most of the others in her class.

Ning had her father programmed in as hotkey three. She paused for a moment to get her story straight. If Ning caught her father in a good mood and played things right, she could get away with a lot.

She'd decided to make out that it wasn't a big deal. She'd say she'd been in a fight. *Miss Xu has packed my things and says it's best if I leave. Could you send one of our drivers to pick me up?* Then if Miss Xu told a different story later on, she could say that the crazy old biddy was angry because she'd lost a paying customer.

Ning took a deep breath before holding down the number three. She almost chickened out and cancelled the call, but nobody answered anyway.

'*Welcome to China Mobile voice messaging. Please leave a message after the tone.*'

Ning didn't know what to say and hung up. As she dropped the phone inside her jacket she saw a music teacher from her school walk up to one of the counters. Mr Shen was slender and still in his twenties. He wore jeans, with a white shirt and a thin tie with piano keys down it.

Ning looked about, wondering whether to hide, but Mr Shen only seemed interested in buying noodles, so she stayed in her seat but turned slightly towards the wall.

Unfortunately, as Mr Shen turned to leave the man on the noodle counter pointed Ning out and spoke loudly. 'Is she one of yours?'

Mr Shen had never taught Ning. He shook his head and told the noodle man that he taught at a lower school, for which Ning was too big. Ning was relieved, but the teacher's brain made a connection a quarter-second before he committed to the escalator. After a wobbly spin on food-court tiles, Mr Shen moved towards Ning with his scrawny neck stooped like some curious bird.

'Fu Ning?' he said, uncertainly. 'Why aren't you in class?'

Ning considered running away. Mr Shen looked neither tough nor fast, especially with a steaming tub of noodles in one hand. Maybe she could dodge between tables and jump down the escalator. Or even charge Mr Shen down and surprise him with her strength. But then what? What would she do all day? Where would she go?

Ning was eleven years old and knew she could only push things so far. Getting kicked out by Miss Xu would make her dad angry. But assaulting a teacher would mean serious trouble with the school authority and this was beyond the limit of Ning's courage.

She stared at Mr Shen and shrugged. 'I just didn't feel like going today.'

'Me neither,' Mr Shen said, as he invited himself to join Ning at the table.

Ning watched the steam rise from the noodle pot, as Mr Shen scooped a hot mouthful with his chopsticks. Most teachers at Ning's school had a strict *do as I say* attitude. Sitting down to talk was radical.

'Don't you have to be in school?' Ning asked.

Mr Shen laughed. 'I think *I* should be questioning. But since you ask, I teach music so I start later and do individual lessons until nine p.m. I'm early today, because I must set up the main hall and prepare the band for the afternoon show.'

Ning had hardly touched her bun and the smell of noodles made her feel hungry.

'Why couldn't you face school?'

Ning shrugged. 'I hate all this memorising for exams. And for parents' day I've got to dress up like a cat and do a stupid dance, and I'm *so* much bigger than the other girls.'

Mr Shen stifled a smile, but then spoke more firmly. 'What will you become if you can't pass exams?'

'Rock star,' Ning said.

'I didn't know you played an instrument.'

Ning felt like she'd been caught out. 'I don't . . . I mean, I'll be a singer or something.'

Mr Shen had briefly seemed, if not exactly cool, then at least more relaxed than most older teachers. But he now gave Ning a stern look.

'You must be careful,' Mr Shen began. 'I can see from how you dress that you take in many western influences, from television and music. But in the West there is lax discipline. If you try and play the rebel here, the school board will classify you as mentally defective. You will be sent to reform school and your parents get no say in the matter.

'I worked in one of those places when I was a student teacher, and believe me they're tough. I saw boys arrive, swaggering like gods. But their heads were shaved, they were given no heat or blankets in winter and their diet was reduced to cold broth. Their spirits were broken most effectively.'

Ning had heard fifty versions of this lecture. She'd spent her early childhood in an orphanage and four years at an elite sporting academy. Monotonous days at Lower School Eighteen drained her spirit, but it was far from the worst place she'd been.

'I know what I *don't* want to do with my life, but I don't really know what I do want,' Ning said thoughtfully.

She looked at Mr Shen, hoping for wisdom, but he felt he'd absolved all responsibility with his lecture, and now his mind was focused on scoffing noodles and the afternoon concert.

6. FACE

Ning sat on a stool behind a privacy curtain. She was dressed in a cat costume: black leotard and leggings, with a pointy-eared hat on the floor between her unshod feet. Her boots and regular clothes were in a mound on the floor, and there were identically dressed but smaller girls on all sides, shrill with pre-show nerves.

Ning grabbed her boot and tipped out the mobile she'd dropped inside for safe keeping. It was against the rules to call during school time, but she was desperate to get in touch with her stepfather.

It wasn't unusual that he hadn't replied. He'd often fly out of the province on business, or spend a day at one of his discount stores in the countryside, where mobile reception could be poor. But she'd also left messages with her father's secretary, who'd never previously failed to return a call.

Dandong was a rapidly growing city. Services sometimes crashed under the strain, and Ning suspected a fault with the telephone network. But she was getting anxious because she'd been kicked out of the dormitory and had nowhere to go when the parents' day show ended.

Ning's step-parents lived twenty kilometres out of the city. No buses went out that far. She barely had enough money for a taxi and drivers were always reluctant to drive so far out. And even if she did make it home, she didn't have a house key. Her stepfather would still be at work, the housekeeper would have finished for the day and the chances of her stepmother being awake were no better than fifty-fifty.

Daiyu straddled piles of clothes, heading towards Ning. 'They'll take your phone if they see you,' she warned.

'Am I speaking to you?' Ning snapped.

Daiyu seemed thrilled to be a cat. Her slim body suited a leotard, she kept swinging the stuffed tail sewn to her bum, while her face was thick with eyeliner, lipgloss, glitter spray and nylon whiskers.

'I don't care if you're speaking to me or not,' Daiyu said, tilting her head and cracking a sarcastic smile. 'But *everyone* else has had their make-up done. Mrs Feng is waiting for you. So you can either go and have make-up like a normal person, or you can make one of your big scenes. I don't care either way.'

Ning dropped her phone back into her boot and almost tripped on her swinging tail as she stood. Her own costume was back at the dormitory and rather than letting Ning out to retrieve it, her teacher made her wear a spare cat suit that was far too small. The leg and ankle cuffs stopped at least ten centimetres off the mark. Ning was getting pinched under the armpits and had a horrible feeling that the arse wouldn't withstand too much prancing about on stage.

The classroom had been divided with a curtain so that the girls could change in privacy, but getting made up involved a trip to the other side. As Ning pushed through the drapes the boys in her class erupted with laughter.

'It's Catzilla!' one shouted.

'Freak of nature,' said another, while Qiang made *boom-boom* noises as if Ning was shaking the floor.

The most annoying part was that while the girls had to dress up like idiots, the boys were doing a basketball display in the tracksuits that they wore for PE.

'Go home and screw your mothers,' Ning said, as she booted the classroom door. 'I wouldn't mind but I'm *better* at basketball than any of you.'

'Meow!' one wag said.

Mrs Feng was a professional make-up artist, and the mother of a girl in another class. She'd set up at a folding table, parked beside the rows of lockers in the broad hallway that ran through the centre of the school. The space was deserted, but the sound of little kids singing wafted from the parents' day show taking place in the main hall.

'I don't want too much gunk,' Ning said, as she sat on

a stool. 'That stuff makes me itchy.'

'You *must* be Ning,' Mrs Feng said.

Ning liked the way that Mrs Feng pronounced her name like some strange and terrible disease, but joy was short-lived because Mrs Feng switched on a powerful make-up lamp and began applying foundation with a cotton wool pad.

'What's that?' Ning asked, as her torturer homed in on her nose with a brush and a small metal tube.

'Look up! Up at the ceiling,' Mrs Feng ordered. 'It's glue for your whiskers. Don't tug them or they'll fall off.'

It took three minutes to complete the look, with copious quantities of lipstick and eyeshadow, but Ning drew the line at glitter spray.

'Enough,' she said firmly, before standing up and heading back towards the classroom.

Qiang and a couple of other boys were out in the corridor and began to laugh. As Ning walked towards the classroom the trio made *boom-boom* noises, but everyone except Qiang backed into the classroom when she got close.

'Let me in the door, turd,' Ning said, as Qiang blocked her way.

Half a dozen other lads stood inside the half-opened door, giggling like idiots.

'If I hit you, you won't like it,' Ning warned.

Qiang laughed. 'I'll not be defeated by a mere cat!' he shouted dramatically.

Ning was keen to get back inside and check her phone,

so she made a quick swoop and flicked the end of Qiang's nose. A roar of laughter erupted as Qiang stumbled backwards, shocked by Ning's speed. When Qiang realised that his mates now laughed at him rather than Ning, he lashed out with a Karate kick.

Ning intercepted the flying leg. With her thumbnail digging painfully into Qiang's ankle, Ning stepped backwards, making him hop helplessly after her.

'Let me go, you elephant!' Qiang demanded.

Ning wanted to humiliate rather than hurt and spotted an opportunity at the end of the hallway. After making Qiang hop a little farther, she twisted his foot so that he buckled with pain. Rather than letting Qiang bang his head on the ground, Ning grabbed him under the armpit, then wrapped her other arm around his waist, crushing the wind from his chest as she tossed him effortlessly on to her shoulder.

With Qiang's head hanging behind Ning's back and his feet kicking in front of her, Ning walked past a startled Mrs Feng to a huge rectangular waste bin planted in the doorway of the school cafeteria.

'You reek,' Ning complained. 'Have you *ever* washed that tracksuit?'

After backing up to the overflowing tub, Ning dropped Qiang head first into apple cores, drink cartons, disposable chopsticks and half-squeezed sachets of soy sauce.

While Qiang thrashed about, buried from head to thighs and desperate to climb out, a dozen boys raced down the hallway towards them, followed by a smaller group of cats.

Ning worried that the boys might attack, but they seemed content to stand back, laughing hysterically as Qiang kicked air and moaned. He was desperate to escape but only managed to rustle garbage and work his way deeper. Two girls who'd also suffered Qiang's jokes thanked Ning for getting revenge.

'What is this outrage?' Mr Ma roared as he stormed across the deserted canteen towards the dustbin.

Ma was the school's deputy head and several kids at the rear of the crowd bolted for their classroom as soon as they heard his voice.

'Where is your class teacher?' Ma demanded. 'Who is responsible for this?'

'It was Fu Ning,' Daiyu announced.

If Daiyu had been within range, Ning would have punched her out.

'Well, who'd have guessed that?' Mr Ma said, as he grabbed Qiang's ankles and picked him out of the bin.

There was laughter as Qiang was planted on his feet, with bits of food stuck in his hair, plus greasy smears and plastic wrappings stuck to his tracksuit.

'I'll wipe your smiles off,' Qiang roared to the other boys, before looking over his back and discovering a chopstick spearing his buttock.

Mr Ma stood in front of Ning. He crouched low and yelled in her face. 'You've already been in trouble for lateness today. Go and sit outside my office. You will be dealt with after the performance.'

But Mrs Feng came to Ning's defence. 'Why punish

her?' she asked furiously. 'Those boys have been ruthlessly teasing girls all afternoon. Their teacher comes and goes, but he does nothing to halt it.'

Mr Ma wasn't used to being dressed down in front of his pupils.

'Well,' he said, shaking with anger as he picked a boy at random. 'You, find the nurse and bring her here to deal with Qiang. The rest, get back to your classroom. Sit still at your desks in the formal position. I expect silence until the time for your performance.'

Ning gave Mrs Feng a respectful bow, before following her classmates back to their room. The better behaved kids had never been shouted at by the deputy head before, and none dared laugh as the girls dived back behind the curtain and the boys sat at desks, with straight backs, hands crossed on the tables in front of them and feet tucked beneath their chair.

'One sound,' Mr Ma roared, as he glowered at the class.

'Fu Ning?' a woman shouted, as she barged in, clouting Mr Ma with the classroom door. 'Is this room twenty-six?'

Ning couldn't see over the dividing curtain, but the appalling scouse-accented Chinese could only come from her stepmother.

Ingrid Fu was originally from Bootle in Merseyside. She had freckled skin and curly red hair down her back. Dandong was a city of eight hundred thousand, but it was off the tourist trail and Westerners were a rare sight.

'Ning babes, you in here?' Ingrid yelled, switching to English.

Ning felt sure the embarrassment her stepmother was about to cause would more than cancel any cred she'd gained by dumping Qiang in the giant food bin.

'Hello, mother,' Ning said, respectful and nervous as she stood up. 'I didn't know you were coming to parents' day.'

'Parents' you what?' Ingrid asked, as she ducked through the curtain and banged her thigh on a desk. 'Oww, ya fecker! I never knew boys and girls were separated over here. It's like a Jew wedding.'

Even kids who hadn't paid attention in English class could work out that Ingrid was drunk.

'It's only when we get changed,' Ning explained, as her face burned. 'Why are you here?'

'You're all dressed as bloody cats,' Ingrid noted, gold bangles on her wrists clattering as she glanced about. 'Is it the school play today or something? That costume goes right up your crack, it looks terrible.'

Ning spoke slowly, hoping to get through Ingrid's thick skull. 'WHY – ARE – YOU – HERE?' she shouted.

Ingrid's head snapped sideways, but her eyeballs took a second to catch up. 'Honey, we've got to get out of here. Grab all your shit, yeah?'

'Is this about the messages I left Dad?' Ning asked. 'I said I needed to be picked up *after* school, not right now.'

Ingrid gasped with frustration and waved her hand

in front of her face. 'Can't be explaining like war and bloody peace or something. I need yous to come with us. Urgent, like.'

Mr Ma spoke in stilted English. 'Ning, Mrs Fu, perhaps you can talk in the corridor without disturbing the other pupils?'

Ning was fine with this if it at least meant she wasn't shown up in front of everyone. Out in the corridor, Ning was caught by surprise as Ingrid shoved her back against the wall.

'Your dad's in trouble,' Ingrid explained. 'You and I have to skedaddle, pronto.'

Ning felt a shot of adrenalin. 'What kind of trouble?'

'Too complicated to explain here. But we've always been all right, you and me, haven't we? I mean, I know I'm not exactly perfect mother material, but you trust me, don't you?'

Ning decided that Ingrid's description of their relationship sounded about right. She wasn't the kind of parent who tucked you in when you were sick, or baked a cake for your birthday, but they'd always got along and sometimes even had a laugh together.

'Do you trust me?'

'Sure, I guess,' Ning said.

'Then you've got to come with me, right now. I can't wait around, they'll be looking for me as well.'

Ning was baffled. 'Who'd come looking for you?'

'Can't wait around,' Ingrid said. 'Come or don't come. No messin'.'

Ning watched as her stepmother started a drunken

walk down the hallway towards the school's main exit, then stopped and turned back.

'I'm dressed as a cat,' Ning shouted. 'Can't I at least go back and grab my clothes?

'No messin',' Ingrid repeated. 'I promised Chaoxiang I'd take you with me, but I can't wait around.'

Ning looked anxiously back towards her classroom, wondering if she could make a dash for her clothes, boots and phone. But the school exit was less than fifty metres away. There was a chance she'd lose Ingrid and a chance Mr Ma would hold her up by asking for an explanation.

'Wait,' Ning shouted, as she raced after her stepmother with her tail swinging from side to side.

7. RIDE

'So you're with me?' Ingrid said, as Ning raced across the car park.

A black 760Li was parked at an angle just inside the school gates, blocking off half a dozen parking bays. It was the biggest BMW you can get and this one was pimped up, with tinted windows and matt black alloys.

Ning expected Ingrid's driver to step out and open the rear doors, but as she closed in she noticed the driver's side mirror dangling from insulated wires, and a scrape stretching from the front wing to a busted rear light.

'Where's Wei?' Ning asked anxiously, as Ingrid climbed into the driver's seat.

'Busy,' Ingrid said. 'Get in.'

Ning hesitated, but Ingrid had made it clear she wouldn't hang about.

'Can you even drive?' Ning asked, as she pressed the button that closed the rear door and lunged for a seatbelt.

'I was doing handbrake turns in nicked Fiestas before you were born, girl,' Ingrid said.

She looked backwards over her shoulder, preparing to reverse out of Lower School Eighteen into the busy main road. Ning clicked her seatbelt on, glimpsing a shopping channel on the headrest TV as Ingrid hit the gas.

The BMW shot forward, ploughing into a parked Honda, with enough force to smash its front headlight and push it sideways into the much newer Volkswagen parked next door. The huge BMW suffered no more damage, but Ning was tempted to jump out while she had the chance.

'I guess that's not reverse,' Ingrid said, as car alarms chorused.

'Are you *sure* you can drive?' Ning asked.

'That's my second accident today,' Ingrid said. 'Third time lucky, eh?'

Ingrid found the reverse selector. The light down the street was red, so they backed into two empty lanes, before Ingrid selected drive and floored the accelerator.

'Christ, this has got some poke!' Ingrid said, as they reached eighty KPH within four seconds, then braked back to nearer twenty-five as they caught the traffic.

After a red light, a right-hand turn and a steep climb up an on-ramp they were on the six-lane Shendan Highway, heading west out of Dandong. Ning realised they were heading home, and calmed down enough to ask a rational question.

'You said Dad was in trouble. Why don't we go to the police?'

'Cos it's the cops that bloody well nicked him.'

'But Dad's not a crook,' Ning said. 'They'll sort it out. We should go to the police station where he's being held and ask to speak to someone.'

Ingrid looked flustered as she used her fingers to comb strands of hair off her face. 'Sweetheart, it's complex. Your father's a businessman. Sometimes in business, you have to bend rules to get things done.'

'Pay-offs,' Ning said.

'Exactly.'

Ning understood pay-offs well enough. She'd been born in a peasant village, which meant she was only eligible for a country school. To get into a more prestigious and better funded city school, her stepfather had handed an envelope fattened with hundred-yuan notes to an education authority official.

'I don't get all the ins and outs,' Ingrid said, as she switched lanes to pass a truck stacked with steel I-beams. 'I think there was an edict from Beijing. A crackdown. Corrupt officials and businessmen are getting rounded up and your dad is caught in the net.'

Ning felt scared. Anti-corruption slogans had been appearing all over Dandong, promising three years' hard labour for those caught.

'Your dad's a good fella,' Ingrid said, trying to sound soothing. 'Important people owe him favours. Even if he's found guilty, it's most likely just a fine.'

'Right,' Ning said, but she didn't stay reassured once her brain kicked in and started asking questions:

Where was Ingrid's driver, Wei? Why hadn't she been able to get her dad's secretary on the phone? And if this was going to blow over, why was Ingrid tearing along the highway in a panic?

'What are you trying to get away from?' Ning asked. 'You've got nothing to do with Dad's business, have you?'

'Not day-to-day, but in a legal sense I do.'

Ingrid was rarely sober much beyond eleven in the morning, so Ning found this hard to believe.

'You never go to the office with Dad, or anything like that.'

'I'm a Brit,' Ingrid explained. 'You Chinese are all tied up with red tape. Regulations on investment, tax, foreign exchange. So your dad sets up foreign companies in my name as a way of getting around the rules. And that's all well and good until the shit hits the fan.'

This made some sense. Ning had seen her stepfather bring home papers for Ingrid to sign.

'But shouldn't we be there for Dad?' Ning asked. 'Why run away?'

Ingrid didn't answer because they were coming up to an exit and she was confused by the road layout. 'Is this the exit to drive through the villages?'

Ning nodded. 'You want seventeen, the exit after this one. It takes us straight to the house.'

But Ingrid scythed in front of a Buick Excelle and

down the exit ramp.

'You'll have to go all through the villages,' Ning warned. 'This way takes ages.'

'I know this way better,' Ingrid said.

This was a blatant lie. The route from seventeen involved driving in a straight line for three kilometres and taking a single right turn, whereas going through the villages involved rutted roads and the likelihood of getting stuck behind a tractor, or some peasant with chicken cages stacked on the back of a moped.

The car felt less comfortable as it left the exit ramp of the modern highway and rattled over cracked tarmac that was barely wide enough for two cars to pass. They'd reached Dandong's outermost suburbs and after passing a drab factory complex that made its surroundings smell like burnt plastic, they reached proper countryside, with wheat and corn swaying under late afternoon sun.

'Does Dad know you're running away?' Ning asked.

'It's his idea,' Ingrid explained. 'He thinks it's better if you and I are out of the country until all this blows over.'

'When did you speak to him?'

'He got a tip-off from a pal in the police department, a few minutes before he got done. There wasn't time for him to scoot, but he made some arrangements and he was on the phone to me as the cops burst into his office.'

'But Dad's not a crook,' Ning said, practically whining. 'This is *so* unfair.'

'Life's not fair, babes. You'd better get used to that. We'll get some things from the house, then stay somewhere like Singapore or Thailand for a few weeks and fly home when this is smoothed over.'

It was a fine afternoon, but Ning studied goosebumps on her legs, caused by fear and the cold blast from the air conditioning. After a couple of minutes with nothing but the sound of the car riding potholes, the tarmac ended and the road forked into two dirt tracks. The big limousine would have bogged down here in the wet, but the province had been going through a hot spell, so the dirt was baked hard and the back wheels spewed up tan-coloured dust.

Ingrid stopped by a stretch of overgrown farmland a kilometre shy of home. The land had been sold to speculators, who'd demolished everything except a small barn, then ringed the plot with wire fencing, much of which had been cut away and stolen by local farmers.

Ning now realised why Ingrid had pulled off the highway at the wrong junction.

'You think there might be cops waiting for us at the house?' Ning said, as she stepped into the dirt, wondering how her unshod feet would stand a cross-country walk.

'Most likely,' Ingrid said. 'We'll come up to the house from behind. If there's a lot of cops we're buggered. But I'm hardly a major villain and they probably don't know that your dad tipped me off before he got arrested. With any luck it'll just be a couple of uniforms expecting me to drive through the main gate.'

'And if we can't get into the house for our passports,

how will we get out of the country?' Ning asked.

'Passports?' Ingrid said, looking surprised. 'Our passports are useless, babe. They'll be on alert at every airport and border post.'

Ning felt a knot in her belly. 'So how do we get to Singapore, or wherever?'

The more Ning heard, the less things made sense. Ingrid had lied about turning off at the junction, what else was she lying about? And Ingrid wasn't exactly stable, so was she lying because she was covering something serious, or because she was a paranoid drunk who didn't understand what was going on?

'There's gonna be time for explanations later,' Ingrid said, as she started walking into the overgrown field, with their house a small outline in the distance. 'We need cash and that house is the only place I know to get it. Once we have money, your father gave me contact details for some people who'll get us out of the country.'

8. HOME

Ning's soles were black as she crept over dusty ground, close to a cedar fence topped with barbed wire. Ingrid was a few steps behind, peering through a gap between planks.

'Can't see anyone,' Ingrid whispered. 'Just a beige car.'

Ning took a look for herself. The villa was large. Two storeys with a reddish slate roof, roman columns and a gaudy dome made from green glass. The large back lawn was immaculately mown, and the centrepiece was a garden square with formal lines of plants and hedges.

The villa had been Ning's home since her adoption five years earlier, but now it felt like hostile ground. The anonymous brown car parked by the garage block had two small roof aerials and on close inspection, blue lights set into the rear bumper.

'Cops for sure,' Ingrid said quietly. 'If I give you a boost, can you climb in?'

The suggestion gave Ning a pang of discomfort. Had her stepdad really asked Ingrid to take her out of China, or did Ingrid just need her to help with the break-in?

Before starting, Ning gave her cat's tail a mighty tug, snapping the nylon threads attaching it to the back of her leotard. Ingrid then stood with one knee on the ground and her palms flat against the fence. Once Ning was balanced on Ingrid's shoulders, she rose up until Ning's eyes were aligned with the wire.

'See much?' Ingrid asked.

It was past five in the evening. Low sun turned the villa's windows into white glare, making it difficult to look at the back of the house. For all Ning could tell, there might be twenty cops inside watching her.

'I'll risk it,' Ning said.

Ning hadn't done gymnastics or strength training in the year since she'd been kicked out of Dandong National Sports Academy, but her skills looked fresh as she moved easily from Ingrid's shoulders. She straddled three lines of barbed wire, then settled into a crouching position with her feet balanced on the top of the fence. As she jumped down, the back of her leotard snagged barbs, throwing her off axis and ripping circular holes over her lower back and right across her bum.

Ingrid stared anxiously through the gap in the fence as Ning hit the grass hard. Ning felt a sharp pain in her right side as she rolled on to her back, but the lawn was regularly watered and the soft earth saved her.

Ning kept low, crawling rapidly over the grass towards the house. After thirty metres, she reached a screened area used to store the household bins. It stank of rotten food and the gravel around the four large plastic bins swarmed with flies picking at a duck carcass.

The rubbish bags were all thrown about and split open, presumably by cops searching for evidence. Ning stood, rather than crawl through the filth. To her relief the pain in her side wasn't too bad when she straightened up.

A metal catch opened the access gate used by garbage collectors. Ning leaned into a paved alleyway, with the fence of the smaller villa next door facing her.

'Nice one, sweetheart,' Ingrid whispered, keeping close to the fence as she ran through the open gate and planted a kiss on Ning's cheek. The alcohol on Ingrid's breath was fresh enough to overpower the garbage.

'Have you got a hip flask or something?'

Ingrid shrugged. 'Needed a quick slug for courage. You ready?'

They moved out of the garbage area. Despite years of boozing, Ingrid was no wimp. They kept low and moved fast, ending up squatting between the brown car and the side entrance of the house, where a trio of air-conditioning units blasted warm air.

While Ingrid peered through frosted glass in the side door, Ning inspected herself. There was a tender spot below her ribs, she had grass stains down both legs of her tights, and the back of her leotard was shredded, exposing black knickers with skulls on them.

Ning looked around as Ingrid unlocked the side door. She twisted the knob slowly, pushed the door and they crept into a large utility room. The floor was covered with limestone tiles. There was a washer and dryer at one end, the cleaner's trolley and an ironing board at the other.

'Everything we need is upstairs,' Ingrid whispered.

As Ingrid crossed to the door on the opposite side of the utility room, Ning grabbed a freshly laundered washcloth and used it to wipe gravel digging painfully into her soles.

Ingrid opened a small gap in the door leading to the main part of the house, but looked shocked and closed it rapidly.

'There's two cops in the kitchen playing cards,' Ingrid said. Then she dug into the pocket of her jeans, pulled out a hip flask and took another slug before offering it to Ning.

The smell of booze made Ning heave and back off.

'Where's the money you're looking for?' Ning asked.

'Up in the nursery,' Ingrid said. 'They seem pretty engrossed in their game. If we pick our moment and keep low they shouldn't see us. I'll get the money. You go to your room and quickly pack a few things in a bag.'

'How do we know they're the only cops?' Ning asked.

'We don't *know* anything,' Ingrid said. 'But there's only one car, and judging by the way they're sitting there playing cards, I'd bet their instructions are to sit around and arrest the dumb English wife when she gets home with ten bags of shopping.'

'They might have heard what happened at the school though,' Ning said.

'Might, might a lot of things,' Ingrid said impatiently, as she reached for the door handle. 'Stick close. Now!'

As Ingrid led the way across polished marble towards a curving staircase, Ning saw the cops on bar stools less than ten metres away. One was practically a boy, the other was fatter with greying hair. Both had gun holsters, but only paid attention to the cards in their hand.

Two cleaners usually kept the house pristine; cops had searched the place, turning everything upside down. There was cutlery and food packets strewn over the kitchen floor, and feathers hung in the air where they'd sliced open sofa cushions.

The stair carpet had been ripped up and Ning placed her feet carefully to avoid the spiked grip rods designed to hold it in place. Her bedroom and the nursery were on opposite sides of the hallway at the top of the first-floor landing.

'Quick as you can,' Ingrid said.

Ning expected her room to be a mess after what she'd seen downstairs, but it still pissed her off seeing all her stuff thrown about. Her mattress, duvet and pillows had all been cut up. Her bed frame had been tipped against the wall, her laptop had been taken away and the contents of every drawer and cupboard were spilled over the floor.

Just entering the room had kicked up a storm of feathers and Ning put a hand over her face because it made her want to sneeze. Most of her bags were at Miss Xu's. The only holdall she could find was a grubby orange pack from her sports academy days. She unzipped it and stuffed in handfuls of underwear, jeans, tops and a brand new pair of Nikes.

With the bag two-thirds full, Ning went into her bathroom to grab some toiletries and was disgusted to find her floor and toilet seat soaking wet where one of the cops had pissed without even attempting to aim at the bowl. Planting her feet carefully between puddled urine, Ning dropped tissues, toothbrush, nail clippers, body spray and a few other bits in the bag. Then she remembered her special box.

Ning found the box tipped on its end between her bedside table and the wall. It was the kind of box a four-year-old thinks is beautiful, made from garish yellow plastic, with peeling gold foil and a picture of a badger in a waistcoat on the lid.

It was the only thing Ning had owned for longer than she could remember. She checked that the cops hadn't interfered, but everything was there: The picture taken at the orphanage with her little playmate who died in a traffic accident, the silver medal she'd won for boxing at the National Tournament in Beijing, a copy of her adoption certificate stapled to a photo taken with her step-parents on the day they'd signed the papers, the autograph of the TV star Ning had a crush on when she was eight, and a bunch of other stuff of no value to anyone but her.

When the box was safely zipped inside the bag, Ning

headed towards the hallway. But she heard a cop coming up the stairs.

'Ingrid,' Ning said, as loud as she dared.

The older cop spoke quietly from the base of the staircase. 'Are you sure this footprint wasn't here before?'

Ning's dirty soles had marked the polished marble at the base of the stairs.

'It's here too, where they pulled the carpet up,' the young cop answered. 'These footprints came after the search. Do you think it's Fu's wife, or the stepdaughter?'

Ning heard the older cop moving up the stairs. 'The girl is only eleven,' he said. 'My daughter is thirteen and her feet are smaller than that.'

Ning thought about crossing the hallway into the nursery, but if the cops were more than halfway up the stairs they'd see her, and she risked getting shot at.

'Mrs Fu,' the older cop shouted. 'We know you're up there. Please step slowly into the hallway with your hands in the air.'

Ning had no appetite for surrender. If the cops got her and things went badly, they'd ship her off to the toughest reform school they could find and keep her there until she was eighteen. With the orange pack slung over her shoulder, she dashed to the window, turned the handle and threw it open. The jump was a metre more than her drop from the fence, and this time she'd be landing on gravel over concrete rather than a soft lawn.

'Let's not have trouble, Mrs Fu,' the older cop shouted,

sounding like he'd reached the top of the stairs.

Ning gulped air and felt sick as she stepped up on to the window ledge, but before she got her other leg up the young cop stood in the doorway with his gun pointing right at her.

'Freeze, freeze!'

He was handsome, no more than twenty-two, and he looked as frightened as Ning felt. She took a look down at the gravel.

'If you jump, you'll probably break your legs,' the cop said. 'And if you don't I'll shoot you in your back as you run away. So show me your hands and step away from the window.'

9. NURSERY

Ning felt beat as she turned towards the cop with her hands in the air. Maybe if she got in close she could knock the gun out of his hand, but that would be tough and even if she pulled that move off his partner would be pointing his gun at her by the time she got the job done.

'Is she alone?' the older cop shouted.

'Was it just you?' the cop asked.

Ning paused for an instant before nodding. Her hesitance dented the young officer's confidence in her answer.

'This isn't exactly the town centre,' the officer said. 'How'd you get way out here on your own?'

'A friend lives in the village a mile away. His dad dropped me behind the field out back.'

By this time the older cop was in the hallway. His red

face and short breathing made him look like a candidate for a heart attack.

'Says she's alone, but I think we need to check the place out,' the younger cop said, as Ning wondered if Ingrid had been brave enough to jump out of a window. 'I'll call for backup just in case.'

'You bloody won't,' the older cop said firmly. 'The boss will rip us one if he finds out we let them sneak in. The wife is no threat, probably passed out drunk somewhere. Get this lady cuffed, then help me look for mother.'

The young cop took handcuffs off his belt and threw them to the floor at Ning's feet. 'Pick them up, and snap them over your wrists.'

Ning bent forward, but a gun went off as she grabbed the cuffs. The younger cop crashed forward. A mist of blood sprayed Ning's face, as she took the best cover she could by diving towards the wall behind her upturned bed.

The next two shots hit the older cop, knocking him down the hallway towards the stairs. Another crack came and this time the bang was so close that it made Ning's ear pop as it smashed through the young cop's skull.

The commotion had thrown up clumps of feathers and Ning fought a cough as Ingrid hopped across the carpet holding a large automatic pistol.

'Where'd you get that?' Ning shouted, over the ringing in her ears.

'Stashed in the nursery, with money and everything else we need,' Ingrid explained.

There was a smell of gunpowder, mixed with shit from the young cop's ruptured intestine. Seeing death up close was a first for Ning, but more shocking was Ingrid's clinical shooting. The young cop had a bullet through the stomach and another through the head. The older one out in the hallway had been hit through the heart, followed by an execution shot through the forehead.

'They're dead,' Ning said, dumb with shock.

'No good to us alive, were they?' Ingrid said.

'When did you learn to shoot?'

'I told you before. I was a medic in the British Army before I met your father.'

Ning had heard Ingrid mention her spell in the army. But it got treated as a joke: like finding out that your fat uncle once ran marathons, or that the cop in the family used to be a car thief.

'I was a crap soldier and a piss poor medic,' Ingrid explained. 'But I could always shoot straight.'

Ning followed Ingrid across the hall to the nursery. She'd always found the changing table and the baby toys depressing. Ingrid had miscarried four babies before the Fus adopted Ning, but the nursery remained, awaiting a biological miracle.

But Ning now saw another reason for keeping the cot. Its foam mattress had been ripped apart in the search, but the officers hadn't discovered the false panel in the cot's underside, which had dropped open to reveal a hidden compartment when Ingrid unscrewed the wooden legs.

As well as the gun Ingrid had already used, there was a second smaller pistol, six clips filled with ammunition and a mound of cling-film-wrapped wads filled with yuan, euros, US dollars and gold ingots.

The presence of this cache caused a radical shift in the way Ning thought of her family. When she woke up that morning, she'd believed her stepfather was a hardworking businessman. Remote, and occasionally scary, but definitely not the kind of man who kept money and guns in the nursery.

'I have to know what's going on,' Ning shouted. 'I have to know *now*.'

Ingrid looked uncomfortable. 'Babes, I swear on my life I *will* tell you, but we can't stick around here.'

Ingrid found a wheeled suitcase in one of the wardrobes, and began stuffing it with money and ammunition.

'There's a red emergency bag already packed in my wardrobe,' Ingrid said. 'Grab that, then wash that blood off your face, but don't take all day over it.'

Ning did as she was told, feeling sick as she wetted a flannel. When she was clean, she ditched the cat suit and slipped into jeans, hoodie and trainers.

She met Ingrid by the utility room door, assuming they'd walk back to the BMW.

'It's a waste of time walking across country again,' Ingrid said. 'It'll be a while before they realise what's happened here. We'll drive the cop car back into the city. It shouldn't take long, we'll be going against the rush hour traffic.'

'Then what?' Ning asked, running around to the

passenger side of the brown car as Ingrid took the driving seat.

When they were belted up and the engine was running, Ingrid handed Ning her mobile. 'Call Wei and tell him I've got the money,' she said.

The villa had a long front driveway with gates that parted automatically as the brown car approached. Ning's heart was thudding, but the ringing from the bullet had died back to a hum and she drew some comfort from Wei's involvement in their escape plan. He was soberer and less impulsive than Ingrid.

'Ning, is that you?' Wei said warmly, when he answered. 'How are you coping?'

'Not brilliantly,' Ning admitted.

The car jolted and nearly went into a dramatic stall as Ingrid slotted the police car into fifth gear, when she'd been going for third.

'Chinky shite box!' Ingrid shouted.

'What's going on?' Wei asked.

'Ingrid just asked me to call you and say that she has the money,' Ning said, fighting a wavering voice.

'Good,' Wei said. 'I've set you up at the Pink Bird Motel. It's dingy, but it's out of the way and any taxi driver will be able to find it for you. You're booked in under the name of Gong. The room has been paid for in cash.'

'Pink Bird, name of Gong. Got it,' Ning said.

'Don't go to the check-in desk. It's room 205 on the second floor. The room is unlocked, you'll find your key in the bathroom, tucked inside a towel. It's better if you stay out of sight as much as you can, but you'll need to eat. There's no room service, but there's a supermarket and a couple of cafes across the parking lot. Someone should be in touch with instructions within forty-eight hours.'

'Will you come and see us?' Ning asked.

'Can't,' Wei said firmly. 'Ingrid understands and you should too. You've *got* to avoid all unnecessary contact. That includes rogue calls to school friends or that boy you fancy. The cops can triangulate your position from a cell phone signal. Both of you to ditch your mobiles as soon as this call is over.'

'Right,' Ning said sadly. 'We might never see you again.'

'Never is a long time,' Wei said. 'But not any time soon.'

Ning hung up and gave the hotel details to Ingrid, who fought the gear lever as they approached the on-ramp leading up to the highway.

'We'll take the car into town and pick up a taxi,' Ingrid said. 'Maybe even a couple of taxis to throw them off the scent. Where's your phone?'

'Inside my boot, back at LS18.'

'Just as well,' Ingrid said, as she snatched her phone from Ning.

With one hand on the steering wheel, Ingrid pressed the button to open her window, then flung her phone into the overgrown area separating them from the oncoming traffic.

'Time to vanish,' she said.

10. PARTICIPATE

Amy had worked hard persuading Dr D to use a CHERUB agent to infiltrate Gillian Kitsell's home, and her new career at TFU depended on the success of the mission. She was too professional to let Ryan sense her angst, but she wanted him on top form and pampered him with a beautifully cooked breakfast of scrambled eggs, crispy bacon and mushrooms.

Ryan was paying the price for pounding the heavy bag the night before, with stiff knuckles and a bruised toe. But he was too proud to admit it and was actually in a decent mood because Amy's plan gave him hope.

Ryan had been enrolled in seventh grade at Twin Lakes Middle School. Santa Cruz had a reputation for good state education, so even wealthy kids like Ethan Kitsell attended regular schools.

For their plan to work Ryan had to arrive late to third

period gym class. He avoided the school bus and Amy drove him an hour later in a Mercedes SL. With the sun up, the roof down and Muse blasting on the stereo, it was a perfect California moment.

Twin Lakes Middle School had grown with the population. Amy parked in front of an old brick schoolhouse that was now used for admin and remedial classes. Beyond was a shabby block of one-storey classrooms built in the sixties and a more recent block with a banked roof that led up to a sports hall at the far end.

'Got everything you need?' Amy asked, as Ryan stepped out of the Merc.

'Checked and double-checked,' Ryan said.

'Great,' Amy said. 'And no pressure, but I was up half the night locating that set of master keys, so if you screw this up I might kick your arse.'

Ryan knew Amy was joking and gave her the finger, before slamming the car door and heading up the steps into the admin block.

The bleeps for the start of third period went as Ryan handed over an absence note, explaining that he was late due to a small burglary at their home.

'I hope they didn't steal anything valuable,' the elderly school secretary said.

'My dad scared 'em off,' Ryan explained, as he stood with his elbows resting on a high counter. 'They didn't get much, but we waited ages for the cops to arrive, and they wanted to question all of us.'

The secretary wheeled her chair back towards the

counter. 'Are you English?' she asked, as she slapped a mauve hall pass on the counter in front of Ryan.

'Yeah,' Ryan said. 'My dad's moved out here for work.'

'My brother was stationed over there. USAF missile base, back in the eighties.'

'Cool,' Ryan said disinterestedly. 'So I show this to Mr Oldfield when I get to the gym?'

The woman glanced at her watch. 'If you move fast, you'll only miss a couple of minutes.'

But Ryan needed to work in an empty changing room, so he ducked into the toilet for a while, before slowly crossing a sunny courtyard and entering the new building.

His trainers squeaked on scuffed tiles as he walked the length of a deserted corridor. When he reached the Phys Ed department, he stood outside the boys' changing room and pretended to drink from a water fountain.

When boys got changed they made a racket, but it was quiet which meant they'd already moved into the sports hall. Unfortunately Mr Oldfield had locked the outer door of the changing room, so Ryan had to walk into the gym, dodging three classes of girls running basketball drills, while seventh-grade boys ran laps around the perimeter, except Yannis who sat on a bench in his regular clothes, no doubt claiming an asthma attack for the seven hundredth time.

Mr Oldfield was bald, thickset and had a moustache. He hadn't got the memo about really tight gym shorts being out of fashion, so he always looked like he'd just returned from a gay pride march.

'Hall pass,' Oldfield said, as he ripped it from Ryan's hand, then looked at his watch. 'This says 10:48. Where you been these past eleven minutes, son?'

'I had to walk right down from the admin unit, sir.'

Oldfield made a contemptuous sucking sound. 'You think kicking your heels means you won't have to participate?' he said, as he pointed across the gym to the inner door of the changing room. 'Well you got that wrong. And you'd better be out here in four minutes or you can see me after school Monday for detention.'

'Yes, sir,' Ryan said sourly.

Ryan had to get into the changing room for his plan to work, but he acted all pissy as he jogged across the gym. He'd shown little enthusiasm in PE class ever since he arrived, because acting the jock wouldn't win favour with a geek like Ethan.

As Oldfield lined the boys up for their next exercise, Ryan's nose got a blast of boy stink. The locker room was designed for a whole year group of 150 boys to change. There was a smart central area, with play boards and padded benches arranged in a horseshoe where coaches could draw diagrams and whip up team spirit before a big game. One side had the coaches' office and shower block, while the rest was slatted benches and rows of lockers radiating out from the centre.

With less than forty boys out in the gym, most of the locker space was free. The seventh grade cliques all had regular spots. Ethan wasn't proud of his body, and changed at the far end of a row with Yannis and some other nobodies.

Ryan's plan was easy to explain, but hard to execute. He had to get a bully pissed off at Ethan, then step in and save the day before Ethan got his butt kicked. The major complicating factors were that the plan couldn't work if anyone knew Ryan had caused the trouble, and the fact that Ryan's class didn't really have any bullies.

There were a few tough kids, but Twin Lakes Middle was in a solid neighbourhood and its seventh graders didn't habitually stab each other or make nerds drink toilet water.

The one source of tension Ryan had picked up at Twin Lakes was racial. Of the fourteen boys in class 7G, nine were white, one came from India and the other four were Latino. A lot of the white kids were rich. They lived in boss neighbourhoods near the ocean and mostly hung out with other white kids. The Latinos tended to be poorer. Many of their parents worked menial jobs, in restaurants, gas stations and even as maids or servants for rich families.

There was no bully in Ryan and Ethan's class, but there was one kid who was tough and volatile. Guillermo was heavyset, ten centimetres taller than Ryan and none too bright. In the three weeks Ryan had been at Twin Lakes, he'd seen Guillermo storm out of classes, punch lockers and throw a massive hissy fit when he couldn't find his homework.

Ryan's first task was to locate Guillermo's locker. He always changed with a big group of Latino boys in the row of lockers furthest from the coaches' office. Once Ryan had checked the toilets and shower cubicles to make sure he was alone he headed up there, placed his pack on a bench and unzipped it to reveal a clear-lidded tackle box. It was divided into thirty small compartments, each containing several keys.

CHERUB agents are taught techniques for picking locks, but it's a slow process and Ryan had to open multiple lockers to find Guillermo's stuff. Luckily lockers are only designed to prevent casual theft. There are always master keys so that teachers, swim instructors or whoever can replace lost keys. After making calls to the FBI regional office in San Francisco Amy had got a set of master keys for all the most common types of locker.

According to the embossed logos on the front, Ryan was looking at lockers made by Nova. The master keys were arranged alphabetically and tagged by manufacturer. Ryan found eight keys for Nova. Four were obviously the wrong shape, two were complicated jobs tagged *luxe* and *golf* which didn't sound right. The final pair were almost identical and tagged *Nova standard A & B*.

Ryan took the A key and used it to open the first two closed lockers, hoping to find Guillermo-sized clothes and his distinctive green and orange backpack. The third locker needed the B key, and confusingly contained the phones and wallets of three lads who'd left their book bags and clothes out on benches.

After deciding that none of the stuff on hooks was Guillermo's, Ryan opened two more lockers before straddling the changing bench to try the other side.

The first one was the jackpot: the green and orange bag, with Guillermo's shorts, basketball vest and hoodie dumped on top of it.

But someone was coming into the room. Shawn was a black kid, not in Ryan's class. The only time Ryan had spoken to him was when they'd been on the same team doing relay runs in gym class earlier that week.

'Oldfield's got some *major* bug up his arse this morning,' Shawn moaned, as he tore off a grey T-shirt revealing good muscles with a light sweat on them. 'Must have worn this shirt for PE twenty times, but today he says I've got to wear the proper shirt with the Twin Lakes logo.'

Ryan tried to sound smooth, though he knew it looked odd, being in front of an open locker in the wrong part of the locker room.

'You're new, ain't ya?' Shawn said, as he disappeared down another row of lockers. 'I'd put your stuff down here, unless you wanna get towel whipped by a bunch of taco eaters.'

'Could be right, yeah,' Ryan said. 'Thanks for the tip.'

Shawn's locker slammed and he jogged out in his proper PE shirt, muttering about Mr Oldfield enjoying sexual relations with his own mother. Ryan gave it a couple of seconds before turning back to Guillermo's locker.

As he rummaged through a pair of shorts with pizza sauce spattered down the legs, Guillermo's phone and keys slid out of the pocket, bouncing off the bottom of the locker and hitting the tiled floor hard. The phone was a Nokia brick from the stone age, covered with marker pen and smiley faces drawn in nail varnish.

Ryan decided it would be good to leave the keys on the floor in front of Guillermo's locker. He then shut the metal door, grabbed his pack and crossed to the area where Ethan and Yannis changed.

Ethan was easier because he always used the same locker, though Ryan had to give master key B a good jiggle before it popped open.

Ryan jumped as Mr Oldfield shouted through the door leading in from the gym. 'Ryan Brasker, you have sixty seconds or I'm in your face holding a detention slip.'

The jolt threw Ryan into a shudder, wasting valuable seconds. Once he was sure Mr Oldfield had gone away, Ryan switched Guillermo's phone from vibrate to the loudest ring setting before reaching inside Ethan's locker.

Ethan's pack was stuffed with books, as well as sandwiches and a wodge of Internet printouts from a chess site. Ryan pushed his hand inside the pack, dropped Guillermo's Nokia down amidst pencil stubs and long-forgotten chocolate bars, then slammed the metal door.

This crucial part of the operation was over, but Ryan still didn't fancy detention. He'd prepared for a quick change by wearing his Twin Lakes PE top under an unbuttoned shirt and his green school issue shorts were revealed as he tugged down baggy cargo shorts and pulled them over his trainers.

Ryan crossed to the back of the room again and shoved his own stuff into a locker a few doors along from Guillermo. He pulled the rubber band with the key attached over his wrist and jogged out. Mr Oldfield was waiting for him by the exit as boys climbed ropes in the background.

'Something's not right with you, Brasker,' Oldfield said.

Ryan wondered if Shawn had become suspicious and snitched. 'I don't know what you mean, sir,' he said warily.

'You pack muscle,' Oldfield said, as he leaned in close. 'You ever wrestled?'

'No, sir,' Ryan said.

'You're built like a kid who could wrestle or play ball. But your attitude stinks.'

Ryan didn't answer.

'Don't it?' Oldfield repeated, loud enough for the kids doing rope work to glance around.

'If you say so, sir,' Ryan said.

'Twenty laps, then join the rest of the group. Now move!'

Ryan stifled a smile as he started to run. Twenty laps of a little gym was nothing, and despite a couple of close scrapes, the first part of the plan was in place.

11. GYM

The lunch bell was ten minutes away as three classes of seventh-grade boys fed into the locker room. A few went for showers, but the majority settled for a squirt of body spray and a dry top.

The six Latino boys grouped at the back with Guillermo were all in the no-shower camp. Ryan stood a couple of metres from them, wiping a sweaty chest with his balled-up PE shirt.

Guillermo discovered his house keys on the floor when he stepped up to open his locker. Just as Ryan hoped, he noticed that his phone was missing when he dropped the keys back into the pocket of his shorts.

Loads of kids were shouting and locker doors slammed, but everyone heard Guillermo's high-pitched shout.

'Which one of you dick wads took my phone?'

Nobody took much notice. Guillermo took everything

out of his locker to make sure it hadn't dropped down at the back, then did a three-sixty look around, before crouching down and peering under the slatted changing bench.

'Have you checked inside your bag?' a skinny kid asked.

Guillermo got right up in his face and spoke aggressively. 'I don't keep my phone in my bag. It goes in my pocket with my keys.'

The kid was half Guillermo's size and he held up his hands as he backed off. 'Just trying to help, man.'

'If someone's messin' they *better* give it up now,' Guillermo shouted.

Despite saying the phone couldn't be in his backpack, Guillermo unzipped all the pockets and pulled everything out to be sure. By the time he'd finished, his face had gone bright red and his movements were all jerky like he was about to explode.

'If one of you is tricking me, man,' Guillermo said angrily. Then he shouted again. 'Who took my bastard phone?'

Ryan was dressed now, and getting tense. The lunch bell wasn't far off. Kids who'd changed were crowding around the exit and the plan would come to nothing if Ethan carried Guillermo's phone out of the locker room before someone tried to call it.

It would seem suspicious if Ryan suggested someone call Guillermo's phone to see if it rang, but he was almost that desperate when a boy called Sal approached Guillermo holding his own phone.

'Don't fret, bro,' Sal told Guillermo. 'What's your number? I'll call it.'

Guillermo looked madder than ever, but Sal was one of the biggest kids in the seventh grade so Guillermo didn't snap at him.

'It's on vibrate,' Guillermo said.

'Still might hear it moving,' Sal said. 'Ain't gonna do no harm. What's your number?'

The ringing sound struggled to be heard over forty hyped-up kids, but it was enough to send Guillermo and Sal on a charge.

Ryan feigned disinterest as the pair barged through the crowd around the door and steamed across the room. They found a mystified Ethan digging down his bag for the ringing phone.

Guillermo grabbed Ethan by the scruff of his hoodie and bounced him hard against a locker. 'What you doing with my phone, bitch?' Guillermo roared. 'You don't like having teeth in your head?'

Everyone had turned towards the action, and Ryan made sure he was close enough to dive in. Ethan was absolutely crapping himself, while Yannis had shrivelled into a corner, acting like he didn't even know who Ethan was.

'I didn't steal your phone,' Ethan said, as he rummaged desperately in his bag.

'Then how come you got it, you skinny piece of shit?'

Guillermo banged Ethan against the locker again as he held out the grafittied Nokia. Ryan stepped forward to make his move, but Sal grabbed Guillermo's arm before he got there.

'That weedy bitch didn't steal your phone,' Sal said.

Guillermo gave Sal a mean stare. 'Then why's it in his hand?'

'You said it was on silent,' Sal said. 'But that thing went off like a car horn. Someone else put that phone in his bag. Someone trying to stir up trouble.'

Guillermo's none too massive brain mulled this over for a couple of seconds, before deciding that Sal made sense. The tension dropped out of the room, but Ryan felt sick because his plan was down the toilet.

Now the threat of violence had receded, Yannis reverted to being gobby. 'Who'd steal a shit phone like that anyway?' he said. 'I had a better one than that when I was eight.'

Yannis had misjudged badly. Guillermo might have his phone back, but he was still angry and suspicious about being tricked.

'What you say?' Guillermo shouted. 'You wanna see if you're still dissing my phone after I've stuffed it up your big fat arse?'

Yannis looked scared, and Sal's reaction came as another surprise. Ryan didn't know if Sal was sensitive to remarks about the Latino kids being poor, or if he had some past beef with Yannis, but he flipped from peacemaker to aggressor and gave Yannis an almighty slap across the face.

Shocked *ooohs* and mean laughs went through the crowd.

'Smack that fatty boy up!' one of the Latino kids shouted.

'We can't all be rich boys like you,' Sal told Yannis, as he drove a finger into his belly. 'So you shut your mouth.'

Ryan realised his rescue plan was back on. Sal and Guillermo were both bigger than him, but he reckoned he could handle both if he moved fast and knocked one of them out with his first blow. Before Ryan got his chance, he was jostled by three other Latino kids.

'Did you hear this?' Sal shouted, as he looked back at his pals. 'Running us all down?'

'Racist,' someone hissed. 'Saying we all poor.'

'I didn't say anything,' Yannis protested. 'Just . . . it's an old phone, so why would Ethan steal it?'

Sal raised his hand again, getting a kick out of the way Yannis was squeezing himself into the corner.

'I bet you taste like KFC, don't you, fatty?'

Ethan could have backed out at this point, because Sal and Guillermo were focused on Yannis. But he stuck up for his friend, even though Yannis had abandoned him a few moments earlier.

'I've got lunch tickets,' Ethan stuttered. 'Have as many as you like. Just leave us be.'

Sal turned furiously towards Ethan, 'You think I'm a charity case, punk? You think your friend can insult me, then buy me off with a two-dollar lunch ticket?'

Besides Sal and Guillermo, there was now a posse of four Latino boys blocking Ethan and Yannis' exit from the row of lockers. Ryan didn't fancy his chances against a gang of six and he felt guilty as Sal slugged Ethan in the guts.

'Nice shot!' one of the posse shouted, as Ethan doubled over in pain. 'Mess him up, Sal!'

The lunchtime bell saved Ethan and Yannis. A good spot in the lunch queue was one of the few things kids valued more than a good view of a fight and there was a rowdy pile-up as bodies and backpacks squeezed through the door.

'Sensible,' Mr Orchard shouted, as he came out of his office to deal with the mob. 'Mr Lowell, stop pushing.'

As Orchard turned back towards his office, he spotted the situation with Ethan and Yannis.

'What's going on?' Orchard shouted. 'It's lunchtime. Out of my locker room, now.'

As the kids dispersed, Sal hissed at Ethan, 'Be seeing you boys after school.'

'Hey,' Mr Orchard said, as he grabbed Sal. 'You've been suspended twice this year already. Would you care to tell me what's going on?'

Sal shrugged. 'Friendly discussion, sir.'

'I've got my eye on you,' Mr Orchard warned. 'Get outta here.'

There were only five kids left in the locker room and Ryan couldn't stick around any longer without looking suspicious. He waited by the exit, pretending to look for something inside his pack while feeling queasy about the situation he'd engineered: it was meant to be over in a minute with a quick flash of his Karate skills saving Ethan from Guillermo, but now it had the potential to be way more serious.

Mr Orchard held Ethan and Yannis back, but Ryan couldn't hear what was said. Yannis came out of the locker room first. Ethan was behind, holding his stomach and with rings around his eyes, like he was close to crying.

Most other kids had raced off to get lunch in the cafeteria at the opposite end of the building, so the corridors were empty enough for Ryan to stay a few metres back and hear what Ethan and Yannis said.

'Should have kept your stupid mouth zipped,' Ethan told Yannis in an angry whisper. 'It was over. They were walking away.'

'Well you offered lunch tickets. That didn't help,' Yannis said.

'I was on the spot. It was all I could come up with to save you.'

'I could have handled them,' Yannis said.

'I saw how you handled them, Yannis. You were like Jell-O.'

'You think they'll really get us after school?'

Ethan shrugged. 'Sal's fierce, but they might just be trying to scare us. I say we go to the chess room now and stay all lunchtime. After last lesson, we run flat out and get straight on the bus, sitting up the front near the driver. With any luck they'll forget by Monday.'

'My dad's got a gun,' Yannis bragged. 'If they do anything to us, I'll bring it to school and shoot them dead.'

'Aww, don't start being a dick. You're *so* full of crap.'

'I'd do it,' Yannis said defensively.

'Yeah,' Ethan scoffed. 'You're going to bring a gun to school. You're going to solve all our problems with a good old killing spree.'

'Don't believe me then,' Yannis said, sounding even more pathetic than usual as Ethan turned towards a staircase.

'Have you even fired a gun before?' Ethan asked. 'And your dad's not a US citizen, so he *can't* own a gun.'

'Where are you going?' Yannis asked, deliberately ignoring Ethan's attack on his revenge fantasy.

'First floor, chess room.'

'I've got to eat,' Yannis said.

'I've got a packed lunch,' Ethan replied. 'Sal and all those guys will be in the cafeteria. If you want to risk that, you're on your own.'

'I'm *starving*,' Yannis protested. 'They do burgers and fries on Fridays.'

'Your blubber will tide you over 'til three-thirty,' Ethan said, still holding his stomach as he started up the stairs. 'You can have one of my sandwiches if you like.'

Ryan didn't belong to chess club so he couldn't follow Ethan and Yannis upstairs. As their voices faded out, he felt almost as bad as he'd done after the meeting on the beach the night before.

12. NEWS

As Ryan ate lunch, the first light of Saturday morning was breaking over Dandong. Ning had barely slept. She woke on a double bed in the Pink Bird Motel. It was after five and she rushed to the bathroom with a bout of nervous diarrhoea. It wasn't cold, but she kept shivering and had to clench her fists under her arms to keep her hands from shaking.

Everything felt wrong. Ingrid promised an explanation, but had said little more about what her stepfather had done, or why they had to leave the country. She'd passed out after draining a litre of vodka and had been snoring ever since.

Ning kept seeing the two dead cops. When her eyes closed she imagined her stepfather under interrogation, or knelt against a wall facing execution. Much as Ning hated her lessons and exam-obsessed classmates, she now craved the certainty of her old life. She felt like she was falling into a bottomless well, grasping at the sides but unable to grab hold.

The Pink Bird was newly built by an unopened highway. The rooms were large but bland, with framed pictures of Cadillacs on the wall. It was a budget place, made for travelling salesmen, visiting relatives and amorous types who could pay by the hour. Each room faced a large parking lot, with a line of flat-roofed convenience stores on the far side.

Ning was sick of Ingrid's snoring and eau de booze. She slipped on trainers, grabbed the room key and crept out. After going down the stairs at the end of the balcony, Ning cut into the parking lot. There were less than thirty cars in a lot designed for hundreds, and it would stay that way until the highway opened.

Something about the silent grey space and the orange sky helped Ning relax. It could get hot at this time of year, but right now the sun wasn't up and a breeze freshened the air. She found herself at the shops without knowing it. The only place open was a twenty-four-hour convenience store.

This part of town probably would have been fields two years earlier. The little shop hadn't had time to decay. The glass in the automatic doors shone. There were no sticky residues in the bottom of the fridges, or dead flies inside the light fittings.

Ning couldn't remember picking up money, but she found coins and a couple of notes in her pocket. Nostalgia drew her towards the instant snacks at the back. She remembered being four or five years old, stopping at a newly opened petrol station on a rare orphanage outing and seeing Pepsi machines, microwaves and fridges filled with bright yellow boxes.

Ning was now old enough to know that great cuisine didn't emerge from microwaves in the back of convenience stores. But her inner five-year-old still loved the yellow boxes: fish in sauce, sweet dumplings, American burger and crispy duck with rice.

Ning dropped an American Burger box into a shiny microwave. As it rotated, she put ice in a cardboard cup and filled it with Sprite.

The burger came out of the microwave spitting hot, with grease soaked through the cardboard clamshell. She opened it, sniffed and defied her nausea with a scalding bite. The meat was dry, the bun soggy, but when you chewed it up with the ketchup it wasn't too bad.

A couple of construction workers in fluorescent bibs were paying for cigarettes as Ning took the Sprite and burger to the service desk. She took another bite of the burger and was reminded of Ingrid as she saw the bottles of spirits lined up behind the counter.

'See you tomorrow,' the assistant told the construction workers, with a strong Korean accent. Then to Ning, 'Just the American Burger and medium drink?'

Ning had been distracted by all the bottles. 'Sorry,' she said as she reached into her jeans. 'Still half asleep.'

'Don't bite until you've paid,' the woman said, though her tone was motherly rather than cross.

Ning peeled out a pair of twenty-yuan notes, but

almost died of shock as she looked at the counter. The construction workers had blocked her view of the morning newspapers, but now she saw a fresh stack of the *Dandong Daily* with a huge photo of her stepdad on the front page and the headline: *Party officials congratulate police as human smuggling ring is smashed.*

Ning's neck snapped back, as if a gutting knife had been thrust between her shoulder blades. The *Dandong Daily* was an official communist party newspaper, filled with dreary articles about party meetings and official appointments. A common joke was that people only bought it because the government-subsidised cover price made it cheaper than toilet paper.

The privately owned *North East China Star* cost ten times the price and had a livelier appearance. The front page showed two pictures of Ning's stepfather. One had him at a function, dressed in black tie and holding a glass of Champagne. The second had been taken after his arrest, and showed him looking scared, holding a sign that read *Fu Chaoxiang J051654.* The headline simply said, *The Slave Master.*

'My dad likes a newspaper,' Ning said, smiling weakly as she grabbed a copy of both.

'Your change,' the woman yelled, as Ning headed for the automatic doors.

Ning stuffed the coins in her pockets and ran out. The construction workers stood nearby, enjoying their cigarettes and drinking tea from thermal mugs. She thought one of them gave her an odd look, but it was just paranoia.

There was a line of deserted picnic tables alongside the store. Ning ignored the drink and burger and began with the front page of the *Star*.

'Businessman' Fu Chaoxiang arrested in police crackdown.
Twenty-eight arrests, including business associates, provincial customs head and six communist party officials. Women's groups petition for death penalty.

An investigation led by the North East China Star *has led to the arrest of businessman Fu Chaoxiang. A well-known figure in the Dandong business community, Fu was known locally for his popular chain of discount stores and sponsorship of Dandong Knights soccer team.*

But while Fu masqueraded as an honest character, his fabulous lifestyle was underpinned by a brutal smuggling racket. According to official documents and evidence gathered by the Star's investigative team, Fu's organisation was responsible for smuggling over eighty women and girls per week across the Yalu River from North Korea. These included children as young as seven years old.

Officials believe that fifty thousand females were

smuggled over the past eighteen years, and some evidence suggests that the actual number could even reach six figures. Smuggling on this scale was only possible with the support from corrupt officials on both sides of the border.

Police say further arrests are possible in the coming days and have published a list of Fu's associates who are wanted for questioning.

Fu's victims were desperate to leave North Korea, where jobs are scarce and food in short supply. Many paid hundreds of yuan to be smuggled into China, where they were promised jobs in factories, but Fu's organisation targeted only females who were youthful and physically attractive.

Some of Fu's victims were passed on to gangsters and

forced to work as prostitutes in brothels all over China. Women who refused to submit were beaten, sexually abused or injected with drugs to make them subservient.

But most victims of the evil slave master were taken far from China and forced to sell their bodies for sex with Western men, or even Africans. In cities such as London, Paris or Los Angeles, Fu's associates were able to sell North Korean women to brothel owners for up to one million yuan.

In the most depraved cases of all, it is believed that wealthy paedophiles in the United States purchased North Korean boys and girls in return for half a million dollars (3.5 million yuan). Authorities in the United States have begun an investigation into several individuals, based upon a dossier of evidence given to them by the North East China Star.

Story continues, page 2–3

More on the Slave Master inside
Full list of arrests and wanted suspects, page 3.
Star Editorial – Fu Chaoxiang must face death penalty, page 6.
One of Fu's victims speaks out – My four years of hell as Amsterdam sex slave, page 4–5.

Ning felt like she'd been smashed in the face with a brick. Part of her wanted to read on, but she could barely see through the tears welling in her eyes. If the article was true, the man who'd clutched her to his chest on water slides, bought her presents, flown to Chongqing to watch her box and cried when she lost on a split decision, was an evil criminal.

At the top of page three the number for the Dandong police hotline was printed in giant red text. Below it was a bank of small head shots. *If you see these people call immediately.*

The pictures were arranged in order of importance,

and each one had a caption. In the top row were two communist party officials, listed as missing. Ingrid was in the third row: *Fu's wife, wanted for questioning.* Ning reckoned Ingrid would be a higher priority by now, because they'd have found the two dead cops. Wei's picture was at the bottom of the page and he was described as a henchman rather than a driver.

The next spread was dominated by a victim's story. A battered-looking woman of thirty with a sombre expression and a half-European baby in her arms. Ning couldn't bear to read on. She abandoned the drink and burger, folded the two newspapers under her arm and stormed back to confront Ingrid.

She was still snoring, enveloped in sweaty bedding and vodka fumes. Ning furiously opened the small cabinet between the two double beds. She grabbed the gun Ingrid had put there in case the cops showed up, then reached under the covers and pinched Ingrid's nostrils.

'Is it true?' Ning shouted, stepping back from the bed with the loaded pistol aimed at Ingrid's head.

Ingrid rubbed her palm across her face, hung over and barely aware of the shout or gun.

'What's up, babes?' Ingrid said.

She still hadn't seen the gun as Ning threw the two newspapers at her face.

'Is this true?' Ning shouted again. 'Tell me the truth, or I swear I'll kill you.'

Ingrid's eyes found focus. She saw the gun and the newspaper headline in the same instant and sprang backwards, knocking the bedside lamp with her elbow.

'It's complicated,' Ingrid said. 'Put the gun down, eh? It might go off.'

Ning shook her head. 'If it goes off, it *won't* be an accident. You've both been lying to me for years. How could you even live with Dad, if you knew he was doing all this stuff?'

'I didn't know,' Ingrid said, spooked by Ning's intense stare and the gun less than a metre from her face.

'Liar,' Ning shouted. 'If you didn't know, why did you go on the run as soon as Dad was arrested? And the money and guns hidden in the cot. You must have known about those.'

'Let me speak, Ning. But take a step back and point the gun down, OK? You can still shoot me, but I don't want any accidents.'

Ning saw sense in Ingrid's argument. She backed up to her bed and sat with the gun in her lap as Ingrid started to explain.

'I know what you're thinking: What kind of woman can live with a man who treats other women like property? But you've got to understand, I didn't find out like you just did. It was gradual.

'When I met Chaoxiang I worked as an exotic dancer at a club in Dalian. I grew up with bugger all. Only thing I've ever had in my favour was big tits and a nice arse, and Chaoxiang likes girls with a curvy Western figure.

'He turned my life into a movie. Suddenly I was being driven around in fancy wheels. Casinos in Hainan, shopping sprees in Shanghai, jewellery worth more than my dad earned in his whole life.

'I knew your stepdad brought girls into some of the clubs, but after I got married I gradually learned more, mainly because your stepdad used my British citizenship to set up companies to avoid tax and regulations.'

'So you turned a blind eye,' Ning spat. 'As long as you got to spend your share of the money, you didn't care what happened to all those innocent girls.'

'Most of 'em aren't as innocent as they make out,' Ingrid said. 'A lot of them do OK. Find husbands abroad, send money home to their families.'

Ning recoiled at Ingrid's attempt to justify. 'But even if one woman was forced to do all that awful stuff against her will, that's one too many. And what about little kids getting sold to paedophiles? How much jewellery did that buy you?'

'I don't know about that,' Ingrid said, as she shuddered and batted away the newspaper. 'I never would have stood for that. And you're forgetting one thing, Ning. Chaoxiang loves both of us.'

Ning let go of the gun and rubbed her eyes. 'I don't love him any more.'

'Then who else is there?' Ingrid said softly, as she slid forward on the bed and put her feet on the floor tiles close to Ning's. 'You hate your stepdad and you want to shoot me. What does that leave you with?'

Ning sobbed as she placed the gun back in the cabinet and slid the drawer shut.

'I've got nothing left,' Ning admitted, as tears streaked down her face.

'You and me both, pet,' Ingrid said. 'I was the one that picked you at the orphanage. Chaoxiang had his eyes on this stick insect in a frilly dress. But I liked you: a little wild thing, rumbling with all the boys in a tracksuit so dirty it could have stood up on its own. I saw myself in you.'

Ning smiled a little. She'd heard the orphanage story before, but it always came up when her stepdad was around and he'd furiously deny all knowledge of the girl in the frilly dress. But then he'd get a cheeky smile on his face and give Ning a cuddle and say that maybe he had at the time, but that Ingrid had made the right choice.

The memory made Ning realise that love didn't have an off switch. She loved her stepdad, no matter what he'd done or what they called him in the papers. She'd probably never see him again. She'd been sobbing for a while, but now she started to cry properly. Ingrid switched beds and gave Ning a squeeze.

'It's you and me now, babes,' Ingrid said. 'Once we're out of China I can lay hands on some of the cash that was put in my name. We'll go back to Britain and make a new start.'

13. HYPE

Ryan felt lonely as he queued for tater-tots, pizza sticks and peanut butter crackers. In ordinary circumstances he'd have a group of friends by now, but he had to remain a loner to stand any chance of befriending Ethan.

With a dollar and eighty cents swiped from his lunch card, Ryan took his moulded plastic tray and sat as near Sal and Guillermo as he could. You could barely hear yourself speak, let alone a group sitting two tables across who used Spanish half the time, but Ryan could tell they were talking about the locker room incident.

Guillermo was hot-headed and none too bright, but Sal was the real bad boy. He'd not changed out of his grey PE shirt and he had big sweat stains under his arms as he stood up from the table, making a dramatic throttling gesture.

Ryan noted chunky calves, and tightness in Sal's biceps, suggesting strength training, perhaps for wrestling or American football.

'I'll wring Ethan's little chicken neck,' Sal said. 'After school we're gonna be right in his shit!'

But to Ryan's eyes, the *we're* part of Sal's talk looked weak. The boys around Sal were entertained by his rant, but they were a bunch of average seventh graders: up for watching a bit of random violence, but unlikely to risk getting into serious trouble.

One lad warned Sal that he'd be expelled not suspended this time and even Guillermo didn't seem keen now that he had his phone back and his temper had cooled.

When Ryan had seen what he needed to, he binned his last two pizza sticks and headed out of the cafeteria. Twin Lakes didn't allow kids to use phones at lunchtime, but there were never any teachers around to enforce it once you moved out of the cafeteria. He jogged between girls playing soccer on the all-weather pitch, sat with his back to a wire fence and pushed a wireless headset into his ear.

'Rybo,' Amy said when she answered. 'How's the master plan?'

'Don't *you* start calling me Rybo,' he said irritably. 'I bloody hate that. Listen, I didn't get to save Ethan in the locker room, but it might all be kicking off after school. Are you home? Can you still log into Twin Lakes' school records?'

'I've had logins for your school's database since we

hacked the system to make sure you got put in Ethan's class. I just need to run inside.'

'You're out on the beach?' Ryan asked, as he heard the distinctive creak of the beach shower door. 'Nice life for some.'

'Right,' Amy said, giving a commentary on her actions. 'The Mac's coming out of sleep mode. Googling Twin Lakes Middle School. *Contact Us, Enrolment, Sports, Departments, Latest News, Calendar* – a-ha – *Secure File Access*. Safari has remembered all the passwords from last time I logged in. So what is it you'd like to know?'

'The first thing I need is anything you have on a kid called Sal,' Ryan said. 'He's a seventh grader, either in class 7B or 7F.'

'Searching for Sal,' Amy said. 'There's a Salvatore in 7B and a Salvador in 7F. Salvador is twelve years old. He was allowed to skip fifth grade as part of a gifted programme. Reports show straight As.'

'I'm looking for a baddie,' Ryan said. 'Read the other one.'

After a pause, Amy laughed. 'Is this bad enough for you? Salvatore, enrolled at Twin Lakes December fifth after expulsion from Mission Hill. He's got about a hundred lines of discipline notes already. His attendance rate is less than sixty per cent.'

'Is there anything about sports?' Ryan asked. 'He's bigger then me so if it turns out he's a kickboxing champ or something I'd really like to know before I start a punch-up.'

'He was removed from the wrestling squad. Coach's

reason: *Persistent violation of attendance code and poor attitude.*'

'Wrestlers don't punch or kick,' Ryan said. 'I can deal with that as long as I don't let him get close.'

'This isn't so good,' Amy said. 'It says Sal was recommended for expulsion less than three weeks ago after being found on school premises with a knife. On appeal the school board reduced it to a final warning and a suspension.'

Ryan tutted. 'Shit.'

'Want me to call in a bomb scare?' Amy said, only half joking.

'I can probably handle it. But last period is a seventh-grade elective, so I need to know where everyone's gonna be.'

Amy sounded confused. 'What, like picking the class representative?'

'Not election, *elective*. Lessons you pick yourself, remember I got stuck with Chorus because I was a late enrolment?'

'And you sing so nicely in the bath now,' Amy said.

'You're a ball of laughs today,' Ryan said acidly. 'I need to know what electives Ethan, Yannis, Sal and Guillermo have, because I have to be in the right place when fisticuffs start.'

'Understood,' Amy said. 'I need to access the seventh-grade timetables. Ethan and Yannis are together – no surprise – in Spanish, classroom L8. Guillermo is in Family and Consumer Science, room G9 and Sal is in Writers' Workshop, room G16.'

Ryan laughed. 'You have to wonder how Sal's novel is coming along.'

'So where are you?'

'I'm in the music block, which is as far from Writers' Workshop and Spanish as you can get. So I'm gonna have to sprint from the music room. With any luck I'll be able to catch Sal and Guillermo as they leave G building, and be on the spot when they get their mitts on Ethan and Yannis.'

*

The rumours were flying in fourth period Science class. *The big fight. Crazed bunch of Latinos fighting Ethan and Yannis. Maybe knives. Maybe a group of tough white kids turning it into a full-blown race war.*

Bored kids can make a big deal out of anything. Ryan knew it was mostly hype, but the talk didn't do his nerves any good. This was the biggest mission of his CHERUB career and even with all his combat training, a big muscly kid like Sal would be no walkover.

Ryan heard no rumours in fifth period because he was lined up with sixteen other kids, holding copies of a songbook called *Middle School Gershwin* and repeatedly droning a version of *I Got Plenty O' Nuttin* while the old granny who taught chorus kept telling them to *Rip into it* or *Show more passion.*

And then it was show time. Ryan muscled his way to the door and burst out on the first pip. Last lesson on a Friday put a spring in everyone's step and he wasn't the only kid anxious not to miss the fight.

The music block was on the eastern side of the

school site and Ryan found himself leading a charge of two dozen seventh- and eight-grade boys through the paved gap between the old and new school buildings. He'd hoped to make it to the front of the new building and pick up Sal and Guillermo as they exited, but by the time Ryan arrived the crowd coming out of the new building was merging with a smaller group exiting the old.

On a normal day bodies filtered quickly, with most kids going left towards yellow buses in the east parking lot, while a smaller number went the other way to walk home or be collected by parents. But today there were enough kids searching for the big fight to jam up the whole concourse in front of the school.

Ryan felt hopeless as his run became a slow shuffle with bodies packed around. None of the teachers knew why the crowd wasn't clearing, but a couple were soon waving arms and ordering kids to keep moving and clear off the main path.

Then some random kid shouted from a first-floor window. 'It's on out back.'

About a quarter of the school knew about the fight. Groups, including the lads that came through behind Ryan, started shuffling back the way they'd come, while others with no idea what the shout meant got in their way.

Ryan pushed bravely between two big eighth graders, skipped over a low chain fence and broke into a sprint across the lawn alongside the old building, which was marked out of bounds.

'Hey you, *boy*, come here!' a teacher shouted. 'And you lot!'

Ryan set the trend and twenty sixth- and seventh-grade boys risked detention to follow him. He burst into a side entrance of the old building and skimmed the dress of a startled Spanish teacher.

Ryan's best guess was that Sal and Guillermo had sneaked out early and ambushed their targets as they left fifth period.

Thirty rubber soles squealed and skidded on the floor behind, but Ryan didn't know the school well. He overshot, missing the short corridor that emerged into the concrete play area on the opposite side of the building. By the time he'd spun around the chasing pack had swept past and he was tangled up with a bunch of sixth graders who'd joined in with no idea what they were running after.

'Out my way,' Ryan shouted, splatting a little kid against the wall as he burst through a set of swinging double doors and back out into the sunshine.

The group who'd overtaken Ryan were thirty metres ahead and about to merge with kids who'd been able to take a shorter route around the front of the old building. Off to the left, three eighth-grade girls and a teacher stood by Yannis, who sat on the concrete making a high-pitched wail.

He'd run twenty-five metres before being caught by Sal and Guillermo. Ryan only got a glimpse, but it seemed he'd suffered nothing worse than a few kicks and punches before the teacher waded in.

CHERUB training had made Ryan fast and fit and as the boys ahead flagged he ran flat out to catch them up. There were kids glued to the windows up on the first floor behind, but Ryan couldn't tell what they were seeing until he'd bounded up sixteen steps at the far side of the play area.

As he neared the top step, the vista opened out into green space, marked out with a baseball diamond. It had a couple of small stands and a fancy electronic scoreboard sponsored by the local GMC truck dealer.

The main event was taking place beyond the far side of the field, more than two hundred metres away. With the sun in his face, Ryan could only see Ethan's skinny-legged silhouette, with Sal close behind. It was like a scene from a wildlife film, with Sal playing the lion and Ethan the poor baby gazelle about to get its throat ripped out.

The chasing pack was about eight strong, though it was impossible to tell if they'd be participants or spectators when Sal caught his prey. Guillermo was even further back, his chubby frame barely capable of a jog.

Ryan had closed to within seventy metres when Sal made his lunge. Ethan fell hard, ploughing into the grass and lucky not to injure his neck as he did a complete head over heels. Sal got a knee across Ethan's waist, but Ethan knocked Sal off and scrambled back to his feet.

'He's been stabbed,' one of the kids running behind Sal shouted.

By this time, Ryan was less than twenty metres from

the action and watched as Sal ripped out the compass stuck in his arm.

'You're dead, faggot,' Sal shouted, as he started running again.

Ethan had opened a twenty-metre gap and Sal was now amidst the chasing pack. Ryan was less than five paces behind, and after going flat out over six hundred metres he was still full of running when other boys were slowing.

After stressing all day, it finally felt like Amy's plan might pay off.

Ethan had no idea that one of his pursuers had both caused his problems and intended to defend him. He ran in terror, clutching a stitch down his side and heading for a wire mesh access gate used by school groundskeepers. The only problem was, he had no idea if it was locked.

A couple more kids had dropped out of the pack. As Ethan stumbled breathlessly into the gate, Sal led the chasing pack, with Ryan and three other kids a few paces behind. Ethan's hands trembled as he reached down and grabbed the metal drop-peg that locked the gate in place.

The hinges squealed as the gate opened enough for Ethan's slim body to slide through. As the peg clanked back into its slot, Sal reached the gate and the pack concertinaed behind him. Ryan didn't know the school's layout well and got his bearings as the boys around him caught their breath.

They were in the far north-east corner of the school

grounds, with a busy four-lane highway less than fifty metres away. Ethan stood in a curved single-lane driveway which Ryan recognised from when Amy had driven into the school with him a few hours earlier.

Sal reached down to lift up the peg, but there was a gap in the fencing so that you could reach it from outside and Ethan used his remaining strength to launch a vicious back kick, catching Sal's fingers and making him howl in pain.

Ryan was impressed: for a kid blessed with neither speed nor strength, Ethan had done a decent job fending off one of the hardest kids in his year. But he was also concerned: if Ethan ran another hundred metres, he'd be in front of the admin building amidst kids, parents and teachers. Sal would be lucky to get a few punches in before an adult intervened, which meant Ryan had no chance to save him.

Stopping had made Ethan's stitch worse and the sweat dripping from his hair blurred his vision. As Ethan turned to run along the curving path, Ryan saw a Volkswagen SUV coming up behind. The mom at the wheel had two little kids in the back and was yelling at one of them.

The sign said ten miles an hour, but the mom was going nearer thirty when the front wing clipped Ethan's shoulder. Ryan gasped as Ethan pirouetted. His head snapped backwards. There was a gut-churning thud and for a second it looked like Ethan would bounce up on to the bonnet, but the car was tall and Ethan got swallowed between the front wheels.

The driver hit the brake, causing squeals and rubber smoke, but she was going too fast to stop before a rear wheel rolled over Ethan's torso. As the braking SUV juddered and threw sparks off the wire fence, the driving force of the rear wheel sent Ethan spinning backwards.

The big VW buckled a concrete post as it finally stopped. There had been more than forty kids chasing across the field. Every one witnessed the accident and there was a collective gasp from kids with rubber fumes in their nostrils.

Ryan felt horror, followed by guilt because this was all his doing. But he'd also learned first aid on campus, so he pushed Sal out of the way and rushed through the gate. Ethan was flat out on the tarmac, convulsing violently with one arm in bits. Ryan crouched down and realised that Ethan was choking as a couple more kids came zombielike through the gate.

Ryan took charge, pointing up the road and shouting. 'Block the road before any more cars come round this corner. Someone call an ambulance.'

Shaking and breathless, Ryan leaned in close. Ethan fought for breath, but gagged every time he tried. Ryan prised Ethan's jaw open and saw that he'd swallowed his tongue. He plunged two fingers and a thumb into Ethan's mouth, but his tongue was harder to grip than the one inside the resuscitation dummy on CHERUB campus.

Once Ethan's tongue had flopped forward, Ryan realised it had triggered a gag reflex. He scooped out as much puke as he could, before laying palms on Ethan's chest and thrusting down hard. Vomit spattered Ryan's face, but Ethan's airway was clear and he drew a long breath into his lungs.

'Oh, Jesus,' the driver said, as she raced up beside Ryan on stupid heels with make-up streaked by tears. 'I just didn't expect to see anyone there. Is he OK? What can I do?'

14. TV

Ning watched her stepdad's picture on the local TV news, as a nasal-voiced government official gave a speech about the successful destruction of a powerful smuggling syndicate. Chinese TV let high-ranking officials ramble on and this dude used his moment of glory to thank detectives, local officials, bureaucrats in Beijing and even North Korean border guards.

The screen cut to a grinning police spokesman with camera flashes lighting up his face. He mentioned the capture of several suspects overnight and confidently predicted the apprehension of more before day's end.

'*These running dogs will be caught and punished!*' he announced triumphantly.

There was no mention of the two cops Ingrid had shot at Fu Chaoxiang's house. Ning was sure they'd have been discovered by now, but this truth would mess up a news story crafted to impress senior party officials in Beijing.

The newsreader was moon faced and pretty, and Ning felt an urge to hurl dung at her fuchsia pink blazer as she bantered with her co-presenter about how she felt better knowing that the Slave Master was behind bars. Then moon face took a long breath and broke into a smile.

'*On a brighter theme, our next story is about a Dandong fifth-year pupil, who has raised over one hundred thousand yuan to pay medical bills for a friend with a rare form of cancer.*'

It was a rolling news channel. Ning couldn't bear to watch the little bald girl in hospital and the young hero being handed flowers for a third time in an hour. She flipped channels, while Ingrid yelped in the bathroom because the shower seemed to freeze or scald, with no setting between.

It was barely noon, but Ning's morning felt a thousand years old when the telephone between the beds rang.

'Be ready to leave at one-thirty,' the man said.

*

Ryan hadn't cried since his mum died two years earlier, but he was close to it as he sat on his bed with the blinds down and the light off. He'd felt guilt before, but only for minor stuff like breaking his little brother's favourite toy and throwing it up on the garage roof. This was turbo-charged guilt that weighed on every breath.

The crash dominated his thoughts. The thump. The way the rear of the big VW rose up when the back wheel went over Ethan's body. The heat and smell as Ethan's tongue slipped between his fingers. Ryan tried to work out what he could have done differently, but his mind wouldn't focus.

He didn't want to see anyone, but Ted Brasker came in anyway. Ted was a big lump from Texas. He was touching sixty, but looked fit, with cropped grey hair and a heavy build. Before being assigned to the Transnational Facilitator Unit his forty-year career had included the Marine Corps, Navy SEALs, diplomatic protection squads and finally the FBI.

'I'm putting laundry on,' Ted said quietly, as he looked at Ryan on the bed with his knees tucked up to his chest. 'This lot's kinda stinking the room up.'

Ryan had showered when he'd got home from school, but the clothes on his floor had done Phys Ed, then been splattered with Ethan's puke and blood. Rather than touch them, Ted grabbed a damp bath towel and balled the clothes up inside.

'Thanks,' Ryan said softly.

'You've not eaten,' Ted said. 'Amy made meatballs. Or there's a stack of menus down there if you want a delivery.'

'Not hungry,' Ryan said, choking back a sob.

'Mind if I sit down?' Ted asked. Though it wasn't a question, because he was sitting on Ryan's bed with the ball of dirty laundry in his lap before the sentence finished. 'I know where you're at.'

Ryan paid no attention, hoping Ted would take the hint and go away.

'I was training special forces back in the eighties,' Ted began. 'Trainees had to swim on the surface of a pool for thirty minutes with full military pack. We'd stand on the edge, acting like total bastards: calling trainees names and describing all the dirty things we'd do to their girlfriends if they drowned. Swimming with that much on your back is brutal, so even the toughest are fighting all the way.

'Now if they go under or start hyperventilating you've got to fish 'em out. But this one guy was always complaining. I figured he was whining and let him suffer longer than I should have. The board of enquiry blamed it on the way the exercise had been designed and the procedure was changed afterwards, but that kid *still* drowned on my watch. It was near thirty years ago, but I can still close my eyes and see him dead on the poolside like it happened just now.'

Intrigued, Ryan turned his head a couple of centimetres towards Ted and saw the faded tattoo of Jesus on his arm.

'That soldier knew there were risks when he volunteered,' Ryan said. 'Ethan didn't sign up for anything. He's a random kid who's in intensive care because I screwed up.'

'You didn't screw up,' Ted said, as he rested his huge hand on Ryan's kneecap. 'Amy suggested it and I approved it, as did Dr D.'

'Does it even matter whose fault it is?' Ryan asked. 'It happened, whoever you want to blame.'

*

Ning and Ingrid's pick-up was an Isuzu van, fitted with special extension pedals for the chain-smoking midget in the driver's seat. Ingrid went for the passenger seat, but the driver barked: 'Don't be crazy. Every cop in town is looking. In the back!'

The rear compartment was full of buckets, mops, vacuum cleaners and a giant floor-polishing machine which gave off eye-watering fumes. The closest thing to a seat was a mound of tangled blue cleaners' overalls.

Ingrid's sunglasses flipped off her brow as the midget hit the accelerator. 'Careful,' she shouted, as Ning grabbed the headrest on the front passenger seat.

'You bastards stitched me up,' the driver complained, as he headed out of the car park. 'I thought four thousand yuan was good for a drive to Dalian. Then I find out you killed two cops. They're turning Dandong upside down. If they catch me with you back there, you think an old cripple like me will see a cell? Not likely! They'll chop my dick off and dump me in the river after I bleed to death.'

'I didn't make these arrangements,' Ingrid said in her awful Chinese, as she reached into her jacket and pulled out a roll of one-hundred-yuan notes. 'Here's five hundred. You get that now if you stop at the next bottle shop and buy me vodka. You'll get another five hundred when you get to Dalian if you stop driving like a damned lunatic.'

Ning gave Ingrid a concerned look. 'Why drink today?' she asked, in her politest English. 'We don't know who we're dealing with or where we're going.'

Ingrid made a hissing sound as the driver snatched his five hundred. 'Don't start lecturing,' she said. 'Me nerves are in shreds. I need something to level out.'

Ning scowled as she rearranged the overalls into a makeshift seat. She'd felt a real connection to Ingrid when they'd hugged the night before, but she was now reminded of her stepfather: When he fought with Ingrid, he'd often say that the only things she ever really loved came in bottles.

*

Ryan's hunger overwhelmed his guilt just before 10 p.m. He trotted downstairs dressed only in shorts and blasted some of Amy's spaghetti and meatballs in the microwave. When it was steaming he walked through to the living area. Ted and Amy sat in darkness in front of a vast projection TV, with the water in the glass-bottomed pool catching moonlight directly overhead.

'What's on?' Ryan asked, as he sat by Amy on a leather sofa.

'*House MD*,' Ted replied. 'Rerun.'

'Good meatballs,' Ryan told Amy.

'TFU is paying our food bill, so I went to that swanky organic butcher and got him to mince up two pounds of filet mignon,' Amy said.

Ted laughed. 'That's my tax dollars you Limeys are spending.'

'You ate enough,' Amy said, as she reached across and plucked a strand of spaghetti from Ryan's bowl before sucking it between her lips. 'Feeling any better?'

Ryan shrugged. 'Pretty much like shit. Did you hear from the hospital?'

'We've got no contacts there,' Amy said.

A doctor was doing a lumbar puncture up on the big screen. It distracted Ryan enough to make him drop spaghetti down his chest.

'All over the sofa!' Amy yelled, as she stood up and ran towards the kitchen. 'I'll get a damp cloth.'

'Can you get me a Diet Coke while you're in there?' Ryan shouted after her.

'And a bottle of Bud for me,' Ted added cheekily.

Amy threw a beer at Ted when she jogged back with the cloth.

'Just this once, as you've had a bad day,' she told Ryan, as she passed him the Coke. 'But don't push your luck.'

The doorbell buzzed downstairs. One quarter of the big screen cut to an image of Ethan's mum on the doorstep. Gillian Kitsell was forty-three and good looking but for a bulbous nose. She seemed tired and wore chinos and a pink striped blouse that was only half tucked in. Amy, Ted and Ryan all felt a kick of excitement.

'You don't know me,' Gillian told the intercom, 'but I understand Ryan lives here? Is he home?'

'We're coming down,' Ted said, before tapping the button on the remote that unlocked the front door.

Amy reached the bottom of the stairs first, by which time Gillian Kitsell – otherwise know as Galenka Aramov – stood in the lobby under a groovy LED chandelier. Ted was a couple of paces behind, with Ryan in last place, cheeks full of spaghetti.

'I apologise for calling so late,' Gillian began. Her

pronunciation was stilted. English obviously wasn't her first language.

Ryan spoke anxiously. 'How's Ethan?'

'Bruised all over,' Gillian said. 'His arm is badly broken. He has cracked ribs and he's in pain so they've sedated him overnight. I'll take a few hours' rest and drive back to the hospital in the morning.'

'I guess it could have been much worse,' Ted said. 'Ryan hasn't been right since he got home. Seeing the crash shook him right up.'

'Ethan will be in hospital for several days,' Gillian explained. 'His arm will need surgery.'

'Have you eaten?' Amy asked, anxious to do all she could to build their relationship with Gillian. 'I made spaghetti and meatballs earlier. There's a mountain left over.'

Gillian patted a flat stomach. 'That's most kind, but I have no appetite. I just dropped by to thank Ryan. The doctor said if he hadn't got Ethan breathing so quickly he might have suffered brain damage.'

Gillian put her arms out and pulled Ryan into a slightly awkward hug. 'I owe you everything,' she said.

'It's only basic first aid,' Ryan replied. 'I did a lifesaver course when I lived in England. I'm really glad I did now, too.'

Ted put a hand on Ryan's shoulder. 'Proud of you, son,' he said.

'Now I will leave,' Gillian said as she backed up to the door. 'Goodnight.'

Ryan was relieved that Ethan was going to live, but he

was still in a state and only managed to focus when Gillian was about to shut the door.

'When Ethan gets out of hospital, can I pop over?' Ryan asked.

Gillian nodded. 'Of course,' she said. 'I'm certain my son will want to thank you personally.'

'You let us know if you need anything,' Ted added, as Gillian left. 'That's what neighbours are for.'

15. WEST

The drive to Dalian was nine hours of hell. Fumes from the polishing machine gave Ning a fierce headache as Ingrid got drunk and the midget driver crept through endless traffic, interrupted only by curses and blasts of the horn.

Ning wasn't a good pupil, but a girl can't spend six years at a Chinese school without a few facts sticking and she'd once written half a page on Dalian: *Population six point two million, China's twenty-first largest city by population. Major industries are shipbuilding, tourism and the manufacture of electrical goods. Thirty-three athletes from Dalian won medals at the 2008 Beijing Olympics.*

The van ditched them at Lao Dong Park in the city centre because it would look dodgy arriving at the swish Q hotel in the back of a van logoed with the name of a Dandong office cleaning company.

Wei had arranged for someone to check in and leave the doors of their rooms unlocked, getting around the legal requirement to show identity cards or passports on arrival. Ning had her own room and was grateful to escape Ingrid's boozy smell. She found the room key tucked inside a towel as she'd done the previous day, but this time it was a huge marbled bathroom with a jetted bath and double sinks.

Ning's room also contained a large wheeled nylon bag, which felt surprisingly light as she lifted it on to her bed. Inside she found two thickly quilted ski suits, with tags and labels still attached. Beneath these were boots and thick gloves, which looked strangely rigid.

Ning found six packets of money inside the gloves. Each newly minted block was sealed in cellophane, with a red band marked *United States Federal Reserve $25,000*. Besides money there was a pair of bright blue passports and identity documents. Ning recognised the flag of Kyrgyzstan on the front – disproving her theory that nothing she'd learned for middle school exams would ever prove useful.

The text in the passport was written in a Cyrillic alphabet, which she didn't understand, but most of it was repeated in English. Ning was no expert, but her new passport appeared to be either genuine or a high-quality fake, with holograms, watermarked pages and a computer chip embedded in the photo page. There was also a Chinese entry visa, claiming that she'd entered the country three weeks earlier, accompanied by her mother, who was on a business trip.

The last items in the bag were hair straighteners, black hair dye and a piece of paper folded into four with *Fu Ning* written on the outer edge. Unfolding it revealed a printout of an e-mail. The sender and recipient's addresses had been deleted, though Ingrid's driver Wei's name remained at the bottom.

Dearest Ning & Ingrid,

Within the next few days you will be contacted by telephone with instructions for your flight out of China. I am on the wanted list and I will have left Dandong before you read this. To my shame, this is the last help I am able to give you.

I suggest you eat in your room and go out as little as possible. Ingrid's red hair is distinctive, and I urge her to change its colour if she has not already done so. Do not use the Internet or telephone to contact friends, or log into any sites where you may have an account.

One hundred thousand dollars in cash will be payable when you arrive at the airport. The remaining fifty thousand should be kept in your possession for emergencies.

The aircraft upon which you will escape will be an unheated cargo plane. Wearing the ski suits should help to make your flight bearable.

Yours with love,

Wei

*

Two nights passed. Ning took a short walk each morning while the maid cleaned her room, but never ventured beyond the shop in the hotel lobby and the Starbucks next door. Ingrid took longer trips, with straightened black hair and sunglasses. She'd return each time with two bottles of vodka and some mixers.

Ning and Ingrid never went out together, because the cops were looking for a Western woman with a Chinese girl, and their conversations never advanced beyond greetings, and recommendations of dishes they'd eaten from room service.

By Monday there was no longer any mention of the Slave Master on television or in newspapers. It was early afternoon when Ingrid got the call they'd been waiting for. At 7 p.m., Ning wheeled out the large bag with the ski suits inside, while Ingrid took everything else.

They'd chosen to exit as two police officers stood in the lobby. Ingrid put one hand on the gun in her handbag and Ning's heart quickened, but they passed unrecognised into the electrically cooled seats of a chauffeur-driven Lexus.

There was a storm as they drove out of Dalian. Ning watched the street light reflected in raindrops pelting the windows. Half an hour later they were in darkness, doing a hundred and fifty KPH on a steeply banked highway. The luxurious car handled speed well, but Ning worried that it might attract the attention of the police.

A convoy of green military trucks passed by and moments later the driver turned off the highway on to an unlit gravel road. After a few kilometres a plane swept overhead, seconds from landing. Ning and Ingrid ducked instinctively as its wingtip lights turned the surrounding scrubland red.

Minutes later they reached a barrier manned by two guards in People's Liberation Army Air Force (PLAAF) uniform. After a respectful wave and a wait for an electronic gate, they were blasting over smooth tarmac with yellow runway markings sweeping beneath the car.

At the end of the runway stood the turbo prop cargo plane that had swept overhead minutes earlier. It was being unloaded by a crew of more than a dozen men. Some were civilian and some wore PLAAF uniforms, but they all had faces covered by balaclavas or scarves.

The men dashed over wet tarmac, between the plane's rear cargo door and a huge truck, carrying sacks marked with the Chinese symbol for rice flour. Ning saw no reason to smuggle rice flour into a military airbase and guessed it was drugs.

Their driver spoke briefly with a titchy PLAAF officer who was running the show, then told Ning and Ingrid to get out.

From close up the plane felt like a wild beast, with its pulsing propellers making Ning's hair and trousers vibrate. The plane was painted dark grey, with PLAAF markings, but all the safety warnings around the fuel hoses and cargo doors were in Russian, and the two pilots up in the cockpit weren't Chinese. It was in horrible condition, with crudely repaired bullet holes across the fuselage and tyres worn down to their steel reinforcement bands.

The little boss shook his head as Ingrid offered four of the sealed twenty-five-thousand-dollar packets.

'Half for me,' he shouted as he took two packets. 'Give the rest to the pilot.'

The propeller noise was painful as Ning straddled a refuelling hose, then climbed steps next to the wing and stepped inside the fuselage. She saw six flip-out plastic seats and the backs of two pilots through the cockpit door.

Down towards the tail was a stamped aluminium floor, fitted with rails for cargo containers. The last few sacks were being unloaded as another truck backed in. Its cargo had been pre-loaded on to pallets and the team of workers dragged the first of them towards the rear cargo ramp as Ingrid leaned into the cockpit.

Ning was a step behind and didn't like what she saw. The cockpit smelled of fuel and cigar smoke. Every dial looked ancient. Some were cracked and more than a few were held in with sticky tape. The pilots' seats had disintegrated and had sofa cushions tied over them. Behind them were mounds of broken components, unfolded charts, fruit peelings, mouldy sandwiches, newspapers and empty vodka bottles.

'I'm Dimitra,' the pilot said, taking Ning by surprise as she offered her hand. 'Do you speak English, or Russian?'

'Good English, no Russian,' Ning said.

Dimitra looked to be in her early forties. She wore a greasy brown flight suit, but while the gloomy cockpit lights were unflattering Ning suspected she'd been beautiful when she was younger. Maks the co-pilot was pudgy and red faced. He wore a gold-buttoned pilot's blazer and the nylon shirt beneath was layered with food stains and cigarette burns.

'Thank you,' Dimitra said, as she took the fifty-thousand-dollar brick from Ingrid. 'When the plane takes off we shut the cockpit door. There's no heat where you sit in the cargo area, but you'll find blankets.'

'Where are we flying to?' Ning asked.

'Near Bishkek, in Kyrgyzstan,' Dimitra said. 'It will take around seven hours.'

'Then we'll fly straight on to Europe?' Ingrid asked.

Dimitra shrugged. 'My instructions are to get you to Kyrgyzstan. Beyond that I know nothing.'

Ning jumped as a loud rattling sound erupted behind them. She looked down the fuselage and saw one of the huge cargo pallets rolling through the body of the plane. The cargo was bound to the pallet by plastic film, and comprised colourfully-printed boxes marked with the brand names of popular medicines.

As Ning and Ingrid kicked off their shoes and stood in the small seating area changing into their ski suits, eight more pallets were loaded. Two were guns and ammunition, one was mounded with fake football shirts, vacuum packed to save space. The remainder were too far back to see what was inside, but it was clear they'd be sharing the sky with weapons and counterfeits worth tens of millions of yuan.

Maks closed the cockpit door after a final conference with the little PLAAF-uniformed boss, then the gaping mouth beneath the plane's tail clanged shut, plunging Ning and Ingrid into echoing blackness, apart from a flickering exit sign above the door.

It would be cold once they were airborne, but it was a warm night on the ground and Ning was slick with sweat as Ingrid slid a gloved hand around her back.

'Doing OK?' Ingrid asked.

Ning nodded. 'Just about.'

The engines blasted up to full power and the wings flexed as the beast began to roll. The cargo clanked and squealed as they picked up speed, and something broke free down at the back. The noise was unreal and Ning clutched Ingrid tightly while keeping her other hand on her seatbelt buckle, partly to make sure she'd put it on, and partly so she was ready to tear it off if they crashed and burned.

There was a bump and a little kick inside Ning's stomach as gravity pushed her down into the hard plastic seat. They were off the ground and rising fast, as the dilapidated Russian plane swallowed its wheels.

16. LADA

After seven hours rattling inside the beast, Ning was relieved to step on Kyrgyz soil. It was dawn. The airstrip sat in a valley and the mountains on all sides made her glad she'd had no window to watch their landing.

In Dandong nothing stayed the same long enough to look old, but this place wore decay on every surface. Years of winter frost had left huge cracks in the runway, a burned-out fuel tanker stood by airplane hulks with missing wings or engines. The buildings in the distance were made from drab concrete panels, roofed with asbestos.

In China the cargo crew was a dozen strong and moved at a jog. Here there were four grizzled men with hands in pockets who looked about, daring each other to make the first move.

'I'm not sure where to go,' Ning explained in English.

'You speak English? Russian?'

The men blanked her, but eventually Dimitra came out of the cockpit. 'Someone from the Kremlin will know what to do with you. We'll walk.'

Ning's shoulders strained with the luggage, until Ingrid stopped and stuffed everything into the big roller bag, which was empty because they were still wearing the ski suits. It was over a kilometre. The last stretch was up a stepped path towards a six-storey building.

'The locals name this place the Kremlin because most of the pilots that live here are Russian,' Dimitra explained, as she shoved a heavy-sprung aluminium door.

They entered a reception area, decked in avocado and beige. A staircase went up on one side, while the other was a lounge area with shabby leatherette chairs and blinking fruit machines. The smell of cigarettes and spilled beer was enlivened by something more pungent from the gents' toilets.

'Aren't we expected?' Ingrid asked.

Dimitra shrugged, as her co-pilot Maks came through the door behind them. 'Whoever comes will look for you here,' she explained. 'I've been in the air for too long. I must go to my room and sleep.'

As the pilots headed upstairs, Ingrid led Ning into the lounge. A man with a gun on his belt laid spark out against a fruit machine. In a far corner beyond the shuttered bar dead-eyed men sat playing poker. They were a mixture of Russians and native Kyrgyz, who could be distinguished by straight black hair and a more Asian appearance.

'What a shit hole,' Ingrid said quietly. 'Reminds us of me dad's working men's club when I was a nipper.'

Ning didn't know what a working men's club was and was too tired to care. The plane had been too noisy for sleep and she'd now been awake for over twenty hours.

Ingrid found a quiet corner away from the poker players and fruit machines and arranged armchairs so they could put their feet up. Ning unzipped her ski suit and sat with her head resting on Ingrid's heavily quilted arm. The strange surroundings made her uneasy, but she could barely keep her eyes open and was soon fast asleep.

*

Ning woke with a jolt. Her eyes shot open, seeing the back of a car seat and a Christmas-tree-shaped air freshener dangling from the hand grip over the door. She'd been laid flat across a back seat. The road was rough and stones pelted the inside of a wheel arch close to her ear.

Her head hurt and her vision was blurry, but she saw the gun on the driver's belt. It was the man she'd seen slumped by the fruit machine in the Kremlin lounge. Her arms were trapped awkwardly behind her back and her fingers felt numb. When she moved her arm, metal bands dug into her wrists.

The clank of the handcuff chain turned Ning's unease to fear. She raised her head and saw that she was in her socks. Her ski suit was gone and her legs were bound together with orange climbing rope, tied so tight that it dug into her flesh.

A youngish male said something in Russian. He looked back over his shoulder at Ning. He seemed about sixteen, thuggish, with spots and a squashed-up face. His neck had a crude one-colour tattoo of a Cyrillic word.

'Where's Ingrid?' was all Ning could think to say, but the muscles in her face weren't moving properly and her words came out slurred. It was like the feeling you get after a dental anaesthetic, but over her whole mouth rather than just one side. She wondered if she'd been knocked out, or drugged.

The older man in the driver's seat spoke perfect English, with a Kyrgyz accent.

'Welcome back, baby,' he purred. 'Maybe you'll think twice before hitting Kuban again, eh?'

He'd only glanced away from the road for an instant, but it was long enough for Ning to see a crust of dried blood around his nostrils.

'You're Kuban?' Ning asked. 'I hit you?'

She racked her brain, but the last thing she remembered was resting on Ingrid's arm in the Kremlin lounge.

'You did,' the youth said, smiling a little. 'Ker-blammo, right on the snout.'

'Shut your mouth, boy,' Kuban roared, raising his hand from the gear stick, threatening to strike the teenager across the face.

Ning's mind grew more focused as they drove on. After a while stones stopped clanking the underside of the car and she saw that they'd moved into a built-up area. They were surrounded by buildings, two or three storeys high. Most were dilapidated and made from the same prefabricated concrete sections as the buildings around the landing strip.

They stopped in a puddled courtyard. The teenager opened the door, giving Ning a view. There were cigarette butts and Styrofoam cups all over the gravel and spewing metal bins at the far side.

Another car had parked up ahead. It was a little Russian-built Lada and she watched a hulking man ordering Ingrid out of the back. She had cuffs behind her back, but her legs weren't bound.

Meantime, Kuban had spotted a frail middle-aged woman crouched amidst the rubbish bags. He shouted in Russian and steamed towards her. The woman wailed as Kuban dragged her out of the rustling black bags. He pulled her through the huge puddle by her hair, then thumped her head against the car, centimetres from where Ning lay.

The woman's desperate groan was sickening. Kuban banged the woman's head again, then threw her to the ground and took a step back before booting her in the stomach. She sobbed and wailed as Kuban shouted to some guys who'd come running out the back of the building, ordering them to get the woman out of his sight.

'Steals my rubbish, breaks the bags open, leaves a big mess,' Kuban told Ning, as he reached into the car and eyeballed her. His teeth were black and his breath had the exact smell of shit.

Ning was helpless as Kuban wound her hair around

his hand and used it to yank her out of the car.

'You like that?' he said, laughing.

Kuban let go and, with her hands cuffed behind her back, Ning had no way to save herself. She crashed down, banging her chin against the gravel. She feared Kuban would take a kick at her like he'd done with the bin lady, but instead he roared at the teenager in Russian.

The boy wore a Barcelona football shirt, filthy jeans and a pair of Adidas with his pinky toe poking through a split in the leather. Ning was no lightweight, but he scooped her off the floor with one hand and threw her up over his shoulder.

Her hair dangled down the teenager's back as he walked her through a metal-plate door and up bare concrete steps. They crossed a polished dance floor, with big loudspeaker stacks against the walls, and ended up in a lightly furnished space, with mirrors and a rail along one wall, like it had been built for ballet training.

Kuban faced Ingrid with a MacBook Pro on the desk between them. Her handcuffs had been removed by her two burly escorts, who now stood with their backs to the mirrors. The teenager asked what to do with Ning.

'Floor,' Kuban said, before turning back to Ingrid.

The teenager sat Ning down with her back to the mirrors. She had gravel stuck all over her jeans, her chin bled and her head stung from being dragged by the hair.

Kuban opened the lid of the laptop and smiled at Ingrid. 'You know what I want,' he said. At the same moment, the teenager turned to leave the room. 'You don't leave,' he shouted. 'You stay and learn.'

Ingrid tried throwing Kuban off with her thickest Scouse accent. 'Dunno what you mean, chuck.'

'Chuck?' Kuban said.

'You know, chuck,' Ingrid said. 'Like mate, pal, chummy. My old bud.'

Kuban sighed. 'Ingrid, we all know Chaoxiang didn't marry you for looks or wit. He sheltered large sums of money under your name. An associate of your husband gave me details of seventeen bank accounts to which you have access, containing approximately eight million euros.

'You will use this computer, the telephone or whatever method you require to access those accounts. You will transfer all of the money to accounts held by my boss.'

'Who's your boss?' Ingrid asked.

Kuban thumped on the desk and raised his voice. 'You *don't* get to ask questions. When the money is transferred, you and your stepdaughter will be taken to the Bishkek international airport and placed on a flight to the United Kingdom. You can return to your ghetto, and eat fish and chips and live in – what is it you English call them? – a *council flat?*'

Ingrid's only response was a scowl.

'My terms are non-negotiable. The only question is how long and unpleasant you make the process of cooperating with us.'

Ingrid tipped her chair back slightly and blew out a long shaky breath. 'You must think I'm proper green to believe that,' she said, before laughing and tapping an index finger against her temple. 'I'm dead the minute you get what you want, and that's why you'll be getting sweet Fanny Adams.'

Kuban smiled and raised one eyebrow. 'We'll see, won't we?'

17. PUSH

Ryan watched from his bedroom as Gillian Kitsell blasted through the beach community's security gates in a Ferrari 458. Ryan's approach to Ethan had to look casual, though he'd been planning it all weekend. He'd even done role play with Amy, working out strategies to steer the conversation towards things they needed to know.

It was a hundred metres across the beach to house five. Ryan peered in through the huge front windows. The layout was identical to house eight, where he'd been staying. The furniture looked top-notch, but there were clothes and dirty crockery everywhere, spoiling the effect.

Ethan's voice came from high up, by the rooftop pool. 'You looking for me?'

Ryan stepped back so that he could see. Ethan leaned over a railing, with his left arm in a cast.

'Heard you got out of the hospital,' Ryan explained. He didn't want their meeting to take place outside, so he let the sentence hang.

'I'll meet you by the front door,' Ethan said. 'Mum says I've gotta thank you.'

Ryan pondered Ethan's words as he walked to the front door. *Meet you by the front door* sounded OK, but *Mum says I've got to thank you* didn't exactly sound like Ethan was grateful, or keen to make friends.

Guilt reared up when Ryan saw Ethan on the doorstep. His skinny legs were a mass of bruises and cuts, some of which had been stitched. The most impressive examples were bruises shaped like tyre tread across his thigh.

'Car one, Ethan zero,' Ethan said, breaking into a smile. 'It's good of you to come around. Doc said I might have ended up a drooling vegetable if you hadn't got me breathing so quick.'

'Just been down for a swim in the sea,' Ryan said, as he tucked his hands under his armpits and faked a shiver. 'Can't believe how cold it's getting.'

'Wind off the ocean starts getting cold this time of year,' Ethan said. 'You wanna come inside for a second?'

Ryan kept his expression to a slight smile and a nod, but on the inside he was whooping it up like he'd thrown the touchdown that won the Superbowl.

'I think you should fire your maid,' Ryan said, as he walked to the kitchen, stepping over coffee cups and newspapers. Ethan's bruises left him creeping about like an old man.

'Mum's got a thing about security,' Ethan explained. 'Says maids steal and stuff, plus with her business and all . . .'

Ryan bit at the opening. 'What's her business?'

'Computer security,' Ethan explained. 'You look pretty cold, you want a warm drink?'

'Got any tea?'

Ethan laughed as they reached the kitchen. 'English people drink heaps of tea, don't they? I think we only have coffee.'

'Whatever's warm and wet,' Ryan said, as he rubbed his hands together.

The kitchen was on a grand scale, like the rest of the house. There was a built-in coffee machine, but Ethan didn't seem sure how it worked, and having one arm in plaster didn't help.

'I never use it,' Ethan said apologetically. 'Hate coffee.'

'I'll do it,' Ryan said. 'Everything at our place is identical.'

'Why no school today?' Ethan asked.

'Asthma,' Ryan said – they'd picked asthma because Ethan suffered too, giving them another potential opening for a conversation. 'My sister had to call the doctor out in the night. I haven't had an attack in years. Doctor said it might be stress: moving to a new country, new school, plus seeing what happened to you.'

'Hate asthma,' Ethan said. 'Freaks you out when you can't breathe. But same as you, I've barely had it since I was eight or nine.'

'It was mild as,' Ryan said. 'But the doctor said rest and I'll milk it for all it's worth. I hate Twin Lakes Middle, I don't know anyone.'

'Is that girl who goes out on the surfboard your sister?' Ethan asked. 'I thought she might be your mom, or stepmom.'

'Amy's my half-sister. Twelve years older than me,' Ryan said.

Ethan grabbed a can of orange juice from the fridge, and looked slightly embarrassed. 'No offence, but your sister's a *total* babe.'

'I'll take it as a compliment,' Ryan said. 'You should ask her out, she totally digs scrawny twelve-year-olds who are into chess.'

Ethan burst out laughing. 'I wish,' he said. 'You might as well have a seat.'

Ryan picked up his coffee and followed Ethan into the lounge area. The tide was in and waves crashed less than thirty metres from the house. The two boys slumped on to sofas, and Ryan drew comfort from Ethan's relaxed body language.

'I think my dad *might* fancy your mum actually,' Ryan said. 'She knocked on our door Friday night to tell us how you were doing and he was totally sucking up to her.'

'He'd be barking up the wrong tree with my mum,' Ethan said. 'She's had a few partners over the years. There was Auntie Theresa, Auntie Helen, Auntie Maritza from Brazil.'

'Guess it's back to online dating for my dad then,'

Ryan laughed, as he sipped his coffee. 'So you're the only one home?'

'Yeah,' Ethan said. 'Mum was gonna work from home, but she's making such a fuss over me and she has this big meeting. So I was like, *go, go, get outta here*. All I need to survive is Pepsi, Pop-Tarts and painkillers.'

'No other family at all?' Ryan asked.

Ethan shook his head. 'My mum's family all come from the back of beyond. You ever seen that Borat movie? She says it's like that – tin huts, horses and carts and shit.'

'What country is it?' Ryan asked. He already knew Ethan was talking about Kyrgyzstan, but was intrigued to know how much Ethan knew, or would admit to knowing.

'Some ex-Soviet republic,' Ethan said. 'Mum gets really cagey if you ask her about it.'

'You've never been over there?'

'Nah,' Ethan said. 'I've met my grandma in Dubai a couple of times, but my uncles and my granddad basically disowned Mum because of the gay thing.'

'Your mum must have shagged at least one bloke for you to pop out though,' Ryan said, wondering if he was starting to push too hard with the questioning.

'My dad was a sperm donor,' Ethan said. 'But don't spread *that* at school. It's bad enough being the chess-playing robot-building geek with the fat best friend, without mixing in lesbian-mom-test-tube-baby shit.'

'At least you've got one more friend than me,' Ryan said.

'You'll make friends,' Ethan said. 'You're a cool guy. I know for a *fact* that Brittany fancies you.'

The idea of a girl fancying him threw Ryan off track. 'Is she the one with the pink braces, in our high set maths group?'

Ethan nodded. 'Has that tight skirt with the camel thingies on it. Yannis lives next door to her and her grandma.'

'Nice tip-off,' Ryan said, smiling. 'Brittany's fit.'

Ryan felt good as he drained his cup of coffee. He'd always suspected Ethan would be more talkative if he could catch him when Yannis wasn't around, but he hadn't expected him to be such a little gossip.

'I'll tell you something funny, but you've got to *swear* not to tell anyone else,' Ethan said.

Ryan laughed. 'How can I say no with a build-up like that?'

'OK,' Ethan said, taking a deep breath. 'I slept over at Yannis' place during summer break. So I'm in his room and I find this pair of girls' knickers. First of all he's like *yeah I had a girl in my room*. And he's giving me all this bullshit about how it was his hot fourteen-year-old cousin. But I know he's lying. I've known Yannis since we were about seven and he ain't got no cousin. So after bugging him forever, I finally get him to confess that they're Brittany's.'

'You what?' Ryan gasped.

'I swear to God,' Ethan said. 'The fat perv snuck into her garden and stole Brittany's frilly pinks from the washing line.'

Ryan laughed so hard he clutched his sides. 'What a sicko,' he screamed. 'Maybe I can sell him a pair of Amy's for fifty bucks.'

Ethan howled with laughter. 'Do you think Yannis puts them on?'

The mental image of Yannis' fat body dressed in girls' underwear was more than Ryan could take.

'Laughing so hard I'm gonna die,' Ryan snorted.

'Hurts my arm,' Ethan said, laughing helplessly. 'Jesus Christ. Imagine if you could get a picture of that. I bet you'd vomit just looking at it.'

A couple of minutes passed before either of them calmed down enough to say anything coherent, and even then they kept getting attacks of the giggles.

'You wanna do something?' Ryan asked. 'I know your arm is screwed, but we're both just kicking around. I've got a PS3 at my place.'

'Can't,' Ethan said. 'Can't move my fingers properly with the cast, but we've got a cinema room downstairs. Wanna watch a Blu-ray or something?'

18. BULBOUS

Kuban had slapped Ingrid, punched her in the face, banged her head against the table and bent back her fingers. Sometimes Ning looked up, but mostly she stared down at the floor. Her hands were numb from being cuffed, she felt nauseous and badly needed to pee, but was scared to ask.

'I was in the British Army,' Ingrid shouted defiantly.

Kuban looked at the two burly henchmen. 'Stand her up.'

Ingrid twisted and grabbed the desk, but she couldn't stop them. As the men held Ingrid in place, Kuban thumped her hard in the stomach. Ingrid groaned and stumbled, but the men kept her upright.

'Anything to say?' Kuban asked.

'Yeah,' Ingrid said. 'Bite me.'

Kuban looked angry as he took a folding knife from

his trouser pocket. 'Grab her hair, keep the head still.'

Ning felt sick as Kuban made two deep slashes across Ingrid's cheek. He then took a small squeezy bottle from his pocket and squirted fluid over Ingrid's face.

'Lemon juice,' Kuban said, smiling as he licked his fingertips. 'Yummy!'

Ingrid groaned and twisted about, trying to free an arm to rub her burning eyes.

'Everyone breaks,' Kuban said firmly. 'You can end this now.'

'Not for you,' Ingrid shouted. 'Never.'

'Your defiance impresses nobody,' Kuban spat. 'Sit her back in the chair.'

As the two henchmen dragged Ingrid towards the desk, she surprised them by lifting up both legs. Ingrid was heavy, and as the man holding her right arm stumbled she freed her left arm and knocked him down with a well-aimed punch on the nose.

Ning had never completely believed that Ingrid had been in the British Army, but you only threw a punch like that if you'd had some kind of training. As the man stumbled back with a bloody nose, Ingrid broke free and charged the desk. She grabbed the MacBook by its screen and threw it as hard as she could at Kuban.

The laptop's hinge snapped as it crashed against the mirrored wall. As Ning dived forward so that it didn't crash down on her head, Ingrid flipped the desk over.

But her freedom didn't last. One of the henchmen grabbed her around the neck as Kuban threw the desk out of his way then punched her in the mouth. The blow caused a mild concussion and Ingrid's head drooped as the henchman dragged her two steps back and dumped her into a chair.

The teenage lad stood by, looking anxiously at the MacBook. 'It's smashed. The boss won't like this.'

'He won't find out,' Kuban said, sounding a little shaky. 'We'll put it back in the cupboard and get another one.'

Ingrid laughed dozily as her head rolled from side to side. Kuban joined the teenager crouching over the laptop.

'Maybe there's a workshop at the market that can fix it,' the henchman who'd been punched suggested.

Kuban stood up furiously and shook the busted MacBook screen in the air. 'You can't fix this, dummy.' he shouted. 'It's ruined.'

The door flew open. Kuban spun around, ready to yell at someone for not knocking, but when he saw who it was he backed up to the desk with an expression like he'd just swallowed a turd.

'Mr Aramov,' Kuban said. 'I wasn't expecting you.'

Leonid Aramov was touching forty, with long black hair and a physique pumped by weight training. He ignored Kuban and stepped straight up to Ingrid. She couldn't see because her eyes were streaming, but she knew his voice.

'Might have known you were behind this,' Ingrid spat.

Leonid cracked a mean smile. 'You looked prettier the first time we met, dancing around a pole with no clothes on.' His tone became more aggressive when he looked at Kuban. 'Tell me you have something.'

'It will take time,' Kuban said. 'She's determined, but they all break.'

Leonid jabbed Kuban in the chest with his pointing finger. 'I hear you fell asleep in the Kremlin lounge.'

'The flight was delayed. You know I've had this flu—'

Before Kuban could finish, Leonid swung his massive arm and punched him in the gut.

'I ordered you to pick them up the instant they stepped off the plane,' Leonid shouted. 'And the scuffle in the bar? What if my mother hears about it?'

'Boss,' Kuban said, badly winded. 'Just let—'

But Leonid wasn't a fan of complete sentences. This time he picked up the laptop screen and belted Kuban around the head with it. 'You will pay for its replacement. And why spray juice in her eyes, you idiot? What if she needs to read a computer screen?'

Kuban groaned as Leonid doubled him over with another punch, then brought his knee up and smashed his nose.

'Go home, you useless drunk,' Leonid roared. Then he addressed the two henchmen and the teenager. 'There's a box of electrical cords in the manager's office – one of you fetch it, one make me some hot black coffee, and boy, you smash the girl's foot.'

As the henchmen hurried out, the teenager stayed still, looking scared and awkward.

'What's your problem?' Leonid shouted, as he pointed at Ning. 'Do as I say, now.'

Ning scuttled back towards the mirrors as the heavy-built teenager moved in. He stamped down, but Ning pulled her socked foot out of the way. With cuffed hands and tightly bound legs, she could only shuffle into the nearest corner.

'Get on with it,' Leonid ordered. 'Stop messing about, boy.'

Ning's corner darkened as the youth loomed over her. He pinned Ning's ankle under his filthy trainer, then rolled her foot on to its side and shifted his weight, so that Ning had seventy kilos crunching the bones in her toes.

After watching Ingrid resist for almost an hour, Ning didn't want to show weakness, but the pain was excruciating and she couldn't help making a low moan.

'You like seeing your daughter suffer?' Leonid asked. 'Or shall we have an adult conversation?'

Ingrid's head still rolled around from the punch, and her eyes were streaming.

'Get some cold water to bring her around,' Leonid told the teenager. 'She's knocked out, she can't see. Why must I work with idiots?'

Ning gasped with relief as the bulky teenager moved off her foot. As he left the room, one of the henchmen leaned nervously in the doorway.

'Sorry, boss, I can't find the box.'

'It's a big wooden crate,' Leonid yelled. 'How can you miss it?'

'Maybe it's been moved,' the henchman suggested.

As Leonid stood in the doorway facing the henchman,

Ingrid stopped rolling her head and looked at Ning, apparently not as unconscious as she'd led her tormentors to believe.

'You both stay still,' Leonid shouted. 'I'll be one second.'

'Get here,' Ingrid whispered.

Despite her pain, Ning quickly shuffled three metres towards Ingrid sitting at the desk.

'I think my toe's broken,' Ning said.

'I grabbed this when I tipped the desk over,' Ingrid said, as she held out the pocket knife Kuban had used to cut her cheek. 'You've got to understand: if Leonid gets our money he won't want anyone knowing what has happened, which means he has to kill us.'

Ning nodded.

'If I'm letting them hurt you, it's because I love you. But I'm going to try getting you out of this room. Use the knife, use your boxing or whatever you can to try and escape.'

'Where to?' Ning asked. 'I don't even know where we are.'

'Babes, I don't have all the answers. But Bishkek is the capital, so there must be something. Try finding an embassy, or a tourist place. Not the police, the Aramovs probably own them.'

Ning still had her hands cuffed, so Ingrid tucked Kuban's knife into the front pocket of her stepdaughter's jeans.

'I love you, sweetheart,' Ingrid said.

'Love you too,' Ning said.

Ingrid reached across to wipe a tear off Ning's cheek, but the teenager had stepped back into the room. He placed a Pyrex bowl and a roll of kitchen towels on the desk in front of Ingrid.

'Mr Aramov say you must wash out eyes,' he said in broken English, before grabbing Ning under the armpits and pulling her back to the mirrored wall.

The teenager then leaned across Ning. For an instant she thought he'd seen Ingrid concealing the knife, but to her surprise the youth pushed a small key into her cuffs and loosened each side a couple of notches before speaking quietly.

'I hope more comfortable,' he said.

Ning was grateful, but wondered if his kindness was part of some grand manipulation. As feeling came back to her fingers, one of the henchmen walked through the doorway with a wooden crate, followed by Leonid, who now held a steaming coffee mug.

'So Mummy is a tough nut,' Leonid said cheerfully, as he stepped towards Ingrid. 'But how much will she let her little girl suffer?'

19. MALMIN

Gillian and Ethan weren't workout fiends, so the basement room that was a gym at Ryan and Amy's place had been converted to a home cinema. The huge projector screen was complemented by speakers built into the side walls and electrically reclining seats. There was even a bar area up back, with a popcorn maker and hot dog grill.

'Mate,' Ryan shouted, as a scene from *Iron Man 2* played up on the big screen. 'Can you pause it, I need a piss?'

Ethan hit a button on an iPad to pause the movie. 'You know where to go?' he asked.

'Same as my house I'd guess, next to the beach shower?'

'You got it,' Ethan said. 'Grab me some M&Ms on the way back.'

Ryan walked back between three rows of cinema seats and out into a hallway with *coming attractions* posters along the wall. He'd now spent over five hours at Ethan's place, and his only major worry was that he might forget some of what he'd found out.

Ryan genuinely needed to pee, but he made it quick and skipped washing his hands because he was intrigued by a small room behind the cinema. The first oddity was that the hallway wall bulged out, suggesting that it had been reinforced. The room's door had an outer layer that matched the other doors in the hallway, but when Ryan rapped on it he heard the distinct ring of metal beneath the walnut veneer.

But it was the lock that really made him curious. It appeared to have two key slots, one above the other, along with a fingerprint panel. Ryan only had a few seconds, so rather than study it he pulled his phone from his shorts and snapped a picture of the front, and a second shot capturing the detail of the markings on the side.

He pocketed the phone and walked back to the cinema, but as Ryan grabbed the door handle Ethan made him jump by opening it from the other side.

'Letting Yannis in,' Ethan explained, before shouting up the stairs. 'I'm down in the cinema.'

Within seconds Yannis was huffing on the stairs. 'How you doing, Ethan? You should have been at school, man. Sal's expelled, Guillermo's suspended for a week. Everyone's asking how you are. So I said you're OK, but I didn't say you were out of hospital in case the teachers tried passing on work.'

Yannis looked confused as he reached the bottom of the stairs and saw Ryan.

'Oh, it's you,' Yannis said sniffily.

'Well, I was me the last time I looked,' Ryan said. He couldn't stand Yannis, but had to try getting along if he was going to stay friends with Ethan.

'We're watching *Iron Man 2*,' Ethan said. 'It's just coming up to the massive ruck at the end.'

Yannis shook his head. 'I thought we could get your robotics stuff out.'

Ethan raised his cast slightly. 'You see me doing any soldering with this on?'

Yannis clearly didn't want Ryan around. 'Why weren't you in school?' he asked bitterly.

'Asthma attack,' Ryan said. 'Doctor said I should rest.'

'You don't look very ill,' Yannis said.

Ryan laughed. 'I'm *not* very ill. But I've got an excuse to miss a couple of days of Twin Lakes tedium, and I plan to make the most of it.'

'Well, if you're watching *that* film, I might as well go home and do my homework. I just wanted to see if you were OK.'

Ethan looked mystified. 'Yannis, why are you being a dick? I'll put the hot dog grill on for you, we can chill.'

But Yannis was heading back towards the stairs. 'I only like seeing a whole movie,' he said. 'Otherwise you don't enjoy it properly.'

Ethan hobbled after Yannis and yelled up the stairs. 'Why do you always act up if anyone else is around?'

'I'm not acting like anything,' Yannis said, his voice sounding all stressed and high-pitched. 'I thought we were friends is all. We usually do things together.'

Ethan was exasperated. 'We asked you to come in, watch a movie and eat hot dogs. It's not like we're throwing you out.'

Yannis didn't answer. The front door slammed. Ethan and Ryan looked at each other.

'Did I do something to piss him off?' Ryan asked.

'He gets jealous if you have *any* friends apart from him,' Ethan said. 'He's the same at chess club. But it's his problem. Let's watch the rest of the movie.'

*

The bloody-nosed henchman grabbed Ning off the floor and threw her down on the desk in front of Ingrid.

'How can you let this happen to your daughter?' Leonid shouted, as Ning stared up at the ceiling tiles. 'What kind of mother are you? What kind of mother lets her own daughter suffer, just for money?'

'Chaoxiang will find out what you did,' Ingrid shouted. 'He knows you have a daughter. Anything you do to Ning, he'll do to her.'

Leonid laughed. 'Chaoxiang upset some very important people. He's nothing but a corpse in a Chinese prison uniform.'

Ingrid leaned forward, so that her bloody face was less than half a metre from Ning's, and spat at Leonid's face. Leonid backed away, wiped up, then pulled up Ning's T-shirt and tipped his steaming coffee over Ning's stomach.

'No,' Ingrid shouted, as Ning screamed in pain.

As the hot liquid scalded Ning's skin, Ingrid tried to stand and one of the henchmen shoved her back down in her seat.

'How can you do that?' Ingrid shouted. 'She's just a little girl.'

Leonid sensed he'd hit a weak spot and looked at the teenager. 'Apparently she doesn't like her little girl getting burned. Go make me another nice *hot* cup of coffee.'

'OK,' Ingrid shouted, as she ran her bloody hands through her hair. 'You win. I'll give you the account details.'

'Good,' Leonid said. 'But you'd better play it straight, or it'll be more than a cup of coffee that I burn her with.'

Ingrid pointed at the water she'd used to rinse out her eyes. 'Give that to her.'

The teenager grabbed the jug and tipped some of the water over Ning's burn. Leonid didn't seem to approve, but he was more interested in getting information out of Ingrid than in yelling at the boy.

'I don't remember the numbers by heart,' Ingrid said. 'In my luggage there's an address book and diary. I can access some accounts by computer, some only by telephone.'

One of the henchmen spoke to Leonid in Russian.

'Kuban already went through her diary and address book,' one of the henchmen said. 'There were no bank details.'

Ingrid snorted. 'Do you think I write them down for any idiot to find if I lose them? They're written in a simple code that Chaoxiang taught me. I'll also need a pencil and a calculator.'

As Ning sobbed from the pain in her burned abdomen, Leonid told the teenager to go and find Ingrid's stuff, and bring a replacement computer so that she could access the internet.

'I'm cooperating now,' Ingrid said. 'Can you at least make Ning more comfortable? Take her cuffs off, give her something for the burn.'

'You are not in a position to make demands,' Leonid said sharply.

'I need to concentrate to extract the numbers *and* sound relaxed when I call the banks to make your transfers. How can I do that with my daughter in agony?'

Leonid saw the logic in this and gave a slight nod. 'She can be made comfortable,' Leonid told Ingrid. 'Food, toilet, a few clothes.'

Ingrid nodded. 'Thank you.'

'Take the girl out,' Leonid told the bloody-nosed henchman. 'But no further than the next room. I'll need her back here if her mother tries any funny business.'

Ning stretched when her cuffs were released and the bindings on her legs cut off. For the first time in almost six hours she was able to move freely, but she hurt all over. The skin around her belly button was blistered, she had a broken toe, bloody wrists, and a dark scab where her chin had hit the gravel.

Ning's newly appointed guard waved her towards the

door. The room outside had been fitted out as a break area for the staff who worked in the club. There were a few random chairs, a sink, a grubby-looking fridge, chipped mugs and wobbly tables. There was a toilet off to the side and Ning headed straight for it.

The henchman insisted on standing in the doorway, but at least had the decency to look away as Ning peed. She then stood by a mirror and washed quickly. Her chin and neck were bloody.

She used a grimy bar of soap to wash the worst of the blood off her face and splashed the burn with cold water. As she came back into the break room the teenager strode through with Ingrid's luggage and a laptop tucked under his arm.

Ning's guard opened up the fridge. She'd expected to see mouldy bread, and half-eaten noodle pots, but to her surprise it was packed with platters on silver trays for some kind of function in the dance hall.

Ning was in too much pain to feel hungry, but she hadn't eaten since the picnic food on the plane and felt she ought to because she didn't know when she'd get another chance. She pulled a paper plate from a cellophane-wrapped stack and made herself swallow a few pieces of fruit, along with a kind of potato salad with chunks of fatty lamb in it. As Ning chewed slowly, her guard tucked into the cling-film-wrapped platters with relish.

'Can I get my trainers?' Ning asked.

Her guard didn't speak English, so she repeated her request, but added gestures like she was pulling on shoes. The guard led Ning out into a passageway. Her backpack leaned against the hallway wall, and looked like it had been pulled about, with bits of clothing spread over the floor.

Unlike the studio and the break room, the hallway had windows. Ning had lost all sense of time and was surprised to see that it was dark.

She dug her spare trainers out of the bag, then leaned against the wall. There was no way to avoid pain as she pushed her injured foot into her trainer, and her toe was much more painful with shoes on, but she could hardly escape in her socks.

As they walked back into the break room, Ning glimpsed Ingrid in the dance studio. She had the laptop in front of her. Leonid sat on a corner of the desk watching intently, while the teenager stood by the wall looking uncomfortable.

Ning's guard had developed a taste for party nibbles and when she turned back he was leaning into the fridge cramming more food into his mouth. She remembered what Ingrid said about taking any chance to escape, and with the guard deep in the fridge, would there ever be a better one?

Ning stood and moved back towards the hallway. She felt Kuban's knife in her pocket, but it made her uneasy because she didn't know the best way to use it.

'I forgot something,' Ning said airily, as she stepped back towards the hallway.

She made it two steps out of the staffroom before the guard grabbed her.

'Nyet,' he said firmly.

The guard was more than twice Ning's weight, so she only had one shot. She packed her strength, rage and everything she'd learned in four years at Dandong National Sports Academy into one titanic punch.

The guard's nose exploded. As he crashed backwards, Ning walked into a mist of blood and threw a second punch at his temple. He slid down the wall, unconscious and minus two front teeth.

Ning looked backwards. She'd made a fair bit of noise and half expected to see Leonid charging towards her, but apparently she'd got away with it. With luck she'd have a few minutes before anyone came out and discovered him.

Ning unbuttoned the guard's coat, and was disappointed not to find a gun. She took his wallet and grabbed her own small backpack from the floor. She had no idea if all of her stuff was still in there, but there wasn't time to stand around and check.

Now she had to work out which way to run. One end of the corridor led towards the club they'd passed through on the way in. It had been empty back then, but it was evening now and she could hear music thumping.

She went the other way, heading for a door at the end of the hallway. It was hard to look through because of the reflections of the indoor lights, but it apparently led outside. She made out a set of emergency stairs through the glass, and saw that it led to the courtyard where they'd arrived that morning.

The gates they'd driven through appeared to be shut, but they didn't look unclimbable. And if the bin scavenger that Kuban beat up had got inside, there had to be a way for Ning to get out. She turned the handle and gave the door a shove. It took some effort to make it budge and she hobbled out on to the metal steps.

20. DOCTOR

The air was muggy and the only light came through the club's windows. Ning had to battle every step, leaning heavily on the handrail to keep the weight off her bad toe. When she got down to the gravel courtyard a rowdy group of men blocked an alleyway leading to the front of the building, so she kept low and limped between parked cars towards the rear gates.

They were a couple of metres high and too close to the ground to slide under. She pulled the wire mesh, hoping to find a loose flap to climb through. When she had no luck, Ning turned towards the bins. They were drum shaped, two metres high, made from aluminium with handles halfway up.

Ning planned to wheel the bin across to the gate, pull herself up to the top and then jump over. If she'd been fit it would have taken seconds, but her toe and burned stomach was agony as she grabbed the bin's handle and dragged it four metres towards the gate.

She glanced about as the wheels juddered on the gravel. There was nobody on the stairs, but the men in the alleyway would see if they'd bothered to take an interest.

With the bin resting against the fence, Ning reached up and grabbed the rim with both hands. Fighting pain, she got one foot on the handle, then pulled a knee up on to the rim. The position was precarious and a rat shuffled over black bags as she stepped into the bin.

She wasn't sure how much the rubbish would settle, but after a wobble she found herself standing inside the bin with the rim coming up to her knees. From here she had to clamber across to the top of the fence and jump down on the far side, but as she reached across she heard footsteps on the metal stairs.

The teenager was first out. Ning lunged desperately for the fence, but her burned abdomen brushed against something sticking out of a bag and her whole body went into spasm. As she crashed backwards into the rubbish bags, Leonid appeared behind the running teenager.

Ning knew she was screwed. She didn't try getting back over the gate, because even if she made it she was in no state to run.

What happened next made no sense. The teenager started gesticulating and shouting in Russian. The motorised gates slid apart as Leonid shouted in Russian, Kyrgyz or possibly a mix of both. The only word Ning understood was *dollars*.

The sound of men running out of the alleyway made Ning realise that Leonid had offered a bounty to whoever caught her. But surely the teenager had seen her drop into the bin?

Ning didn't dare peek, but there were voices and footsteps in the gravel nearby. She spent a couple of minutes sharing the bin with at least one rat, until someone decided to wheel it back to its usual spot.

After a thump against the courtyard wall, Ning was shocked by fat fingers curling over the metal rim, followed by the squashed-up face of the powerfully built teenager. She braced herself, expecting to be grabbed and yanked out, but instead he made a shush gesture.

'I tell them you jump over and run up hill,' the teen said, struggling with his English. 'I come back. But it be long time, yes?'

'Yes,' Ning said.

'Do not move. I must go.'

'Thank you,' Ning said, as the face disappeared.

*

Ryan was bursting with information when he got home. Amy did a full debriefing, talking him through everything Ethan had said, and everything he'd learned about Gillian Kitsell: the stuff about Gillian being disowned because of her sexuality, Ethan's sperm donor father, the secure room in the basement.

Amy typed up detailed notes and sent them by secure e-mail to an Information Manager (IM) at TFU headquarters in Dallas, together with the pictures of the lock on the secure room.

The IM would work through the night, checking out everything Ryan had unearthed and following up any leads. When Ryan woke in the morning he'd have a detailed report in his inbox, telling him which facts did and didn't check out, along with suggested lines for further questioning and things they hoped he could learn from Ethan over the coming days.

'Hear you had a good day,' Ted said, as Ryan strolled through to the kitchen.

'Yeah,' Ryan said, as he rubbed his eyes. 'It's knackering though. You're only sitting about, but the whole time you've got to judge what you can and can't say and work out what to ask next without the guy losing his temper and calling you a nosy bastard.'

'He wasn't shy though?' Ted asked.

Ted had an apron on and stood by a five-ring hob with rice steaming at the back and a sizzling pan of strip beef and peppers up front. He was also jiggling his bum to a Phil Collins tune coming through the ceiling speakers.

'Ethan's quite the gossip queen once you get him going,' Ryan said, as he leaned towards the pan. 'Your Mexican smells good. Less sure of your taste in music.'

'You can't beat old Phil,' Ted said. 'Only thing better than Phil's concerts is Texas A&M in a play-off game!'

'Is that baseball or something?' Ryan asked.

Ted balled up an oven mitt and laughed as he threw it at Ryan. 'College football, boy! Don't you know sport?'

'We have rugby in Britain,' Ryan explained cheekily.

'It's similar to American football, but we don't need all those girly pads and helmets because the players are *real* men.'

'I'll put you over my knee if you ain't careful,' Ted laughed. 'We're about done here. There's guacamole and sour cream in the fridge. Can you get that out, and set the table for four?'

'Four?'

'Didn't Amy tell you? The boss is coming. Called on her cell a while back. Must have hit traffic cos I thought she'd be here about now.'

Ryan sighed as he opened the cutlery drawer.

'No fan of Dr D?' Ted asked.

'I've only met her a couple of times,' Ryan explained. 'She's annoying, with the high-pitched voice and the wavy arms and the, *Hi I'm Denise, but you gotta call me Dr D.*'

Ted laughed. 'You've got her accent to a tee. I know she's odd, but she's very good at her job. She's also the head of TFU, which means she's my and Amy's boss. So try keeping her sweet, OK?'

'No worries,' Ryan said, as he peeled cling film from the guacamole and tasted a dab on his little finger. 'Will she be staying over?'

'For a few nights,' Ted said. 'Anyone asks, she's your grandmother on your late mother's side, as per the mission background.'

'I remember,' Ryan said, as the doorbell rang.

Ted pressed the button to release the front door and Dr D found her own way to the kitchen. She came in, placed a large gold box on the table and kissed Ryan on both cheeks.

'I read Amy's message to the IM,' Dr D said. 'Boy-o-boy, that's progress. I got you a gift. I really think it'll help with the mission.'

The gold box made Ryan think it was a large cream cake, but he popped the lid and discovered a rounded pebble and a bonsai tree.

'It's for your room,' Dr D said excitedly.

This wasn't the sort of thing you expected from a senior American intelligence officer. Ryan thought Dr D was bonkers, but Ted's request to play nice was fresh in his mind.

'It's umm . . . lovely,' Ryan said. 'I've always liked tiny trees.'

'It's a feng shui kit,' Dr D explained. 'When I saw your bedroom, with the toilet and shower pointing towards the bed, I knew the energy was all wrong. Place the tree on your window ledge and the stone on the shelf above the toilet. The chi in your room will be rebalanced and you'll feel properly energised when you wake up in the morning.'

'Ryan could do with more energy,' Amy said, as she came in and gave Dr D a kiss. 'He can be a right miserable bugger when he first gets out of bed.'

Ted whispered in Ryan's ear as he reached into a cupboard to grab the plates. 'Google feng shui when you get a chance,' he said. 'And be grateful, she once bought me a purple healing shirt.'

Dr D sat at the dining table as Ryan spread out plates

and cutlery.

'I reckon our best bet will be finding a new lady friend for Gillian Kitsell,' Dr D said. 'Ryan, we need to know Gillian's type. Next time you're over at the house, look out for any photos of Gillian with one of her exes.'

'TFU not finding out that Gillian's a lesbo must be a bit of a cock-up,' Ryan said. 'I mean, people she works with must know. And she travels so there must be airline records of her flying with female partners.'

Dr D bristled at the suggestion that someone at TFU hadn't been thorough. 'Young man,' she said firmly. 'We ran a background check. But Gillian runs a computer security company. She's a cautious lady, surrounded by employees who are instructed to report anything unusual to their company's internal security team.

'At present, Gillian has no idea she's under investigation, or that we know she's related to members of the Aramov Clan. But all she needs is one tip-off that someone checked her name on the United Airlines database, or an ex-girlfriend calling up to say that someone's been asking questions, and Gillian could jet off to Kyrgyzstan, where we can't lay a finger on her.'

21. DAN

Ning waited for hours. Rubbish bags landed on her head, flies and rats freaked her out and the stench of decay lined her throat. She heard men coming back through the gates, disappointed not to score their bounty, but Leonid didn't seem too fussed. He'd gone back upstairs to work on Ingrid.

It was impossible to get comfortable, especially with her toe and stomach competing to be the most painful. Lying in rat piss and maggots made her worry about the burn getting infected. She wondered if Ingrid knew she'd escaped and tried not to imagine what Leonid was up to.

Ning also thought about her saviour. The teenager had crushed her foot when ordered to, but he'd also loosened her handcuffs. Leonid would surely kill the teenager for lying about her escape, so it was brave to intervene. But had he done it because he was good and wanted to save her, or bad and wanted an eleven-year-old girl for reasons that didn't bear thinking about?

As night turned to morning the club got busier, until the courtyard was heaving. Everyone seemed drunk. Bottles smashed, cigarettes got flicked into Ning's bin and there was at least one fight.

Ning had no watch, but she guessed it was past 3 a.m. when the door staff came to clear everyone out. Her back ached and desperate thirst made her consider climbing up and making a break. But how far would she hobble on her bad foot before someone spotted her? Waiting for the teenager was her only realistic chance of getting more than a few hundred metres.

'Still there?' the boy asked, when his face finally appeared over the edge of the bin. 'We go now. Everyone gone.'

The teenager took a precautionary backwards glance as Ning held up her arms. He grabbed her under the pits and pulled her out, painfully dragging burned flesh across the rim of the dustbin.

Ning felt around her chest to make sure she had her backpack as the teenager carried her towards a rusting Lada, with mismatched body panels.

'Not far,' the teenager said as he sat Ning in the open boot.

She had to tuck her knees into her chest to fit inside, amidst snow chains and muddy boots.

'Do not cry. I help,' he said gently.

Ning had been in pain for so long that she didn't

even realise there were tears down her cheek. The slam of the boot popped her ears. Her position was even less comfortable than inside the bin, but she felt some relief as the car pulled through the gates and turned on to a road.

The ride was less than ten minutes. The boot creaked open at the base of a three-storey block. Nobody was about as the teenager gave Ning a piggyback to the first floor. He fumbled for a key and set her down in the hallway of a tiny apartment.

'What's your name?' Ning asked, as she leaned against the wall.

'Daniyar,' the teenager said. 'But everyone say Dan.'

He slid open a tiny plastic door, revealing a cramped space with a shower, sink and toilet with lopsided seat.

'You smell bad,' Dan said. 'Water, yes?'

Ning nodded as she limped into the bathroom. Dan was clearly no fan of cleaning products: the floor was covered in some appalling examples of used underwear, with mouse turds dotted around the sink and along the skirting.

She turned on the shower and began to undress. The mirror showed the filth soaked into her clothes. Her burn stung badly and had darkened since she'd last seen it, as had the wounds on her chin and wrists. She was down to her socks when the rattling door made her jump.

Ning was jittery and hopped back, but Dan had only put his arm inside the door. He felt blindly along the wall, attached a pink towelling robe to a hook inside the door, then reached back in holding out a small bar of fancy soap.

'My sister leave this here when she marry,' Dan said.

At home Ning had been used to designer toiletries, but there was something comforting about the crumbling pink bar with a swan moulded into its surface.

Removing her sock was excruciating and revealed a broken pinky-toe pointing up at an alarming angle. But emotionally Ning felt stronger as she stepped under a weedy shower head and washed the stench out of her hair. She had to keep soap away from her burn, but she felt almost human as she stepped into the hallway.

The rest of Dan's apartment comprised a single room, five paces in any direction. Besides his bed the space was dominated by a flat-screen TV, an exercise bench and a mountain of barbells and cast-iron weight discs. The posters on the walls depicted large-breasted women dressed in skimpy leather costumes.

The oppressive maleness made Ning feel vulnerable with nothing under her robe, but Dan didn't seem threatening, as he stood by his kitchen cabinet slicing an apple and dividing the chunks between two plates.

'You sit my bed,' Dan said.

As Ning sat, Dan came across with a mug of tea and a small plate. There were cubes of cheese, apple slices, a lump of processed meat shaped like the can from which it had been pulled, and a triangle of flat bread, which Ning eyed suspiciously.

'Lepioshka,' Dan said. 'You not like?'

Ning smiled as she bit. 'Yes I like,' she said, smiling.

'I've never had bread like this before.'

Dan sat beside Ning on the bed. He'd kicked his trainers off and his socks stank, but she could hardly complain. Dan's plate was the same, but with larger portions.

'Sorry about foot,' Dan said, as he chewed a piece of the canned meat. 'I have much guilt.'

Ning nodded and spoke extra slowly so that Dan could understand. 'You were brave to help me.'

'Kyrgyzstan is very poor,' Dan explained. 'You saw lady in bins?'

'The one Kuban beat up?'

'Yes,' Dan said. 'Many here live like that. Old get no money. Young have no job. Even in Africa many people more rich than Kyrgyzstan. You understand?'

'Understand,' Ning said.

'I would much like to work as mechanic, or shop. Maybe even educate. I work for Aramov Clan because I am very muscle.'

To make his point, Dan pulled up the sleeve of his Barcelona shirt and showed off an enormous bicep.

'I hate many thing Aramov Clan do. But I have no mother, father. Sister marry, go far away. If I no work for Aramov, no money, no apartment, electricity, food. I be like bin lady. Yes?'

Ning put her hand on her chest. 'You have a good heart,' she said. 'How old are you?'

'Sixteen. You?'

'Eleven,' Ning said, 'nearly twelve.'

'Kuban tell me to hurt people. Much bad things if

you not obey Aramov Clan. They kill me if they find you. Much painful, make example.'

'Can you get me away from here?' Ning asked.

Dan looked uncertain. 'Many things I must find out. It take time.'

Ning had checked her backpack while she was in the bin and located the twenty-five-thousand-dollar brick rolled inside an old pair of shorts. But while Dan seemed trustworthy, she decided not to mention it for now.

'Don't look scared,' Dan said. 'Tomorrow I see nurse. Old friend of sister. She look. Make better.'

'You trust her?' Ning asked.

Dan didn't know the word. 'Trust?'

Ning tried to think of another way to put it. 'Your friend, I still be safe?'

'Safe, yes!' Dan laughed. 'She hate me working for Aramov. They murder her father brother.'

Ning wasn't sure if *father brother* meant father and brother, or father's brother, but either way it sounded better than going untreated.

'Are you sure they won't look for me here?' Ning asked, as she ate the last corner of the bread.

'Leonid does not need you. Ingrid give everything he ask for.'

Ning hadn't thought to ask about Ingrid. She gulped air: Ingrid believed she'd be killed as soon as Leonid had what he wanted.

'Where is she now?'

The look on Dan's face told Ning that Ingrid had been right.

'Oh *God*,' Ning gasped, as tears welled in her eyes.

'Please no scream,' Dan said, ready to clamp his hand over Ning's mouth. 'Wall very thin. People hear above.'

'How?' Ning asked. Then angrily, 'Why didn't you say something?'

Ning saw that Dan looked hurt. 'I want you strong before I tell.'

'How?' Ning repeated.

Dan didn't know the word, but made a throttling gesture with his hands.

'Strangled,' Ning said.

'Not much hurt,' Dan said, as he reached into the pocket of his jeans and pulled out a gold ring, studded with three minuscule diamonds.

'Leonid took ring with big, big diamond. He give other man gold necklace, and this for me. But you must have now.'

Ning felt like she'd been blown to bits as she took the ring and twirled it slowly in front of her eyes. Her stepfather had bought Ingrid some fine jewellery, but this battered old piece was the only thing Ingrid always wore, along with her wedding ring. She always called it her *Argos Catalogue ring*, though Ning had no idea what that meant.

As Dan put a hand on her back and said sorry again, Ning moved the ring close to her nose. She gave the inside an experimental sniff and caught Ingrid's vodka and sweat aroma.

'My bed is yours,' Dan said, as Ning cried softly. 'You need much to sleep.'

22. NURSE

Ning couldn't leave Dan's apartment. The first night she'd lain awake in pain, wondering if he was too good to be true. But it turned out that the only offensive things about Dan were his odorous feet and volcanic night-time farts that soon became a huge joke between them.

Dan's nurse friend made Ning comfortable. She set her toe and swaddled it in a tight bandage; she cleaned the burn and tweezered gravel from the deep cut on her chin. Ning gave Dan some of her US dollars and he came back with a carrier bag full of elasticised bandage, antiseptic ointment and a special cream for healing burns.

Most days Dan went to work early and came back after dark. He said he did jobs for Leonid Aramov, but clammed up when pressed for details. They'd make dinner together and sleep head to toe on a double bed.

For the first couple of days, Ning wasn't fit for much. She spent hours on Dan's X-box and worked through his pirate DVDs, which mostly comprised gruesome slasher flicks and ultimate fighting videos. By the third day she was more mobile and decided to wage war on filth. She swept the floor, cleaned the bathroom, scrubbed down kitchen cabinets and tossed all the rotten food in the fridge.

Washing had to be done by hand, but over the following days she worked through Dan's underwear mound, the bed sheets – which she suspected had not been washed since the day they'd been bought – and several pairs of jeans which were so filthy that they still turned water black after being soaked and wrung out three times. The only things Ning didn't wash were the curtains, because Dan told her to keep them shut at all times.

It was hard work, but being busy kept dark thoughts out of her head.

Dan had a date on their third night and Ning felt jealous as he rushed about changing from his work clothes into a shirt and jeans that she'd washed. She secretly hoped he'd be home by eight with a slap mark on his cheek, but when he rolled in at 2 a.m. there was lipstick on his collar and he sang while he brushed his teeth.

'Did you make love?' Ning asked, as he climbed under the bed covers.

Dan didn't understand. 'What is *make love*?'

'Sex,' Ning said, making an in-and-out gesture with her index finger.

Dan laughed. 'I wish much to have sex. But she live with mother and you are here.'

That was the only time Ning had felt like a burden, and Dan's poor English made it tricky to judge his true feelings.

The next night they discussed plans for escape. Bishkek was near to a highway that took trucks carrying goods from China to Russia. They considered using some of Ning's money to pay a Chinese truck driver to smuggle her into Russia. But this would involve a two-day drive across Kazakhstan and Ning spoke no Russian, so it was likely she'd be picked up on the streets and sent back to China as an illegal immigrant.

Dan's second suggestion showed more promise: flying to Europe aboard one of the Aramov Clan's planes and then travelling to Britain. Ingrid had been a British citizen, and as her legally adopted daughter, Ning should be entitled to British citizenship.

She'd end up in a British orphanage, or perhaps living with a relative of Ingrid's, but either option seemed preferable to China, where her history of indiscipline and involvement in the murder of the two cops guaranteed that she'd spend the rest of her youth under strict discipline in a reform school.

Ning's fifth day was a Sunday and Dan didn't have to work. He went for a drink at the Kremlin and came back with information. Apparently the Aramov Clan ran thrice-weekly flights from their mountain airstrip to Plzeň in the Czech Republic.

'Chinese or Kyrgyz need apply for visa to enter most European country,' Dan explained. 'But for Czech Republic you only need passport. You still have the Kyrgyz passport?'

Ning had only seen Dan and the nurse over the past six days and speaking slow and simple English had become habitual.

'Passports are in my bag,' Ning said. 'Kyrgyz and Chinese.'

'I have beer with pilot called Maks. He say he get you on board plane, no problem. When you arrive Czech Republic, he take you to meet person he knows. Once there it is easy to get France, Spain, Italy. He say Britain more hard, but you can smuggle in truck, pay maybe one thousand dollar. Or you can get a good European passport. This take longer. Pay maybe two, three thousand dollars. Good yes?'

Ning smiled. 'Yes, good. I have more than enough money. I know Maks, he was co-pilot when I flew here.'

'He flies Plzeň tomorrow. You pack things. I set alarm to four in morning and drive you.'

It was already late evening and Ning felt sad. It would be impossible to live her life cooped up in Dan's tiny apartment, but she felt safe here and part of her wished that she could.

*

Dan stopped his battered Lada on a gravel track. The sky was dark, but a bluish glow rose from the runway of the Aramov Clan's landing strip in the valley below.

'Follow path,' Dan explained. 'Steep, be careful. At bottom you see three broken aircraft. Keep from sight until Maks come. He light cigarette when is safe for you. He want three thousand dollar. You have it ready, yes?'

'All counted out,' Ning said.

Her eyes glazed with tears as she leaned across from the passenger seat and gave Dan a hug.

'I owe you my life,' she said. 'You are very kind and very brave.'

Dan smiled and looked emotional. 'I think you more brave: no other girl dare wash my dirty underwear.'

Ning laughed as she kissed Dan on the cheek.

'I will try to call your mobile when I am safe,' Ning said. 'And I give you two thousand dollars.'

Dan raised his hands. 'Your money, I no want.'

Ning smiled. 'No choice,' she said. 'I leave in your room, under mattress. Buy new curtains.'

They gave each other a final hug, before Ning grabbed her pack off the back seat and set off down the path. The light from the runway gave a rough idea where to place her feet, but the path was steeper than she'd imagined and it was hard on her broken toe, because the downward slope meant every step pushed her foot towards the front of her trainer.

Maks sat on the deflated tyre of a tailless Antonov cargo plane. He seemed relaxed as he puffed a cigarette and counted his three thousand dollars. At the same time, Ning eyed an approaching convoy comprising an E-Class Mercedes and a pair of bashed-up minibuses with luggage lashed to roof racks. All three vehicles had Chinese number plates.

'The count is good,' Maks said, as he pocketed the money. 'When you get to the plane you go to the back. Sit in the single seat. Avoid speaking and do not give your name.'

'Dan bought books for me in the market,' Ning said. 'I'll read. How long is the flight?'

'Eight hours, including a stop in Volgograd to refuel. In Plzeň, I will take you through customs then put you in a taxi, to meet a lady called Chun Hei.'

Ning looked confused. 'Dan said you'd go with me.'

'*Nyet, nyet!*' Maks said, shaking his head. 'I am the pilot. I must fly back here after one or two hours. Don't worry, you will be safe.'

Ning's ride was a thirty-five-year-old, ex-Soviet Antonov AN-24. As the fifty-seat turboprop made regular trips into the Czech Republic, it had to meet European safety standards and looked in much better shape than the junk heap that had taken her out of China. The hull was painted white with red and gold stripes – the Kyrgyz national colours – and *Clanair* was stencilled along the side.

As Ning neared the aircraft she followed Maks through a forty-strong scrum, trying to cram their stuff into the plane's hold. Apart from a smartly-attired couple who'd emerged from the Mercedes, the passengers were all women aged from mid-teens to early twenties.

They were a mix of Chinese and North Koreans. The Chinese girls had accents from impoverished Sichuan and Qinghai provinces. They wore bright clothes, had wheeled suitcases and squealed like they were on a school outing. The Koreans were quieter, wore drab clothes and kept their few possessions in old-fashioned suitcases or vinyl shopping bags.

The one thing all the women had in common was beauty. Some were small and curvaceous, others tall and catwalk thin, but there wasn't a moustache, pug nose, missing tooth, saggy breast or flabby stomach amongst the whole lot of them.

Ning had learned a lot by watching and reading all the news about her stepfather's human smuggling operation. She shuddered as she realised she was standing amidst Grade-A human stock, destined for the European sex trade.

Until now Ning had consoled herself with the thought that her stepfather's arrest had at least saved thousands of young women from suffering, but apparently the trade in pretty girls was getting along fine without him.

A Kyrgyz customs official stood at the bottom of the steps into the plane. The women all had to hand him a small amount of Chinese or Kyrgyz currency before he'd inspect their passports and put a stamp inside. Ning worried that she only had dollars, but Maks gestured like he was raising a drink to his mouth and the official let her through without even opening her passport.

Ning passed the wealthy couple who had a row at the front with extra legroom, then did as Maks instructed, finding the single windowless seat at the back of the plane. There was a small galley alongside, but the fridges, ovens and water heaters had been stripped out, leaving holes which had been stuffed with litter.

After tossing her backpack into the luggage rack above her head and tucking Kyrgyz and Chinese passports inside her jeans, Ning fastened her seatbelt. The North Korean girls were boarding and gawped at the interior of the plane as if it was an alien mothership. They didn't start sitting down until a big-arsed stewardess yelled in Korean.

Ning rested her head against the curved fuselage. She tried not to think about Dan because she was sure she'd start crying. Everything around her felt corrupt and dirty and after all she'd been through in the past ten days, this felt like the natural state of things.

She hoped it would get better when she landed in Europe, but she wasn't confident that it would.

23. PLZEŇ

Monday was Ethan's first day back at school and Ryan hung out with him most of the day. Yannis had grudgingly accepted Ryan, partly because it was also Guillermo's first day back from suspension and Ryan provided physical protection, but mostly because Ethan made it clear that he liked Ryan and was going to speak to him whether Yannis liked it or not.

Yannis and Ethan had chess club after school.

'You can come along,' Ethan said, as the trio rolled out of last period English class.

Yannis jumped at an opportunity to swat Ryan down. 'Mr Spike won't let him join this late in the term,'

Ethan laughed. 'He won't care. We've only got twelve members, and half never turn up.'

Ryan had to learn about Ethan's background by spending as much time as possible with him. Normally he'd have said yes, but he'd woken with a scratchy throat that morning and over the day it had morphed into a full-blown cold, complete with bunged-up nose and thudding headache.

'I'm getting the bus home,' Ryan said. 'I feel crappy and can't play chess to save my life. I always forget how the horsey moves.'

'You mean the knight,' Yannis said, missing the fact that Ryan was making a joke.

Ethan smiled. 'Don't want your germs anyway,' he said. 'Expect I'll see you at the bus stop tomorrow if you're feeling better.'

'Expect I'll be in,' Ryan said. 'I usually shrug colds off fast.'

Ethan couldn't easily carry his backpack with his broken arm in a cast, and Yannis looked delighted as he grabbed it and headed upstairs to chess club.

Ryan's beachfront house was a fifteen-minute drive by car, but the school bus detoured to drop kids off at every housing development so it took nearer forty minutes for Ryan to get home.

'Hey, Amy,' Ryan croaked, as he leaned into the kitchen.

Amy sat on a stool reading through a slab of TFU briefing documents.

'Oooh, you sound rough,' she said, as she stood up and put her hand on Ryan's forehead. 'You're burning up. You want me to drive to the drug store and get you something?'

'Nah,' Ryan said. 'I've got paracetamol in my medical

pack upstairs. I'm gonna swallow a couple and soak in a hot bath.'

'Drink some orange juice,' Amy said. 'Vitamin C is good for colds.'

'Are Ted and Dr D back yet?'

Amy looked at her watch. 'Their flight from Dallas should have landed by now. They'll be in by dinnertime, which is roast chicken before you ask.'

Ryan headed upstairs to his room. It wasn't like CHERUB campus was a dump, but it would definitely seem like a comedown when this mission ended. His room was at the end of the second floor, with a balcony overlooking the sea, ten metres of wardrobes and a giant bed with a huge circular tub at its foot. Most impressively, Ryan could dial in his required bath temperature, press a button and a torrent would fill the tub in under three minutes.

As he soaked he watched a dumb police-chase show on a Bang & Olufsen LCD. Amy brought up a tray with orange juice, peppermint tea and some buttered toast.

'If you're gonna be sick this is *definitely* the way to do it,' Ryan said, as Amy turned out the pockets of his dirty school clothes.

Ryan finally got out when he started to look like a raisin, but he could only be bothered to walk three paces and crash forward on to his bed, rolling up in his duvet rather than towelling off. When he woke an hour later, Dr D stood over him looking cross.

'Is it dinner already?' Ryan asked, looking down anxiously and reassured that all his private bits were covered up. The headache had gone off slightly, but his nose was clogged.

'You didn't brief Amy when you got home from school,' Dr D said.

Ryan noted that she was wearing ginormous sunglasses and an odd dress with huge shoulder pads.

'Nothing much happened,' Ryan said. 'I went to school. Yannis was there all day. You can't really talk properly when he's around, and most of the time it's lessons and stuff.'

'You need to engineer a situation,' Dr D said. 'You'll never attain the level of intimacy required to find out everything we need to know about Gillian Kitsell. We need to set her up with a female agent, but I need information on the type of woman she goes for. What do her ex-girlfriends look like? How did they meet? Does Gillian frequent gay bars or clubs?'

Ryan blew a stream of snot into a tissue before he spoke. 'I've tried, but there are no photos around the house. Gillian's study has an electronic lock, her bedroom is on the top floor where I've got no business going. And I can't keep asking Ethan questions about his mum's sex life without risking our friendship.'

Dr D folded her arms and sounded hostile. 'Well you seem to have spent a lot of face time with Ethan for precious little result.'

'It's only been a week,' Ryan said angrily. 'Ethan and his mum are close. I actually think Ethan knows more about his mother's business and family background than he's admitting to. Give it another couple of weeks and

I'll *engineer your situation*. I'll invite Ethan over here when everyone else is out, confess a few of my darkest secrets, and hopefully he'll open up with a few of his in return.'

'You could arrange it for this weekend,' Dr D suggested.

'It's too soon,' Ryan said. 'Besides, his mum won't let him stay out till he's feeling better.'

'And what about today?' Dr D said. 'Amy says Gillian arrived home with Ethan and Yannis in the back of her car. So it's Ethan's first day back at school, and you've allowed them to fall back into their familiar pattern of hanging together without you there. If that goes on, Yannis could easily cut you out again.'

Ryan jumped out of bed, holding his duvet around his waist and yelled furiously. 'I'm sick,' he shouted. 'I'm a trained agent and I know what I'm doing. I *will* stay friends with Ethan. I *will* get information about Gillian. I *will* fix the burglar alarm sensors and break the lock on their back door so that you can get a man inside the secure basement room. But it all takes time, and you being pushy, and nagging me every five minutes and generally getting on my tits, is doing no good whatsoever.'

Amy heard Ryan shouting and ran up the stairs. 'Are you OK?' she asked as she ran in. 'What's going on?'

Ryan pointed at Dr D. 'Either she goes back to TFU headquarters in Dallas and stays there, while I get on with my job, or I'm quitting and going back to campus.'

Amy looked at Ryan, who seemed upset, and Dr D,

who looked furious. Her position was awkward, because CHERUB had assigned Amy responsibility for looking after Ryan, but her pay cheques came from TFU and Dr D was her boss.

'Ryan, you need to stop shouting,' Amy said.

'Oh, take her side,' Ryan growled.

'I'm not taking sides,' Amy said, struggling not to raise her voice. 'I'm just saying that *nothing* ever gets accomplished by people yelling at each other. I suggest that we calm down over dinner, and talk things through properly afterwards.'

'I don't think she even understands how CHERUB operations work,' Ryan said, slightly calmer.

Dr D reared up angrily – at least as much as you can rear up when you're barely five feet tall. 'Young man, I was running undercover operations for a decade before you were even born. You're doing well, but you need to pick up the pace.'

As Ryan opened his mouth to reply, Amy noticed two black figures running purposefully across the beach outside. They were male, in black wetsuits and carrying rubberised backpacks.

'Something's up,' Amy said, as she dashed towards the window to get a better look. Her voice turned from curious to urgent as she spotted a high-speed dinghy moored in the harbour. 'They're all kitted out like Special Forces and I think they're heading for Gillian's house.'

*

Plzeň airport had a single runway and a modern terminal

building, built in the hope of attracting budget airlines to the Czech Republic's fourth largest town. Maks was allowed through a special fast security channel for airline staff and Ning half expected never to see him again as she followed arrows and stood in line with the passengers.

'Purpose of stay?' a customs officer with pink lipstick asked in English.

'Two weeks' holiday,' Ning said, pointing to the Chinese girls waiting on the other side of the customs barrier. 'I'm with the tour group.'

Ning's heart skipped as the woman swiped her dodgy Kyrgyz passport through a scanner. But no cloud of burly customs officers came running. The woman stamped the passport and passed it back.

'Enjoy your holiday.'

The men meeting the Chinese and North Korean girls in the arrivals hall held bright red banners marked *Clanair Holidays* but they wore sunglasses and leather jackets, looking more like nightclub bouncers than tour reps. One of these men eyed Ning suspiciously as she walked off, but Maks was waiting for her.

'I got you some local currency,' Maks said, as he handed Ning a small pile of Czech banknotes. 'This should be enough to pay for some food and a taxi. This is where you need to go.'

Maks handed Ning a postcard with an address and phone number on the back.

'Show that to the taxi driver. Chun Hei will meet you there at twelve-thirty.'

'What time is it?' Ning asked, as she looked around for a clock.

'Just after eight a.m.,' Maks said. 'You don't have a watch?'

'Kuban took it from me.'

'I'll tell Dan you arrived safely,' Maks said, as he unbuckled the cheap digital watch on his wrist. 'Take this. It's still on Kyrgyz time, you need to take off five hours.'

'Are you sure?' Ning said.

She wasn't sure if Maks' sudden outbreak of kindness was caused by genuine concern or by fear of what Dan might do if he found out that he'd reneged on his promise to travel with her in the taxi.

'I buy for fifty som in the market,' Maks said. 'Don't worry about it.'

'Thank you,' Ning said, as she found that the innermost hole just about held the man-sized watch on her wrist.

'I hope you get to wherever you want to go. Now I must leave to prepare for return flight.'

Maks started walking and turned left at a sign marked *Private – Pilot Lounge*. Ning pocketed her fistful of Czech crowns as she looked around the arrivals hall. It was a desolate space, with a few shuttered shops and a coffee bar with airport cleaning crew as its only customers.

Ning had three hours to kill and considered getting a quick breakfast, but according to the arrivals board the next plane wasn't due to land for over an hour, and she reckoned some bored cop or customs officer might stick their nose in if she wandered around on her own for too long.

She walked through electronic doors with a multilingual sign over them that read *Welcome to Czechia* and turned towards the taxi rank.

24. GRAPPLE

Gillian Kitsell was on a lounger by her rooftop pool, enjoying a warm evening with Scotch on the rocks and *Wired* magazine. A clunking sound made her peek over her Ray-Bans, but there was nothing to see and she blamed it on a gremlin with the pool filter.

'Ms Kitsell,' Yannis said politely, as he waddled out on to the roof terrace. 'Ethan says he's getting hungry. We were thinking about ordering some Chinese food, but we need your credit card.'

Gillian nodded as she reached around the back of her shorts to grab a wallet. 'Not a bad idea, Yannis . . . Hang on a second. My cards are in my work trousers. I'll come down with you. I'll need to peek at the menu anyway.'

As Gillian drained her Scotch and got ready to stand up, a hooded man in a black wetsuit peered over the end of the glass-bottomed pool. The noise Gillian heard had been a grappling hook snagging the safety rail around the edge of her pool. The intruder had scaled the side of the building in under ten seconds.

He whispered into a headset. 'I have Gillian and Ethan on the roof terrace. I'm moving in.'

The intruder swung his leg on to the end of the terrace, partially obscured by a planter. As Gillian rose up from the sunlounger and Yannis padded back towards the French windows, the intruder slid the small pack from his back, unzipped a pocket and pulled out a silenced pistol fitted with a laser sight.

The red dot flickered on Gillian's shirt between her shoulder blades. The bullet barely made a sound as it left the gun, but there was a thud as it hit Kitsell's spine with enough force to shatter two vertebrae. Fragments of these bones punctured Gillian's heart and lungs before exploding out the front of her chest.

The hit knocked Gillian forward towards the pool and Yannis spun around in time to see his best friend's mum plunge face first into the water. He thought Gillian had tripped until he saw the intruder jogging across the terrace towards him. Then he saw the jiggling red dot on his T-shirt.

'No,' Yannis gasped.

As Yannis started to turn, the first bullet hit him in the side. The effect was like the ultimate dig-in-the-ribs. His whole body spasmed as he stumbled through an open section of the French windows and fell into a leather lounge chair. The gunman finished Yannis off with a shot in the back and a bullet through the temple.

'Mother and son dead,' the intruder told his headset. 'Meet you by the front door.'

But Gillian's son was actually down in the kitchen, holding a menu and struggling to decide between king prawn chow mein and barbecue pork with cashews. The splash was unusual, but Ethan walked through to the living-room expecting to see his mum taking a rare swim. Instead he saw her face down on the surface. Coins from her pockets were spiralling towards the pool's glass bottom as she bobbed in a growing cloud of blood.

Ethan's first instinct was to run up and see what was going on, but he saw a black silhouette running beside the pool and then heard footsteps on the stairs that were way too fast for Yannis.

Escape was Ethan's only option. He made a dash for the front door, but his bruised legs didn't have much speed. He was less than three metres from the hallway as the intruder rounded the bottom of the stairs and opened the front door. The second figure wore an identical black wetsuit, but carried an equipment pack that was much heavier.

'Nice one,' the new arrival said, patting the gunman on the back as Ethan backed into the living-room. 'I'll handle downstairs. You might as well take a look around for a little bonus: see if she's got jewellery or something.'

'How long will it take you to set up?'

'Four to six minutes.'

As the intruders spoke, Ethan backed up into the kitchen, grabbed a telephone off the wall and dialled triple zero. This should have alerted the armed guard on the front gate, but the phone was dead. He thought about his cell phone, but it was upstairs in his school bag and the intruder was blocking his path to the front door and the staircases.

Ethan's heart thudded as he tried to think. The only way out that didn't involve getting past the intruder was the small rectangular window above the dryer in the laundry room. But it was up near the ceiling and it would be tough getting through with his arm in a heavy cast.

*

While the intruder clambered up the side of house five, Amy had vaulted down the stairs in house eight and found Ted in the basement fiddling with the air conditioning.

'Where's your guns?' she asked. 'There's some guys running up the beach towards the Kitsells' place.'

Ryan was behind Amy in the amount of time it takes to pull on shorts and a T-shirt. 'I've got my mobile,' he said. 'I'm gonna stroll out on the beach and take a peek.'

'Could it be innocent?' Ted asked. 'Couple of divers low on fuel, pulled into the nearest harbour.'

Amy shook her head. 'That's not what it looked like. The body language was all wrong. They looked like guys on a mission.'

'Guns are up in my room,' Ted said. 'Let's go get.'

'Stay close to the house, Ryan,' Amy shouted.

An adrenalin rush muted Ryan's cold as he walked through the beach shower. He tucked a boogie board under his arm as he stepped outside, hoping to look like a regular kid heading for the surf.

The tide was going out and the sun dazzled off the wet sand as he peered down towards the harbour and ocean. The dinghy had been lashed to the underside of the harbour jetty. It was black, with a pair of chunky outboard motors. A woman knelt at the rear of the boat and she kept looking up the beach towards the Kitsells' house. Everything Ryan saw confirmed Amy's opinion of a professional crew up to no good.

With the woman looking up the beach and most likely in radio contact with her two colleagues, Ryan realised they couldn't approach Ethan's house from the beach. As he threw the board back into the beach shower Amy yanked him back inside.

'We'll go up and out the front door,' Amy said. 'Ted's gonna circle around the outside of the harbour. Dr D is calling the local cops for backup, but whatever's going on is likely to be over by the time they get here.'

'What about the guards on the main gate?' Ryan asked.

'Rent-a-cops,' Amy said contemptuously as she handed Ryan an automatic pistol. 'More likely to hinder than help, so hopefully they're oblivious.'

'Walther P99,' Ryan said. 'Like James Bond.'

'It's loaded, but if you use it, our cover is blown. So last resort only, OK?'

Ryan tucked the P99 into the waistband of his shorts as Amy led him out of the front door. The land at the rear of the eight houses was mostly lawn, with a stretch of road leading from each house's garages towards the security gates.

Amy's phone bleeped as they walked barefoot in front of house seven. Her voice rose an octave as she read the text to Ryan. 'Ted's made it over the dunes to the jetty. Says there's a body floating in the pool.'

'Rope,' Ryan said, as he got close enough to see into the gap between houses five and six. 'Threw up a grappling hook and climbed up.'

Amy backed up to the garages of house six and waved Ryan back. 'No further,' she ordered. 'They're pros. They'll be wearing body armour. Most likely carrying sniper rifles or machine guns. I'm not going up against that with handheld pistols in our beach shorts.'

But as Ryan took his first steps back, Amy yelled, 'Wait up.'

A small window just above ground level had swung open and they both heard a frustrated moan.

'That's Ethan,' Ryan said, 'cover me.'

Without waiting for Amy's permission, Ryan bolted across the gap between houses, keeping low until he reached the small window. Ethan was red with frustration as he stood on top of a dryer, frantically trying to pull himself through the window with one weedy arm.

'I've got you,' Ryan said, as he reached inside and grabbed Ethan by his wrist.

The cast on Ethan's arm split as Ryan dragged him through the narrow opening, making him groan with pain.

'He's in the kitchen now,' Ethan said. 'He's got a gun.

I thought he was gonna kill me.'

Ryan helped Ethan to his feet and they sprinted back towards the garages in front of house six.

'Yannis and my mom are dead,' Ethan said. 'But I think I was their target.'

'Is it just two bad guys in the house?' Amy asked.

'Yeah,' Ethan said, clutching his broken plaster cast as his face twisted in pain.

'Ryan, get him inside,' Amy said.

'What are you gonna do?' Ryan asked.

Amy looked annoyed. Ryan realised she didn't want to say anything that might compromise their cover story around Ethan. As the two boys jogged back towards house eight, Amy called Ted on his mobile.

'Two hostiles in the house,' she told him. 'We've got Ethan. Yannis and Gillian are dead.'

'Right,' Ted said. 'I'm in the sand dunes. I've got my rifle and clear sight of the boat.'

'You a good shot?'

'I can kill 'em for sure,' Ted said. 'But Dr D's instructions are not to shoot unless they're an immediate threat to someone. She's trying to get a chopper up to see where that dinghy goes and what it leads us to. Our priority is to seal off the murder scene, then get down in that basement room and see what Gillian's been hiding.'

25. SECRETS

Ryan led Ethan through the front door and kicked it shut.

'You're safe,' Ryan said urgently. 'Just gotta do something.'

He rushed through to the kitchen where Dr D was on her mobile. He stuck his gun in a cupboard beside the cereal boxes and told Dr D to keep her voice down because Ethan was in the house. When he got back to the hallway, Ethan was leaning against a table. Tears streaked down his face and he was clutching his broken cast.

'My gran is speaking to the cops, they'll be here any minute,' Ryan said. 'You wanna come up to my room and lie down?'

Ethan nodded. He was trembling and had pale sweaty skin, which Ryan recognised as symptoms of shock.

'What if they saw us?' Ethan asked. 'What if those guys come over here?'

'My dad's got a gun, if they come near this house he'll shoot them. You're shaking so much, you have to lie down.'

As Ethan moved towards the stairs he retched and threw up over the hallway tiles.

'I'm sorry,' Ethan sobbed. 'I'll clean it up.'

'Don't even think about it,' Ryan said, as he tried not to catch the smell of puke in case it set him off too. 'Can you make it up to my room? I'll be right behind you.'

'You've saved my life twice now,' Ethan said. 'You must be my guardian angel.'

'Maybe,' Ryan said, laughing uneasily.

As Ethan crept up the stairs, Ryan dashed back to the kitchen to get a cloth. Dr D was off the phone.

'The hostiles are heading back to the boat,' Dr D said. 'I've tried FBI and local but they can't get a chopper up in time, so we'll hedge our bets: I've told Ted to take one man out before he gets in the boat. Amy's circling around the dunes to act as his backup, and the local cops are trying to contact any civilian or coastguard choppers that might be in the air, in case one of them can help.'

'What about our cover?' Ryan asked.

'As far as the media is concerned, Ted will be a have-a-go resident who pulled out his gun and shot a bad guy. California's even got a law that enshrines your right to blast a burglar.'

'Have we any idea why this has happened?' Ryan asked, as he ripped off two squares of kitchen towel and wiped a blob of puke off the top of his foot.

Dr D shook her head. 'Not a clue. Stay with Ethan, see if you can open him up.'

'He's heading up to my room, but he spewed in the hallway. I was getting something to clean with.'

'I'll deal with that,' Dr D said. 'You get up there. He's vulnerable and the next twenty minutes are crucial. Keep his brain ticking over. He's just seen his mother and best friend killed. If you don't keep his mind active he could go catatonic and then we'll get nothing out of him.'

'Right,' Ryan said. 'I'm on it.'

The excitement had subdued Ryan's cold, but the virus was fighting back. He was burning up as he dashed into his bedroom, but a fever and stuffy nose was nothing compared to some of what he'd been through during basic training.

'You OK, mate?' Ryan asked.

He'd expected to see Ethan huddled on his bed but he stood by the windows, looking out to sea.

'Your dad took out one of the bad guys,' Ethan said, matter-of-factly.

Ryan saw one of the intruders lying in the wash where the sea met the beach. He had a red splatter where his head should have been and the high-speed dinghy was blasting away from the shore in a cloud of spray. Ted and Amy were emerging from the sand dunes. Their manner seemed cool and professional and this would undermine their cover story about being a regular family if Ethan saw too much of it.

'I don't think you should see this,' Ryan said.

'You look like you're about to puke again. You need to lie down.'

Ethan sounded slightly aggressive. 'Good on your dad,' he said. 'That shit killed my mom.'

'Come on, mate,' Ryan said, before putting his arm around Ethan's back and gently nudging him away from the window.

Ryan was surprised to see a phone in Ethan's hand. 'Is that my cellphone?'

'I didn't think you'd mind,' Ethan said.

Ryan took a backwards glance at Amy and Ted as he took his phone back. They were heading up the beach towards Ethan's house. The retired basketball player who lived at number six had also emerged into the sand, looking confused and a little scared.

'Who'd you call on my phone, the cops?' Ryan asked, as he helped Ethan settle on a trendy leather sofa in front of the wardrobes.

'No,' Ethan said, as Ryan sat alongside. 'Some lawyer called Lombardi. My mom said I had to call him if anything bad ever happened. She even made me memorise the number. Like, so I could call even if I lost my phone and everything.'

Ryan realised this info was gold, but his fever made it hard to concentrate. 'Sounds like your mum was expecting something to happen,' he said finally.

'It's complicated,' Ethan said, and left it at that.

Ryan struggled to find the line to get him talking again. 'Is it something to do with her business?'

'Family,' Ethan said, as he ran the back of his good

hand across his tear-filled eyes. 'Mom swore me to secrecy, but now she's dead I guess it doesn't matter.'

'I won't tell anyone, I swear,' Ryan said. 'And it might help to get it off your chest.'

'My mom's real name wasn't Kitsell, it was Aramov,' Ethan began. 'My grandma Irena runs an airline. But not an eighty-nine-dollar return ticket to Miami type thing. She bought up a bunch of old cargo planes when the Soviet Union collapsed and uses them for every kind of dodgy op you can imagine.'

'How do you mean?' Ryan asked.

'You name it,' Ethan said. 'Gunrunning, cocaine, fake Hermès handbags. My mom used money off my grandma to set up her software company, but she never wanted anything to do with the family business.

'Then last year my grandma got sick with cancer. She's already lasted longer than the doctors expected, but it's incurable. My mom's got two brothers. Josef is the oldest, but he's a little simple. My other uncle, Leonid, is apparently a stone-cold psycho. Leonid always assumed that with my mom in America and Josef a retard, he'd take over the family business when my grandma died.

'But when she started getting sick my grandma said she wanted my mom to come back into the business, because Leonid is too hot-headed to run things on his own. Mom didn't really want to. I mean, would you want to give up what we have here to go live some place where they eat sheep's eyeballs for breakfast? But it was her dying mother's wish.'

'Wow,' Ryan said. 'And I thought my family was a

bunch of lunatics. So you think it's Leonid who sent those guys to kill your mum?'

'Has to be,' Ethan said. 'I heard one guy say, *I've killed both targets, mother and son*. Now it's possible my mom had another enemy, but only Leonid would target me as well, because if I'm alive my grandma might still leave me a share in the family business.'

'They think you're dead,' Ryan said.

'For now,' Ethan said. 'But when they read the news they'll find out it was Yannis.'

Keeping Ethan talking had helped with his state of mind. He had some colour back and now sounded more frightened than shocked.

'How can this lawyer protect you?'

'Not exactly sure,' Ethan said. 'I expect my grandma's involved somehow. The only certainty is that Leonid will come for me if I stick around here.'

'So what did this lawyer say?'

'Just to keep my head down, and that he'll be in contact very soon.'

Ryan planned to suggest that maybe police or FBI protection would be more useful than some random lawyer, but as Ethan said *soon* there was a humongous bang. The whole house felt like it had been thrown to the right. There was the sound of car alarms, shattering glass and bits of furniture toppling over.

'Christ,' Ryan said, seeing a crack in his bedroom ceiling as he rushed towards the window. 'Was that an earthquake?'

Ethan shook his head. 'I think it was my house. I

forgot all about the second guy going downstairs. He must have rigged explosives in my basement.'

'What was down there?' Ryan asked.

'Something my mom was working on for Grandma Irena.'

But Ryan lost interest in Ethan's words as he remembered that he'd last seen Amy and Ted walking up the beach towards the house that had just exploded.

'Stay right there,' Ryan said, as he raced out of the room and sprinted down to the ground floor.

Dr D was down in the hallway. She was trying to get the front door open, but the explosion had made the house flex to such an extent that the door had become wedged in its wooden frame.

'Where are they?' Ryan yelled, as he pushed Dr D aside and used all his strength to rip the door open.

'You've got no shoes on,' Dr D shouted, as Ryan shot through the door and sprinted down the side of the house towards the beach. 'The sand could be full of broken glass.'

But Ryan didn't care. 'Amy?' he shouted. 'Amy, where are you?'

26. DEAD

The houses had been built to withstand a California earthquake, but no engineer had ever modelled the effect that a huge explosion would have on several tonnes of water in the glass swimming pools. Gillian Kitsell's corpse had been flung up more than thirty metres and now lay in the middle of the beach, while the retired basketball player had been decapitated by a flying slab of fifteen-centimetre-thick pool glass.

It was like a giant sick version of a bug splattered on a car's windscreen and Ryan probably would have spewed if his mind hadn't been focused on Amy.

'Hello?' Ryan shouted, as his feet ran through sand warmed by the blast.

Ethan's house had been utterly wrecked. All that remained were shreds of reinforced concrete attached to a twisted steel frame. The heat coming out of the basement had turned sand to glass, which now steamed from the water that had landed on top of it.

'Ryan,' Amy shouted, as she appeared from the far end of house one.

He broke into a huge smile, but Amy was waving her arms urgently.

'There might be a secondary,' she shouted. 'Get back.'

Ryan swung away from the house as he bolted past and then ran into Amy's outstretched arms. The two homes at this end had no obvious damage, though the terrace on top of house two was home to smouldering chunks of Yannis and BMW.

'I thought you were dead for sure,' Ryan said, as he pulled Amy into a hug.

Ted stood alongside. Several cop cars were parked on the lawn out front with a fire truck close behind.

'Luckily I went straight for the basement,' Ted explained. 'Saw a dozen sticks of mining explosive near the bottom of the staircase and told Amy to run for it.'

'Another thirty seconds and we'd have been toast,' Amy added.

'That basketball player is dead,' Ryan said. 'He was pretty famous, wasn't he?'

Ted nodded. 'Famous enough that you'll have every news outfit in California camped out here for the next two days. I'd better head off those cops and tell them it's a Federal matter before they mess with our crime scene. You two stay in the house. Keep doors shut, blinds down and don't speak to anyone.'

Ryan walked back to house eight with Amy and ran up to his room.

'Ethan, mate?' he shouted.

Ryan's heart skipped as he saw the room was empty. He thought Ethan might have disappeared, but then he saw that the bathroom door was shut.

'Are you OK, mate?' Ryan asked, as he tapped on the door. 'Can I come in?'

The door wasn't locked and Ryan found Ethan sitting on the toilet lid sobbing helplessly.

'My mom is all I had,' Ethan said. 'I loved her so much.'

Ryan stood close and put a hand on his shoulder. 'I don't know what to say.'

'My grandma's gonna want me to live with her,' Ethan said. 'I don't know anyone out there. I can only speak a little bit of Russian and my mom always said she'd never go back because it's really horrible.'

'Well maybe you don't have to,' Ryan said. 'I don't know how it works, but I don't think a granny who you've only met once can take you out of the country without any say-so.'

'Maybe I shouldn't have called that lawyer,' Ethan said. 'But Mom always drummed it into me.'

'We have to leave,' Ryan said. 'The fire department want all eight houses evacuated until they've been inspected by an engineer. There could be unseen structural damage, or gas leaks. I've got to pack an overnight bag. You can borrow some of my clothes and stuff. The FBI want to question everyone, so we've all got to go to a motel down the road.'

'Is everything in my house wrecked?'

'Pretty much,' Ryan said.

'Shit,' Ethan shouted.

He knocked Ryan back as he shot up and swung his fist at the mirrored cabinet over the sink. Fortunately for the mirror, Ethan was weedy and instead of smashing the glass he only succeeded in hurting his hand.

'Jesus Christ,' Ethan screamed. 'I've got nothing. I might as well be dead.'

'You need to calm down, mate,' Ryan said, as Ethan kicked a toilet roll holder and cursed his injured fist.

Ryan grabbed Ethan, pinning his arms to his side and walking him backwards out of the bathroom.

Ryan pushed Ethan over his bed. 'You're going to hurt yourself. You need to take deep breaths and calm down.'

'My mom's dead,' Ethan sobbed. He was trying to break free, but Ryan was much stronger.

'I need a hand up here,' Ryan shouted. 'Can anyone hear me?'

Dr D was first up the stairs, with Amy close behind.

'In my wardrobe, second door along,' Ryan said.

Amy realised Ryan was asking for his CHERUB medical kit, but they didn't want Ethan asking questions about why he kept sedatives in his room. She found the nylon case, unzipped it and stood out of sight as she found a syringe of sedative.

'You bastards!' Ethan shouted. 'Let me up.'

Ryan pulled Ethan's shorts down, exposing part of

his bum, as Amy opened the syringe's plastic packaging with her teeth.

'Calm down, mate,' Ryan said soothingly.

As Ryan pushed Ethan down into the mattress to keep him still, Amy stabbed him with the needle. Ryan kept Ethan pinned as his breathing slowed and his muscles relaxed.

'Poor bloody kid,' Ryan said breathlessly, when he finally stepped away.

'And we've still got no idea why this happened,' Amy said.

Ryan grabbed a tissue from the box beside his bed and cleared his nose before replying. 'He actually told me a whole bunch of stuff. You'd better go get your laptop, I want to get it all down before I start forgetting.'

27. CHOPS

Ning rode a Mercedes taxi to a small shopping precinct on the outskirts of Plzeň and killed off three hours walking between shops. It was a school day and she tried keeping out of sight, worried that cops or some do-gooder might try to interfere. Her mood swung between optimism and despair, reaching its blackest when she thought about Dan and the fact she'd probably never see him again.

Chun Hei met her outside a Lidl supermarket, and was just late enough for Ning to start getting anxious. She was in her early thirties. She had her hair in a bob and dressed in a leather jacket and black jeans.

She spoke Chinese with a heavy Korean accent. 'Sorry to keep you waiting, it's been chaos all morning. Did you enjoy your chocolate cake?'

The only thing Ning had eaten was an éclair from a

posh-looking bakery at the opposite end of the precinct.

'Have you been following me?' Ning asked.

Chun Hei laughed as she pulled a wet wipe out of her handbag. 'It's all over your face.'

Ning was pleased by the wipe's lemony scent, and Chun Hei's motherly air put her at ease.

'You must have children,' Ning said.

'Only mums carry wet wipes,' Chun Hei laughed. 'I have two daughters, who I must collect from school soon. I've made calls on your behalf. There's a man out on route five who knows about bringing people into Great Britain. It's expensive, because you must cross the water. He says two thousand five hundred euros up front. Three thousand if your family pays when you arrive in Britain.'

'I have US dollars,' Ning said. 'Will he take those?'

'I'm sure he would,' Chun Hei said, looking surprised. 'Are you carrying a lot of money with you?'

'I can pay him,' Ning said, deliberately avoiding details. 'How do you know this guy?'

'I wheel and deal,' Chun Hei said. 'I drive my van about, buying and selling whatever comes my way, without paying too much attention to where it comes from.'

'You're a fence,' Ning said.

Chun Hei nodded. 'That's how I meet Maks and the other men who fly from Kyrgyzstan. They smuggle things hidden inside toilet rolls, I buy the toilet rolls. They smuggle inside toys, I buy toys. Do you know what a brothel is?'

'Where men go to pay for sex,' Ning said.

'If you travel west from here on route five, you reach the border with Germany. Near the border are at least a hundred brothels. German men drive across because they pay less for sex in the Czech Republic, and the laws are more relaxed.

'I go up there a lot, because brothel owners are always keen to buy cheap gear: bed sheets, bras, toilet cleaner, instant noodles, and always for cash. But as well as the brothels a lot of girls pass around behind closed doors, before being moved on to other countries.'

'Like a slave market,' Ning said.

'That's what it is,' Chun Hei said solemnly. 'And you *must* be careful. A girl your age could be worth a hundred thousand euros to a brothel owner. This is so dangerous for you.'

'I can defend myself,' Ning said. 'I was a boxer.'

Chun Hei looked surprised. 'A girl boxer?'

Ning nodded. 'Next year women's boxing becomes an Olympic sport. I grew too tall for gymnastics, so they trained me as a boxer instead.'

'The Chinese like their gold medals,' Chun Hei said, with a chuckle. 'I'm taking you to a man called Derek. As far as I know he's decent – but how decent can any person in that business be?'

'Not very,' Ning said uncomfortably.

'The important thing is not to pay up front,' Chun Hei explained. 'Hide your money in as many places as you can. I'll tell Derek that you have family who will pay when you reach Britain. He's much less likely to rip you off if he hasn't been paid and thinks there are family members who will come looking for you.'

'That makes sense,' Ning said. 'I think I can afford three thousand.'

'There is also my fee,' Chun Hei said. 'I'll charge you two hundred and fifty euros for the drive to the border and the introduction. OK?'

'I don't have anyone here,' Ning said. 'I don't really have any choice.'

*

Amy typed up everything Ryan could remember, interrupted only by a fire officer telling them to pack up and leave the building. Once they'd e-mailed everything through to the Information Manager in Dallas, they packed bags and drove out of the estate. It was a warm evening, but Amy put the roof of her Mercedes up, because a TV van was setting up at the gates of the development.

'Reckon I'd have to win the lottery to stay in a house like that again,' Ryan said, as Amy opened up the throttle.

'Those houses go for close to ten million,' Amy said. 'So you'd probably have to win it twice.'

The motel was a grotty sort of place a few minutes' ride inland. The sign out front offered *HBO* and *beach in walking distance*, but the entire motel had been cordoned off. There were signs up denoting the area as an FBI incident zone and rows of government issue Ford sedans and 4x4s.

'Identification,' a uniformed cop said, as he dazzled

Amy with his torch. She flashed her Secret Service credentials and he all but doffed his cap as he waved her through.

The surviving residents of the eight houses were a well-heeled bunch, thoroughly out of place in this dive. Amy and Ryan grabbed their bags and threaded past the elderly couple from house three as they argued with a Special Agent who insisted that nobody could leave until they'd been interviewed.

'Our daughter lives two blocks away,' the woman whined. 'My husband has diabetes.'

Ted and Dr D had arrived an hour earlier and bagged adjoining family rooms. Ryan leaned into a side room fitted with two bunks and saw Ethan, dead to the world.

'I feel so shit about what's happened to him,' Ryan told nobody in particular.

He walked up to a set of filthy net curtains and peeked at the traffic on the highway behind the motel. It was just past eight, but with his cold and everything he'd been through he felt ready to crash.

Dr D had her laptop open at a small desk less than a metre away. 'I've just read through Amy's e-mail report. Looks like Ryan did a great job opening him up.'

'Thanks,' Ryan said. 'If that bomb hadn't gone off, I think I would have got a lot more.'

'There's always tomorrow,' Amy said. 'With Yannis and his mother dead, you're Ethan's only friend.'

Ryan shook his head as he sat on a flower-patterned couch with a brown stain across the arm. 'That can't be good, can it?' he said. 'Your only mate is a spy who almost got you killed.'

Amy laughed. 'Well, he thinks you're his guardian angel.'

Dr D read something off her laptop screen. 'Message from the IM back in Dallas. The number Ethan dialled on Ryan's phone was an unregistered pre-pay cellphone.'

'Big surprise,' Ted said.

'The signal routed through a cellular tower in Paolo Alto,' Dr D said.

'That's where Gillian's company is based,' Amy said. 'It's about fifty kilometres from here. Probably an employee.'

'Do you think this Lombardi will show up?' Ryan asked.

'For sure,' Ted said. 'Gillian must have put security measures in place on the assumption that Ethan would be taken into custody by child protective services if something happened to her. Lombardi will want to find Ethan and take him to safety as soon as possible.'

'We'll have to decide exactly how to play it,' Dr D said. 'This Lombardi character almost certainly knows far more about Gillian Kitsell and the Aramov Clan than Ethan does. But if we spook him, we'll get nothing of value.'

Ted nodded in agreement. 'Especially if he really is a lawyer.'

'Is it me, or does *Gillian Kitsell and the Aramov Clan* sound like the name of a sixties pop group?' Ryan asked.

Amy cracked up laughing, but Dr D and Ted looked at Ryan like he was nuts.

'Sorry,' Ryan said. 'My headache's getting really bad again. My brain's scrambled.'

'Well you've done your debrief,' Amy said. 'Ethan's not gonna wake up for three or four hours, so why don't you get some rest?'

Ted picked a key from his pocket and gave it a jangle. 'Two doors down.'

'Are you sure you don't want anything to eat first?' Amy said. 'There's a couple of places across the road.'

'I'm not hungry,' Ryan said, as he grabbed the key from Ted, picked up his bag and walked up to the door.

'You know a boy's really sick when he stops eating,' Ted said. 'You sleep well, boy.'

'Yeah,' Amy said. 'I'll be in the next room. Knock if you need anything, even if I'm asleep.'

Ryan was amused by all the sympathy. 'It's just a cold,' he said. 'There's a good chance I'll live until morning.'

28. KNUCKLES

Ning rode to a primary school in Chun Hei's van, and had a wriggly five-year-old on her lap for the final two-kilometre drive to a third-floor apartment. The home was stacked high with produce, from giant bottles of fabric softener, to bath towels, baby milk and canned pineapple.

Ning had to shift eight boxes of cat food to get in Chun Hei's shower cubicle, but she felt much better for a wash. Once she'd dressed, Ning sat at a circular table and ate microwaved frankfurters and spaghetti hoops, while Chun Hei's daughters babbled away in a tangle of Czech and Korean.

The banality of the situation made Ning realise that while her life had been torn apart, the rest of the world had carried on. Kids had been studying at LS18 in Dandong. People had driven to work, done the supermarket shopping, unblocked sinks and yelled at their kids. The thought of normality carrying on without her made Ning feel insignificant, but it was also comforting to think about these lives, instead of the dangers and risks in her own.

After sponge cake, two episodes of *The Simpsons* dubbed into Czech and a role alongside bears and dolls in an imaginary tea party, it was time to drop the little girls with an elderly neighbour and take Chun Hei's van west.

The journey along route five took just over an hour. It was all fields until they got within a few kilometres of the border. Here there were fast food joints, petrol stations and mildly sinister buildings with boarded windows and provocatively dressed girls at the entrance.

'The best-looking Czech or Russian girls get to stand on the street,' Chun Hei explained. 'Some are touting for sex, but most hand out advertisements for the brothels. Once you're inside you'll find a lot more dark-skinned girls: Chinese, Vietnamese, Pakistani.'

'How many girls altogether?' Ning asked, as she noticed a woman wearing next to nothing leaning into the window of a big Audi.

'Thousands, I'd guess,' Chun Hei said. 'Girls come and go. One week they're closed down in a police raid, the next they're open again.'

'Men are gross,' Ning said, as she shuddered.

They pulled off the highway and rolled into a near-empty parking lot. The building was like all the others: two storeys, dirty curtains at barred windows and peeling grey paint. Swinging doors took them into a lobby with velvet sofas and a vague smell of sick, but there was no sign of any girls.

Chun Hei spoke to a man sitting behind wire mesh. 'I'm looking for Derek,'

'Downstairs,' he said.

The twisting stairs were bare boards, and damp hung in the air.

Chun Hei seemed slightly suspicious as she looked back at Ning. 'There are usually girls here, and Derek's usually up by the door.'

A rotting door led through to a cellar with mildewed walls and junk piled under dust sheets. Ning only got a brief glance into the room, but she saw enough to get scared: a bald man wearing a barman's apron was tied to a chair. His face was bloody. Two hulking figures stood over him and there were more off to the side.

'Ning, run,' Chun Hei shouted.

As Ning spun, one of the thugs grabbed Chun Hei, smacked her across the face and shouted something in Czech. Ning thought about trying to save her, but the men were much too big.

The guy who'd been behind the wire spread himself out to catch Ning at the top of the stairs. She barged into his chest with enough speed to knock him back. He wasn't as bulky as the thugs downstairs, but he still had no problem grabbing Ning and bouncing her off the wall.

He shouted something in Czech, but Ning had no idea what. As she twisted out of his grip Ning saw a gun holstered under his jacket. She might have thought twice if she'd seen it a second earlier, but she'd spotted an opening.

Ning's first punch hit the man in the ribs. He stumbled back, giving Ning enough space to attack properly. The man was too tall for her to be able to get much power behind a head shot, so she went for his stomach. After five hard punches in two seconds, Ning had her opponent gasping for breath against the far wall.

She hadn't trained in a year, but she hadn't lost her fighter's instinct. As soon as the man crumpled forward, she went for the temple. The thinnest part of the skull is the most vulnerable and Ning only took one good shot to leave her opponent sprawled unconscious over sticky carpet.

Boxing gloves don't just protect the person being hit and Ning's knuckles hurt so bad she could hardly move her fingers as she looked around, planning her next move. Downstairs she could hear men shouting and Chun Hei in tears.

Ning looked at the holstered gun, considering a rescue mission, but she'd never fired a gun in her life. She had no idea how many men were down there or what kinds of weapons they had. Her only realistic option was to run.

Ning raced outside. In one direction was the parking lot and the highway, in the other an access road, with shabby one-storey houses and a burned-out barn in the tall grass beyond. With no strategy other than getting clear before someone came after her, Ning sprinted off.

As she neared the end of the alleyway a man sprang out of the tall grass, waving his arms.

'Are you Ning?' he asked, in English.

Startled by her own name, Ning stopped running but kept back, with her fists bunched. The man was mixed race Asian-European, in his twenties with green streaks in his hair.

'How can you know me?' Ning asked, keeping one suspicious eye on the stranger and the other on the building she'd just left.

'Name's Kenny. I was waiting for you to arrive,' he explained, speaking perfect English. 'Luckily I was taking a piss when those goons turned up and I squeezed out of a back window.'

Kenny beckoned Ning with his arm. She thought for half a second before stepping into the tall grass.

'Keep down,' Kenny said, as he went down on all fours.

The ground was strewn with litter and Ning's knuckles were agony as she crawled along, a few centimetres behind Kenny's boots. After thirty metres they jumped down into a concrete drainage channel, with graffiti sprayed up the sides and all kinds of debris underfoot.

Although Kenny wasn't very old, he was breathless and stopped moving before breaking into a rattly smoker's cough.

'What was going on back there?' Ning asked. 'The guy tied to a chair, was that Derek?'

'Yeah,' Kenny said. 'They're Russian mafia. They

asked Derek to take Russian women to England for them, but they won't pay what he wants. What you saw was their technique for getting him to lower his prices.'

Kenny started walking briskly along the ditch as Ning asked her next question. 'Where does that leave me and Chun Hei?'

'Look out for syringes,' Kenny warned, as he pointed one out. 'Step wrong and they'll go right through your sole. I wouldn't worry about Chun Hei. Knowing her sweet-talk, the Russians will end up buying a lorry load of cheap carpet tiles off her.'

'And me?'

'Derek's the boss, but I run the route,' Kenny said.

'So there's a regular schedule of trucks going to Britain?' Ning asked.

'Not exactly regular, but there's always drivers coming and going and over time a guy like me gets to know which ones are reliable. As far as you're concerned, I've got your pick-up set for tonight and there's nothing any Russian can do to stop it. There's just the small matter of my two and a half thousand euros.'

'Chun Hei was going to talk to Derek about that. My uncle will pay three thousand when he collects me in England.'

Kenny stopped dead, looking unhappy. 'I heard nothing about that. Do you have money or not?'

'Three thousand when I arrive,' Ning said firmly.

'I've got a situation,' Kenny said, shaking his head. 'Derek is over there getting battered, you understand?

When people pay on arrival, their money comes back through him. But for all I know, he won't even be my boss this time tomorrow. If I'm lucky I'll end up working for a bunch of Russian psychos who'll pay me less and treat me worse. At worst, they're gonna want me dead.'

Ning had money, but she was reluctant to hand it to a guy she'd just met, who could easily run off with it.

'I need money to book myself the Easy Jet back to England,' Kenny said. 'Keep my head down for a few months. Work in my ma's cafe and generally not tangle with any crazy Russians. So I appreciate you're a kid, but you must have *some* money for food and shit. I'm just asking for a taste, you hear?'

Kenny's desperation seemed real enough, but Ning wanted to hang on to as much money as she could.

'All I have is a few hundred US dollars.'

Kenny pondered this. 'I can change dollars easily enough. How many is a few?'

'About four hundred,' Ning said. 'I'll pay you three. That leaves a hundred for me when I get to England.'

'Show me.'

Ning had split her money as Chun Hei had recommended. She leaned against the wall of the trench, pulled off her trainer and peeled out three hundred and fifty dollars tucked beneath the inner sole.

'Kinda smells of feet,' Ning said, as she passed it over. Then she made a big thing out of rummaging in her jeans for what she'd said was her last fifty.

'Smells like money and it's enough for a flight,' Kenny

said happily. 'Unfortunately my wheels are parked outside Derek's place, but we're only a couple of Ks from where I can put you on a lorry heading for Britain. You up for walkies?'

29. CHIPS

The truck stop wasn't designed for pedestrian access, so Kenny and Ning took their lives in their hands, straddling roadside barriers and carving through six lanes of speeding traffic. The place was recently built, with a cheap hotel, shops and two restaurants.

Ning's eyes were drawn to a parked cop car as they pushed through a hedge and walked briskly across tarmac marked out with truck-sized parking bays.

'Don't sweat over the fuzz,' Kenny said, as he headed for a burger joint. 'Derek keeps them happy.'

Kenny had a pal called Steve, who was skinny and kind of weird looking. They found him in a quiet corner tucking down a bacon cheeseburger and fries.

'Watch what you say in front of this one,' Kenny warned, as he pointed at Ning. 'She's got perfect English.'

'Looks bad with Derek,' Steve said, sounding

depressed. 'I told him not to dick with those Russian headcases, but he wouldn't have it. You think we're even gonna get paid for this?'

'I reckon it'll blow over,' Kenny said. 'Whatever happens someone will need lads to run the route.'

'You said you'd go home sooner than work for Russians,' Steve said.

'I've reconsidered,' Kenny said. 'I'll stick by you, mate, don't lose any sleep over old Kenny.'

Ning knew Kenny was lying. But was he lying to Steve about staying, or had he lied to her just to shake her down for a few hundred dollars? Whatever the truth, Kenny clearly wasn't happy having Ning around and pointed out two women sat a few tables across.

'Go sit with the old grannies,' he said. 'I'll get you some chips in a minute.'

Ning felt uncomfortable as she joined the two women. One was a Chinese lady called Mei; she was about forty and looked like she'd led a hard life. The other was a slim Bangladeshi who spoke English with a posh accent.

The women said hello to Ning, but their expressions were disapproving, most likely because she was young and they suspected she was destined to become some paedophile's plaything. Ning fidgeted with drinking straws and listened to the women's conversation. It hadn't occurred to either that she might understand English and they chatted away like she wasn't even there.

Mei was travelling to Britain to work; she'd apparently

spent years working in a biscuit factory near Birmingham, only to be deported after an immigration department swoop. The Bangladeshi didn't say her name, but told Mei that she was returning to Britain after going home to look after an elderly relative.

Mei seemed impressed as the Bangladeshi explained that she was a fully qualified British driving instructor, who could earn twenty pounds an hour teaching girls to drive in Southall on the outskirts of London.

Kenny threw a packet of soggy chips and a can of Coke on the table and gave Ning a wink. 'Thanks for keeping your trap zipped,' he whispered. 'Best if nobody knows I'm going until I've gone, you understand?'

Mei took a few chips when Ning offered, but the Bangladeshi lady recoiled. 'They're probably fried in beef fat,' she explained.

The Russian gangsters had rattled Ning, but her mind was eased by this scene with the two middle-aged women, who apparently regarded being smuggled across borders as little more than an inconvenience.

'Steve's had a call from your driver,' Kenny said. 'Truck's only about six Ks out, so if you ladies need to use the shitter you'd best make it quick.'

'Did you hear the route?' the Bangladeshi lady asked.

'Straight through Germany and France. Ferry from Dieppe to Newhaven. He's a good driver, used him a million times.'

But the two older women looked unhappy.

'What's so bad?' Ning asked, surprising them by speaking English.

'Six hours at sea,' Mei explained. 'The Calais–Dover route is much faster, or the Eurotunnel.'

'But I've heard Eurotunnel is most risky,' the Bangladeshi woman said. 'More searches and suchlike.'

'I just hope the driver gives us fresh air when he takes his break,' Mei said.

'How long will it take?' Ning asked.

'Sixteen hours if we're lucky,' Mei said. 'But it can be much more if the driver stops overnight, or you have to wait for the ferry.'

Ning followed the two older women to the bathroom. Steve was in a big hurry when they came out because their truck had pulled in earlier than expected. By the time they reached it, Kenny had opened up the back doors. He tied a scarf over his face, before reaching in and grabbing a lidded plastic drum. He then waddled a few steps before tipping it up, spilling a stew of turds and urine around the base of a small bush.

As Ning gagged from the stench, Steve ran across from a nearby car, carrying a crate of half-litre water bottles and a carrier bag filled with chicken pies, chocolate bars and individually wrapped muffins. Someone inside moaned that it was hot.

'I can't leave the doors open,' Steve said unsympathetically. 'There's cops swarming, now get back, people need to get in.'

Mei looked unhappy as she threw her bag into the truck. Ning came next and was shocked by the heat and a smell that was like a blocked toilet mixed with bad socks. The official cargo was boxes of copier paper, stacked a metre high on wooden pallets. There was about sixty centimetres between stacks of paper and one or two bodies could wedge into each gap.

Fifteen people were inside already. There was one family with three small boys curled around them and two young men. The rest were all pretty young things aged between fifteen and twenty.

'Find a good spot before the doors close,' Mei told Ning, in Chinese.

A sweat-soaked girl touched Ning's hand as she walked by. 'Are we near the ferry now?'

'Czech–German border,' Ning said, to the girl's obvious disappointment.

A second later the back doors clanged and they were in darkness. The only light came through small vents in the ceiling. Someone lit a small torch to help the new arrivals find space. Mei took Ning's hand as she felt her way forward, apologising when they stepped over someone or had to shift a piece of luggage.

'This isn't bad,' Mei said, when they were almost up by the driver's cab. 'If we squeeze together, we won't get thrown about when the truck moves.'

The air was so hot that Ning could hardly breathe. She didn't understand how anyone could eat in such a stench, but she heard muffins and pies being torn from wrappings. Someone down by the doors was banging on them, demanding they be left open until the truck moved.

'Shut your yap or I'll come in and belt you one,' Steve shouted.

Mei's body fat made a good cushion and Ning settled with her head against her arm.

'Keep hold of your backpack,' Mei said. 'Someone robbed eighty pounds from me the last time I came over.'

'It's *so* hot,' Ning said. 'I'm dripping already.'

'Mind over matter,' Mei said, as she patted Ning's leg. 'Breathe slow and keep sipping your water. It's the ones that yell and panic who pass out.'

As Ning shuffled about to get comfortable, the engine came to life. There was a hiss of hydraulic brakes and a clank of metal as the big truck rolled out.

30. TEXAS

Ryan woke up in the T-shirt, shorts and Converse trainers he'd worn the evening before. His eyes were gluey, his nose clogged and the bed was full of sand. He sat on the edge of the mattress blowing his nose and feeling achy and miserable.

Ryan didn't remember anything about the room. He'd crawled under the sheets without even bothering to switch on the light. There were two double beds, and judging by the ball of blankets and the roller case with *Don't mess with Texas* sticker, Ted had spent the night in the other one.

After grabbing toiletries from his bag, Ryan brushed his teeth and took a shower. Ted had already used the only bath towel, leaving him with a skimpy hand cloth. He felt tired, but was curious about the progress of the mission and decided to get dressed.

Ryan assumed it was about half-eight, but when he clipped his watch on he saw it was nearer ten. The sun was bright as he stepped outside, heading for the family room two doors down. Two black-suited FBI dudes guarded the ends of the balcony, and a scrum of press reporters and TV news vans had been penned into the farthest corner of the parking lot.

'How you feeling?' Amy asked brightly, as she let Ryan in. She looked like she'd been out for a run, dressed in Lycra shorts and a sports bra, and dripping sweat.

'Shitty,' Ryan said.

There was no sign of Ted or Ethan. Dr D sat at her laptop, almost as if she hadn't moved since he'd left the room the night before.

'You hungry?' Amy asked. 'We're thinking of going across the street in a minute. The FBI guy said they do a good steak and eggs.'

'I could eat something,' Ryan said, as he leaned into the side room with the two bunks. 'Where's Ethan? You want me to try getting more out of him?'

'We're tracking him,' Dr D said, tapping her laptop screen.

'Pardon me?' Ryan said.

'After you went to your room, we got intel from headquarters in Dallas,' Amy explained. 'The duty IM used the Echelon monitoring network to scan cellphone traffic in the Paolo Alto area, trying to detect anyone using the keywords *Kitsell* or *Aramov*.

'She picked out a few calls. We haven't identified the Lombardi who Ethan spoke to, but we found his associates. They knew Ethan was staying at this motel with a neighbour's family. Their plan was to send people posing as child protection officers to come and collect Ethan from us.'

'Did we get them?' Ryan asked.

'Not exactly,' Amy said.

'We fitted a tiny tracking implant into Ethan's buttock,' Dr D explained. 'A man and woman claiming to be child protection officers got here just before midnight. They showed impeccable fake credentials to the FBI teams outside and we let them leave with Ethan while he was still sedated.'

Ryan wasn't impressed. 'Tell me you're kidding?'

'Ryan, this is *fantastic* news,' Dr D said, as she stood up with a huge smile on her face. 'This tracking device opens a potential doorway to the deepest roots of Aramov Clan operations in the United States and worldwide.'

'Bravo for you,' Ryan said. 'But what about Ethan? He's been run over, his mum and his best mate have been murdered, and now he's gonna wake up in a strange place with people he's never met. He's gonna be terrified.'

'I know it's not ideal,' Dr D said. 'But we had to make a rational calculation. TFU's job is to bring down sophisticated criminal networks. We can track Ethan's movements and mount surveillance operations on everyone he comes into contact with. It's likely we'll unearth Lombardi and other key players.'

'I was only scratching the surface with Ethan last night,' Ryan said angrily. 'We were really connecting. I think he had a lot more to tell regarding what his mum was up to. We could have helped him *and* got the information we needed.'

'Ryan, you need to calm down,' Amy said firmly.

But Ryan ignored her. 'I *never* would have signed up for this if I'd know we were going to use a kid as a pawn, without any consideration of how it would affect him.'

Amy put a hand on Ryan's shoulder. 'It was a finely balanced decision,' she said calmly. 'It's not that we don't see what you're saying, but you must understand the other side of the argument. You know what the Aramov Clan does. How many people die from one Aramov Clan shipment of guns, or fake pharmaceuticals?'

Dr D took a step closer to Ryan. 'You're filling our space with negative energy,' she said. 'You should take some deep breaths. Positive vibrations will help you feel better, and strengthen your immune system against your cold.'

'Positive vibrations!' Ryan said incredulously, stepping up to Dr D and yelling right in her face. 'How can you be so full of this new age crap, yet not give a damn about Ethan? You saw him when he was freaking out last night. What if he tries to kill himself?'

'That's *enough*,' Dr D said furiously. 'Maybe you don't share my personal philosophy, but here's the bottom line, Ryan. *I* am a senior officer in a unit of the United States Secret Service. *You* are a twelve-year-old kid assigned to work for me. You're entitled to voice your opinion, but I had to make a difficult decision. Now I expect you to obey the chain of command like a grown-up.'

'So it's great when I help you, but now I'm just a kid?'

'Ryan, that's not what she's saying,' Amy said, as she put a hand on Ryan's arm. 'You need to back off.'

'Stop touching me,' Ryan shouted. 'You're just sucking up to your new boss. CHERUB wouldn't treat someone like this.'

'Ryan, give over,' Amy said. 'CHERUB is like any other intelligence organisation. They'll try and avoid it, but sometimes the little people have to suffer to help develop the bigger picture.'

Ryan was furious and felt outnumbered with Amy taking Dr D's side. 'I'm telling you, I could have got *so* much more out of Ethan.'

Dr D glanced impatiently at her watch. 'I have a million things to do this morning. Ryan, you have no further role to play in TFU operations. Amy, take him across the street to get some breakfast. I'll call Dallas and get him booked on the first available flight back to Britain.'

Ryan had a pretty even temper, but he'd become fond of Ethan and felt that Dr D was patronising him.

'You're just a hard old bitch,' he told her, before turning towards Amy. 'And you're not who I thought you were, either.'

'Let's get breakfast,' Amy said, tugging Ryan's arm for a third time.

Ryan resented Amy grabbing him, and the self-satisfied smile on Dr D's face made him so mad that it felt like a bomb going off. He lunged forward and gave Dr D an almighty two-handed shove.

'Ryan, no!' Amy shouted, as Dr D went flying.

The elderly American tried saving herself by grabbing the desk, but it was out of reach. She crashed hard on her bum and thumped the back of her head against a wooden chair.

Ryan was tempted to swing at Amy as she dragged him back and threw him across the double bed, but he'd seen her kickboxing skills and fortunately the red mist cleared before he gave her an excuse to kick his ass.

'Have you *any* idea how hard I had to work to persuade TFU to use you?' Amy steamed. 'You've wrecked my credibility with a stupid childish tantrum.'

Ryan rolled on to his back, as Dr D rubbed her head. Amy tried helping her off the carpet.

'Don't touch me,' Dr D screamed. 'Just get *him* out of my sight.'

Amy held open the motel-room door, and Ryan got a gut-churning feeling that he'd just blown his career as a CHERUB agent as he stepped out on to the sun-bleached balcony.

31. TRANSIT

They got ten minutes' fresh air and five extra passengers when they stopped in a picnic area near Dieppe. Ning's only previous nautical experience was a hovercraft between Hong Kong and Macau when her stepdad wanted to gamble, but this was creepier, sealed in a swaying container in pitch darkness. She threw up four times and Mei was a saint, holding back her hair, wiping her face and fetching water to help wash out her mouth.

Nerves peaked as they disembarked from the ferry. All smuggling works on the principle that customs can only search a small proportion of what enters a country, whether it's a drug mule flying in with a kilo of cocaine, a fishing boat picking up a crate of guns, or illegal immigrants hidden amongst a hundred and fifty trucks coming off a ferry at Newhaven.

The odds of getting caught are always slight and after twenty hours in stinking darkness, Ning jumped from the back of the truck on to British soil. Her eyes took a while to adjust to fading light. It was a blustery autumn evening and they were at the back of a dilapidated warehouse. It wasn't raining but it had been, and a group of thuggish-looking men didn't want them standing around outdoors.

'Inside, out of sight. Move it.'

The warehouse interior was stacked high with bundles of old newspapers. Crumpled and sweating, the illegal immigrants queued in front of a small Asian woman holding a clipboard. First to be ticked off and set free were the family with the three boys, four black men who'd boarded in France and the Bangladeshi driving instructor, who stopped to wish Mei luck before heading to a waiting taxi.

It was Ning's first chance to study her fellow travellers in the light and she realised the remainder divided into two groups. Nine were young women destined for the sex trade. Most were Chinese girls in their late teens, but there were a couple of Russians who looked slightly older. The other six were like Mei: older women who'd travelled from China to work illegally in low-paid jobs that British people turn up their noses at.

During their long journey, Mei had told Ning that she came from a poor peasant family in Western China. A criminal gang had paid for her to be smuggled from China to Britain and now she'd have to work for the gang until her debt was paid off. If she ran away, or her work wasn't satisfactory, the gangsters would punish her family back in China.

Ning felt awkward because she clearly didn't belong with either group. There were too many thugs around for her to try sneaking away, so her strategy was to stick close to Mei and hope for the best.

The woman with the clipboard dealt with the young girls next. The Chinese all got ticked off and sent over to stand by a pair of nasty-looking thugs. But one of the Russian woman had been moaning ever since Ning boarded the truck. She started ranting at clipboard lady, rambling in bad English about being lied to, and bad food and the smell of the bucket making her feel sick.

The Russian got to run her mouth off for almost a minute, but when she gave clipboard lady a shove, one of the thugs swooped. An extendible baton came from his trouser pocket, sprang out to a half-metre length and was smashed brutally against the back of her legs.

Women gasped as the Russian crashed to the floor. The thug then dragged her several metres by her hair, before dropping her and standing with his heel pressed against her throat.

'I'm the complaints department,' he shouted. 'What's your complaint?'

The Russian woman couldn't breathe, let alone complain.

'Anyone else?' the thug shouted, as he turned towards the shocked Chinese teenagers. 'Any of you bitches speaks unless I ask you something and you'll be well sorry.'

The Russian sobbed as she stood up and limped across to join the Chinese. When the second Russian was ticked off clipboard lady's list, the four thugs marched eight frightened-looking women out of the doorway towards a waiting van.

Ning was queasy from the ferry crossing and the shocking outburst of violence made her feel even worse, but at least all the heavyweights had departed with the young girls. Their only chaperones now were clipboard lady and a beady-eyed Chinese driver, who squatted on a bale of old newspapers reading a fishing magazine. These workers didn't need security, because their husbands and children back in China faced violent retribution if they ran.

'And you?' clipboard lady asked, when she got to Ning. 'I have no information. Where did you board?'

Mei answered for Ning. 'She joined with me at the Czech border.

'You stowed away?' clipboard lady asked angrily.

'I paid a man called Kenny, he works for someone called Derek.'

'You lie,' the woman said, shaking her head. 'Derek would e-mail me with any extra passenger details. And you are so young, how old are you?'

'Thirteen,' Ning said.

'Do you have a passport, or Chinese identity card?'

Ning pulled the dodgy Kyrgyz passport from her jeans.

'This says you are *eleven*. What am I supposed to do with you?'

'I can just leave,' Ning said.

Clipboard lady considered this, but the driver lowered his magazine. 'What if she leaves and the cops pick her up?' he shouted. 'She knows this place. She can recognise the truck.'

'I can lie,' Ning said. 'I'll say I sneaked inside a truck in Dieppe.'

'If you let her go and she belongs to someone, there'll be hell to pay,' the driver warned.

'Then what *am* I supposed to do with her, know-all?' clipboard lady asked the driver furiously.

'Take her with the others,' the driver said. 'Then the boss will have to decide.'

Neither clipboard lady nor the driver looked particularly large or fast. Ning reckoned she could run if she wanted to. But it was getting dark, she didn't know where she was and she decided it would be best to stick with Mei until she'd put some more thought into what she was going to do next.

*

Ryan had passed through airport security, but still had over an hour until his flight from San Francisco to London. He was feverish as he wheeled his flight bag through shops selling sunglasses and golf accessories.

He found a newsagent and decided to kill a few minutes flicking through magazines, but he couldn't find anything interesting and he was distracted by flashbacks to the moment when he'd shoved Dr D. It felt like someone had hacked into his brain and planted a fake memory from some other kid who was dumber and more impulsive.

And the more Ryan thought, the more he realised that as much as he felt sorry for Ethan, Dr D had only done what most – if not all – senior intelligence officers would have done. They were trying to bring down one of the world's largest criminal organisations and that's never a painless process.

As Ryan left the shop, he noticed a boxed chocolate shaped like the Golden Gate Bridge and decided to buy it as a present for his seven-year-old brother, Theo.

He was pocketing his change when the phone rang and he saw *campus* flashing on the display. It was Zara Asker, the chairwoman.

'Ryan what happened?' Zara said, sounding more exasperated than angry. 'Dr D called me. She's furious.'

'I don't know,' Ryan said meekly. 'I'm sorry. I was feeling really rough and this flash of anger came over me. Am I going to get kicked out of CHERUB?'

Zara laughed slightly. 'Ryan, I called because Amy said you were in the airport on your own and I wanted to know if you were OK. You obviously can't go round assaulting senior American intelligence officers. You can expect a serious punishment, but CHERUB is your home. We don't kick kids out for one stupid lapse of judgement. Frankly, if we did we'd probably have about three agents left.'

A tear welled in Ryan's eye as he leaned against a circular post. All he could manage to say without blubbing was, 'OK.'

'There'll be a car waiting to pick you up when you

arrive in London,' Zara said. 'I'll text you the driver's details once we've booked it. When you get home and you're feeling better I'll sit down with you and your handler. OK?'

'Right,' Ryan said. 'Thanks for calling. I now feel slightly less like stabbing myself through the heart with an airline fork.'

'You relax and have a good flight,' Zara said. 'You're going to be punished, but you're a good kid and this isn't the end of the world.'

*

Clipboard lady let Ning, Mei and the other five Chinese ladies into a grim shower block at the back of the warehouse before setting off on the next leg of the journey. Ning hoped to see some of Britain, but they travelled on wooden benches in the windowless rear compartment of a white van.

After three hours they arrived at a dilapidated brick-built factory. Ning had studied Britain on a map when she'd been in Dan's apartment in Bishkek, and while she had no idea where she'd ended up, she estimated that three hours would have taken her from the south coast to somewhere in the middle of the country.

The building might have been old, but everything inside sparkled. Despite it being the early hours of the morning, there were more than a hundred Bangladeshi and Chinese women crammed into a noisy but well-ordered factory space.

They all wore identical hairnets, face masks and white overalls, and worked at stainless steel tables in groups of three. At one end, a woman frantically spread mayonnaise over bread, the next person laid on a filling and topped it with salad leaves or tomato, while the third person cut the sandwich in half and dropped it into a triangular plastic box.

A ginger-bearded supervisor rushed across to greet the new arrivals, then turned angrily to clipboard lady. 'Only seven? I was told twelve to fifteen.'

'Maybe more tomorrow.'

'I'm short-staffed,' the supervisor said sourly. 'I'm working on the line myself, that's how bad it's got.' He then turned towards the new arrivals and spoke in bad Chinese. 'Ladies, follow me please.'

'Not you,' clipboard lady told Ning, as Mei and the others were led into a cloakroom where they'd receive nets, masks and overalls. 'I'm taking you up to the boss.'

Ning was shown upstairs to a shabbier floor, set out with sewing machines that hadn't turned a stitch in decades. Clipboard lady led Ning across cracked tiles to an office fitted out with a wooden executive desk and mahogany shelving.

The man behind it was in his thirties. Chinese, dressed in a polo shirt and checked slacks, with a gold Rolex and diamond-studded bracelet. Ning thought he was like a younger version of her stepfather.

'Who is this?' the boss asked furiously, as Ning stepped in. Her eye caught a large globe and a picture of two boys of around her own age on the wall.

'I left a message on your mobile,' clipboard lady explained. 'Her name is Ning. Says she's thirteen, but her passport says eleven. Stowed away in the truck in the Czech Republic. I didn't let her go in case she got picked up and led the cops back to the meat warehouse.'

The boss shook his head. 'So you brought her here and showed her this place as well? How bright is that?'

'We use the white van so people don't see them coming and going,' clipboard lady said. 'I left you a message. I'm sorry, but I didn't know what else to do.'

The boss glanced at Ning, then back at clipboard lady. 'I've been awake since seven yesterday morning,' he shouted. 'We're eighteen people short down there and I can't make full orders. So right now, I want anything with two eyes and two hands downstairs putting shit between slices of bread.'

'A girl that age might raise eyebrows among the other women.'

'It'll raise more if I lose the supermarket contract and have to sack the bastard lot of them. In the morning call around and ask who she belongs to, but tonight she works with everyone else.'

32. CUT

Ning was tall for her age. With a face mask and hairnet she didn't look much different to the older women. She'd worked on the production line for six days straight and nobody had questioned her role since the boss put her to work on the night she'd arrived. The factory was short-staffed and the only thing anyone in authority cared about was getting sandwiches out the door.

Each shift began at 3 p.m. It was supposed to last twelve hours, with two fifteen-minute breaks, but in reality nobody was allowed to leave the factory until the production quota was met, so thirteen or fourteen hours was common. The shifts were divided into prep, where vegetables were chopped, meat sliced and dressings mixed, then assembly where the women made the sandwiches.

The factory was kept cool so that food stayed fresh,

but the pace kept workers sweating. The equipment was modern and everything had to meet the strict hygiene standards set by a supermarket chain.

The supervisors would gently tell workers to get a move on if they worked too slowly or spread an ingredient too generously, but only grew angry if someone breached a hygiene rule. One failed bacteria test, or a hair in a sandwich, could lose the supermarket contract and cost everyone their jobs.

The work was monotonous rather than hard, but long working hours wore everyone down. After each shift, the women were crammed into windowless vans and driven a few streets to the houses where they lived.

Because the sandwiches had to be delivered to the supermarket warehouse by four-thirty each morning, the women would eat dinner an hour before most people got up, then sleep through the early part of the day. By the time they woke it would be early afternoon, giving just a couple of hours to wash and eat before they were driven back to the factory.

Ning needed more sleep than the adult women and it always took a poke from Mei to get her up. Their room was in the basement, with six bunks and boards across the windows to help the women sleep through daylight.

'If you don't move soon you won't even get to eat before work,' Mei said.

Ning had never liked getting out of bed. She felt sour at the irony of it all: she'd started in a cramped, noisy dormitory in Dandong, risked her life travelling to the other side of the world and ended up in some unknown part of Britain, doing something even more futile than school and living in a cramped bedroom that was worse than the one she'd started off in.

'You sleep like the dead,' Mei said, as Ning rubbed her eyes.

Ning was fond of Mei and smiled a little. 'I feel like the dead. All I see in my dreams is sliced bread and prawn mayonnaise.'

'How's your hand?'

Ning had forgotten that she'd gashed the back of her hand on a meat slicer. The wound stung a little, and blood had seeped through a luminous green sticking plaster, which was designed so that it would be easily spotted if it fell off into someone's lunch.

'Looks worse than it feels,' Ning said, as she experimented, moving her thumb and fingers. 'I'm going to try getting a shower.'

'You'll be lucky,' Mei said.

The detached house had four bedrooms. There were four or six bunks in each one, plus eight in the living-room, giving the house a maximum total occupancy of twenty-eight workers, plus Leo the supervisor, who occupied what had originally been the dining-room.

Presently there were only twenty-two women in residence because of the labour shortage, but that was still too many for a dingy basement toilet and a small bathroom with shower on the first floor.

Ning padded upstairs in a nightshirt, with her towel thrown over her shoulder. There was no lock on the bathroom door because women were expected to use the toilet while someone was showering, and vice versa.

Steam and smoke hit Ning as she pushed the door open. The quartet who lived in the most spacious upstairs bedroom formed a mean clique who acted like they were better than everyone else. Especially in front of recent arrivals slumming it in the basement.

'Out,' one shouted in Chinese, as Ning looked around.

One of the quartet was showering, one was towelling off, one sat on the toilet with her jeans around her ankles and the last was propped against the sink smoking a cigarette.

'How long are you going to be?' Ning asked.

The girl by the sink flicked cigarette ash at Ning. 'We'll be as long as we want,' she said. 'You want this stubbed out on your arm?'

'Beat it,' the one towelling off shouted, as she pushed Ning towards the door with her foot. 'Can't you take a hint?'

Ning felt humiliated as she backed into the hallway while the four women laughed inside.

'How old is that girl?' one asked bitchily. 'She hasn't even got tits.'

'Nor have you,' another woman said, before howling with laughter again.

Ning needed to pee and was tempted to cross the hall into the quartet's empty room and do it on their carpet. But she didn't need four new enemies, so she went back to the basement like a good girl and joined the line for the grubby toilet.

After another scrum in the kitchen to get breakfast, Ning spoke to Mei as she put on the clothes she'd worn the day before.

'When do you think we'll get paid?' Ning asked.

Mei laughed. 'In a month if we're lucky. They always promise, then stretch it out. It's a way of keeping you here, even after you've paid off debts. When I was deported, I lost five weeks' pay. When I first came to Britain I spent three weeks fruit picking. There were about sixty of us and nobody saw a penny.'

'Didn't you complain?'

'To who?'

'Won't the gangsters who paid for your journey get angry?'

'Here's how it works,' Mei said. 'The boss at the sandwich factory pays the local gangsters for however many women he wants.'

'Who are the local gangsters?' Ning asked.

'The guys who drive us back and forth for our shifts, set up houses like this one, employ Leo to keep us in line.'

'I thought those guys worked for the factory boss,' Ning said.

Mei shook her head. 'The factory boss is just a businessman who wants cheap labour. So he pays the local gangsters, and must pay on time unless he wants a beating. The gangsters here in Britain pay seventy-five per cent of what I earn to the gangsters in China who paid for my trip. The traffickers in China get paid because they'd cut the supply of new arrivals if they didn't. And guess who gets paid last?'

Ning sighed. 'Us?'

Mei nodded. 'We get paid when the local gangsters feel like it, and if you ask too often they'll smack you about for your trouble.'

'I was thinking in the night,' Ning explained, lowering her voice so that the woman across the room couldn't hear. 'I've got no reason to stay here, but I thought if I worked until payday, I'd have some English money to travel around with.'

'What would you do?' Mei asked.

'I thought I'd go to Bootle and try to find Ingrid's sister. I'll tell her what's happened and hopefully she'll help me. If that doesn't work, I'll hand myself in. I was legally adopted by Ingrid, so I should be able to claim British citizenship.'

'Are you certain of that?' Mei asked.

Ning nodded. 'Ingrid and my stepdad used to say that they were planning to work for a few more years, and then retire to England and live in a big country house.'

'Now there's a dream,' Mei said, as she glanced at her plastic watch. 'Looks like time to head upstairs.'

The twenty women queued in the upstairs hallway as a white panel van reversed up the front drive. As the van driver walked around and undid the back doors, Leo, the brutish Chinese man who ran the house, took a chain off the front door and turned a mortise lock.

The instant the front door opened, the women piled into the van. Ning was near the front and got a seat on one of the two planks that made benches along the sides.

But out of respect, she stood up and let Mei sit.

This left Ning squashed up on the bare metal floor as the van took its familiar six-minute drive. They'd almost arrived when the van braked suddenly. Bodies slammed and limbs tangled in the darkness, Ning thumped her head against the metal divider separating them from the driver's compartment and there were high-pitched screams.

'Sorry, ladies,' the driver shouted. 'Cyclist just tried getting himself killed.'

The women were still straightening up when the van pulled off. Someone had stepped on Ning's hand, slightly reopening her wound from the previous day. When the van's back doors opened at the factory, the light revealed a bead of blood creeping out from underneath the sticking plaster.

It didn't amount to much and Ning wiped it on to her jeans as she stepped into the factory, but the bead of blood set off a chain of thoughts:

Ning didn't owe any gangsters money, but she didn't want to stick around for weeks waiting to get paid. She somehow doubted they'd just let her walk out even when she did.

It would be difficult to escape from the factory, or from the house when every room was crammed. But the factory's strict hygiene regulations meant that no matter how short-staffed they were, workers always got sent home if they were sick, and Ning reckoned it wouldn't be that hard to escape the house in the daytime when it was mostly empty.

As the newly arrived workers formed a scrum, trying to get inside the cloakroom to change into their work gear, Ning cut around the back and headed for the ladies' toilets.

She shut herself in a cubicle, bolted a bright blue door and peeled the plaster off her hand. The dried blood made it look more dramatic than it was as Ning dug her nail into the cut and picked off the scab. As the wound broke open she gave it a squeeze. This was excruciating, but had the desired effect and sent two streaks of blood dribbling down her arm.

Ning pressed a few squares of toilet tissue into her bloody palm and headed out of the toilet. She made sure that several drips of blood hit the spotless hallway floor as she headed for the food preparation area.

'Hey,' a fat supervisor shouted, as she raced up behind Ning and grabbed her arm. 'Where are you going, young lady?'

Ning copied Ingrid's trick of rolling her eyes and acting like she was close to fainting. 'I'm looking for Mei,' Ning said, as she slumped against the wall. 'It's been bleeding all night. I think I'm going to be sick.'

Someone spewing in the food preparation area was a supervisor's worst nightmare. The fat woman grabbed Ning and led her towards a tiny first aid cubby under the staircase.

'You can't work like that,' the supervisor said, as she settled Ning into a plastic chair. 'You stay there. I'll come back and dress it once the shift has started. Then one of the drivers can take you home for a rest.'

33. HOME

Less than an hour after she'd left, Ning stood back at the front door of the house waiting for Leo to answer. He was in his forties, well over six feet tall, with thick rectangular glasses and a stubbly beard. As far as Ning could tell, Leo's wardrobe didn't extend beyond tracksuit bottoms and Chelsea shirts.

'What's going on?' Leo asked, as the van driver gave him a wave and drove off.

Ning held up her neatly bandaged hand.

'Right,' he said grumpily. 'Get down to your room and stay out of the way. I'm expecting people.'

Leo kept his door closed when the women were around, so Ning got her first glance inside as she passed down the hallway. The room was a tip, with overflowing ashtrays and empty beer cans everywhere. Pride of place went to a huge TV, which was currently showing a PS3 game with *PAUSED* written across the screen.

'Snout out, nosy parker,' Leo said. 'If I hear a peep out of you, you'd better be dying.'

Ning tried to think as she walked down to her room. The basement windows were all boarded and she reckoned her best escape route would be out of the back door into the garden, or possibly through the kitchen window – smashing the large central pane if necessary.

But the other women wouldn't be home for another twelve hours and her escape was more likely to succeed if she took time to prepare. She still had her American dollars, but British money would be of more immediate use for buying food and travelling, and so would a better idea of where she actually was.

Women like Mei who still owed money to the gangs that trafficked them weren't allowed to leave the house, but women who'd paid off their debts could go out on their days off, if Leo gave them permission.

From what Ning had heard, two of the quartet who'd bullied her that morning were the only ones apart from herself who didn't owe gangsters. A search of their room might unearth something useful, such as money, a local bus map, or a letter with an address. If she was really lucky she might even find a mobile phone that would enable her to give Dan a call and tell him that she was OK.

Ning badly wanted a shower, and this would also give her an excuse to go up to the first floor and have a quick rummage. She grabbed clean clothes, towel and soap and headed upstairs.

Leo had made it clear that he wanted Ning to stay out of the way, but although he yelled a lot none of the women seemed properly scared of him and when she reached the ground floor she was reassured to find his door was closed and his PlayStation blazing.

With the shower in constant use, the bathroom floor was always puddled. The smell of cigarettes lingered and the bathtub had a layer of grime in the bottom and a plughole clogged with hair. Ning didn't want to get the fresh dressing on her hand soggy and solved this by tearing the plastic off a new pack of toilet rolls and winding it over her hand.

Even though the bathroom was grotty and her hand was in plastic, Ning still enjoyed the blast of hot water and took longer than she should have. She was washing the last shampoo out when Leo barged in.

'Are you deaf, missy?' he shouted. 'What did I tell you?'

Ning was naked and backed up behind a thin white shower curtain.

'What did I say?' he repeated.

'I don't remember,' Ning said, shivering as her shoulder blades touched the wall tiles. 'Can't this wait?'

'I told you to stay downstairs,' Leo said, as he lifted the toilet seat and started taking a piss. 'You're going the right way about getting a slap.'

'I didn't think you'd mind as long as I was quiet.'

The doorbell rang before Leo could answer. 'Bloody bollocks,' he shouted, as he shook off hastily and raced outside doing up his belt. 'Always when you start pissing.'

As Leo raced downstairs and answered the front door, Ning decided it was best not to antagonise Leo by sticking around in the shower. She finished rinsing her hair, towelled off fast, dressed in clean underwear, jeans and a sweatshirt. As she stepped on to the first-floor landing she caught a putrid smell and overheard a man talking to Leo.

He spoke in Chinese, and his tone made it clear he was Leo's boss.

'What are we supposed to do with them?' Leo asked, sounding slightly worried.

'Clean up and keep them out of sight, until someone comes to pick them up.'

The reference to cleaning up made Ning think someone might be coming up to the bathroom, so she hopped across the hallway and dived into the evil quartet's room. As she did she glanced downstairs, seeing Leo's small but stocky boss, and two black-haired girls slumped against the hallway wall.

'Christ, Ben, what happened to them?' Leo asked, as Ning listened from the doorway of the quartet's bedroom.

'Driver was Polish,' Ben explained. 'Van and driver went missing a few days back. Last night I got an anonymous phone call telling us where to find it.'

'Why would a driver abandon his truck?' Leo asked. 'Who called?'

'Russians,' Ben explained. 'There's a bunch of them trying to get a slice of our trafficking operations. We've got no idea if they killed the driver or just scared him off. But the vehicle was missing for six days and the women didn't have much water.'

'Why here?' Leo asked.

'You were nearest, the house is empty in the day. They'll be gone before the workers get home.'

'There's a girl here,' Leo said.

'You said it was just you,' Ben roared.

'I *was* alone when you called, but they dropped her off from the factory with a busted hand.'

'And you don't bother to tell me?' Ben shouted. 'Where's she now?'

'She was upstairs taking a shower.'

'Find her.'

Ning shut the door and backed into the quartet's room as Leo bounded up two stairs at a time. She jumped on to one of the women's beds, grabbed a crossword magazine and pretended like she was reading it as Leo burst in.

'Why are you in here?' Leo shouted.

Ning saw that she'd stupidly left her wet towel and toiletries bag by the door, making it obvious she'd been standing there listening.

'I *told* you to stay in the basement,' Leo said, as he picked up the toiletries bag and threw it furiously at Ning's chest. 'It was for your own good.'

'What's going on?' Ben shouted. 'Get her down here.'

'You heard him,' Leo shouted. 'Get up.'

Ning slid off the bed and Leo held the door open as she stepped out on to the first-floor landing.

'My oh my,' Ben gasped, as he looked up at Ning from the bottom of the stairs. 'What a pretty little thing.'

Leo gave Ning a little jab in the back, nudging her down on to the top step. The intense smell coming up the stairs reminded Ning of the bin Dan pulled her out of in Bishkek. As she looked beyond Ben's gold watch and tattooed arms, she saw that what she'd thought were two black-haired girls when she'd glimpsed between the stair rods were actually bodies. They were wrapped in cheap black bin bags that had split in several places as they'd been dragged up the hallway.

34. MATES

Ryan had been back on CHERUB campus for a week and lay face down on his bed when Max Black and Alfie DuBoisson dropped by. He'd bounced between a few different groups when he'd first joined CHERUB, but had formed a bond with Max and Alfie during basic training and they'd been tight ever since.

Max was twelve and about the same height as Ryan, but with a slimmer build. His freckled skin and blond hair gave him an innocent look, but he was always getting into trouble and sometimes it rubbed off. It was never for bad-boy stuff like fighting or drugs. Max just had the boredom threshold of a two-year-old and was more or less allergic to sitting still, doing what he was told and following instructions.

When Ryan first arrived on campus he'd been scared to talk to Alfie. Although he was still only eleven, Alfie was a head taller than Ryan and Max, with a chunky build that meant he'd have been fat without CHERUB training. Beneath menacing dark eyes and bushy eyebrows, Alfie was quietly spoken and had a posh French accent. He played flute and guitar and was irritatingly smart, even by the exalted standard of CHERUB agents.

'So, Mr Ryanator,' Max said eagerly. 'How did the big showdown in the chairwoman's office go?'

Although Ryan had been home for six days, he'd been sick for the first three and ended up on antibiotics for a chest infection. By the time he was well enough to speak two sentences without hacking up phlegm, Zara had jetted off to New York to celebrate her wedding anniversary with her husband Ewart.

'Fairly terrible,' Ryan said, as he rolled on to his chest.

Alfie spoke from back near the door. 'So what's the tariff for granny bashing these days? Max's money was on ditch clearance, but my bet was on one-on-ones.'

Both were common punishments for CHERUB agents in big trouble. Ditch digging was a coverall term for various kinds of manual labour that involved clearing the undergrowth and drainage channels in the wooded area at the back of campus. One-on-ones were painfully intense sessions with a physical training instructor.

'Neither,' Ryan said. 'I'm suspended from all missions except recruitment missions for three months, loss of allowance for two months, confined to campus for one month and work duty in the recycling centre.'

Max looked shocked. 'You beat up some little old lady and all you get is the recycling centre? I got ten hours of one-on-ones just for crashing an electric buggy. You shouldn't be sulking, Rybo. You should be celebrating.'

'With buxom mademoiselles,' Alfie added. 'And deep-fried Mars bars!'

Max looked back over his shoulder. 'Alfie, can we leave your fantasies out of the conversation for once?'

'Maybe the recycling centre isn't as hard as one-on-ones,' Ryan said, 'but I'd rather do twenty one-on-ones than five hundred hours in recycling.'

Max gasped, then laughed. 'Five hundred! Holy shitting shit. Nobody ever got a five hundred hours of *anything*. That's gonna take you months to work off.'

'Zara says if I do two hours a night on weekdays and three hours on a Saturday and Sunday I can do it in six months.'

'I doubt it,' Alfie said, shaking his head. 'Training exercises and missions will delay things. I'd say more like eight or nine.'

'Five hundred hours,' Max said. 'At least it'll teach you not to go round bashing up old ladies.'

Ryan found Max's tone irritating and he sat up sharply. 'I only shoved her. It's not my fault she happened to be a thirty-kilogram midget who'd fall down in a stiff breeze.'

'Calm down, tiger,' Max teased. 'You know what you're like with those violent mood swings of yours.'

Ryan simmered as Alfie started to laugh.

'Are you guys here for any reason other than to take the piss?' Ryan asked.

'I think we've covered the piss-taking now,' Max said, before looking back at Alfie. 'Was there anything else on the agenda?'

Alfie saw that Ryan looked upset and gave Max a look that said *stop it*.

'You need a girlfriend, Ryan,' Alfie said. 'You're gonna be on campus for at least the next few months.'

'Grace,' Max suggested. 'Nice bum. Not a great deal in the boob department yet, but that's bound to improve and she totally fancies you.'

'The last time I saw Grace she squirted half a can of whipped cream down my shorts,' Ryan said.

'Blatant flirting,' Max said.

'I'm pretty sure she hates me and I'm not even bothered,' Ryan said. 'I can get a girlfriend when I'm fourteen or something.'

'I'd lick honey off Grace's belly,' Alfie said.

Ryan and Max both laughed.

'I swear, Alfie,' Max said, 'you seriously need help. You're an eleven-year-old sex fiend. Have you ever considered an iced bath, or going for long runs?'

'I'm half French,' Alfie said. 'We're the greatest lovers in the world.'

'Grace is tiny, Alfie,' Max said. 'If you got married you'd roll over in the night and she'd disappear up your arse crack.'

Ryan felt slightly less miserable now that Alfie was the butt of the joke. 'Yeah,' he said. 'You need a *big* woman.'

Max agreed. 'Like Irene: you know, the canteen lady with the huge rack and the mole with hairs growing out of it.'

Ryan burst out laughing. 'I bet when Irene takes her clothes off, she's got more giant moles,' he said. 'Whole massive clumps of them, growing under her pits like mushrooms.'

'Aww, don't,' Max said. 'You're making me gag.'

'Isn't that your phone?' Alfie asked.

Ryan had his mobile on vibrate, but he hadn't noticed over the laughter. Max took the phone off its charging stand and threw it across.

'Hello?' Ryan said, but there was nobody on the other end.

The phone's screen said, *1 Missed Call – Amy Collins.* Ryan didn't know what it was about, but he didn't want Alfie and Max dicking about in the background.

'Mission stuff,' he said.

For security CHERUB agents aren't supposed to share details of their missions, so Alfie and Max left without fuss.

'Meet you downstairs for lunch in ten,' Alfie said.

'I'll try,' Ryan said.

He didn't know what to think as he read Amy's name on the screen. Ryan understood why she hadn't taken his side when he'd hit Dr D, but he'd grown fond of her when they'd lived together in Santa Cruz and on an emotional level he still felt betrayed by the way she'd sided against him.

'Hi, mate,' Amy said. 'Are you OK? I feel really bad

about how stuff turned out last week.'

'I've gotta write Dr D an apology,' Ryan said. 'How's she doing?'

'No damage,' Amy said. 'Ted reckons he's been working with Dr D for years and quite regularly gets the urge to knock her on her arse.'

Ryan laughed awkwardly. 'Maybe that'll be some consolation as I do my five hundred hours in the recycling centre.'

'Five hundred,' Amy gasped. 'Wowee! Zara really threw the book at you, didn't she?'

'Yes she did.'

'I was going to call to see how you were doing,' Amy said. 'But this isn't a social call. We've lost the tracker we implanted in Ethan's thigh.'

'Seriously?' Ryan said. 'Did it break, or do you think it was found and pulled out of him?'

'Impossible to say at this stage,' Amy said. 'We thought we'd lost all trace of Ethan. But HQ in Dallas kept monitoring the phone and Internet accounts you set up under the name Ryan Brasker. An unknown number tried to call your Ryan Brasker mobile and we think it's probably Ethan.'

'Must be,' Ryan said thoughtfully. 'Nobody else had that number.'

'I need you to go over to the mission control building,' Amy said. 'They can route comms so it'll look like your call comes from a mobile phone in California. After I hang up I'll send you an e-mail that the IM put together. It's got a background story, saying where your Ryan

Brasker persona is living now and what you've been doing since Ethan last saw you. You need to read and memorise the details.'

After what had happened the previous week, Ryan didn't appreciate Amy's bossy tone, nor the way she just seemed to assume he'd do whatever she asked.

'I'm suspended from missions,' Ryan said.

Amy sighed. 'Ryan, this isn't exactly a mission. You don't even need to step off campus. We just need you to re-establish contact with Ethan and try to find out as much as you can about where he is and what he's doing.'

'I don't know,' Ryan said. 'Cherubs have the right to refuse any mission, don't they? I'd just like to put Santa Cruz behind me; work off my punishment hours as fast as I can and move on.'

This wasn't really true, but Ryan wanted to make Amy sweat.

'But what about Ethan?' Amy asked. 'He could be in danger.'

Ryan laughed. 'So Dr D cares about him again now that it suits her?'

'Look, Ryan, I understand why you're sore. I'll have to talk to Zara to revoke your mission ban anyway. What if I try to bend her ear? I'll tell her Dr D has forgiven you, and get your punishment hours reduced, or something like that.'

Ryan broke into a big smile at the thought of this, but he made sure his emotions didn't come through in his voice. 'I suppose I'd have more time to help you if the punishment was reduced.'

'I'll ask her to knock a hundred hours off,' Amy said. 'How does that sound?'

'Pretty good,' Ryan said. 'Do you think you could get her to reinstate my allowance as well?'

'Don't push your luck,' Amy said, as she gave a dry laugh. 'I'll send that e-mail over, you can start reading and I'll talk to Zara.'

35. HOSE

Ning tried going back to the basement, but Ben made her stay upstairs in the kitchen, with the door open so that he could keep an eye on her. Leo went out for about twenty minutes and came back with thick plastic dust sheets, reels of tape, plastic masks and cartons of bleach from a DIY store.

'Put the kettle on, sweetheart,' Ben said.

As Ning made mugs of tea, she thought about throwing the boiling water and making a run for it, or grabbing a big knife from a kitchen drawer. But Ben had a bulge under his shirt and she was sure it was a gun.

Out in the hallway, Ben and Leo rolled the bodies in dust sheets and wound whole reels of tape around them. Then a van backed on to the driveway. They threw the bodies inside and it pulled away.

Ning thought uneasily about the creepy way Ben

spoke and touched her face when they'd met on the stairs. She was pretty sure it was dollar signs not lust she'd seen in his eyes, and she recalled what Chun Hei had said about how much money a girl her age would be worth to a brothel owner or a paedophile.

It had been stupid staying here so long.

'You're just a lazy piece of shit,' Ben shouted from the hallway. 'You'll do as I say.'

Ning's ears pricked up, and she took a sideways step so that she could see the two men through the kitchen doorway. Leo was on his knees, scrubbing a red mark off the hallway wall, and Ben stood over him with his hands on his hips.

'You could have burned out the van,' Leo said angrily. 'Saved all this mess and stench.'

'It's a two-year-old van,' Ben yelled. 'You think I'm just going to throw away ten thousand pounds?'

'You have insurance.'

'You think smuggling vans are legit, you dipshit?' Ben shouted. 'I don't care if you're too much of a sissy to put up with a little bit of stink. You get your hose and disinfectant, you put on a mask and you hose out that van like I tell you.'

'Why'd you even bring it here?' Leo shouted. 'I'm a caretaker. Shit like this is above my pay grade.'

'You were nearby. This house has tall hedges, it isn't overlooked. I expect everyone who works for me to pull together in a crisis. So are you going to do it, or do you and I have a big problem?'

Leo towered over his boss, but he took a step back

and raised his hands in a surrender gesture. 'You know we don't have a problem.'

'That's good for you, *and* for your mother back in China,' Ben said threateningly. 'I have to go home and change for a dinner appointment. Once you've cleaned out the van, get Nikki to come back and pick it up. Then I want you to drive up to the country place with Ning. Clear?'

'Yes, boss.'

'Do you know where you're going?'

'I've been there before,' Leo said.

Ben started clicking his fingers in Leo's ear. 'From now on, when I click you jump. Click, jump. Click, jump. Clear?'

Ning didn't know what the country place was, or what to expect when she got there, but she was certain it wouldn't be good. As Ben kept clicking his fingers and yelling at Leo, she quietly pulled open a kitchen drawer and started hunting for a weapon.

*

Amy called Ryan back fifteen minutes after she'd hung up.

'Zara has no problem with you helping to relocate Ethan and she's agreed to knock seventy-five hours off your punishment. And I'll get TFU to pay your two months' allowance, if you find Ethan. Do we have a deal?'

'I guess we do,' Ryan said, as he smiled and silently shook a jubilant fist in the air.

'Did you read through the e-mail?'

'Yeah, it all seems straightforward.'

'Great,' Amy said. 'If you go over to the mission control building they'll set up a communications room for you.'

As Amy hung up, Ryan grabbed a printout of her e-mail and took a brisk ten-minute walk across to the mission control building.

The high-tech, banana-shaped building was barely six years old, but it'd had a troubled history, with dodgy security systems, faulty heating and burst pipes. Presently the whole place was covered in scaffolding while a team of army engineers replaced large sections of the roof.

After using his fingerprint to unlock the main door, Ryan found sixteen-year-old black-shirt Lauren Adams waiting for him. She had shoulder-length blonde hair and an athletic build, sort of like a younger, less stunning version of Amy. Ryan didn't know Lauren well, but she'd given him some one-on-one Karate lessons before he'd entered basic training.

'Haven't seen you in ages, Ryan,' Lauren said cheerfully, as she led him down a curved corridor. 'Good to see you in a grey T-shirt.'

'I didn't know you worked over here,' Ryan said.

Lauren shrugged. 'Just for a few weeks, maternity cover. It's good to get experience in areas like Mission Control, because it means you stand a better chance if you want to come back for a summer job when you're at uni. Here we are.'

They'd reached the door of a small office, with a soundproof door. A pair of Windows PCs and a Mac sat on a long desk inside.

'I'll leave you to it. Just yell if you need anything,' Lauren said.

Ryan sat in a bouncy office chair and saw that Lauren had printed off a sheet with logins for all of the various Internet and social networking accounts that had been set up for the Ryan Brasker identity he'd used on the mission.

California was eight hours behind the UK, which made it just after eight in the morning. Ryan jiggled the mouse to wake up one of the Windows PCs and started a monitoring program that would log every piece of information passing through the computer, including keystrokes and audio. Then he put on a wireless headset and logged into a program routed through TFU in Dallas. This would make it appear as if he was talking from a mobile phone in California rather than the UK.

The screen showed three missed calls, all from the same unknown number. Ryan clicked the *call back* button and waited for about twenty seconds. Ethan's voice came on just as he was about to hang up.

'Ryan, is that you?' Ethan whispered.

'Good to hear your voice, mate,' Ryan said. 'Where the hell are you? What happened?'

'I'm not supposed to communicate with anyone,' Ethan explained. 'I'm with Lombardi's people. You know the guy I called on your phone?'

'I remember,' Ryan said.

'I wanted you to know I'm OK,' Ethan said. 'And to talk.'

'Where are you?'

'Somewhere near Denver, Colorado,' Ethan said. 'I'm in hospital. The plan is to send me back to live with my grandma in Kyrgyzstan, but the hospitals out there aren't great, so they're fixing my arm here while they wait for fake ID to arrive so that I can leave the country. My cell blew up with the house, but the hospital shop sends a trolley around and I got them to sneak me a piece-of-crap pre-pay phone.'

'Do you need help?' Ryan said. 'Can't you call the cops so you can come back?'

'It's not safe for me in California,' Ethan said. 'My uncle Leonid wants me dead.'

'But surely it'll be *easier* for him to get at you in Kyrgyzstan.'

'They seem to think my grandma can protect me once I'm over there; bodyguards or whatever. To be honest I'm not keen. My mom always said Kyrgyzstan is a total dive, but it's not like I have a choice now she's dead.'

'I'm sorry,' Ryan said. 'I wish there was something I could do.'

'It's just nice to talk to someone normal,' Ethan said. 'I'm going *mad* lying here, worrying about what's going to happen. The only thing is, I'm already low on calling credit.'

'Text me your account details,' Ryan said. 'I'll make sure your account stays topped up. Then you can call me to talk any time you like.'

'Are you sure you don't mind?' Ethan asked.

Ryan laughed. 'It's not like my family can't afford it.

And after everything you've been through, it's the least I can do.'

Ethan sounded close to tears. 'You don't know how much that means to me, Ryan. You've saved my life twice and you're the only person in the world I can talk to.'

*

Leo was in a vile mood as he stood in the house's driveway hosing out the filth left behind by the two dying girls. Ning thought about making a run for it, but the back door was locked and the garden had a high wooden fence on all sides, while Leo blocked off the front.

But with Leo out front, Ning was at least free to roam the house. She went to the basement to pack her bag, which still contained eighteen thousand dollars and the lurid yellow treasure box containing her adoption papers, boxing medals, family photos and other junk that connected her to her past.

Then she dashed back upstairs to the quartet's room and quickly found a five-pound note and some coins lying on a bedside table.

It was getting dark by the time Leo reeled in the hose. Ning thought again about running off, as Leo washed himself at the kitchen sink and put on a clean shirt, but he always turned the mortise key in the front door, the windows all had security bolts and if she smashed the glass he'd surely hear and grab her before she made it through. It was better to stick to her plan.

Nikki rang the bell and collected the keys for the van. Leo yelled at Ning as its engine clattered to life in the driveway.

'Get your stuff, we can leave now.'

As Ning grabbed her backpack, Leo held out some lengths of washing line.

'It's a two-hour drive,' he said. 'Get in, lie across the back seat and keep your head down so you can't see where you're going. If you fidget I'll pull over and tie you down with this.'

'I'll be good,' Ning said.

Leo's car was a newish Peugeot. The rear windows were heavily darkened, making Ning suspect that she wasn't the first person to travel against her will. For the first ten minutes she kept still, seeing nothing but Leo's hand changing gear. She wasn't sure if she was just imagining it, but the corpse smell seemed to hang in the air and it made sense because Leo hadn't bothered to change his trainers or tracksuit bottoms.

The noise of the car grew louder as they moved on to a faster road. Leo put a talk radio station on, and a woman with a high voice was complaining about how kids on her estate kept tipping her bins over.

Ning reached into her jeans. She had a short kitchen knife in the big pocket in the front of her sweatshirt, but she went for a reel of string instead. She'd found it under the sink. It was the kind of cord you'd use in the garden to train plants.

As she pulled the reel out, a couple of coins rolled across the seat fabric and dropped into the footwell, but Leo didn't notice over the radio and road noise. Ning turned to face the upright of the seat before winding three loops of cord around her good hand. She pulled out a length of eighty centimetres and then made three loops around her bandaged hand with the reel dangling off the end.

'What are you playing at?' Leo asked, as he glanced back quickly. 'I told you: face down.'

'I've got a stiff neck.'

'You'll have more than a crick in it if I have to pull over,' Leo said, raising his voice slightly.

Ning turned back on to her chest, but she had to keep her hands tucked uncomfortably beneath her body or Leo might look back again and see the cord stretched between them.

Attacking Leo while they were moving risked a serious accident, so Ning had to wait until they stopped. But they were on a fast road and her hands grew numb as radio callers covered gypsy camps, neighbours who played Reggae until 4 a.m., kids on skateboards and Britain going to pot ever since they abolished national service.

Finally the car began to slow as they turned off the fast road. Ning almost made her move the first time they stopped, but it was just a roundabout and Leo pulled away before she'd even turned around.

At the next stop, Leo pulled on the handbrake. Ning sat up quickly and saw a red traffic light at a junction, six cars ahead.

'Hey, I told you once already,' Leo shouted.

But this was Ning's moment. She lunged forward, reaching over the headrest with the cord stretched tight. She whipped it down and pulled it tight around Leo's neck, then wedged her feet against the back of Leo's seat to maximise pressure.

Leo's legs spasmed as he gasped, making him floor the accelerator pedal. But with the handbrake on, the car only managed to shoot two metres forward and hit the car in front. The cord cut into Ning's wrists, but she didn't let go as she looked around the side of the headrest and saw Leo's head lolling as the cord tightened across his windpipe.

Up ahead, a furious man climbed out of his dented car as the lights turned green. Leo seemed to have stopped fighting as Ning unwound the cord from her bloody wrists. As she reached into the footwell to grab her backpack, cars trapped behind honked and traffic started moving in the other lane.

Ning threw a door open and stepped into the road. There was a tiny gap between moving cars and she forced a taxi to brake as she ran to the kerb. When she reached the pavement, she started running as fast as she could.

PART TWO

FIVE WEEKS LATER

36. GREEN

It was late afternoon and Ryan was logging his eighty-first hour in the recycling centre on CHERUB campus. He wore a blue overall and thick gloves as he wheeled a giant plastic bin towards his nine-year-old brother Leon and Leon's best mate, Banky. The two red-shirts had earned themselves thirty hours' recycling duty for sneaking out of bed with a cache of fireworks.

'Mind your toes,' Ryan said, as he grabbed the base of the bin and tipped it up.

A wave of clothing spewed out across the floor, accompanied by a whiff of socks and BO.

'Aww,' Banky moaned, as Leon pulled his overall up over his nose.

'There's masks in the changing area if you want them,' Ryan said, as he picked out a muddy sock and held it up. 'People are *supposed* to only put clean clothes in the recycling bins, but as you've noticed it doesn't always work that way.

'You need to sort all this lot into four piles. Pile one – anything that's clean and still in reasonable condition gets packaged up and sent to Africa. Anything with a label saying it's pure wool or cotton can be recycled and goes into pile two. Pile three – synthetics, mixed fibres and clothes that are really filthy can't be recycled. These go to landfill. Finally, pile four is anything that has a CHERUB logo on.'

'What happens to them?' Leon asked.

'Nothing with a CHERUB logo can leave campus for security reasons,' Ryan said. 'It all goes in the incinerator.'

'Can we use the incinerator?' Leon asked.

'Nope,' Ryan said. 'One of the maintenance staff burns secure waste in the incinerator every Wednesday. And it's all automatic, so all you see is a few wafts of smoke coming out the chimney on top of the building. Any more questions before you start?'

'Yeah,' Banky asked. 'Is it true you got five hundred hours because you're a granny basher?'

Ryan smiled. 'Not true. I got five hundred hours because I slapped the piss out of an annoying little red-shirt who asked me dumb questions.'

Banky and Leon looked at each other and smiled.

'Oooh, isn't my brother clever,' Leon said sarcastically. 'He turned things around so that the joke was on us.'

Banky spoke in a pompous professorish voice. 'Yes, Leon, old bean, I thought it was a terrific use of humour. Jolly clever indeed.'

'All right, smart arses, get on with it,' Ryan said, as he started walking away.

'Where are you skiving off to?' Leon asked. 'We can't do all this on our own.'

'I've got to fetch all the glass bottles from the kitchens,' Ryan said.

As Ryan walked towards the exit he felt a smartphone vibrating in his back pocket. He pulled off his filthy gloves and checked the screen. Ryan still had his normal phone, but this extra one was set up just for communicating with Ethan. It recorded every word, logged every message and automatically relayed everything to TFU headquarters in Dallas.

Ethan's arm had multiple complex breaks from the car injury and the doctors in his Colorado hospital weren't happy with the way it was healing. His message to Ryan read: *May be out of touch 4 a bit. Texting from hospital toilet! Op in an hour. Kinda shitting self cos it was painful last time.*

The broken arm was partly Ryan's fault and he felt guilty as he tapped a reply: *Hope op goes well m8. Been reading a book on chess. Gonna beat you soon!*

As Ryan pushed the phone back in his pocket he noticed someone ducking under the opened portion of the recycling centre's main roll-up door. To his surprise it was Amy Collins.

'Hiya,' Amy said brightly.

Ryan smiled involuntarily. 'What you doing here? I thought you were in Dallas.'

'Touched down at lunchtime,' Amy explained, as she

waved a cardboard folder. 'TFU have been trawling US and European intelligence and police files for anything relating to Kyrgyzstan or Aramov Clan operations. I'm following up something we found at a Scottish IDC.'

'IDC?' Ryan asked.

'Immigration Detention Centre,' Amy explained. 'It's where they send illegal immigrants before they get deported.'

'Right,' Ryan said. 'And you're telling me this because . . . ?'

Amy didn't answer immediately. She'd been distracted by what was going on behind Ryan. 'Your co-workers don't seem very motivated,' she said.

Ryan turned and saw that Leon and Banky weren't sorting. Instead, they'd both dug the biggest bras they could find out of the clothes pile, put them on over their overalls and were now helping one another to stuff them with things to make giant false breasts.

'They're lazy little shits,' Ryan moaned. 'I'm supposed to be in charge, but there's no way my little brother's gonna do what I tell him, and Banky just follows his lead.'

'Is he one of the twins?' Amy asked.

'Yeah,' Ryan said.

'I can see the family resemblance,' she told Ryan, before striding purposefully into the middle of the recycling area, putting her hands on her hips and yelling, 'What on *earth* do you think you're doing?'

Leon and Banky weren't old enough to remember Amy as a CHERUB agent. But while they didn't have a clue who she was, her tone still made them jump.

Amy pointed her finger up at the roof. 'You do know there are CCTV cameras in here, don't you?' she said. 'I've been watching everything you're doing and I'm going to make a report to Zara. She'll double your punishment hours if you don't start pulling your weight.'

Ryan hid a smile as Banky and his brother started frantically pulling the bras up over their heads.

'What cameras?' Ryan asked, when Amy came back towards him.

'Let that be our little secret,' Amy said. 'But I expect you'll get more work out of those two from now on. Now, where was I?'

'IDC,' Ryan said. 'And where I fitted in.'

Amy nodded. 'Are you and I on speaking terms after everything that happened in Santa Cruz?'

'I think this counts as speaking,' Ryan said, keeping one eye on Leon and Banky as they rapidly sorted clothes.

'You know what I mean,' Amy said. 'Things were awkward when I left you at the airport in San Francisco, and things weren't exactly rosy when we spoke on the phone. I should have been more supportive.'

Ryan shrugged. 'It's awkward when you're in a new job,' he said. 'I basically acted like a tosser when I shoved Dr D, so I reckon we're about even.'

'Cool,' Amy said. 'Because you're up to speed with most information on the Aramov Clan and Zara says she's happy for you to be involved in a recruitment operation.'

'Now you've lost me,' Ryan said. 'First you said Aramov Clan, now I'm recruiting a new CHERUB agent. Which one is it?'

'Both,' Amy said. 'I've prepared this file for you. If half is true it's a hell of a story. It also contains personal information that mustn't be spread around campus. Treat this file as you would a mission briefing document.'

Ryan took the folder and saw a centimetre-thick wodge of interview statements, translations of Chinese newspaper articles, e-mails and photographs. The sheet stapled to the front cover of the picture was a standard form CHERUB used for potential recruits. Ryan saw the photo of an Asian girl and began reading aloud.

'Fu Ning,' he said. 'Turned twelve last Wednesday. Speaks fluent English and Mandarin. High IQ, champion boxer. Sounds like CHERUB material to me. So what's the Aramov link?'

'Fu Ning was picked up at Liverpool Central station just over a month back. It was near midnight. A station guard alerted the transport police because she was alone. She'd been travelling around for a few days trying to find an aunt who came from Bootle. She was dirty, she had cuts on her hand and wrists, a broken toe that hadn't been set properly, a burn on her chest, and eighteen thousand US dollars in her backpack.'

'Sad,' Ryan said, as he tried to imagine how all those injuries could have happened to the innocent-looking girl in the picture.

'Ning claims to have travelled from China to the Czech Republic, via Kyrgyzstan. Along the way she encountered Leonid Aramov. Ning is currently in an IDC in Scotland and I'm booked on a train. I'll meet Ning this evening and try to find out how much she learned in Kyrgyzstan.'

'Then she'll come back here for recruitment tests and you want me to look after her?' Ryan said.

Amy nodded. 'On paper Ning is prime CHERUB material, but she's suffered a lot in the last two months. Until I actually meet Ning, I can't gauge how it's affected her mentally.'

37. BLUE

Whatever hand fate dealt, Ning always seemed to end up in a room filled with bunks. This one was in Kirkcaldy Immigration Detention Centre. Her two roomies were Veronica, a sixteen-year-old Jamaican who was awaiting deportation after serving a short sentence for smuggling cocaine, and Rupa, who was eight months pregnant. She couldn't be sent back to Bangladesh until after her baby was born.

The regime at Kirkcaldy was relaxed. People wore their own clothes and picked and chose when to eat or sleep. But there were still bars on the windows, the showers and toilets were grim and every expense was spared on the food.

Ning's block held women under twenty-two and quite a few of them had babies or toddlers. There was a cute little chap who gave Ning cuddles and sat on her bunk playing with toy cars, but at other times the screaming babies and brats charging up and down the hallways did her brain in.

The staff were mostly OK, though like any place some were better than others. Lucy Pogue was a tough-looking officer who ran Ning's block. She was usually grumpy, but had reason to be: in the three weeks since Ning arrived, she'd seen Lucy punched and kicked, get piss thrown in her face after a search team confiscated drugs, and dealing with a detainee who'd tried killing herself by slashing her wrists.

'So, how's it going?' Lucy asked casually, as she came into Ning's room.

Rupa was at a doctor's appointment and Veronica had her iPod blasting, so Ning's was the only reply.

'Dull as,' Ning said.

'Have you been to school this week?' Lucy asked.

Girls under sixteen were supposed to attend school, but it wasn't strictly enforced.

'It's pointless,' Ning said. 'Five- to fifteen-year-olds in one class, speaking twenty different languages.'

'I need you to come over for an interview,' Lucy said. 'Bring your immigration papers. They're waiting for you.'

Ning was surprised. She'd had several meetings with the immigration officer dealing with her citizenship application, but the others had been scheduled in advance. Ning took a minute to slide on trainers and get copies of her paperwork out of her locker before Lucy led her downstairs.

The route to the administration building took them across a blustery courtyard with swings and a roundabout. The interview room was small. It always seemed stuffy and a couple of degrees too hot. Ning's Immigration Case Officer was called Steve. He had red hair and a shaving rash, and you could see nipples through his thin white shirt.

'Afternoon, Ning,' Steve said politely. 'Take a seat.'

Ning sat in an orange plastic chair, while Lucy stayed back near the door.

Steve clicked his pen and spoke. 'I have the usual boxes to tick,' he said. 'First of all, I understand that you speak English and do not require a translator?'

'Yes,' Ning said.

'Secondly, your legal aid representative cannot be present this afternoon. But he will be notified of this meeting. You'll get an opportunity to talk to him by telephone if you wish to do so later.'

Ning nodded. Steve ticked another box on his form, then tapped his papers against the desk.

'Now,' Steve said seriously, 'I have some unfortunate news today. I'm going to read a prepared statement as it's a legal requirement: *After consideration of your application for British citizenship, it has been decided that you have no proven basis to obtain British citizenship, or to remain in Great Britain for any other reason. You will be given full details of why we reached this conclusion. You have a limited right of appeal as per the provisions of the 2002 Immigration and Nationality Act. We have notified the Chinese authorities of our intention to return you to the People's Republic of China.*'

Ning felt like she'd been punched. 'I don't understand,' she said shakily. 'Ingrid was British, I was legally adopted.'

Steve tipped his chair back and interlocked his fingers. 'Unfortunately, we've been unable to trace any details of this *Ingrid*.'

'She worked as a stripper,' Ning said. 'Maybe Ingrid Hepburn was her stage name. And weren't you going to check with the army?'

'The army has no record of an Ingrid Hepburn,' Steve said. 'I also had a fellow officer visit the address in Bootle where your aunt is supposed to have lived. The current residents had been there for two years and we were unable to trace previous occupants.'

'Well what about my accent then?' Ning said desperately. 'Everyone here takes the Mickey and says I speak English like a Chinese scouser. I got that from Ingrid. Where else could it have come from?'

'An accent is not grounds for citizenship,' Steve said. 'I'm sorry, but I've thoroughly investigated your interview statements. There are no grounds for you to remain in the United Kingdom.'

'What about compassionate grounds, or refugee status?' Lucy asked.

Steve looked uncomfortable. 'China has a functioning child welfare system. Child protection officers will meet Ning when she lands in Beijing.'

'Child protection,' Ning said angrily. 'They'll dump me in some reform school a thousand miles from anywhere.'

'Ning, I'm not unsympathetic,' Steve said. 'But I work within a framework of rules and guidelines. I have no personal discretion.'

'What's the bloody point?' Ning shouted as she shot up from her seat, lifted the desk and slammed it against the floor. 'Why do I bother with anything?'

Lucy put a reassuring hand on Ning's shoulder.

'There's only one flight a day from Edinburgh to Beijing,' Steve said. 'I believe there are seats available on tomorrow's flight.'

Ning was shaky and had tears welling in her eyes as she walked back across the courtyard with Lucy.

'China probably won't be as bad as you think,' Lucy said, as she left Ning at the door of her cell.

Lucy meant well, but Ning was irritated because she'd spent the first four years of her life in a Chinese orphanage, while Lucy knew nothing about them.

'You look beat up, girl,' Veronica said, pulling an ear bud out as Ning sat down. 'They booked your flight?'

Ning got on OK with Veronica, but her mix of London and Jamaican slang was tough to follow.

'Looks like tomorrow,' Ning said sadly.

'It's a rip-off,' Veronica said. 'End of the month, innit? They gotta meet their quota and a whole buncha girls gets marching orders. I'm flying out tomorrow, man. Not that I care, cos I haven't seen my mum or my cousins in like the *longest* time. We'll party and the drug people owe me money for six months of my life, innit?'

'It's not really their fault,' Ning said. 'Steve tried to help me.'

'Don't believe none a that shit,' Veronica snorted. 'Them people don't lift a finger, right? No *way* any decent country should send you home to Chinaland. No way!'

'I suppose,' Ning said weakly.

'I've got a tradition,' Veronica said, as she reached into her locker and pulled out a small bottle of whisky. 'When I leave a place I make my mark.'

Booze always made Ning think of Ingrid and she shook her head. 'I hate the smell,' she said.

Veronica laughed as she unscrewed the cap. 'Who says it's for drinking? You got anything valuable, pack up now cos I'm burning this room up.'

Ning watched as Veronica splashed the whisky over her mattress. Seeing that Veronica was serious, Ning raced to her locker and grabbed her backpack. They'd taken her money away when she'd arrived, but she still had her yellow box and some clothes.

'What about *your* stuff?' Ning asked, as she threw the backpack over her shoulder.

'Don't want none of it,' Veronica said. 'Everything stink like prison.'

'But Rupa,' Ning said, as Veronica scrunched up pages of a magazine and threw them on to her bed to act as kindling. 'She's really poor. People have given her clothes for the baby and stuff. It'll all go up in smoke.'

Veronica pulled on a sweatshirt and stuffed her iPod and charger in the front pocket.

'Rupa's stuck up. Looks down her nose at me.'

'She's just shy,' Ning said. 'She can hardly speak English.'

'Why you take everyone side but mine?' Veronica said accusingly, as she threw deodorant cans and bottles of perfume from her locker on to her whisky-soaked mattress. 'Aerosol gonna explode. Boom!'

Ning thought about all the baby stuff, plus the immigration papers Rupa would need for her appeal.

'Stop it,' Ning ordered.

'Who do you think you are?' Veronica said. 'Try stopping me, see what you get.'

Ning thought about running down the hallway and yelling for Lucy, but Veronica smoked. She could use a match and light up the bed in an instant, so Ning closed in and shoved Veronica back against the wall.

Veronica turned swiftly and aimed a slap at Ning's face. Ning ducked, then bobbed up and slugged Veronica in the gut. Ning moved forward to hit Veronica again, but she stepped on to one of the torn magazine pages and her foot slid. It wasn't dramatic, but it gave Veronica time to shove Ning backwards.

As Ning crashed against the frame of her bed, Veronica grabbed a matchbook from her bedside shelf. Ning found her feet, but Veronica lit and threw the match. The whisky erupted in a sheet of blue flame as Veronica ran for the door, laughing madly.

The magazine pages caught light. As Ning grabbed her pack and headed for the door, Veronica yelled down the hallway, sounding like a wounded cat.

'Ning set my bed on fire. All my stuff is burning! Oh my sweet lord, Jesus!'

Veronica gave Ning a *screw you* smile, then turned to

run. Ning punched Veronica in the back. It was only a glancing blow, but it knocked her off balance. She sprawled across the hallway floor as the smoke alarm went off.

Girls hurried out of their rooms into the corridor as Ning jumped on to Veronica's back. She was angry at everything and punched Veronica out with a ruthless left-right combo to the head. As Lucy appeared from her office by the stairs, a stocky Nigerian detainee ripped Ning away from Veronica. But Ning's flailing arms and legs meant she couldn't keep hold of her.

'Evacuate,' Lucy was shouting, as Ning began sprinting down the corridor. 'Fire marshals, check rooms. Quickly, quickly. Make sure you've got all the kids.'

The flames from Veronica's mattress were now licking the ceiling and a curtain of dark grey smoke was forming along the roof of the hallway. As Ning and a bunch of other girls raced down the stairs the sprinklers kicked in, drizzling them with cold water.

Six kids and two dozen women emerged sopping wet into the courtyard. Ning found herself encircled by wet, angry bodies.

'Why'd you start a fire?' a tough-looking Russian shouted. 'All my stuff is in there. Are you gonna pay for what's ruined?'

'It wasn't me,' Ning said desperately. 'Veronica started the fire.'

'I saw you come back from interview,' a black girl standing behind Ning said. 'You just got marching orders, didn't you?'

'I did,' Ning said, 'But Veronica . . .'

Ning didn't get to finish because the big Nigerian lady had grabbed hold of the pack on her back.

'Veronica's things are burning,' she shouted. 'Our things are all getting ruined, but guess who kept all of hers?'

If any of the mob doubted that Ning had set the fire, the realisation that Ning had walked out with all her belongings snuffed them. With the Nigerian gripping her backpack, Ning couldn't defend herself as a woman smacked her hard across the face.

As the mob roared approval, the Russian spat in Ning's face, followed immediately by three or four others.

'Lucky you're leaving cos I'd stab you up,' someone shouted, as Ning held her arms up to stop the torrent of spit.

'All right, ladies,' a male guard shouted, as he jogged towards the scene with a burly colleague close behind. 'Break it up. Move calmly towards your assembly point.'

As the women peeled away, the Nigerian gave Ning an almighty push, sending her sprawling out by the feet of the approaching guard.

'Ooopsy,' the guard said, pretending he hadn't seen anything.

As Ning rolled over on to a grazed elbow, she saw Lucy glaring down at her.

'What was the point of that?' Lucy said angrily. 'It's going to take *weeks* to get my unit straight.'

Ning didn't bother denying that she'd started the fire. Nobody ever believed anything she said and she felt so worthless that she didn't even wipe the spit off her face.

Lucy looked up at the burly guard. 'Take her to C building, put her in a segregation cell.'

'Is she being charged?' the guard asked.

'That's probably what she's hoping for,' Lucy said, with no hint of the sympathy she'd shown earlier. 'I'll make a couple of calls and tell the deportation unit she's a priority. I can't hold a girl her age in seg for more than a day and she won't be safe back amongst the other girls. I just hope they can get her on tomorrow's flight.'

38. TRAIN

It was after nine and Ryan still had a stack of homework to do, but he sat at the desk in his room with the pages of Amy's report spread around him. He had Google Maps up on his laptop screen, centred on the point where the police had found Leo unconscious behind the wheel of his Peugeot.

Ning didn't know where she'd been held captive, but told the police that it had taken forty minutes to drive from the house to the point where she'd run off. Leo had regained consciousness in an ambulance and discharged himself from hospital before the cops were able to question him.

All signs pointed to Leo being an illegal immigrant. He'd made no attempt to reclaim his car from the police impound. The vehicle had no insurance or registration documents and carried a cloned number plate from an identical vehicle. Like the police and TFU before him, Ryan couldn't see any way to trace the house where Ning had been staying, or the sandwich factory stuffed with illegal immigrants.

'You don't have a lot of luck, do you?' Ryan told himself, as he looked at Ning's picture.

The door swung open and Max burst in, dressed only in luminous orange stretch briefs and brandishing a large black gun.

'Hold on to your girlfriends, cos Max Blaaaaaack is here,' he yelled cheerfully.

'Nice pants,' Ryan said. 'I seriously doubt any female on earth will be able to resist you.'

'Exactly,' Max said as he slammed the gun down on Ryan's papers. 'Now, stop focusing on my pants and check this baby out.'

Ryan knew a real gun when he saw one, and this wasn't. 'It's paintball.'

'Yeah,' Max said. 'But saying that this is only a paintball gun is like saying a Lamborghini is only a car. This is an RAP4 T68. Three hundred rounds per minute, upgraded for automatic burst fire. Comparing this to those weedy little guns they've got in the campus paintball zone is like comparing a rat turd with a big ball of elephant dung.'

'Great,' Ryan said wryly. 'You have a totally awesome gun, which means you can shoot the crap out of everyone. Which means nobody is ever gonna want to go paintballing with you.'

Max smiled. 'That's where you're wrong, smarty pants.

Because I've got eight of 'em, along with all the trimmings: hoppers, loaders, compressed air tanks. Even some decent goggles that haven't got five years of crud stuck all over them.'

Ryan looked suspicious. 'And where did the money for all that lot come from?'

Max gave a sly smile. 'Let's just say I was on a mission and a small quantity of cash found its way into my hands.'

Ryan tutted. 'It's against the rules for us to keep money we make on missions.'

'Is it?' Max said, grinning. 'Guess I forgot.'

'I'm already in Zara's bad books,' Ryan said. 'So no offence, but find someone else to play with, OK?'

'Come on,' Max begged. 'You, me and Alfie plus some other guys. Tomorrow night, as it's getting dark. Running round, getting muddy, having a laugh. Where's your spirit of adventure?'

'I expect I'll be in recycling,' Ryan said, as he pointed at a mound of textbooks. 'Or working my way through that lot.'

'So what's this?' Max asked, as he snatched a photo sticking out from Amy's folder. 'Aww, that's revolting. What happened to her?'

Max had picked out a copy of a photo of the burn on Ning's stomach, taken by a doctor who'd examined her the morning after she'd been picked up.

'No joking around,' Ryan said angrily, as he snatched the photo and gave Max a little shove. 'She's a potential CHERUB recruit, but what she's been through is awful.'

'So what are you doing with it?'

'I'm helping Amy with her candidate assessment. And if she does come here, you'd better not say anything about seeing that picture because I'll kick the shit out of you.'

'Christ,' Max said, raising his hands and taking a step back. 'You're wound up tight. You *need* to chill out.'

'I'm sorry, but reading this file doesn't put you in the mood for joking about,' Ryan said. 'I'll *try* and make time for paintballing tomorrow night. But I can't promise cos I've got so much on.'

*

Amy's train was due into Edinburgh at eight-thirty. She was supposed to pick up a hire car and drive to Kirkcaldy IDC, where she'd arranged to interview Ning at a quarter to ten. But the train in front broke down and Amy spent an hour marooned near the Scottish border, without even a mobile phone signal.

When her train finally got moving they were stuck behind a slow-moving freight train. She reached Edinburgh at a quarter to eleven, only to find the car-hire desk had shut fifteen minutes earlier.

Amy called Kirkcaldy, but got a recording on the other end.

'*We only accept telephone enquiries between eight-thirty a.m. and seven p.m., Monday to Saturday, and between twelve and six p.m. on Sunday. If you'd like to leave a message, please speak clearly after the tone. All messages will be forwarded to the relevant staff member or detainee within twenty-four hours.*'

'Hello,' Amy said, rapidly trying to think what to say.

'My name is Amy Collins. I spoke with Officer Lucy Pogue in section D early yesterday morning. I was supposed to interview detainee Fu Ning, but my train into Edinburgh was very late and the car-hire desk is closed. I'm also jet-lagged, so I'm going to book into a hotel and try making it up there early tomorrow morning. Thanks, bye.'

*

The segregation cell was designed so that inmates had nothing to break. The plastic mattress and pillow were moulded to the floor, there were no sheets, and the toilet, shower and sink were a single pressed aluminium moulding, with water controlled by heavy-duty floor pedals. To minimise suicide attempts, the lights stayed on 24/7 and inmates were stripped of everything but underwear.

There was no TV, books or radio and the only sounds Ning heard were footsteps passing by and a man two cells down who was completely mental and kept screaming that rats were biting him.

She spent hours rolling about, sticking to a mattress that reeked of disinfectant. It was three a.m. when she dozed off, but she was woken just over an hour later.

'I'm Joan Higgins,' the woman said, as Ning sat up, rubbing her eyes. 'We're going to be alongside each other all the way to Beijing, so I hope we can be civil.'

'Whatever,' Ning said. 'They took everything away when I got in here. Have you got my bag?'

Joan nodded. 'It's outside. I've found you some clean clothes, shampoo, a towel and a flannel. It's a long journey. There's time to freshen up if you'd like.'

Joan waited outside while Ning showered and put on clean clothes.

'I'm told you're a wild one,' Joan noted, as they walked to the front of the building. 'You don't seem wild to me, but I have to put plastic cuffs on until we board the plane.'

Ning said nothing as she went through formalities in the detention centre's processing area. She signed a form to say she had all her personal property and another saying that she accepted the verdict of the immigration officer. The government had no grounds to seize her eighteen thousand dollars, so she was also given an envelope containing a cashpoint card, pin number and *thanks for opening an account* letter.

Joan fitted the plasticuffs, but left them loose so that Ning could have fought her way out of them if she'd wanted to. But she'd lost the will to fight or run away. Coming to Britain now felt like a childish fantasy and while Ning didn't want to kill herself, there didn't seem much point in being alive either.

Joan led the way into an empty visitors' car park. The sky was black and the floodlights illuminating the perimeter of the detention centre had an eerie blue shimmer.

'How long will it take?' Ning asked when they reached a Ford Focus.

'Our flight to Beijing leaves at seven-fifty, total flight time is about thirteen hours.'

Joan popped the button for the central locking and

opened the driver's door.

'What happens when I arrive in China?' Ning asked, as she got in the passenger side.

'Someone from Chinese immigration will meet us in Beijing. I'll pass you over, and after that you're in their hands.'

39. PLANE

Amy's journey had been crap, but she'd compensated herself with a room in the five star Balmoral Hotel next door to the station and eight hours' sleep in a huge cashmere-topped bed. She wanted to be at Kirkcaldy IDC by ten, so she ordered breakfast in her room for half-seven and was downing porridge and black coffee in bed when her mobile rang.

'Amy, it's Lucy Pogue from Kirkcaldy. I got your message, but I'm afraid Fu Ning's deportation papers came through yesterday. She was booked out of the detention centre shortly after four this morning.'

Amy practically choked. 'How did this happen?' she spluttered. 'I've flown all the way from Dallas to interview her.'

'We had problems involving Fu Ning yesterday afternoon and we took the decision to accelerate her departure. I know we spoke, but with everything that was going on your interview request slipped my mind.'

'Do you have her flight details?'

'There's only one daily flight from Edinburgh to China,' Lucy explained. 'I don't know the exact time.'

Amy did a quick mental calculation. The drive from Edinburgh to Kirkcaldy took just over an hour, so Ning would have been at the airport by five-thirty. For an international flight she'd need to check in two hours before departure, so her flight could be leaving at any point from about seven-thirty onwards.

'Thanks for getting back so early,' Amy said, with angst in her voice. 'I'll try catching her before the plane leaves.'

Amy's phone said 7:42 a.m. She tapped the screen to open the browser window and Googled *Edinburgh Airport Departures*.

The phone was only connected using 3G, so she had an agonising wait while the main page of the Edinburgh Airport website downloaded. Another click took her to a departure board. She scanned down the list and found Ning's flight:

CI208   Beijing   7:50   Last Call

Throwing her breakfast tray aside, Amy yanked jeans up her legs as she called 999 using the hotel landline. She asked to be connected to the Edinburgh Airport emergency number.

'That isn't how it works,' a soft-spoken operator

explained. 'If you explain the nature of the emergency, I will direct your call as required.'

Amy grunted angrily. 'I'm an American security agent. There's a person on board a plane who I *need* to interview. I need you to connect me to the airport security chief.'

The operator sounded confused. 'Did you say you're a security agent?'

'Yes,' Amy yelled. 'Please, I'm begging you, just put me through.'

'I'm going to have to speak to a supervisor,' the operator said. 'Can you hold for a moment?'

'For Christ's sake,' Amy shouted.

The clock on Amy's phone was now on 7:45. As she held the landline to one ear waiting for the operator, she flipped through her mobile phone's memory until she came to U for Unicorn Tyre Repair.

'It's Amy Collins, former agent 0974,' she yelled, when someone picked up. 'I need a passenger stopped at Edinburgh Airport. Name of Fu Ning. She's on flight CI208 to Beijing.'

Amy was reassured by the voice of Chief Mission Controller Ewart Asker.

'You're cutting things fine,' Ewart said. 'But I'll see what I can do.'

Meantime the 999 operator had come back on the landline. 'Hello,' the woman said. 'I've spoken to my supervisor. She wants to know if you're reporting the possibility of an imminent threat to an aircraft.'

Amy decided to leave stopping the plane to Ewart, but she was still furious and gave the operator a mouthful.

'No there's not a terrorist threat,' she yelled. 'And the speed you work at it's a bloody good job as well, isn't it?'

*

Jean put her hand on Ning's knee as CI208 taxied towards the runway. The safety demonstration had just ended and the seatback screens had gone blank. Ning was in a window seat and she looked out, wondering if the sunrise and the expanse of concrete would be her last ever sight of Britain.

A woman with a Chinese accent came over the intercom. '*Good morning, lady and gentlemen, this is your co-pilot speaking. Welcome to China International. Sorry we are a few minutes late backing away from gate, but I am pleased to say we have not lost our departure slot and are expecting to take off within the next few minutes. Weather forecast for our arrival in Beijing is eighteen degrees with light showers. Our flight time will be twelve hours twenty minutes. Flight crew, secure doors and take positions for take-off.*'

Ning had flown often, but still felt a jolt of anticipation, glimpsing the runway lights as the Airbus turned into its pre-take-off position.

*

Amy didn't bother with niceties such as socks or a bra, just a T-shirt, jeans and trainers. She bounded down to the Balmoral's lobby with a bag slung over her shoulder and her mobile in hand. There was a taxi rank right outside.

'Really sorry,' Amy said as she bumped an elderly American couple from the head of the taxi queue and jumped into a waiting cab. 'Airport,' she told the driver. 'Any idea how long it takes to get there?'

'Twenty minutes if the traffic's good,' the driver said. 'Twice that if it isn't.'

Fortunately they were half an hour from peak morning rush hour, and once out of the city centre they were going against the traffic.

Amy called TFU headquarters in Dallas, and asked them what the chances were of stopping a China International flight once it was in the air.

'Not a hope in hell,' the duty officer told her. 'Unless there's an immediate security threat you'd be creating a huge diplomatic shit storm. Your best bet would be to put in a request to interview Fu Ning when she reaches China.'

'That's what I thought you'd say,' Amy said. 'I just hope we caught her before that plane took off.'

When Amy hung up, she saw that she'd missed a call from CHERUB campus. Ewart had left a voice message.

'Amy, it's Ewart. Fu Ning is a confirmed passenger aboard CI208. I got a call through to Air Traffic Control at Edinburgh. They were going to try pulling the flight, but I don't know if we've caught it in time.'

Amy tried calling Ewart back, but he was engaged, so she opened her web browser and refreshed the flight information page:

CI208   Beijing   7:50   Gate Closed

By this time Amy's taxi was passing a big yellow and black sign saying Welcome to *Edinburgh International Airport*. She saw that it was quarter past eight, and realised there was no point panicking: Ning had either flown or she hadn't. Running around wouldn't change a thing.

'Good drive,' Amy told the cabby as she handed him a twenty-pound note and jumped out. 'Keep the change.'

'Excuse me,' the driver shouted after her.

Amy turned back, thinking she hadn't given the driver enough money, or that she'd left something in the taxi, but the driver pointed at her face.

'I know you're in a hurry, lass,' he said, 'But I thought you'd like to know that you've got a blob of something on the end of your nose.'

Amy smiled as she rubbed her hand across her face, then looked at porridge smeared across her palm.

'Messy eater,' she explained, as she gave the driver a thumbs-up. 'Thanks, mate.'

All the junk Amy had hastily stuffed into her bag rattled as she walked through the automatic doors into the airport check-in area. She looked up at the giant destination board and liked what she saw:

CI208   Beijing   7:50   No Information

She wasn't sure where to go next. She figured airport security was best and headed for an information counter, but her phone rang before she got there. The man on the other end had a thick Scottish accent.

'Miss Collins?' he asked. 'When you reach the airport

I'm at the fast-track security gate at the extreme left of the terminal.'

Amy looked up and saw a stout little police inspector speaking into a mobile phone less than twenty metres away.

'Did you stop the plane?' she asked, as she dodged baggage trolleys and rushed across the concourse.

*

The pilot told the passengers that they'd been called back to the terminal for technical reasons as he peeled off the runway. The plane rolled across the airport for more than ten minutes, passing the entire length of the terminal building and stopping on a stretch of bare tarmac.

'This is odd,' Jean said, as Ning watched airport security police wheeling metal steps towards the main door at the front of the Airbus.

People in the rows on either side spoke with a mix of curiosity and suspicion as four armed policemen raced up the steps and moved swiftly down the plane's single aisle. Jean and Ning were surprised as the lead officer stopped by their row and spoke after a quick glance at the seat numbers.

'Fu Ning?' the officer asked. 'We've been asked to remove you from the plane.'

'What's going on?' Jean asked, as she pulled out her immigration service ID. 'I'm accompanying her.'

'Nobody tells us anything,' the officer said. 'We need you to come with us.'

Everyone looked around as Jean and Ning walked towards the front of the plane.

'Ladies and gentlemen, this is your co-pilot. As you can see we've been called back to the terminal for the removal of two passengers. Unfortunately regulations do not allow us to fly with checked baggage unless the passenger is present. We're hoping that a baggage cart will be available shortly, but we may be subject to . . .'

The airport security police seemed pleased to have a bit of drama on their hands. Besides the four cops who'd boarded the plane there were two more at the bottom of the stairs and another bunch in the arrivals lounge when they reached the top of a long metal staircase.

Ning looked about curiously as she re-entered the warm carpeted world of the airport terminal.

'Does anybody know what's going on?' Jean asked, as she pulled a BlackBerry out of her coat pocket.

Nobody answered, but the girl who did know was hurrying towards them in jeans, trainers and a scruffy grey T-shirt. She broke into a huge relieved smile as she shook Ning's hand.

'Hi, Ning,' Amy said. 'Looks like I caught you just in time.'

40. BURGER

Amy took Ning to the airport Burger King. They faced each other across a glossy table top, with a plastic tray between them.

'So,' Amy said, as she blew on her coffee, 'I expect you're confused.'

Ning smiled awkwardly as she peeled waxed paper away from her cheeseburger.

'I've got a picture that you might find interesting,' Amy said, as she rummaged in her bag. She pulled out a photo printed with a dodgy inkjet cartridge, so that it looked all pink.

Ning gawped as Amy slid it across the table. There were three women in British Army uniform, and the one on the right was Ingrid, looking about twenty.

'That's my stepmum,' Ning gasped.

'I was able to access a version of the UK military

personnel database that isn't available to agencies like the immigration service,' Amy explained. 'It wasn't hard to find her, because Ingrid isn't a very common name in the UK. Your stepmother's real name was Ingrid Miller, born in 1970 in Bootle, Merseyside. The woman on Ingrid's right is called Tracy Hepburn. She wasn't your stepmother's sister, she was an army friend, and I suspect she's the lady who sent you presents on your birthday.'

'Ingrid claimed she was thirty-seven,' Ning said. 'But I guess she lied about her age along with everything else. So does Ingrid have any real relatives?'

'Her parents both died before you were born. Ingrid does have a real sister called Melanie. She's married and lives in Manchester. I don't think she's the kind of auntie you'd want to end up living with though. She's been in and out of prison for drug and shoplifting offences and two of her own children have been taken into care.'

'That about sums up my luck,' Ning said.

'Don't worry,' Amy said. 'I looked into Ingrid's background purely to determine how much truth there was in the statements you gave to the police and your immigration officer.'

'It's *all* true,' Ning said.

'I know,' Amy said. 'You don't need to worry about being shipped back to China. The British secret service will support your application for citizenship, provided you agree to help us. The organisation I work for is investigating the Aramov Clan and I'll need to give you a detailed debriefing on everything that you saw in Kyrgyzstan.'

'I don't mind that,' Ning agreed. 'Though I didn't exactly see much.'

'You'd be amazed how often tiny details can turn out to be critical in an investigation,' Amy said. She glanced around to make sure nobody was close by and then spoke in a lower register. 'I'd also like you to visit a place called CHERUB campus, with a view to becoming one of their agents.'

English wasn't Ning's first language and she thought she might have misunderstood. 'Agent?'

'The principle behind CHERUB is simple,' Amy said. 'Adults rarely suspect that children are spying on them.

'For instance, I'm twenty-three. If I went undercover, became a drug dealer's girlfriend and started asking a lot of questions about his business, he'd probably suspect that I was an undercover policewoman. But if you started hanging out on that drug dealer's patch, maybe you'd approach the dealer and ask if you could earn some pocket money working as a lookout or something. As far as the dealer is concerned you're a kid. You can't be a snitch or an undercover agent because you're eleven years old.'

'Twelve,' Ning said. 'I had my birthday last week.'

'CHERUB agents need to be a cut above,' Amy explained. 'Physically strong and clever. Trained to run fast, or fight their way out if things get hairy. You'll have to undergo a set of recruitment tests before CHERUB can accept you. After that you'll face a hundred days of basic training which is very tough indeed. But according to your school records—'

Ning looked surprised as she interrupted. 'I went to school in *China*.'

'I've done my homework on you,' Amy said, wagging her finger. 'We got a Chinese-based CIA officer to bribe an education official in Dandong. I've read through copies of your entire education file, going back to when you were three years old.'

'I'd *love* to read those,' Ning said. 'I've always wondered what people were writing while I was getting yelled at.'

'I doubt any of it would surprise you,' Amy said. 'Apparently you're clever but easily bored and disrespectful towards adults. The English translation that I read had the phrase *heading for trouble* a hundred and six times.'

'But you still want me?' Ning asked.

'Kids who are clever and obedient tend not to make the best CHERUB agents. Troublemakers tend to be bolder and more creative, and CHERUB needs people who can think for themselves on undercover missions.'

Ning felt hopeful for the first time in weeks as she pushed the last piece of her cheeseburger into her mouth.

'I always used to wind my teachers up by saying that I wanted to be a rock star or a terrorist,' Ning said. 'I never thought about being a secret agent, but I guess that could be fun too.'

*

After stopping at the hotel to pack up and pay the bill, Amy and Ning boarded the next London-bound train. They had a first class carriage almost to themselves and they sat facing each other.

Amy had a list of over two hundred questions for Ning, covering everything from whether the Aramov Clan's pilots had seemed happy with their lot, to whether Leonid Aramov favoured his left or right hand. But she decided to leave a tough and potentially upsetting questioning until she'd had more time to gain Ning's trust.

As the scenery whizzed by, Ning sprawled over her seat as Amy told her life story:

Her parents died in an accident when she was a baby, she'd joined CHERUB at five with her older brother John. She'd become a successful agent, gone to university in Australia, run a diving school, lived with an older guy who'd been a jerk, worked as a bodyguard, and then six months earlier accepted an offer to work for TFU in the United States.

In return, Ning took Amy through her story, from being one of thousands of female babies abandoned in the Chinese countryside every year, into orphanages, getting adopted by Chaoxiang and Ingrid, joining the National Academy for Sport, getting kicked out of the National Academy for Sport . . .

Amy didn't want Ning to get sad and changed the subject when they got to Chaoxiang's arrest. She reduced Ning to laughter as she tried speaking Chinese phrases learned during a language course many years earlier.

'You're asking to ride on a cup of coffee,' Ning explained, as they rolled into a platform.

Amy panicked when she saw the sign. 'This is us,' she

said, jumping up and grabbing Ning's pack from the overhead rack.

*

Because CHERUB campus is a secret facility, new agents only discover its location after they've been recruited. The standard procedure for potential recruits aged nine or over is to be drugged and brought to campus with no prior knowledge.

The recruit then wakes up in a bed on campus, naked and with a set of CHERUB uniform laid out for them. The way that the candidate reacts to this bewildering and frightening experience forms part of their recruitment process: kids who stay composed and try to understand the situation stand a better chance than kids who start screaming for their mummy at the first sign of stress.

But Ning had been burned and tortured. Waking up groggy and naked might freak her out, so she'd receive the gentler introduction usually reserved for the under-nines.

A van and driver waited in the station car park. The rear compartment had four comfortable chairs, along with a selection of magazines and books, a fridge containing bottles of juice and water and a flip-down TV. The driver's cab was blocked off and there were no side windows, but it wasn't dark when the doors closed because there was a smoked glass panel in the roof.

The station was only twenty minutes' drive from campus, but the driver took a tortuous route through nearby towns and villages designed to give Ning the impression that they'd travelled much further than they really had. When he opened the back doors, they were in a gravel parking lot with the entrance to a small reception building off to one side and helipads behind it.

'I'll be right back,' Amy told Ning as she jumped out of the van and broke into a sprint. 'I'm *absolutely* busting.'

Ning smiled as she watched Amy charge through a set of doors. She looked across lawns and trees at a large white building.

'That's the swimming and diving complex,' a boy said, startling Ning as he stopped behind her.

He was decent looking, with scruffy black hair and a silver stud earring. He wore combat trousers and a grey T-shirt that gave Ning her first glimpse of the CHERUB logo.

'Ryan Sharma,' he said. 'They've asked me to show you around.'

Although Ning was the one on strange turf, it was Ryan who felt awkward as they shook hands. He'd read Ning's file so that he could help with the recruitment process, but it felt weird meeting someone for the first time when he'd already read her school records and seen pictures of her injuries.

'That's the pool complex up there,' Ryan explained, then he turned and pointed back towards the eight-storey building behind them. 'That's the main building. Archives in the basement, admin and canteen on the ground floor. More admin on the second and third, staff quarters fourth and fifth and the kids live on the sixth through eighth.'

'How many?' Ning asked.

'Three hundred-ish,' Ryan said. 'But about seventy of those are red-shirts, which means they're too young to go on missions. And at any given time you've got maybe half the qualified agents away on missions or training exercises, which means there's never more than about two hundred kids actually on campus.'

'The lawns look beautiful,' Ning said.

Ryan laughed. 'If you misbehave, you'll get plenty of chances to mow them. We'd better step inside reception and get you kitted out.'

The reception area was built underneath a helipad. Ryan led Ning down metal steps into a slightly gloomy windowless space. There were X-ray machines and airport-style security barriers, but these were only used when adults arrived, or when there was a big event such as a campus reunion.

As Amy came out of the toilet, Ryan was going through a metal-doored cabinet, trying to find an orange CHERUB T-shirt, combat trousers and boots in Ning's size.

'Can't I have a black T-shirt?' Ning asked, as Ryan handed Ning a pile of stuff.

Amy and Ryan both laughed.

'The orange T-shirt is for new arrivals on campus,' Amy explained, as she went into a cabinet and grabbed a white T-shirt for herself. 'It's like a warning signal, so that people don't discuss secret stuff in your presence, and agents can only talk to you if the chairwoman authorises it. The other T-shirts are based upon your rank and black is the highest. Ryan's grey, which is for newly qualified agents, and I'm putting on white, which is for staff and retired agents.'

Ryan looked away as Ning and Amy changed.

'I've got some work to prepare on your debriefing,' Amy said, as she stood up. 'Ryan will take you to meet the chairwoman, then he'll give you a tour of campus.'

'When do I start the recruitment tests?' Ning asked.

'It's nearly two already,' Ryan said. 'There won't be time today, so tomorrow most likely.'

41. AUTOMATIC

Ning had been awake since 4 a.m., but she felt reinvigorated and was well up for the campus tour. Zara let Ryan use one of the electric buggies that were usually reserved for staff and he drove Ning on a grand circuit, taking in all the main campus features, from the mission control building, through the basic training area, past the lake, the martial arts training dojo and the athletics track.

They stopped a few times along the way. Ning didn't like the look of the height obstacle. She petted the guinea pigs and beagles in the junior block, got introduced to Ryan's youngest brother Theo, talked Ryan into letting her drive the buggy and watched a couple of overs of cricket while he tried to explain the rules.

Their final stop was the pool and a tear streaked down Ning's cheek as they stood by the huge windows watching campus' youngest residents splashing about in a kiddie pool, accompanied by a platoon of bright yellow ducks.

'You OK?' Ryan said, reaching across to put an arm around Ning's back but then deciding that she might not like it.

'It's cool here,' Ning said, as she looked Ryan right in the eyes. 'This is a chance of a new life, but what if I fail the recruitment tests?'

Ryan shrugged. 'There's no point stressing over it. All you can do is try your best.'

'But where would I end up?'

'CHERUB won't abandon you,' Ryan said. 'Zara would find you foster-parents or something. But I don't think you've got much to worry about. You look like a tough nut to me.'

'I've been in better shape,' Ning said nervously. 'Apart from a couple of basketball games at Kirkcaldy I've not exercised in weeks.'

'They take factors like that into account,' Ryan said, but he didn't want Ning getting depressed and changed the subject. 'So, are you hungry?'

Ning drove the buggy for the final few hundred metres from the pool to the main building. Once Ryan had plugged the buggy into its recharging socket he led Ning to the dining-room. It was almost five, and there were about forty kids either queuing at food stations or eating at the tables. Being a Friday, most of them were happy and many were rushing because they were heading out for the cinema or bowling in the nearest town.

'Food smells all right,' Ning said.

Ryan nodded. 'It doesn't look much different to a regular school canteen, but the cooks have mostly worked here for years and they're decent. If you like steak they do *great* steak on Fridays. It's organic, from one of the local farms. The only thing is it's cooked to order so you have to wait a few minutes. Or do you only like Chinese food?'

Ning didn't reply, but Ryan caught a look that made him realise he'd said something stupid.

'Steak medium, with mushroom, chips and pepper sauce,' Ryan said, when they reached the service counter.

'I'll call in about ten minutes,' the chef said, as he passed Ryan a numbered ticket. 'What about your orange friend?'

'I'll try the steak,' Ning said. 'It can't be any worse than the filth I've been eating at Kirkcaldy.'

They grabbed drinks and cutlery and headed for a table.

'Yo-yo, Rybo!' Max shouted, then more quietly. 'Oh, you've got your orange-shirt with you.'

'Come meet my mates,' Ryan told Ning.

'Is Rybo your nickname?' Ning asked.

'No it isn't,' Ryan said irritably, as he led Ning to a table where Max sat next to Alfie. A couple of Ryan's other mates sat nearby, while Grace, Chloe and a few younger girls were at the next table.

'This is Ning,' Ryan said, loud enough for the whole group to hear. 'She's in an orange shirt, but Zara says people can talk to her. Just use common sense and don't give all our secrets away.'

Most people said hello, but Max always had to be a smart arse and greeted her in a dreary sing-song voice. 'Hello, Ning, it's lovely to meet you and welcome to CHERUB campus.'

'All right, Black, stop stalling,' a black boy called Aaron said as he sat opposite Max and banged his elbow on the table. 'Time to put your money where your very large mouth is.'

As Ryan and Ning found empty seats, they saw a little mound of pound coins on the table between Aaron and Max.

'Do you have arm-wrestling in China?' Ryan said, as Max and Aaron eyed each other up and gripped hands.

'I think I've seen it,' Ning said.

Alfie was acting as referee, and knelt at the end of the table as Max and Aaron gripped each other's hands.

'Ready?' Alfie asked. 'Three, two, one, wrestle.'

Max and Aaron's faces contorted as they tried pinning the other's hand to the table. Aaron got the early advantage, but Max had stamina. It took half a minute, but Max shot up and yelled to celebrate his victory.

'You suck,' Max shouted. 'It's my money.'

Ning looked at Max. 'Can I try your game?'

Max looked at Ning and scoffed. 'No offence, but we're all highly trained. I don't think you'd be much competition.'

'I'm not in the best shape,' Ning said politely, as she curled her arm to show off a rather impressive bicep. 'I'd just like to try it.'

Max seemed slightly mystified. 'Maybe you should ask one of the girls?'

Ryan knew Ning had some boxing experience and was pretty strong, but Max was in top shape and did a line in explosive one-armed push-ups that he couldn't match.

'No, with you,' Ning said. 'I know I won't win. But can't you just show me?'

'Well, if you insist,' Max said awkwardly.

Aaron gave his chair to Ning as Max sat back down.

Ryan compared the two arms as they lined up across the table. Max was about the same height as Ning, but her arm was much longer, giving her a reach that would be a huge advantage in the boxing ring.

He didn't notice an even more important difference until Max and Ning grasped each other's hands. Max's arm was bulkier, and had more muscle, but the tendons in Ning's arm were different to any others Ryan had ever seen.

With her wrists clenched, the lower half of Ning's arm formed a thick triangle that looked like the sail of a boat. You can build muscles with fitness training, but the position of the tendons that transmit the power of your muscles is purely down to genetics. As soon as Ryan saw it, he understood why sports scientists had picked Ning as an elite boxer out of the twenty million kids born in China each year.

Nobody else knew Ning's background, but a dozen kids jumped up when they realised Max was in trouble.

For the first ten seconds of the bout, Max gritted his teeth and used all of his strength, but Ning's arm stayed upright, like it was bedded in concrete.

Max was turning bright red and grunting like a pig, while Ning smiled sweetly and didn't even break a sweat.

'You're getting caned, Max!' Chloe shouted. 'Come on, thingy whatever your name is.'

'Ning,' Ryan said.

'Well, I'm getting bored now,' Ning said casually.

She cheekily raised one eyebrow, took a breath and started to push. Max made a superhuman effort to resist, but within three seconds Ning had his hand pinned to the table. The crowd erupted and, as Max was always a bighead, everyone took great joy rubbing it in.

'Crushed by a girl,' Grace said happily. 'How old are you, Ning?'

'An orange-shirt *girl* wiped you out, bitch!' Chloe added.

Ryan was killing himself laughing, and to Max's credit, he took defeat with good humour.

'Well, you've got to let the little lady win, haven't you?' Max said jokingly. 'Make her feel welcome and all.'

'I'd be happy to make it best of three,' Ning said.

Max glanced at his watch. 'Oooh, is that the time? I'd *love* to but I've got to go and see a man about a dog.'

Ryan took a couple of steps back and enjoyed Ning being the centre of attention until an impatient-looking chef holding up two plates of steak caught his eye. 'Sharma!' he shouted. 'Stop chatting up the girls and come get your dinner.'

42. BREATHE

Ning was given a room at the far end of the sixth floor. Like all rooms on campus, it had been decorated and refurbished when its previous occupier left CHERUB. It wasn't as plush as some of the swanky hotels Ning had stayed in with her father, but it was a palace compared to Kirkcaldy IDC.

The tiles and fittings in the bathroom were all new. Ning spent an hour with bubble bath up to her shoulders and cocoa butter conditioner nourishing her hair.

Since leaving China she'd rotated two pairs of jeans, three T-shirts and three sets of underwear. As well as making up the bed and leaving fresh towels and toiletries, the person who'd prepared the room had left new socks and underwear, along with a swimming costume and a spare CHERUB uniform.

Kids raced by outside as Ning sat on her bed combing

her hair. Their easy banter reminded her that she didn't belong here yet. The prospect of British foster-parents was better than what she'd faced when she'd woken that morning, but CHERUB campus felt like the thing she'd been longing for her entire life: somewhere you could make a difference now, not just after hundreds of exams and years of boring school.

There was a quiet knock, followed by Amy's head peeking cautiously around the doorframe.

'Come in,' Ning said.

'I thought you might be asleep,' Amy explained as she stepped into the room. 'I wanted to catch up earlier, but I've been reading briefing documents over in mission control and I lost track of time.'

'Ryan said I should try to sleep because of the tests tomorrow,' Ning said. 'But my brain's shooting off fireworks after all that's happened today.'

'How was Ryan?'

Ning smiled. 'He's really nice. His friends were too, and campus looks *amazing*.'

'I printed this off properly and had it laminated,' Amy said, as she passed Ning a copy of the photo of Ingrid in her army uniform.

Ning reached down into the backpack alongside her bed and pulled out her yellow box. 'I'll put it in here,' she said.

Amy smiled as she sat on Ning's bed. 'Have you had the box for long?'

Ning looked a touch embarrassed. 'I know it's naff, but I've had it longer than anything else. I use it to keep medals, nick-nacks, random junk.'

'It's not naff,' Amy said. 'It's good that you've kept hold of a few things, even after all you've been through. I think CHERUB can sort you out a new backpack though. That one looks like it's seen some action.'

'Hasn't been the same since it spent three hours in a bin at the back of a Kyrgyz nightclub,' Ning said. 'Zip's busted as well.'

'I've been working on questions for your debriefing on the Aramov Clan,' Amy said. 'It's going to take a long while, but it can wait until after the weekend. However, I was intrigued by how little information you had about the sandwich factory and the house you stayed at.'

Ning looked uneasy. 'The police asked over and over. They thought I was hiding something, but I told them everything I remembered.'

'I'm not accusing you of lying,' Amy said. 'But the human brain often blocks out the memory of stressful or distressing events. It's a kind of coping mechanism. My boss at TFU has taught me a relaxation technique that might help jog your memory.'

'I don't mean to be awkward, but I am knackered,' Ning said.

'The technique actually works better when a subject is drowsy,' Amy said. 'If we can find the sandwich factory and the house where you stayed, it could open up a whole new front in the battle against people smuggling.'

'How?' Ning asked.

'Police surveillance teams, most likely. They'd start off watching the factory. Track the vans bringing the women to and fro and find out where all the houses are. Hopefully they'll pick up on the people who deliver new workers.'

'One of the cops who interviewed me said I'd given them a few other leads.'

'Oh yes, lots,' Amy said. 'For instance, we could try tracing the warehouse you were taken to when you first arrived in Britain, staking out the truck stop in the Czech Republic, finding Chun Hei, or tracking down female Bangladeshi driving instructors working in south-west London. But I really want to find the factory and the house where you stayed, because if we find Leo we should be able to track down Ben.'

'Why's he so important?' Ning asked.

'Ben is clearly a boss,' Amy said. 'He knows what was done with the bodies of the two dead girls and was clearly planning for you to be exploited sexually if you hadn't managed to escape when you did. Chances are, if we track Ben down we'll find other girls who weren't so lucky.'

'Makes sense,' Ning said, chilled by the reminder of how much danger she'd been in. 'Let's give it a go.'

'It should be easier to identify a factory than a house,' Amy explained. 'So that's where I'd like to take you first.'

'Is it like hypnosis?' Ning asked.

Amy nodded. 'Some people are more susceptible to hypnotic states than others. This is a bit of a long shot, but I'd really like to try.'

'OK,' Amy said, as she adopted a softer tone and slower speech. 'Lie back on the bed and find a position in which you're comfortable. Then I want you to focus your eyes on a single spot on the ceiling.'

Ning plumped her pillows, then lay back as Amy turned out the room's main light, leaving the dim glow from a desk lamp.

'Stare at the spot,' Amy said. 'Focus on your breathing. Don't think about anything except the rhythm of your breathing. In and out, in and out.'

Amy let Ning breathe for a few seconds before continuing.

'Now I want you to relax your fingers and your toes. Feel the relaxation coming up your body. Your stomach is relaxed. And your shoulders. Now all the muscles in your face are very, very relaxed. Your eyes are getting heavier and you're focused on your breathing. In and out, in and out.

'Now your eyes are closing. When I snap my fingers, you're going to close your eyes and focus on my voice. You're going to be arriving at the sandwich factory for the first time. Remember everything around you. Remember what you're wearing and how you feel. Your eyes are getting heavier and now I want you to completely close your eyes.'

As Ning's eyes closed, Amy set a small digital voice recorder running and then snapped her fingers.

'You stepped out of the van,' Amy said. 'Tell me the first thing that comes into your head.'

'I'm sucking a boiled sweet,' Ning said. 'One of the ladies in the van handed them out. It doesn't taste nice, but I can't spit it out without upsetting her and I don't want to crunch it because Ingrid says that can break your teeth.'

'Good,' Amy said gently. 'Focus on the taste of the sweet. As you do, look up at the building and tell me what it looks like.'

'It's dark,' Ning said. 'Two storeys. Bricks, covered in black dirt. The windows downstairs are boarded. There's no light at the windows upstairs, and some of the glass is broken. There's a fan running.'

'And who is with you?'

'There's a lady with a clipboard. Mei is next to me, and the lady with the sweets, and a couple of others.'

'Tell me where you go next.'

'The door is grey. There's a space, like a rectangle for a sign, but it's been unscrewed. Inside my backpack scrapes along the wall, because it's narrow. There are brown trays that we put the sandwiches in. All stacked up.'

'Are there any markings or names on the trays?'

'No, they're plain.'

'You're inside with Mei and the others,' Amy said. 'What happens now?'

'Roger is there. He's big. Ginger beard. He argues with clipboard lady because he expected twelve of us. Mei and the others go inside to the cloakroom to put on overalls and masks, but I have to go upstairs to see the boss.'

'Feel yourself walking up the stairs,' Amy said. 'What's around you?'

'Upstairs is dusty,' Ning said. 'Old sewing machines and it smells oily. There's a big roof outside with lots of pigeons, but it's too dark to see. You can just hear them warbling. The lady is in front of me and the boss makes us wait outside his office.'

'Is there a sign on the office door?' Amy asked.

'Can't see. The door is open.'

'What's the boss doing inside? Is he making any kind of noise.'

'I don't think so. But it feels like clipboard lady thinks he's toying with her. Wasting her time.'

'What else is around you?'

'A photocopier and water bottles. And there's a desk. For a secretary or something.'

'Does the boss call you into the office?'

'Yes. I've been in the dark and the office is really light, so my eyes hurt.'

'Does the boss have a name?'

'Clipboard lady calls him Mister or Sir. He reminds me of my stepfather, but younger. It looks like he's wearing golf trousers. And there's a big globe resting on a glass shelf.'

'Is there anything else on the shelves?'

'Files, but there's a picture of two boys on the wall above.'

'Tell me about the boys.'

'They're the boss's sons.'

'How do you know that?'

'They look like little versions of him. One is maybe a year older than the other. The younger one has dirt on his cheek.'

'Dirt?' Amy said curiously. 'Is it a school photo? Are they in uniform?'

'They're both quite muddy,' Ning said. 'They're wearing football kit.'

'Can you see the colours?'

'Orange and maroon striped socks. Maroon shorts and orange shirt.'

'Good,' Amy said. 'Is there anything else in the picture?'

'I can't think,' Ning said, raising her voice.

Amy realised she'd raised her own voice, and that Ning had responded. 'You don't need to think about anything because you're in the room,' Amy said. 'The boss is there. You can see the picture. With the two boys in their muddy kit.'

'The younger one is holding a little silver cup,' Ning said. 'And there's a sponsor's logo on their shirts.'

The sponsor's name might be crucial, but Amy kept her voice calm. 'What does the logo look like?'

'It's a square man. Cartoon, with a smile.'

'Is there writing on it.'

'I'm too far away,' Ning said. 'There is writing but I can't read it.'

'OK,' Amy said. 'And what else do you see. Is there anything else? On the boss's desk, perhaps?'

'Pen pot, laptop, Sellotape dispenser.'

'No more photographs? Nothing you can read?'

'2011, on the front of his diary. He has a blotter with a map of the world.'

'OK,' Amy said. 'And what are the boss and the lady saying?'

'He's stressed. Ranting about *the supermarket*. And not having enough staff. He never looks at me.'

'Does he have a name for the supermarket?'

'They never said,' Ning said, speaking louder as she opened her eyes and rolled over to face Amy. 'It was always a big secret.'

A more experienced hypnotist might have kept Ning in her trance state for longer. Amy had violated one of the rules that Dr D had taught her: you must lead the subject gently through a trance with hints and suggestions. Asking direct questions such as *Did the boss ever give a name for the supermarket?* pulls the subject out of their trance and back into rational conscious thought.

'They always spoke about *the supermarket*,' Ning explained, sitting up and stifling a yawn. 'But the name was like top, top secret. Once we'd packed up the sandwiches, someone in another room would stick labels on the boxes.'

'I'm a beginner with hypnosis,' Amy said, 'but we might have got somewhere. I hadn't seen the bit about the globe, or the photograph, in any of your statements.'

'That was really powerful,' Ning said, in a state of awe. 'I actually did feel like I was there. Do you want to try again?'

'At some point,' Amy said. 'It's good to know you're susceptible to hypnosis, but you should probably get some sleep now. It's past ten and you've got a big day tomorrow.'

'I saw a hypnotist on TV once,' Ning said. 'He told this woman that onions tasted like oranges and she sat there biting great chunks out of them.'

Amy laughed. 'Whatever happens I promise not to make you eat any onions.'

43. SUPPLY

CHERUB agents miss out on regular schooling when they're away on missions and they have to catch up with Saturday morning lessons.

Ryan felt a sense of dread as he packed his books for history, maths and English literature. He hadn't been able to understand most of the maths homework and he was relying on summaries he'd found on the web to make up for only having read fifteen pages of *To Kill a Mockingbird*.

In between breakfast and history class Ryan had to take Ning across to the medical centre where she'd begin her recruitment tests. It was a drizzly morning with a biting wind.

'Campus seems bigger without the buggy,' Ning noted, as she rubbed goosebumps on her bare arms.

'You can't get training hoodies in orange,' Ryan said.

'But the tests will warm you up.'

The medical unit was state-of-the-art and included a six-bed hospital ward, a dental suite and a sports medicine facility used for fitness assessments and rehabilitating the kind of injuries CHERUB agents commonly pick up in training.

'Good morning,' Dr Kessler said, with a thick German accent. 'Two more recruits for the mincer, eh?'

'Two?' Ning said, as Kessler led them down a short corridor.

The sports medicine and fitness testing facilities were similar to ones Ning had been in at Dandong National Sports Academy. Amy was already in the examination room and Dr Kessler bit her head off for sitting on a worktop.

'This is a medical facility,' he yelled. 'Your bottom may look very nice, but it does not belong on my sterile work surface.'

Amy put on an *I'm sorry* face as she jumped down. The other person in the room was a boy who looked about ten. He wore the same boots, trousers and orange shirt as Ning. He had a slim build, with glossy black hair and a Mediterranean complexion.

'Ning, this is Carlos. Carlos, Ning,' Amy said. 'You'll be going through all the recruitment tests together.'

Carlos was shy and it took a nudge from Amy to get him to come forward and shake Ning's hand. Ning felt sorry for Carlos as she studied his slim wrist and long slender fingers with chewed nails.

'Good luck,' Ning said.

Carlos narrowed his eyes. 'I don't believe in luck,' he said.

Ning thought Carlos sounded arrogant, but she was keen to make nice so she smiled and said, 'Maybe you're right.'

Dr Kessler glared at Ryan and Amy. 'If you see Lottie the nurse on your way *out* of my medical unit, tell her to come immediately.'

Amy and Ryan took the hint about leaving and exchanged smiles as they headed into the hallway.

Ryan wagged his finger at Amy and mocked Dr Kessler's voice. 'You will not sit on my sterile surface. If you do I'll have you shot by the Gestapo.'

'Kessler's Jewish,' Amy said. 'I wouldn't make any Nazi cracks in front of him, unless you want to end up with a thermometer up your butt next time you stop by to get your blisters popped.'

'Good call,' Ryan said, laughing as he and Amy backed up to the wall to let Lottie the nurse get by. She was pushing a trolley laden with heart monitoring equipment and two rather sinister-looking sets of pincers that were used for muscle biopsies.

'Kessler's waiting for you,' Amy told Lottie.

'He's a grumpy old sod,' the nurse said. 'And he wonders why everyone quits.'

A cold gust blasted Amy and Ryan as they passed through the automatic exit doors. The rain was coming down quite hard as they set off along a gravel path towards the main building.

'The height obstacle's gonna be tricky in this weather,'

Ryan said, as he looked up at a darkening sky. 'And Ning didn't seem keen on heights.'

'If you haven't got plans I was hoping you'd come over to the mission control building,' said Amy. 'I need someone with half a brain to bounce ideas off.'

Ryan reached over his shoulder and thumped on his book-laden pack. 'I've got lessons.'

Amy smiled. 'It's funny how you forget stuff. I used to *loathe* Saturday morning lessons, but I haven't even thought about them since I left campus.'

'When you get as old as you are, it's only natural for the mind to start going.'

'Watch it, cheeky,' Amy said, as she gave Ryan a little dig in the ribs.

'I'm happy to help,' Ryan said. 'But I'll have to clear skipping lessons with my handler.'

The rain started blasting in marble-sized balls as Ryan took out his phone. He pulled his hood up as he spoke to Meryl, but by the time she'd agreed to let him help, Amy had jogged about thirty metres ahead.

'She's good,' Ryan said, when he'd caught up. 'What are we brainstorming?'

'Football kits,' Amy said cryptically. 'But I'm getting bloody soaked, so let's leave it until we get to mission control, eh? Race you.'

Before Ryan could answer Amy bolted off along the gravel path. It was a kilometre from the medical unit to mission control, but they were both in shape and ran at a good pace. Ryan won, but only because he was prepared to get muddy by crossing the grass, while Amy stuck to gravel.

When they got into mission control they were sodden and breathless. Ryan stood inside the main entrance unlacing his muddy boots as Lauren Adams walked towards them.

She adopted a sarcastic tone. 'Oooh, is it raining out?'

'You've noticed,' Amy said. 'Anything exciting happening?'

Lauren shook her head. 'Nice and dull, which is good because I'm trying to revise my AS physics. Ewart's gone to get a late breakfast, I'm manning phones in case an agent calls in with an emergency.'

'Are there any towels around here?' Amy asked, as she flicked water out of her hair.

'I'll grab a wodge of paper ones from the bathroom,' Lauren said. 'Just listen out for any calls in the control room.'

As Lauren hurried off to the bathroom, Ryan peeled the soggy bottoms of his trousers away from his legs. When he looked around, Amy was pulling her T-shirt over her head and her wet bra left little to the imagination.

'Stop perving,' Lauren said loudly, as she walked out of the bathroom.

'I wasn't,' Ryan said, turning red.

Once they'd done the best they could drying off, Ryan and Amy walked to the operations centre in the middle of the building. One or two mission controllers were always on duty here, providing emergency support for mission controllers and agents in the field.

Because it was always in use, the operations centre never got tidied properly and there were mounds of paperwork, coffee cups, broken computer components and Post-its spread over six workstations arranged in a semicircle under a double-height ceiling.

'OK,' Amy said, as she stood by a white marker board mounted on a side wall. 'Last night I used a hypnosis technique on Ning. She mentioned seeing a photograph on the wall in an office. Two muddy boys, aged between ten and twelve. They were wearing football kits: maroon and orange hooped socks, maroon shorts and orange shirts. The shirts also had a logo, which Ning described as a *square smiling cartoon.*'

Ryan sat in one of the office chairs, rocking it from side to side as he faced Amy. Lauren was further away with her face in a physics textbook, but half listening to what Amy had said.

'Why's the kit so important?' Ryan asked.

'Because if we can identify the team that these boys play for, we can get their names. Once we have their names we can find out where they live and who their parents are. Once we know that we can find out who Daddy is and where Daddy works.'

'At least maroon and orange is unusual,' Ryan said. 'Millions of football teams must wear red and black, or blue and white, but who plays in maroon and orange?'

Amy nodded and wrote *maroon and orange* on the whiteboard.

'How do we know it's football?' Lauren asked. 'I mean. What if it's rugby, or hockey?'

'Fair point,' Amy said, as she added *Rugby?* and *Hockey?* to the board. 'Although it makes our task harder, not easier.'

Lauren laughed. 'Sometimes the truth hurts.'

'You said the boys were muddy,' Ryan said. 'Which makes rugby more likely. And hooped socks are quite common for rugby teams.'

'What happens when you Google football teams?' Lauren asked.

'I had a quick mess with the web,' Amy said. 'You get thousands of random teams. I tried searching for *orange and maroon kit* too and all I got was a Sydney rugby union side.'

'And the Internet's not geographical,' Ryan said. 'You can't narrow your search down to teams in specific areas, unless you know an exact place name. But what about local newspapers? You know, they always report kids' football matches and have team photos and stuff. We know the approximate area where Ning was. We could get copies of local newspapers from all around. There might be a hundred or so and you'd have to go through lots of back issues. It would take a while, but it's far from impossible.'

'Worth thinking about,' Amy agreed, as she wrote *local newspaper archives* on the whiteboard. 'I suppose you could even try calling the newspapers up, because a local sports correspondent might know which teams play in which colours.'

'But you'd tip people off that we're looking,' Lauren said.

'I don't think that's critical,' Amy said. 'We can easily find an excuse. Say we're police looking for a young burglar or mugger seen wearing those colours, something like that.'

'What about the sponsor's logo?' Ryan asked. 'Like, I know you can't type *square cartoon man* into Google, but there must be a place where trademarks are kept. And they must be indexed somehow.'

'Long shot,' Amy said. 'But that's what brainstorming's all about.'

As Amy wrote *trademark registry?* on the whiteboard, Lauren shot out of her seat.

'I played under-nines' football before I joined CHERUB,' she said excitedly. 'My mum ordered a kit and got this local shop to sponsor us, in return for which she agreed to stop robbing them.'

Ryan looked confused. 'What was your mum, a stick-up merchant?'

Lauren laughed. 'She ran the biggest shoplifting gang in London. And none of that really matters.'

'So what are you getting all excited about?' Amy asked.

'Kit suppliers,' Lauren said, as she typed *football kit suppliers* into the computer in front of her. 'My mum ordered three or four catalogues, I can remember looking at them, picking out the colours.'

'I get it,' Ryan said. 'There are tens of thousands of kids' football teams in the country. Hundreds of leagues, hundreds of local newspapers, hundreds of schools, youth clubs and churches that run them, but you're saying there are probably only a dozen or so companies that supply printed football kits. And most of them would have records of who they've sold kits to and what colours they were.'

Amy broke into a smile. 'Nice one, Lauren,' she said, as she wrote *KIT SUPPLIERS!!!* up on the board. 'And if it's like most businesses, the market for kits is dominated by a few big companies. If we can identify the biggest kit suppliers, then get them to send us a list of everyone who's ordered an orange and maroon kit in the past five years, there's a decent chance we'll locate the team we're looking for.'

'I'm extracting a list of—' Lauren began, but a phone rang before she could finish and she reached out to grab it. 'Unicorn Tyre Repair, how may I help you?'

As Lauren dealt with a stricken CHERUB agent at the other end of the country, Amy stepped across to Ryan.

'We'll get a list of kit suppliers off Google,' Amy said. 'Then we'll crosscheck company names against Companies' House business records, so that we can pick out the ones with the biggest financial turnover. Then we'll start making phone calls, starting with the biggest and working our way down.'

'A lot might be closed on a Saturday,' Ryan said.

Amy nodded. 'But I'd still like to get on with this. We'll get the company directors' names and crosscheck against bank databases to get home addresses and contact details. I don't care if they're golfing, sailing their boat or visiting Granny. We'll find out who sells orange and maroon football kits, then who's been ordering them and where they play.'

'Might take a while tracking all these people down,' Ryan said.

Amy nodded in agreement. 'You got any mates who wouldn't mind getting out of Saturday morning lessons?'

44. TREADMILL

Dr Kessler's idea of a little pinch was closer to Ning's idea of complete agony, but the small piece of muscle tissue that had been removed from her thigh would give a wealth of information on her physical potential when stained and viewed under a microscope.

After the biopsy, Carlos and Ning had full body X-rays to determine any skeletal defects, then they were wired up with heart monitors, fitted with breathing masks and given a treadmill workout to test their heart and lung capacities.

The speed at which you recover from a bout of exercise is a key sign of your fitness levels, so Ning and Carlos still had the heart monitors attached as Dr Kessler disappeared to his lab and gave them a chance to rest.

Ning wasn't as fit as she'd been when she lived at the sports academy, but she was still a natural athlete and recovered well. Carlos on the other hand was gasping and kept rubbing the plaster stuck to his thigh.

'If you scratch you'll make it worse,' Ning said.

'What do you know?' Carlos said. 'And why do you speak with such a stupid accent?'

The girls at Kirkcaldy had taken the mickey out of Ning's Sino-Scouse accent and she'd grown self-conscious about people thinking she sounded stupid every time she opened her mouth.

'I've had muscle biopsies when I was at a sporting academy in China,' Ning explained. 'If you scratch, it will start bleeding again.'

Lottie the nurse dropped by with cups of water, which they both downed quickly. Ning threw her empty cup at the recycling bin, but it bounced off the rim. Carlos approached to dispose of his own cup as Ning bent over to pick hers up, but made a retching sound and shot a torrent of puke down the back of Ning's shirt and trousers.

'Aww, bloody hell,' Ning shouted angrily, as Carlos staggered off to the other side of the room and broke into a coughing fit.

Ning didn't know whether to clean up or help Carlos first.

'Nurse,' Ning shouted, as she spotted a dispenser filled with paper towels.

Lottie comforted Carlos and gave him water to wash his mouth out as Ning did the best job she could cleaning off the back of her T-shirt and trousers.

'Is there anywhere I can get a clean set?' Ning asked.

'Can I run back to the main building, I know there's a uniform store somewhere?'

'I'm sorry, but I can't authorise you to leave during recruitment testing,' Lottie said. 'Please sit still, the heart monitors are supposed to be measuring your recovery time.'

Ning felt sorry for Carlos, but at the same time she was angry with him because there were a million places where he could have thrown up without hitting her.

Now that medical procedures were over, chairwoman Zara Asker would conduct the rest of the tests.

'I've got three kids and they've all thrown up on me dozens of times,' Zara told Ning when she arrived. 'We need to get to the dojo and I'm not taking a twenty-minute diversion just because you've got a little wet patch on your trousers.'

Ning felt miserable as she followed Zara through light drizzle towards the dojo. Carlos was still fighting for breath and twice Zara turned back and yelled at him to keep up. The chairwoman had seemed much nicer the previous afternoon and Ning guessed Zara was just having a bad day.

The martial arts dojo was one of the swankier buildings on CHERUB campus. The construction cost had been donated by the Japanese government after a CHERUB operation infiltrated a Russian spy syndicate stealing valuable Japanese technology.

It was built in traditional Japanese style, with a vaulted roof shaped from huge single-trunk beams. Outside was a traditional Japanese rock garden and a carp pond spanned by a wooden bridge. The inside was more functional, and apart from the spectacular roof, could have been any modern gymnasium, with banks of fluorescent lights and a hum from the ventilation system.

After leaving shoes and socks outside on a porch, Ning, Carlos and Zara crossed springy blue matting in the main part of the gym. You'd usually see Miss Takada teaching martial arts here, but presently a group of cherubs in their late teens had a ghetto blaster pumping out an old show tune as they practised a dance routine.

A sliding screen took them through to a side room which had a square of red matting in the centre and wooden benches around the edge. Two sets of safety gear had been left in the middle of the floor: lightly padded martial arts gloves, gum shields, head protectors and a protective cup for Carlos.

'The rules are simple,' Zara said. 'Use any technique to floor your opponent, except kicks to the genitals, jaw wrenching or eye gouging. It's five rounds, first to get three submissions wins.'

Ning looked awkwardly at Zara, as Carlos tried to figure out how to properly tighten the Velcro straps on his padded gloves.

'Amy wrote a file on me,' Ning said. 'I don't know if you read it, but I've done a *lot* of boxing and Carlos is way below my weight class.'

'Of course I read your file,' Zara snapped. 'But who says getting into CHERUB is easy? If Carlos is small and skinny in here, he won't suddenly get big and strong on an undercover mission, will he?'

Ning wondered about Zara acting so differently to how she'd been the previous afternoon. Ryan had refused to give any details on the recruitment tests, but he'd hinted that she should expect the unexpected. As Ning pulled on her headgear she wondered if Zara's mood was a deliberate way to make her feel uneasy.

'Line up,' the chairwoman said sharply.

But Carlos hadn't mastered his combat gloves and Zara tutted impatiently as she fixed the Velcro straps for him.

'Touch gloves and fight.'

Carlos moved aggressively, swinging wild fists and making a few soft contacts with Ning's shoulders. But he had no idea what he was doing and Ning could have planted a brutal fist in his face any time she liked.

As Ning backed up Carlos almost did for himself, coming off balance with his own swinging fist. Ning saw the opportunity to floor him without serious damage and swept his feet away. Carlos hit the mat hard and Ning straddled his back.

'Give up,' Ning said, as she sat on Carlos' back.

It's tough to speak with gum shields in, but whatever Carlos said wasn't polite and he kept wriggling even though his situation was hopeless. Ning didn't want to hurt Carlos, but she needed to do something extra to make him submit, so she put her hand on to his shoulder and dug her thumb into his armpit.

'Oww,' Carlos yelled. 'I submit.'

Carlos steamed as he stood up and shouted like a spoiled brat, 'That wasn't fair. I tripped.'

Ning couldn't help but laugh. 'I thought you didn't believe in luck.'

'Get your gum shields back in,' Zara said firmly. 'Line up, touch gloves.'

Carlos had nothing in his tactical arsenal beyond the wild swinging thing. But he didn't trip this time, so Ning moved in and gave him a fairly gentle punch in the face, hoping it would be enough to knock him back without hurting his nose. To Ning's surprise, Carlos' legs went wobbly for about half a second, but as she backed off Carlos charged again. She shoved him backwards, but not before he'd caught her with a heel in the stomach.

Unfortunately for Carlos, it was only enough pain to make Ning angry. She ducked into a proper boxing stance for the first time and threw three quick punches. The first to the head knocked Carlos backwards, the second to the gut doubled him over and the third pounded the side of his ribcage and left him sprawling on the mat.

Carlos had landed face down, but he soon rolled on to his back and made a high-pitched wailing noise.

'I'm sorry,' Ning said, as she rushed over. 'There's nothing to be ashamed of. I've always been strong and I've won medals for boxing.'

Carlos had this weird expression and Ning backed off because she thought he might puke again. She turned to face Zara.

'What's the point of this?' Ning asked. 'All it proves is that an experienced twelve-year-old boxer can batter a skinny ten-year-old. That's hardly a big surprise.'

Zara eyeballed Ning. 'Maybe *you* should remember who you're talking to and follow the rules.'

Ning bristled. She'd woken up that morning thinking she'd found a place where she wanted to be, but now she was facing a strict teacher laying down stupid rules and telling her to remember her place, exactly like school in China.

Ning trembled as thoughts raced through her head.

'I'm not hurting Carlos again,' she said, as she ripped off a glove and threw it down. 'I submit three times, so Carlos wins three to two. Just hope I'll do better on the next test.'

Zara took a long slow breath before nodding. 'Fine, Carlos wins.'

Ning had expected Carlos to show gratitude, but he instantly leapt up off the floor and started jumping around shouting, 'I win, I win. In your face!'

'Aww, give over,' Ning said irritably. 'You didn't even know how to put the damned gloves on.'

'The next stage tests your brainpower,' Zara said. 'A simple written exam, testing mathematical abilities, language skills and general knowledge. You'll have ninety minutes and I expect you to complete it while sitting in *complete* silence.'

*

It took Amy and Ryan an hour to make up a list of eighteen companies that produced the majority of Britain's printed team kits. By the time they'd finished, Ryan's mates Max and Alfie had been roped in and Amy divided the list so they each had four or five companies to call up.

The team of four used the six desks in the control areas to make their calls. They each started by calling the phone number on the company's website. Ryan's first call was to a company called Kitmeister UK.

After listening to an *open Monday to Friday* recorded message, he started looking up the names of company directors. Then he accessed mobile phone network databases and got the number for half a dozen mobile phones whose bills were paid by Kitmeister UK. He was about to start dialling them in turn, when Amy approached.

'Think of it like cracking nuts,' she said. 'Deal with the easy ones first, and return to the tough buggers if you need to later.'

It was Max who made the first breakthrough. He waited for everyone to finish the call they were making before explaining his scribbled notes.

'I called Matthews & Son,' Max explained. 'It took about six attempts to explain what I was asking for, but the receptionist put me through to this old-timer. He sounded doddery, but he's been in the kit business over forty years and he definitely knew his stuff.

'He says that basic kits without logos are produced by several different manufacturers, and then customised with sponsors' logos and player numbers by companies like his. He reckons that none of the big name manufacturers currently make an orange and maroon hooped sock. The only one that does is a Taiwanese kit producer called SoccaAce.

'He says he wouldn't sell SoccaAce because their stuff is *cheap for a good reason.* He also said that there are only two companies he knows who do print on SoccaAce kits. One is called Oberon Sports, the other is Kitmeister UK. He's really got it in for Kitmeister. Apparently they're the biggest company in the market, but their quality is poor and their customer service is appalling.'

'Nice one, Max,' Amy said, as she cracked a big smile.

'Did I earn a kiss?' Max asked cheekily, as he leaned back in his chair.

Amy laughed and gave him a peck on the cheek.

'Eww,' Ryan said. 'Have you any idea where he's been?'

45. PAPERS

Ning's exam took place in an empty office on the ground floor of the main building. The door was left ajar so that Zara's assistant could keep watch as the potential recruits worked at small wooden desks.

Ning had taken exams or practice exams at least twice a week at school in Dandong, during which she'd developed a routine of quickly checking through the entire paper before starting work. It didn't take a genius to work out that it would take way more than ninety minutes to complete the whole paper, so she noted the questions offering the highest marks and targeted those first.

Carlos' attitude seemed more relaxed and he drove Ning mad by rustling his paper, humming and drumming his pencil on the desk. After twenty minutes Ning was starting to wish she'd knocked him out in the dojo.

She finally snapped when Carlos started putting his finger in his mouth making pop noises.

'Will you shut up,' she said, in an angry whisper.

Zara's assistant overheard. She came out from behind her desk and stood in the doorway wagging her finger.

'One more sound, young lady, I'll take that paper from you and tear it up.'

To make matters worse the lead inside Ning's pencil kept breaking and she had to keep stopping to sharpen it. But for all the frustrations, Ning didn't feel she'd done too badly when Zara came to collect the papers.

The chairwoman had entered the office holding a metal cage covered with a checked cloth. Removing it revealed two fluffy white rabbits.

'Meet Duster and Bouncer,' Zara said, as she pulled a carrot stick out of her pocket and fed an eager bunny through the bars of the cage. 'Aren't they sweet?'

The rabbits were cute and Ning crouched in front of the cage to look at them.

'Can I feed them?' Carlos asked, and Zara handed him a carrot stick.

Zara spoke as Duster munched his carrot stick. 'I'll just need both of you to kill a bunny by stabbing it through the throat with your pencils and then we can get a spot of lunch.'

Carlos jumped back from the cage as if he'd received an electric shock. 'Why?' he asked, horrified.

'Well you eat meat, don't you?' Zara said. 'Every animal you've ever eaten must have been killed by someone.'

'I . . . I don't like blood,' Carlos said.

Zara looked at Ning. 'What about you?'

'Sure,' Ning said.

Ning opened the rabbit cage and reached in to grab Duster – or possibly Bouncer because it was hard to tell. The rabbit was jittery and tried to escape Ning's arms, but she calmed the animal with a series of long slow strokes from the top of her head down to her tail.

'Good girl,' Ning said soothingly.

With a sudden movement, Ning brought a heavy Karate chop down on the back of the rabbit's head to stun it.

'Shit!' Carlos shouted, backing up to the wall as Ning grabbed her pencil and hung the limp animal over the bin by its hind legs.

She then trapped the rabbit's head between her knees and jammed the pencil into the main vein running down its throat. The spurt of blood sounded like peeing as it hit the bottom of the bin. After he'd got on her nerves all morning, Ning turned slightly and made sure Carlos saw plenty of blood and gore.

As Carlos turned green, Zara found a tea tray for Ning to place the rabbit on when it had bled out.

'You've done that before,' Zara said, clearly impressed.

Ning nodded as she squeezed the rabbit's body to force out the last drips of blood. 'Some of the ladies who worked at my first orphanage used to breed and sell rabbits. We were allowed to play with them, but our diet wasn't great so we ate them too. If you give me a sharp knife I can gut it. I've cured the pelts too. When I was little I had a rabbit fur hat that tied around my chin when it snowed.'

'You have no problem with killing and eating animals?' Zara asked.

'I think animals should be well treated while they're alive, but humans come first,' Ning said. 'There are many rich people in China, but millions of peasants still go hungry in the countryside.'

Zara nodded, then looked at Carlos. 'She's shown you how it's done. Are you sure you don't want to have a go?'

'I just can't,' Carlos said. 'That was the horriblest thing I've ever seen.'

'Oh well, Duster,' Zara said, as she put the cloth back over the cage. 'Looks like you'll live to see another recruitment test. Now, let's get some lunch.'

Ning looked at Carlos and spoke in her politest *butter wouldn't melt* voice as she followed Zara towards the dining-room.

'I wonder if they have stir-fried rabbit on the menu?' she teased. 'It's delicious.'

*

Over in the mission control building Alfie plucked warm sheets of paper out of a laser printer.

'This is the e-mail the woman from Oberon sent me,' Alfie said, as he waggled the papers in front of Amy. 'They've made twenty-eight sets of kit with maroon and orange hooped socks since 2002. Three football and two rugby clubs, they've given me all the customer addresses and postcodes.'

'Nice,' Amy said brightly as she fired up Google Maps on the computer in front of her. 'Give me postcodes, let's see how many are within an hour's drive of where Ning got pulled out of that car.'

Oberon Sports was based in the south-west and the first four postcodes were all in Devon or Cornwall. The final kits had been delivered to a youth club in Milton Keynes. Amy typed in *Wigan to Milton Keynes* and got an answer of 155 miles and two hours forty minutes' driving time.

'It must be Kitmeister UK,' Amy said, as she walked over to Ryan and Max. 'How are you getting on?'

Ryan huffed with frustration. 'I spoke to Kitmeister's managing director, but he's at his cottage in Yorkshire for the weekend and can't get into the office until Monday, because only the building manager has the code for the alarm. To make matters worse, he says he'll have to talk to his solicitors before giving any information to any government department.'

Amy tutted. 'Sounds like he's being awkward for the sake of it.'

Ryan shook his head. 'Then he went into a rant about government harassment and the Inland Revenue strangling small businesses like his with red tape. After he slammed the phone down on me, I looked up Kitmeister's Inland Revenue files. Apparently they're under investigation for non-payment of taxes.'

'That's gonna make it tough to get info,' Amy said.

'If you want my opinion,' Max said, 'we should

drive round to his house and threaten to nail his balls to a door.'

Alfie put on a mock gangster voice. 'And even if he does cooperate we nail one of his balls to a door anyway, because that's the kind of guys we are.'

Amy laughed. 'Somehow I can't see your testicle nailing scheme getting past Zara or the CHERUB ethics committee.'

'Leaving the psycho nailing fantasies aside,' Ryan said, 'Kitmeister UK's headquarters is only about forty minutes' drive from here. Breaking in and having a little rummage through their filing cabinets and computer systems isn't completely out of the question.'

Amy nodded. 'I work for TFU not CHERUB, so I'll have to get a mission controller on board, but if Kitmeister are being stroppy about cooperating with us it could be our best option.'

*

There were four pools in the CHERUB campus swimming complex: A twenty-five-metre learner's pool, a full fifty-metre Olympic pool, an extra-deep diving pool and finally the leisure pool, where the fourth of Ning and Carlos' five recruitment tests would take place.

Even at its deepest point the leisure pool was only two and a half metres. It had all the standard equipment: three water slides, a play castle, miniature islands with plastic palm trees and a wave machine.

For the test, seventeen-year-old identical twins Callum and Connor Reilly had spread over a hundred plastic balls around the pool. They'd also set the wave machine to its highest setting so that you had to fight half-metre waves to swim up to the deep end.

'These are the rules,' Zara said, as the slim-but-muscular twins stood behind, towering over her in their swimming shorts. 'There's a red bin for Ning on the island and a blue bin for Carlos next to it. You've got twenty minutes to put as many balls as you can in your bin. Green balls are worth one point, yellow three, blue five and red ten. You can throw balls, but you must only carry one at a time. There's no physical contact allowed and you can use the poolside to access the slides, but you'll be docked fifty points if you use the poolside to move around. Is all that clear?'

'What are the ball scores again?' Carlos asked.

Ning surveyed the pool as Zara repeated the scoring system. The low-value green balls were all bobbing in the water at the shallow end near the bins, while most of the higher-value ones were in inaccessible locations. The ten-point reds were in the furthest-flung locations, at the top of water slides, or on the upper level little kids' castle.

'Away you go!' Zara shouted.

Carlos dived straight in and swam towards his bin, while Ning waded through knee-deep water towards the castle, feeling like a contestant in a TV game show. She'd spotted three red balls and managed to climb on to the castle and throw two of them into her bin, but the third bounced off the edge and Carlos grabbed the rebound and dunked it.

Ning picked the wrong moment to slide off the castle

and almost lost her footing as a fast-moving wave knocked her sideways. She grabbed a blue ball worth five points as she waded on towards the island with the bins, but she was horrified to see Carlos rapidly scoring ones and threes by scooping up the easy balls that the waves had pushed to the edge of the pool.

Ning got her blue ball into her bin with a short throw, then joined Carlos in a mad scramble for greens and yellows. As balls flew, Callum clambered on to the island. As he threw the collected balls into an empty jet pool, Connor stood with a notepad and pencil keeping score.

'Ning thirty-eight, Carlos fifty-one,' Connor shouted.

By this time most of the easy balls near the island had been cleared. As Carlos picked the last few, Ning began swimming towards a larger island in the middle of the pool that had about a dozen five-point blue balls on it.

Ning had good strength and stamina, but a poor stroke meant that she found it tough swimming against the waves surging down from the deep end.

'New balls,' Zara shouted as she tipped a dozen ten-point reds into the end of the pool.

Ning hadn't realised more balls would be added as the game progressed. As she dithered between sticking to a plan and getting the blue balls from the island or going for the reds in the deep water, Carlos skimmed past underwater.

Carlos might have been weak on land, but he made Ning feel clumsy as he swam fifteen metres without surfacing for breath. She decided to compete for the reds, but by the time she'd reached deep water Carlos had thrown ten of the twelve balls in the rough direction of his bin and was heading back.

After battling with the waves, Ning was gasping as she grabbed a single red ball. Carlos was already back at the shallow end, picking up the reds he'd thrown down and dropping them into his bin.

Ning desperately threw her red ball from the deep end. She came close to getting it into her bin, but it bounced off the edge and Carlos swept in ruthlessly and took it for himself.

'Sixteen minutes to go,' Zara shouted.

'Ning forty-one, Carlos one hundred and eighty-seven,' Connor shouted.

Ning punched the water with frustration as she headed for the blue balls on the island. She was getting completely thrashed.

46. HEIGHT

To get the Kitmeister UK break-in approved, Amy had to type up a mission briefing, get senior mission controller Ewart Asker to read and approve it, track down chairwoman – and Ewart's wife – Zara to sign off on it, then e-mail the details through to two members of the CHERUB ethics committee, requesting an urgent response.

Amy wore her best poker face as she stepped into the hallway.

'And?' Ryan asked.

'It's all set,' she said. 'I had to play up the yobbo angle, so you might have to smash a few things up.'

'I can do mindless vandalism,' Alfie said, grinning and thumping on his chest. 'I'm actually rather partial to it.'

Ewart overheard and shouted a warning from inside

his office. 'Nothing too extreme, boys. We don't want anything that gets publicity and makes the police start a big investigation.'

'Gotcha, boss,' Max said, as he leaned into the office and gave Ewart a cheeky salute.

'Good luck,' Ewart said firmly. 'Now close my door and bugger off.'

'Right, boys,' Amy said as she led the excitable trio towards the exit. 'You'll need to change out of CHERUB uniforms. We might as well have radio links so bring your communications stuff, as well as your break-in equipment. I'll sort out a car and meet you in the dining-room in about twenty-five minutes. We can grab a quick bite, and set off by two.'

'Sounds good,' Ryan said, as he slid his feet into the muddy boots he'd left by the main door.

*

Ning was bigger and stronger than Carlos, so she changed strategy, staying close to the bins, trying to intercept anything that Carlos threw and only swimming when Zara threw new balls into a shallower part of the pool.

It was a reasonable strategy, but when the twenty minutes were up, Ning was completely exhausted and still more than a hundred points off Carlos' score.

'Well done, mate,' Zara told Carlos enthusiastically, as she tousled his hair. 'You cut through that water like a little tadpole.'

Ning resented the compliment and seethed with jealousy as she towelled off and switched her swimming costume for her blood- and puke-spattered T-shirt and combat trousers.

To make matters worse, she could hear Callum and Connor laughing and joking casually with Carlos as they changed just out of sight a few metres away. Ning had been trying really hard, but although she thought she'd done well on the written exam and killing the rabbit, she wasn't confident that she'd done enough to be accepted as a trainee CHERUB agent.

The final test was the height obstacle. Ning hadn't liked the look of the creaky wooden structure, with its narrow poles, ropes and beams, when Ryan had toured campus with her the day before. She liked it even less as she stood at the base of a wobbly thirty-metre rope ladder, looking up with slanting rain hitting her face.

Callum was already halfway up the ladder with Carlos and they'd left slippery clumps of mud from their boots on the rungs. Identical twin Connor would accompany Ning, while Zara had gone back to her office to catch up with e-mails and paperwork.

'Will I die if I fall?' Ning asked.

'You won't die,' Connor said. 'But the tree branches will lash you and the rope nets are strung tight. I've known a few people hurt themselves, and one guy who got his boot caught in the netting and broke his leg.'

Ning managed an awkward smile. 'Best to avoid falling off then?'

'Absolutely,' Connor said. 'Start climbing and try to remember that nothing good ever came of looking down.'

As Ning made it up the ladder, Connor stayed a few rungs behind. Up above, Carlos was shuffling across a scaffold pole, aided by shouts of encouragement from Callum.

Ning's strong upper body meant she had no difficulty crossing the pole and by the time she was over they'd caught up with Carlos, who'd lost his nerve at the first jump. There were trees all around the height obstacle, but they'd been cut away to make this first leap seem scarier. The two wooden boards jutted dramatically over open space.

'I can't,' Carlos said.

'Just think about the jump,' Callum told him. 'It's just over a metre, barely more than a step.'

Carlos looked like he was going to spew again, but he took a short run-up and made it across, with a rather alarming wobble as he landed on the opposite side.

Ning felt less scared on the obstacle than when she'd been looking up at it, and this was an easy leap compared to feats she'd performed on a much narrower gymnastics beam when she was six years old.

The mid-section of the obstacle comprised a zigzagging walk along narrow planks, with occasional leaps. As the course progressed, jumps grew longer and the beams narrower and more steeply angled. The final section was a pair of beams less than five centimetres wide, set half a metre apart and sloping down forty degrees.

Carlos wrapped himself around the beam and began shuffling down on his bum, but he had a mini freak-out halfway across and Callum had to grab hold and rescue him. Ning went last and copied Callum and Connor, balancing one boot on each beam and walking down in four bold steps.

'Nice,' Connor said, as Ning joined him on the final platform.

There were two routes to the ground. The first was a jump through the trees on to a crash mat, but this quartet would be using a steeply angled zip wire with a muddy pit at the far end of its landing zone.

As Callum grabbed a set of padded handles and prepared to make his jump, Connor pointed at a tree and gave Ning instructions.

'The trick is to let go at *precisely* the right moment,' Connor explained. 'Too soon and you'll fall from a great height and hurt your ankles, or even break a leg. Too late and you'll end up in the pit. And that pit may look like regular mud from here, but that's just a dry crust over absolute filth. I'm talking about horse crap, cattle slurry, rotten fruit and chicken feathers. Speaking from experience, it takes about five days' showering to completely wash the stink off of your skin.'

Ning looked mildly horrified as she watched Callum speed down to the ground. He made a textbook landing five metres from the pit and rolled forward on to his knees.

'Try not to plant your feet,' Connor said, as he fitted a grab handle over the wire and helped Carlos to line up. 'Fall forward like my brother did.'

After he'd beat her in the pool and generally been a pain all day Ning wouldn't have minded seeing Carlos plough into the filth. He came agonisingly close, but Callum grabbed him as he tilted towards the dirt.

Now it was Ning's turn. It looked a long way down as she reached up and grabbed the handles.

'Step off gently when you're ready,' Callum said. 'Let go when you see your feet a metre and a half from the ground.'

It was a slow start, but once Ning got going it felt way faster than it looked. About a third of the way down the wire was anchored between two trees, after which the incline grew steeper. Ning looked down as the ground closed in. She almost let go, but decided it was still too high. But the angle was so steep that before she knew it the pit was almost under her.

She pulled her knees up to her chest, but that only bought her a fraction of a second. The crust caught her boots, creating enough drag to rip her fingers off of the handles. She put her hands out to save herself, but her outstretched arms punched through the crust, closely followed by her entire body in a dramatic belly flop.

Beneath the crust was half a metre of brown water, while the bottom was a gloopy layer so thick Ning had to use all her strength to pull her wrists out. She got up on one knee, but she couldn't see with her eyes full of dirt.

She'd pressed her lips together, but an abominable taste still filled her mouth, and the stench clinging to the inside of her nose was beyond description. Before Ning found her feet she felt something prod her in the belly.

'Grab the pole,' Connor shouted.

Ning reached blindly and grabbed the shaft of a long pole. Connor gave it an almighty tug and there was a sucking sound as Ning's boots were dragged out of the mud. She managed to hold on until she reached the embankment and as she crawled up she felt a hose on the top of her head.

'Keep your mouth shut and try not to swallow,' Callum advised, as he aimed the hose up high so that a torrent rained down over Ning's head.

Her ears were clogged, but the first thing she heard after she'd dug the muck out was Carlos screaming with laughter.

'Oh God, God, God!' he howled. 'That's the funniest thing I *ever* saw. Ning, do you realise that most of what's stuck to you came out of a cow's arse? Oh, man! I'm gonna piss myself.'

Callum and Connor were smiling a little too as Ning got her eyes open.

'Here, take the hose,' Callum said, as he threw it towards Ning. As she reached down to grab it Carlos started impersonating her accent again.

'Me Ning. Me the Chinese Scouser. Me covered big, big cow poo. Smell worse than Chinese take away.'

Ning snapped. She threw down the hose and began storming towards Carlos.

'You little sprat,' Ning shouted. 'If you don't shut your face I'm gonna punch every tooth out of your head and make—'

As Ning came forward, Carlos dived behind Callum, giving the teenager no choice but to intervene.

'Ning, calm down,' Callum shouted.

Ning tried to get behind Callum and grab Carlos, but the seventeen-year-old pushed her back.

'If you start fighting you'll both fail the recruitment tests for sure,' Callum said.

Ning glowered for a few seconds before taking a step back, followed by a deep breath. She picked up the hose as Callum and a still laughing Carlos started walking back towards the main building.

'At least it's over now,' Connor said. 'Hose yourself off as best you can. Then you can go back to your room in the main building and have a proper hot shower. They've got this special soap that neutralises smells. If I can find some I'll bring it up to your room.'

'Thanks,' Ning said, as she bent forward, hosing off strands of muddy hair.

'Try not to swallow too much until you've used some mouthwash and brushed your teeth. I'd bet that broth will turn your stomach out if you drink too much of it.'

'Did Zara give any hint of how well she thought I was doing?' Ning asked.

'No,' Connor said. 'And if she had I wouldn't be allowed to tell you. Just clean up in your room and wait for a call. Zara will make her final assessment once your exam is marked and all your test results are through from Dr Kessler. It'll probably be a few hours.'

47. ALARM

The Saturday afternoon traffic was awful, so it was gone three when Amy turned a black Mercedes E-class wagon into a trading estate. There were about twenty warehouse units and Kitmeister UK's metal-sided box was one of the biggest. Most units were closed for the weekend, but there was quite a bit of traffic coming out of Kitmeister's neighbour which sold timber and doors.

'Could have done without the DIYers,' Amy said, as she stopped the Mercedes in the access road leading towards the Kitmeister warehouse.

Max lowered an electric window in the back and studied the building, looking for security cameras and alarm boxes.

'I'm seeing a couple of old-school CCTV cams over the main door and side entrances,' Max said. 'Burglar alarm box has the name of a company called Titanium Security.'

As Max said the name, Alfie sat next to him typing it into a laptop which was linked to a list of every police monitored burglar alarm in Britain. The file also had a list of passwords, which were used when an alarm company detected a fault or did maintenance work.

Once Alfie had all the details, Amy called up the local police station and spoke in her politest voice.

'Hello, my name is Eileen Smith . . . I'm calling from Titanium Systems. Our diagnostic software is reporting a fault with the alarm at Kitmeister UK, Unit sixteen on the East Lane trading estate. One of our engineers will be on site in a moment and it may trigger an alarm signal at your station . . . Not a problem, the deactivation password is DGCD 24425 . . . Oh, I expect he'll be on site for two hours at most, but don't worry I'll give you another call when the alarm is fixed . . . You have a good afternoon too, officer.'

Amy smiled as she dropped her phone into a tray by the armrest and pressed the button to open the boot.

'Radio check,' Amy said, as she pushed in an earpiece. 'Amy, check.'

'Max check.'

'Ryan check.'

'Alfie check.'

'All OK,' Amy said. 'Someone might get suspicious if I'm parked here. So I'll drive out by that little kids' playground thingy we passed on the main road. Do you remember where that was?'

'No sweat,' Ryan said, as he opened the front passenger side door. 'Meet you there.'

The three boys stepped out and went around the rear to grab their backpacks, along with a large hammer and a collapsible ladder. As Amy drove away the trio donned baseball caps and pulled hoodies over their heads.

Max took a can of spray paint from his pack as Ryan and Alfie stretched out the ladder. Alfie leaned it against the wall close to the alarm box, because although they'd dealt with the alarm's link to the local police station the sound from the bell box would still attract attention.

Ryan climbed up and used the hammer to knock the plastic cover off the bell box. This unveiled a standard arrangement of a large plastic siren, attached to a backup battery.

It took three swift belts with the hammer to shatter the siren. The alarm's anti-tamper system was activated, but all that came out were crackling noises.

'Job done,' Ryan said, as he slid down.

Meantime, Max had sprayed black paint over the lens of the security camera. He'd established that there was a deadlock and an electric card swipe on the door. He had the skills to override both, but they were supposed to be yobs, so he attacked with a crowbar.

The double doors were made from a soft wood and Max punched a hole above the main lock with the crowbar's sharp end, then he pushed the hooked end through the hole and tried wrenching the lock out of the doorway.

'Weed,' Alfie said, as he pushed Max out of the way.

Alfie needed all his strength and bulk to rip the deadlock out of the door frame. The electronic lock was much weaker and it simply took a shoulder charge to burst in.

'Right, now what?' Max said, as Ryan looked around a lobby with foam chairs and a fancy reception desk.

'Alfie, stay here and keep lookout,' Ryan said. 'Me and Max will split up and search. We need to find a computer which can access Kitmeister's invoices. It's most likely to be in an office: accountant's, director's or something like that.'

Amy's voice came through the boys' earpieces as Ryan headed down a narrow hallway with a whiff of drains. 'Ryan, are you in yet?'

He touched his earpiece to activate a microphone. 'We're in.'

'It's all restricted parking,' Amy said. 'Give me a call when you're ready and I'll pull up somewhere near that green mound thingy by the estate entrance.'

'No worries,' Ryan said.

He'd reached an open-plan office, with three desks and a separate room at the far end. He jiggled the mouse on all the computers, hoping that one had been left on. He had no luck, so he went into the separate office, sat in a big leather chair and switched on the computer.

'It's all clear here,' Alfie said over the com.

'You only need to tell us if it's not,' Max answered.

Ryan drummed his gloved hand on the desk as the computer booted up. The machine asked for a log in password, so he switched it off, plugged in a USB stick and rebooted, pressing CTRL and F10 to enter the machine's set-up mode. From set-up he quickly changed the computer's settings so that it would boot up from his USB stick, bypassing the computer's hard drive.

'Now you're my bitch,' Ryan told himself, as he rubbed his hands together.

The USB was configured with a special cut-down version of Windows which was customised to mirror all the host machine's settings and turn its hard drives into slaves. When it finished booting, Ryan searched the C drive for accounting software, opened up Sage Accounts and selected the invoicing module.

He'd been taught a few things about accounting software, but Ryan was no expert and felt out of his depth as he flipped through screens showing Kitmeister invoices, starting with the most recent. The problem was that the invoices had stock codes and said things like *Kit 43566 size L QTY3* rather than something useful like *orange and maroon hooped socks*.

But Ryan had noticed Kitmeister catalogues stacked up outside, so he grabbed one and flicked through pages of shirts, shorts, balls and shin pads until he came to socks. There was a double-page spread of SoccaAce socks, one colour, two colour, tricolour, striped and hooped. The order code for orange and maroon hoops was SAOM- followed by another letter depending upon the size.

Ryan opened up the accounts program's search function and did a search for SAOM*, which ought to give him all the invoices with orange and maroon hooped socks of any size.

14 Results Found

If there was an option to print fourteen invoices in one go Ryan couldn't find it, so he began printing them off one at a time.

Ryan touched his earpiece. 'Looks like I've got what we came for,' he said happily, as the first sheet rolled out of a laser printer under the desk.

'Excellent,' Amy replied. 'Don't forget to make a mess before you leave.'

'There's something else,' Max said. 'Ryan, when you've got the invoices meet me back here in the warehouse.'

The printing was complicated by the paper running out, but all the printers were identical so he just swapped a tray from another machine. When Ryan had all the invoices, he pocketed the USB key and jogged back the way he came. He passed Alfie in the doorway and headed through swinging doors to meet Max in the storage and manufacturing area.

'Took you long enough,' Max moaned. 'Get a look at this.'

'Kiss my arse,' Ryan said, as he walked between rows of shelving stacked with packets of sportswear, tracking Max's voice to a spacious area filled with the equipment used for making transfers and fixing them to football shirts.

Max stood along the back wall, pointing at rows of file boxes. 'They're templates for designs,' he explained. 'I looked at the orders in progress, and each one has a code. If the code is on the invoices you've printed, we might be able to find the template for the design that Ning described.'

'I've heard worse ideas,' Ryan said, as he spread the invoices across a workbench in front of a thermal transfer machine.

Of the fourteen invoices Max had printed, six included charges for printing sponsors' logos. Four of these were nowhere near where Ning had been pulled out of Leo's car, leaving two decent bets.

'Design code 1207-381,' Ryan said.

Amy sounded slightly alarmed as she spoke through the earpieces. 'If you guys have the invoices, why am I still sitting here?'

'Give us a minute,' Ryan said. 'We're on to something, but it'll be done by the time I've explained it to you.'

The boxes with the design templates were all filed in date order. Max located 1207-381, but the logo was for a pen company.

'And the other one?' Max asked.

'0809-017,' Ryan said.

As Max ran along the row of boxes, a man shouted, 'What are you Herberts playing at?'

He was beefy with cropped hair, dressed in a sawdust-covered sweatshirt carrying the logo of the timber place next door. Ryan's first thought was *what's happened to Alfie?*

'We're here doing work experience,' Ryan said.

'Do I look like a prat?' the man said aggressively. 'I went for a smoke and saw half the bloody lock ripped off the door. You boys better stay right where you are. The cops are on their way.'

Before Ryan could answer, the man heard footsteps behind and spun around. Alfie launched a full-stretch roundhouse kick, catching him viciously in the side of the head. The man crashed sideways into a shelving unit and came out swinging, but while he was big he had no skills. Alfie ducked under the fists, bobbed up and thrust his palm under the man's chin. His head snapped backwards and he crumpled to the floor in serious pain.

'Give me your phone,' Alfie shouted.

Alfie was big for an eleven-year-old, but he had a boyish face and the man couldn't believe that he'd been floored by two hits from a kid.

'Don't eyeball me, tubby,' Alfie said. 'Phone, now.'

As Alfie took the man's phone and threw it up on to a high shelving unit, Ryan touched his earpiece.

'Amy, we've been spotted by a local. Bring the car in. We need to be ready for a fast exit.' Then he let go of the earpiece and tore into Alfie. 'What the hell are you playing at? You were supposed to be on lookout.'

'It's a long drive back,' Alfie explained. 'I needed the toilet.'

'How old are you, five?' Ryan shouted. 'Couldn't you just whip it out and pee against the wall?'

Alfie shook his head. 'It was a number two and I can't ride back to campus with a shitty arse.'

'OK, that's too much information,' Ryan said, torn between losing his temper and laughing.

A triumphant shout made Ryan spin around and see Max holding a stencil outline for a cartoon character shaped like a slice of bread and the name *Nantong Bakery* beneath it.

'Holy crap,' Ryan said jubilantly, before touching his earpiece. 'Amy, we've *definitely* cracked it. Max has found the logo. The square cartoon man was a sandwich.'

'I'm pulling into the estate's main entrance,' Amy said. 'Kick up a quick storm and I'll meet you out front in two minutes.'

Max grabbed the invoices and the stencil design. Alfie heard the man from the wood shop groan, but he didn't look like he was up to much more than that, so he let him be.

'Make sure we've got everything,' Ryan said. 'Alfie, have you got the ladder?'

As the trio headed out they created a wave of destruction, knocking printers and LCDs on to the floor, scooping stuff off desks, tipping over a water dispenser and ripping plants out of pots.

Max managed the most spectacular piece of damage by lifting up an office chair and shattering the glass partition behind the receptionist's desk.

Ryan was first out of the building and alarmed to see a posse of four blokes striding purposefully across the car park towards him. They were all big, and all but one wore safety boots and the wood shop's distinctive green sweatshirt.

'Oi-oi!' the one in the lead shouted. 'Stop walking right where you are.'

'Thieving little bastards,' another added.

Ryan turned back inside and shouted, 'We've got company.'

Max raced out, closely followed by Alfie, who had the collapsible ladder in one hand and held a yucca plant like a spear in the other.

'You poofters can't catch us!' Max shouted, making a wanking gesture as he started running after Ryan.

Alfie's bulk made him slower than Ryan and Max, but he still had an edge over the chasing pack. Ryan pushed through a waist-height hedge and reached the approach road. He saw Amy driving the Mercedes into the trading estate's entrance about a hundred metres away and realised they had a problem.

The road Ryan stood in reached a dead end at the locked gates of a toner supply company. To get to Amy they'd have to get through the four men, two of whom appeared to be brandishing lengths of wood.

'Why run this way, dick brain?' Alfie asked, as he emerged from the hedge.

Ryan knew he'd get into a pointless argument if he replied.

'They're old and slow,' Max said contemptuously. 'Let's have 'em!'

'Put your stuff down and wait for the cops,' one of the men shouted.

'Slags,' Max shouted, shaking his fist in the air as he led a charge.

Ryan wasn't convinced that taking on four well-built blokes was a better course of action than getting arrested by the cops and waiting for CHERUB to arrange their release, but on the other hand he'd never live it down if he left his mates to fight alone.

As Max launched a two-footed flying kick, Alfie brandished the yucca plant like a lance and used it to fend off a bloke swinging at him with a two by four plank. Ryan was a few metres behind and faced a mad-eyed fellow who'd circled behind Max and Alfie.

'Stay,' the man ordered, as he swooshed a plank of wood through the air. 'Wait for the cops or I'll give you a pasting.'

'Make me,' Ryan said as he kept jogging.

The man swung with the plank, but Ryan kicked back explosively. The plank shattered against the sole of his trainer. He caught its pirouetting end out of the air and swung it around, belting his opponent hard across the knuckles. As the man stumbled back, Ryan dropped him with a kick in the guts.

Up ahead, Alfie had triumphed medieval style with a yucca plant sword and the collapsible ladder serving as a shield. Max's opponent was crawling away holding his stomach, while the fourth man didn't like what he'd seen and was running for cover.

Amy pulled up fifty metres away. She blasted her horn and shouted into her earpiece.

'Move your butts, the cops will be here any minute.'

Max got in first. Alfie climbed in the other side and rather than faff about opening the front door Ryan dived in quickly beside Max. Amy set tyres squealing as Ryan pulled up the door. The boys flew across the car as she launched into a high-speed reverse, followed by a squealing handbrake turn.

'Not exactly textbook,' Alfie said, as Amy put the car in drive and sped off, 'but that was the best ruck I've had in months.'

Amy sounded cross as she blasted her horn and cut on to a section of dual carriageway. 'Please tell me that amidst that carnage you kept hold of the invoices.'

'I've got them,' Max said, as he pulled them from the pack still strapped to his back.

It was only as Ryan reached around to put on his seatbelt that he considered the clump of muddy roots resting in his lap, stretching across Max's knees and ending up with spiky leaves sprouting up around Alfie.

'Why have you still got the bloody yucca plant?' Ryan asked.

'I'll find a new pot for it when we get back to campus,' Alfie explained. 'I'm thinking of naming it Doris.'

48. RESULTS

Ning felt down as she showered in her room. She'd strained her shoulder in the pool, and it really hurt as she scrubbed and scrubbed with a watery deodorising soap that smelled of alcohol and left her skin raw and dry.

When she stepped out, she saw that someone had been in her room. They'd left a tray of sandwiches, juice and tea on the bed, taken the foul-smelling kit away and replaced it with a clean set. As she sat down in a robe, pulling the sandwiches apart to see what was inside, Ning noticed a piece of folded paper tucked between the tea pot and the milk jug:

Please report to my office at 6 p.m. Do not leave your room unless you hear a fire alarm. If you need anything urgently dial 75 on your phone and speak to my assistant.

Zara Asker, Chairwoman.

It was just after three and Ning knew the wait would be agony. She nibbled sandwiches and flipped through news channels on the TV. Some actor had died, someone had been blown up in the Middle East, an MP had resigned.

She'd seen the news regularly at Kirkcaldy and the fact that there were hardly ever any stories about China always made her feel homesick. The news also made her wonder about her stepdad. Was he in prison? Had his trial begun? Had he already been executed?

Ning spotted a pencil next to the bedside phone and used the back of the note to write down her prospects:

> Fight – Did better than Carlos, but argued with
>   Zara.
> Exam – Did pretty good ???
> Rabbit – Good.
> Pool – Carlos crushed me.
> Height – Did OK, except at the end. Lost temper.

She'd hoped things would seem clearer in writing, but the results looked as mixed on paper as they'd been in her head.

At half-five she flicked off the TV and started getting dressed. She felt like a visiting alien as she peeked into rooms, and saw CHERUB agents having Saturday afternoon video game competitions, or watching sport on TV. In the lift down to the ground floor, she was accompanied by two girls dressed for tennis. They chatted confidently as Ning stood in the back corner of the lift with an intense feeling of paranoia.

She reached Zara's office eight minutes early, but Zara let her straight in and she sounded warm as she told Ning to sit down.

'You did well,' Zara said, making Ning break into a smile. 'Amy didn't give me much time to read through your personal file, but I quickly realised you were going to match or exceed all the physical requirements for joining CHERUB.

'However, I was less certain about your suitability for working undercover. You have a history of discipline problems, in terms of following instructions, being disruptive and getting expelled from schools. So, I arranged the tests to make you uncomfortable, to stress you mentally, try and irritate you, or make you blow up and quit.'

'I did kind of lose it with Carlos at the end,' Ning said.

Zara laughed as she pressed a button on her intercom. 'You can all come in now.'

Carlos led the way, holding out a leather cushion with a carefully folded blue CHERUB training T-shirt resting on it. He was followed by Ryan and Amy and Connor.

'Welcome to CHERUB,' Zara said. 'You did really, *really* well today. I was especially impressed with the rabbit, and the way you didn't let me bully you into seriously hurting Carlos in the dojo.'

Ning smiled, but didn't fully understand. Had Carlos also been accepted? Then she realised he was wearing a grey CHERUB T-shirt which meant . . .

'You're not a recruit,' Ning blurted.

'Carlos is small for his age,' Zara explained, as Carlos, Amy and Ryan all laughed. 'He qualified as a CHERUB agent last year. I asked him to find every possible way to irritate you: taking the Mickey out of your accent, taking credit when he didn't deserve it, puking on you, humming during the exam, dropping your pencil from his eighth-floor balcony so that the lead inside kept breaking.'

Ning shrieked and put her hands over her face. 'AAARGH!' she yelled. 'You have *no* idea how much I wanted to beat the crap out of you.'

'I got a silver in the last campus kickboxing tournament,' Carlos said, as he held out the blue training shirt. 'You might have a harder time if we ever do fight again. So are you expecting me to hold this thing up all day, or what?'

Ning didn't want to strip in front of everyone, so she pulled the blue shirt over her orange one.

'Don't give Carlos all the credit though,' Amy said. 'The zip wire was Ryan's idea.'

Ning looked confused again. 'What did you do?'

'There's two different kinds of handles,' Connor explained. 'Some have special gears so that you go down more slowly. We usually use slow handles for little kids so that they get used to the jump. But today we all used the slow ones, and you had a normal one. We figured there was at least an eighty per cent chance you'd get the timing wrong and end up in the shit.'

'You're evil,' Ning screamed, then burst out

laughing. 'I can't believe you all knew about this. I hate all of you!'

'The good news is you're not gonna catch E. coli or something from the crap either,' Ryan said. 'It's actually mud and clay, mixed with fruit peel and a few chemicals to give it that authentic farmyard pong. But don't tell any red-shirts that, we like to throw them in once in a while.'

'The puke was fake too,' Carlos explained. 'Mashed potato, sour milk, carrot and apple juice. I had it in a little squeezy bag and squirted it over your back.'

'Damn, I feel stupid now,' Ning said, but she was grinning and had tears of happiness streaking down her face.

'It's Saturday night,' Ryan said, as he patted Ning on the back. 'I'll introduce you to everyone, and we'll have a laugh, yeah?'

Ning bounced on her toes as she went around hugging everyone in turn, leaving Zara until last.

'Thank you so much for letting me join,' Ning said. 'I was starting to hate my life.'

'Can you give Ning and me a few moments?' Zara said.

Ryan was last out and spoke to Ning as he stood in the doorway. 'When you're done, come up to my room and I'll introduce you to a couple of the girls.'

Ning nodded. 'Great, but I don't know how long I'll be.'

'Only a few minutes,' Zara said, before telling Ning to sit back down.

'I was sitting upstairs, worried sick,' Ning confessed.

'I've got a few things to explain,' Zara said. 'Basic training lasts a hundred days and the next session begins in just under a month. I'll set up a meeting with a handler, who'll sort out your education program and run you through the rules for life on campus. The athletics department will give you a training program, so that you're close to peak fitness when basic training begins.

'I'll also arrange for a dental check-up, some money and a shopping trip to buy new clothes and personal items. Amy's going to be doing your Kyrgyzstan debriefings and finally I'll arrange some sessions with a speech therapist, because *that* accent will stick out a mile on undercover missions.'

'Thank God,' Ning said. 'Ever since I got to Britain I feel like everyone's sniggering every time I open my gob.'

'We've corrected strong accents before,' Zara said. 'There's absolutely nothing to worry about. Any questions?'

'Not that I can think of right now.'

'Well, you know where I am if you think of any. You're going to be a busy girl over the next few weeks, but there's usually corridor parties and things around here on Saturday nights. So let your hair down and have fun. It's what you need after all you've been through.'

49. CHESS

The beds on CHERUB campus were really comfy and Ning didn't wake up until half ten, when Amy knocked on her door.

'You have fun last night?'

Ning rubbed her eyes and smiled slightly, as Amy eyed a white mini dress on the floor.

'We didn't really do much,' Ning said. 'Hanging around, playing music and stuff. I met some nice people. I'm not exactly sure about that dress.'

'Did someone lend it to you?'

Ning nodded. 'People said I looked nice, but it's so not me.'

'It's good to doll yourself up once in a while,' Amy said. 'I've been working on the information you gave under hypnosis and I've got some pictures I'd like you to look at.'

Amy pulled them from a plastic wallet. Ning instantly recognised the logo in the first one.

'Nantong Bakery,' Ning read. 'That's *definitely* the logo I saw on those football shirts.'

'Hoped you'd recognise it,' Amy said, as she tucked it back in the file wallet and handed over three pictures printed from Google Street View. 'Now take a look at these. These premises are all owned or rented by Nantong Bakery, and are within an hour's drive of the spot where you escaped from Leo.'

The first picture was of a modern aluminium-sided building, surrounded by car parking with a giant Nantong logo on the side.

'That's nothing like it,' Ning said, but her eyes lit up as she flipped to the second image. It was taken from the road and slightly blurry, but she instantly recognised the grubby brickwork and boarded windows on the upper floor. 'That's it.'

'You're sure?'

Ning nodded. 'Hundred per cent. I even recognise the battered van parked in the courtyard. How did you find it?'

'Me, Ryan, Max and Alfie did some detective work yesterday, while you were doing your recruitment tests.'

Ning had a sudden thought and felt anxious. 'Does this mean you'll send the cops in to raid the factory and deport all the women? My friend Mei already got sent home once, but if you owe the gangsters money they force you to go back.'

'CHERUB and TFU don't mount operations just to

send a few illegal immigrants home,' Amy said. 'Our goal is to bring down major criminal networks like the Aramov Clan and the people smugglers. I've already spoken to a senior police officer with SOCA and they'll take the people smuggling investigation forward.'

'SOCA?' Ning asked.

Amy smiled. 'That's the Serious Organised Crime Agency. Their first step will be to mount a surveillance operation on the factory. It shouldn't be too hard to trace the vans going backwards and forward to the houses. Hopefully they'll track down people like Leo and Ben. And who knows where the investigation will take us after that?'

'How long will it take?' Ning asked.

'Months,' Amy said.

'Will CHERUB be involved?'

'Possibly.'

'And what about the bastards who killed Ingrid?'

'Leonid Aramov sits at the top of the tree,' Amy explained. 'His family are rich and powerful, and nobody has touched them in two decades. I can't promise we'll get them, but I can promise TFU will do everything we possibly can.'

'Cool,' Ning said, smiling slightly. 'So will you start debriefing me today on what happened in Kyrgyzstan?'

'It's a Sunday,' Amy said. 'Go hang out with your new friends. We'll start on that tomorrow.'

*

Ning found her own way to the campus dining-room. She got cereal and yoghurt and was pleased when

Ryan came up behind and started dishing himself a full English.

'So, how you doing?' Ryan asked. 'Sleep well?'

'Beautifully,' Ning said.

'Enjoy yourself last night?'

'Sure,' Ning said, as she grabbed a glass of fruit juice and followed Ryan to a table by the window. 'Everyone kept trying to wind me up about basic training. It *can't* be as bad as everyone's making out.'

Ryan laughed. 'We'll see if you agree with that statement in a hundred and twenty-six days' time. I think you'll be doing basic with my twin brothers, Leon and Daniel. They turn ten next week.'

'Is that good or bad?' Ning asked.

'Let's just say rather you than me.'

'Don't you get on with your brothers?'

'Theo, the little guy, is OK,' Ryan said. 'He sleeps over in my room sometimes and stuff. I've got nothing against the twins, they're just a pain like most brothers.'

'Theo's cute,' Ning said. 'I always wanted a brother or sister.'

'I don't reckon you should worry about basic training,' Ryan said, as a fork load of scrambled egg tumbled down his sweatshirt. 'You've got the physique for it. The only thing that could floor you is some random injury and there's not much you can do to prevent that.'

Chloe and Grace came towards the table as Ryan shook the egg off his sweatshirt.

'Mucky pup,' Grace said, as she gave Ryan's ear a gentle flick. 'So, Ning, the shops in town open at noon today. You want to come with us and spend some of that fat clothing grant Zara's giving you? We know *all* the best places.'

Ning wasn't massively into clothes, but the limited selection she'd taken out of China reminded her of unhappy times and she could have happily burned the lot.

'I'd like to,' Ning said, as she looked at Ryan. 'But aren't we paintballing, or something?'

'That's this evening,' Ryan said. 'You can do both.'

'In which case I'd love to come shopping,' Ning said.

'Oooh, paintballing rocks,' Chloe said. 'What time's that?'

Ryan shook his head. 'That's with me, Max and Alfie. And it has to be an even number.'

'No problem,' Grace said. 'Three against three.'

'You'll have to ask Max,' Ryan said. 'He's trying out his new guns.'

Grace laughed and spoke quite loudly. 'Do you mean the guns he bought with money he's not supposed to have? The ones he'd be in lots and lots of trouble for if any senior staff happened to find out that he had them?'

Chloe smiled and spoke in the same kind of voice. 'Not that we'd ever dream of blackmailing him.'

'OK, I'm sure Max would *love* you to come,' Ryan said, as the girls sat at the table on either side of him.

'So do you want to come shopping with us?' Ning asked him.

Ryan laughed. 'Girls' clothes shops do sound enticing,

but I'm afraid it's homework and then a session in the recycling centre.'

'That'll teach you to batter old ladies,' Grace said.

Before Ryan could reply, he heard the distinctive ring of his Ethan phone. As he pulled it out of his sweatshirt, he stood up and jogged through a glass door on to a patio outside.

'Hiya, mate,' Ryan said. 'How's tricks? How's the arm doing?'

'Arm still hurts like shit,' Ethan said. 'I'm in Dubai, man.'

'What?'

'Dubai,' Ethan repeated. 'All my Kyrgyz documentation came through, so they shipped me out. Fourteen-hour flight, at least it was first class.'

'Where you at now?' Ryan asked.

'Some hotel,' Ethan said. 'I don't know how much this call is costing, Ryan. Are you sure your dad won't mind?'

'My dad's company has like a billion cellphones. Don't sweat it, they'll never notice your bill. So who's with you?'

'Just this dude who met me at the airport. He works for my grandma Irena.'

'Did you get my latest chess move on Facebook?'

'Yeah,' Ethan said. 'But you didn't get that good that fast. You're getting help from a web forum or something.'

'I may have asked a friend for some advice,' Ryan said guiltily.

'I'll play you in a live game online,' Ethan said. 'That's when we'll see how good you've really got. So I'm just mooching around and there's Internet on my TV. Can you get online?'

Ethan still thought Ryan was in California and Ryan quickly calculated the time difference.

'It's three in the morning,' Ryan said. 'I need my beauty sleep.'

'Aww, shit!' Ethan said. 'Sorry to wake you. I'm *so* jet-lagged.'

'What time is it in Dubai?'

'Early evening. We're driving to Sharjah Airport tomorrow morning – that's one of the other Emirates. I'll be flying off to Kyrgyzstan in one of my family's shit box Russian planes. Then I've got to meet my grandma and all my cousins and stuff.'

'It might be nice to meet your family,' Ryan said.

'Don't take the piss,' Ethan said. 'I'm freaking out. I'm a California boy. Grew up on the beach. Palm trees, malls, Silicon Valley. Now I'm heading off to live with a bunch of peasants who think playing football with a goat's head is the height of sophistication.'

'It might not be that bad,' Ryan said. 'And whatever happens, keep hold of that phone and stay in touch, yeah? When I get time, we'll go for some Facebook chess.'

'Of course I'll stay in touch,' Ethan said. 'You're my only friend. Plus you saved my life twice, so you're my guardian angel too.'

'I'm too far away to save your life in Kyrgyzstan,' Ryan

said. 'So look after yourself.'

'Chess,' Ethan said. 'I'll be waiting.'

As Ryan pushed his Ethan phone back into his pocket, he looked back inside the dining-room and was pleased to see Ning jabbering away comfortably with Chloe and Grace.

50. NEW

It was half-seven and pitch dark as Ryan and Ning strode across CHERUB campus, heading for the paintball range.

'Good day?' Ryan asked.

'Really good,' Ning said. 'Got some cool jeans. Trainers, shoes, loads of new tops and a backpack. You?'

'Logged another five hours recycling. That's eighty-six down. Only three hundred and thirty-nine to go.'

'I just can't see you losing your temper like that,' Ning said. 'You seem so . . . Nice makes you sound wimpish, but you know what I mean.'

'I've got no idea what came over me,' Ryan said. 'Pushing Dr D probably wasn't the stupidest thing I've ever done, but it's definitely in the top three.'

'And how was your Facebook chess game?'

'Ethan thrashed the pants off me, like always. I feel really sorry for him. I'm the only friend he's got and I'm basically manipulating him to try getting information about the Aramov Clan.'

'His life would be even worse if you weren't involved,' Ning said. 'And I hope you do get information. I've got personal reasons for wanting to see Leonid Aramov strung up by his balls.'

By this time they'd reached the mesh fence around the paintball zone. There was a big red sign up saying *Face masks must be worn beyond the red line* and *Paintball range must not be used without permission.*

'You ever done paintball before?' Ryan asked, as they turned into a grimy concrete changing shed.

Most things on campus were kept neat, but this was where people changed after shooting paint at one another. Over the years all the paint stains got smeared together into a brown sludge that covered every surface and squelched underfoot.

'Now you see why we dug up those old clothes for you,' Ryan said.

'Took you long enough,' Max moaned. 'We were about to start without you.'

Max, Alfie, Chloe and Grace were already kitted out with gloves and masks, and had a few paint splats where they'd tried out the new weapons.

'Evening all,' Ryan said. 'So what are Max's guns like?'

'Fragging awesome,' Alfie said. 'I put mine on automatic, shot at a tree and there were bits of bark flying off.'

'I think I prefer the old single-shot weapons,' Grace said. 'It's more skilful than random blasting.'

'No way,' Max said exuberantly. 'Automatic is *so* extreme, Ryan. There's like a hundred times more bullets flying around with these babies. It's absolutely mental.'

'Are we playing or yapping?' Alfie asked. 'Doris is expecting me back by ten.'

'Who's Doris?' Chloe asked.

'Alfie's new girlfriend,' Max explained. 'She's a yucca plant.'

'Ok,' Chloe said, as she gave Alfie a stare. 'That's so weird, I'm not delving any deeper.'

Ryan reached into a box and found gloves and face masks for himself and Ning. 'Never go into a room with guns without your mask fitted,' he explained. 'The triggers are really light, so they can go off by accident and you could lose an eye or something.'

'Right,' Ning said. 'Does it hurt when you get shot?'

'You might have some little bruises tomorrow,' Chloe said, as she patted Ning's back. 'But Ryan's layered you up with clothes, so it won't be much.'

'What about teams?' Ryan said. 'Maybe I should stay with Ning and then balance it up with Alfie because he's the best player.'

'Nah!' Chloe said, as she grabbed Ning. 'Battle of the sexes: boys versus girls. Are you with us, Ning?'

'I guess.'

'Woo-hoo, girl power,' Grace shouted. 'Remember, Ning, if you see a boy aim for the balls.'

Ryan rapped his knuckles between his legs. 'I'm

wearing my cup.'

They fitted their masks, then walked through to the next room, where the paintball guns and ammunition were all set out on racks.

'Pop off the lid and load ammo in the hopper,' Chloe explained, as she helped Ning. 'Then stuff as much spare as you can carry in your pockets.'

It had rained on and off the last two days and the ground was squelchy as they headed out into the gloom.

'The game is hunt the flag,' Chloe explained. 'We start at one end, boys at the other and flag in the middle. To win, we've got to get the flag to the boys' end. If you get shot by a paintball, you have to run to the back and wait thirty seconds before you can start again.'

'The thirty seconds is on the honesty system,' Grace added. 'Which basically means everyone cheats. You wanna give your gun a test fire?'

Ning pulled her trigger and got a little backwards kick as six paintballs flew out of her gun and cracked off the surrounding trees.

'Nice,' Ning said.

'Is everyone in position?' Max shouted, from the opposite end of the range. 'Three . . . two . . . one . . . charge!'

Ning belted through the trees, with her gun ready as Chloe and Grace raced ahead. Mud spattered her trousers, plants whipped her legs and the visor made it hard to see.

For the next two hours Ning ran, jumped, slid down

embankments, shot her gun, got shot, tripped on tree roots, crept, ambushed, won, lost, cheated, bundled, scrapped and finally watched in despair as Ryan ran the flag into their end zone to beat the girls by five rounds to four.

Ning got back to her room after ten, muddy and breathless. It took ages showering mud and paint out of her hair. When she got out she straddled bags filled with all her new clothes and crashed face first on to her bed. She was exhausted, happy and her whole body shuddered with excitement.

She'd stepped out of darkness into a bright new world.

The adventure continues in CHERUB: *Guardian Angel*

Ning must get through a hundred days of basic training, before being sent back to Kyrgyzstan.

Ethan faces a new life with his extended family in Bishkek, but his grandmother Irena – the head of the Aramov Clan – is sick with cancer and his uncle Leonid wants him dead.

Ryan uses his online friendship with Ethan to get information that could destroy the Aramov Clan. But when TFU's scheme goes wrong, the clan splits into two heavily-armed factions engaged in an all-out war.

GUARDIAN ANGEL
Robert Muchamore

Ryan has saved Ethan's life more than once. Ethan thinks he must be a guardian angel. But Ryan works for CHERUB, a secret organisation with one key advantage: even experienced criminals never suspect that children are spying on them. Ethan's family runs a billion-dollar criminal empire and Ryan's job is to destroy it. Can Ryan complete his mission without destroying Ethan as well?

OUT NOW

THE RECRUIT
Robert Muchamore

A terrorist doesn't let strangers in her flat because they might be undercover police or intelligence agents, but her children bring their mates home and they run all over the place. The terrorist doesn't know that one of these kids has bugged every room in her house, made copies of all her computer files and stolen her address book. The kid works for CHERUB.

CHERUB agents are aged between ten and seventeen. They live in the real world, slipping under adult radar and getting information that sends criminals and terrorists to jail.

Also available as an ebook

WWW.CHERUBCAMPUS.COM

Hodder
Children's
Books

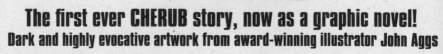

CHERUB™

MAXIMUM SECURITY

Robert Muchamore

Under American law, kids convicted of serious crimes can be sentenced as adults. Two hundred and eighty of these child criminals live in the sunbaked desert prison of Arizona Max.

In one of the most daring CHERUB missions ever, James Adams has to go undercover inside Arizona Max and bust out a fellow inmate!

CHERUB

THE KILLING
Robert Muchamore

When a small-time crook suddenly has big money on his hands, James Adams is sent on a mission to determine where it came from.

But the plot James begins to unravel isn't what anyone expects. And it seems like the only person who might know the truth is a reclusive eighteen-year-old boy.

There's just one problem. The boy fell from a rooftop and died more than a year earlier.

WWW.CHERUBCAMPUS.COM

Hodder
Children's
Books

CHERUB

DIVINE MADNESS

Robert Muchamore

When CHERUB uncovers a link between eco-terrorist group Help Earth and a wealthy religious cult known as The Survivors, James Adams is sent to Australia on an infiltration mission.

It's his toughest job so far. The Survivors' outback headquarters are completely isolated and the cult's brainwashing techniques put James under massive pressure to conform.

NO.1 BESTSELLING AUTHOR OF *CHERUB*

ROBERT MUCHAMORE

ROCK WAR

MEET JAY. SUMMER. AND DYLAN.

JAY plays guitar, writes songs for his band and dreams of being a rock star. But seven siblings and a rubbish drummer are standing in his way.

SUMMER has a one-in-a-million voice, but caring for her nan and struggling for money make singing the last thing on her mind.

DYLAN'S got talent, but effort's not his thing ...

These kids are about to enter the biggest battle of their lives. And they've got everything to play for.

Hodder
Children's
Books

Also available
as an ebook

ROCKWAR.COM